CLAN NOVEL
SETITE

BY KATHLEEN RYAN

WHITE WOLF

Galatea rose with one motion: an undulating flexion of every muscle, ending arm's length from the Egyptian. She bent over the litter, reached under it, and drew forth a compact, blocky journal, four inches thick. Handing it to him, she tried to make their fingers touch; Andreas took great pains to see that she failed. He opened the book, read a few sentences on the first page, flipped randomly through six or seven others, and studied the final entry carefully. It seemed genuine. He would have to assume it was mainly lies, cover to cover—the proverbial ounce of wheat in a ton of chaff. Unless the author were slavishly enthralled to the Toreador—a possibility worth considering—he would have written only truths that Galatea was already known to know, and told Malachite exactly what he was doing.

If one could find out whether the Nosferatu had been her slave... Andreas determined he would have the book, at least, and make what he could from it.

"I accept."

"Good." Galatea smiled again, and the sun shone. "I will follow Lord Valerian's lead, and wake where he does." She sank gracefully to her silken bed, and composed herself. "What do we do now?"

"I—I have others still to see." *Pathetic*, he thought. *I sound like Willem talking to the blacksmith's daughters. Thank Set, the boys will pack her away in the morning.*

"Pity."

"You go into your casket in the morning," Andreas said, as quickly as possible. "My men will wake you in Sofia." He fled.

Dark ages SETITE ™

Kathleen Ryan

AD 1205 to 1208
Fourth of the Dark Ages Clan Novels

For my brother, Captain Mike Ryan, Signal Corps, U.S. Army.
Hooah!

And the place was named Massah and Meribah, because the Israelites complained and put the Lord to the test when they asked, "Is the Lord with us or not?"

—Exodus 17:7

Go to, let us go down, and there confound their language of all the earth.

—Genesis 11:7

What Has Come Before

It is the year 1205 and the mighty city of Constantinople has not recovered from the Fourth Crusade, a misguided army that sacked and looted the city in the spring of the previous year. Now, the crusaders and Venetians have cooperated to establish a new "Latin Empire" in the place of the old Byzantine Empire, further shocking the Greek citizenry.

Away from the eyes of men, vampires lurk on both sides of the conflict. The predators of the Byzantine night have found their city torn open and Michael, the ancient vampire who led them, destroyed. They now desperately seek a new leader, and the most wretched have gathered in a makeshift camp near the city of Adrianople, where they lick their wounds and make ready for the coming struggle.

Meanwhile, the vampire Andreas has agreed to guide the vampiric necromancer Markus Giovanni to Venice, where he has business to conduct. After that, he is to head to Adrianople where he expects to find clients among the refugees and the crusaders, both of whom need safe passage away from the war zone.

Prologue

Constantinople, Byzantine Empire
Ash Wednesday, 1204

His name was Sarrasine. He failed to kill his father.
Sarrasine followed him into the tunnels beneath the Hippodrome and fell upon him there. The deed took time, for Khay'tall was strong in everything save faith and discretion, but the younger man was crueler, and his teeth buried in the withering neck. He tried desperately to drain the last drops and the essence that remained when all blood was gone—the dark water of the afterlife and Khay'tall's soul along with it—but in vain. In terror, his talons dug deep into the lifeless flesh, and he saw that his sire's chest was empty.

Soul, lifeblood, dark water. All had been bound into his heart and removed. Hidden in some receptacle—what the traditional priests of Set called a scarab.

Sarrasine stood over the dry husk of his father bloody-mouthed, not sane.

Now began the frenzy of Sarrasine. First, the frantic search for the hiding place, mindlessly and without hope or reason. He pried open the hollow where his father thought to betray him. He clawed into limestone, into marble, into the sodden earth. He found nothing.

After the flooding madness, it dawned on Sarrasine that this was the second time of tasting his father's blood. Already, nauseating fondness enveloped him—the false love of the hardening blood oath between Khay'tall and himself.

He realized then what his failure meant. Khay'tall would

not forgive. As soon as his heart quickened the flesh, he would exact his vengeance for this attempted patricide. How soon this might be, Sarrasine could not know. Twisted and sinister hope rose within him. The heart would need blood. Who was there to feed it? He hauled the carcass out of doors, up to the highest part of the arena rooftop, and left it on an east-facing wall. This body, at least, would not serve Khay'tall again.

Then came the slaughter. The deed had been done in secrecy thus far. No one with orders to tend the scarab had reason to go near it yet, but on the next night, with the master missing, someone would act. And so Sarrasine went to Khay'tall's haven and massacred servants, priests, women, children, old men, dogs, cats, cattle, beasts—every creature who might bring blood to the heart of his vengeful sire. He could not even let them live to go to the spot, to lead him where he most wanted to go. There were too many to watch.

At sunset the next night, he made his display of outraged innocence before the various Byzantine worthies. A month later, when the agent of Thebes arrived to investigate the murder, Sarrasine had vanished, and no two accounts agreed on why or where.

Chapter One

The girl stood on the roof of the custom house and watched ships come into port. She wore a bone-white cloak. It was closely wrapped about her—it hid her death-pale skin and her hell-red hair. She leaned on a broken pikestaff, motionless. Only those whose hearts have ceased to beat can stand so still.

She was patient.

In the rooms beneath her, the guards changed twice. Hour by hour, the tide crept slowly in. The lagoon, fleeing that invasion, sought refuge on the lowest steps and walkways; the buildings of Venice subsided a little farther into the waters. The wind changed, blowing bitter cold from the north. Silver frost blossomed on the girl's cloak, hair, staff, and skin. And at last the ship she hoped for sailed into view.

On her prow was gilded a pair of ancient eyes—Egyptian eyes, such as the pharaohs carved into stone—shining faintly in the moonlight. Large, heavy, and built for cargo, she was nonetheless very nimble with her holds half-full. The *Golden Virtue* glided gracefully into the quay, and the men on shore scurried out to welcome her, to bind her, to supply her and to tax her.

The watcher shook herself and stretched, grinning down at the ship. A thin, blue-white hand brushed the ice from her clothes, swept back her hood and rubbed vigorously at her chin. She leaned over the low wooden parapet, straining to pick out one man among the crowd. When she found him, she gave a little, hopeful hop. The master of the *Virtue*, with another man she did not know, was walking toward her along the quay. She turned on her heel, moving lightly, and sprang down the stairs. On the last step, she stopped and listened cautiously. Someone was speaking.

"Young man. Will you carry us?" These were deep tones in the local dialect—a native Venetian, if she were any judge.

"Where do you go, my lord?" came the higher-pitched answer.

"Does that matter, boy?" A third voice, speaking a very clean but unplaceable Latin, foreign, without the accent of any one city.

The girl in the cloak stepped out of the covered stairwell, crouched down, and peeped around the corner of the custom house. She had a fine view between two barrels. Her quarry had come to a small boat tended by a small boy.

"No, sir," said the gondolier. He had to rub the sleep from his eyes, but he was already at work, seizing his customers' baggage, anxious not to lose the fare.

"Please step in, my lord." The boy helped the first gentleman to a seat of honor on the center thwart. The stranger was European—a Frank, guessed the watcher, or Rom, from the east. His hose and cotte were the shade of black only the wealthy could afford. There was fur on the hood of his vast black cloak and the cuffs of his fine leather gloves. He was tall and broad-shouldered. He looked colossal beside his slender companion and the half-grown gondolier. The watcher could not see his face.

"And you, sir. I will take you wherever you like." Andreas Aegyptus, master of the *Golden Virtue*, stepped onto the tiny foredeck and squatted on it as if he owned it. He was altogether lean, brown, and hawk-like. He balanced himself the way a falcon would: heels together, toes apart and curling his thin sandals around the plank's edge. With his chest pressed against his thighs, he wrapped his arms around his knees and held his fawn-colored robes neatly and smoothly tucked between them. He had a high-domed, shaved head; a thin, fine-cut nose (crooked where it had been broken in mortal life); a strong and narrow mouth; a sharp chin graced by a short, braided beard.

It was not an easy face to disguise or hide, but it was a very obedient mask. He had fine control of it. Tonight, it was sternly vigilant, and the watcher crouched a little lower into her hiding place.

"I can go anywhere. Very quick, too, sir." The boy took his place at the stem and pushed away from the landing.

The watcher bit her lip wistfully. She told herself that she hadn't really wanted to talk to her man in front of anyone else, but it was no less disappointing to watch the opportunity glide away.

"Clearly, I am going to have to be clever," she mused, and stalked cheerfully across the planks, farther into the islands of the city.

On the journey, there were three: a youth, a man, and a god.

The boy, living, thought only of the boat. He had painted it red, trimmed with yellow, eighteen months before. By day and from a distance, to a sympathetic eye, it was the very image of the doge's bright and gilded scarlet flagship. By the light of the moon, it was dull and blistered black, with a bit of flaking brightness on the gunwales. The boy saw that it was shabby, and he was ashamed of it. He poled his fares slowly up the Grand Canal, dreaming of new and better colors he would buy, now that Constantinople's treasures had come to Venice.

The man, dead and damned, thought most about his losses. Markus Musa Giovanni sat enthroned in the middle of the boat. He began the trip with his sable hood thrown back, as was his habit, to better see the world, but as the gondola glided into a smaller, narrower waterway, he stopped admiring the view and listened. He heard music playing, babies crying, women scolding and men cursing, but he could not catch the noise of the sea. He knew that great waves crashed on the sandbanks just a few miles east of here, but however he strained, the sound eluded him. From his palace in Constantinople, he had heard the Sea of Marmara crashing on the cliffs below the city every night, and he had dreamed of the ocean as he slept in his crypt every day. He folded his hands on his lap, watched the tame waves of the lagoon lap against the boat and tried not to think of home.

The god—a small and modest one, the servant of a greater deity, still earning his power, learning his trade and uncertain of his inheritance—an apprentice god, in fact—thought only of his mission. Andreas, known to the courts of Europe as Andrew of Egypt—known to the courts of his god as Ankhesenaten—perched at the prow of the gondola and looked into the darkness before him. In each of his aspects, he was perturbed.

As Andrew of Egypt, he had been paid for his services, and his reputation was at stake tonight. He was obliging the great Cappadocian matriarch, Lady Constancia, and if he did not make safe delivery of her protege to the Giovanni house in Venice, it would be known. Other customers might think again.

As Ankhesenaten, servant of Set, he devoted himself to protecting his charge. The great work he would begin tomorrow depended on success tonight—Andrew's reputation was vital to Ankhesenaten's mission. Then, too, the Giovanni were said to have powers over the spirits of the dead, and he might one night need their services. A relationship with this one, young in years, yet very powerful in blood and influence, was surely worth cultivating.

And Andreas, in his own heart, was really concerned for his passenger. Markus, whom he liked, had joined a war. He was involved, very publicly, in the schemes of the mighty. Though he had proven himself in both battle and intrigue, he seemed open and lighthearted, not suspicious enough to survive the special enmity he might now have earned. Andreas determined to bring Markus safely through this wretched swamp of a city. The Setite would feel far better when he saw his friend received into the stronghold of his kinsmen; until then, Andreas kept his vigil and guarded against an ambush.

"Markus," he said eventually. "Is that the house?" The enormous Cappadocian craned his neck to see around the prow. Through an alley that led off the canal-side street, he could see an open square. The little campo was bordered on all sides by tall houses, one of which was well-lit and very solid-seeming. Built of stone to the second story, its upper floors were thick, timber-frame constructions. Its deep and narrow windows were open now, but heavy, iron-bound shutters hung ready at every one. "It is," Markus answered.

"This is a poor landing-place," Andreas warned. "Is there a better one?"

"Unless they have changed the arrangements drastically, yes. Around this corner, to your right, boy. That's the spot. Pull in beside those steps—no, the ones with the railing. Very good."

Behind the rail, a very frail old man lay on a rough pallet, sleeping. His lids fluttered weakly as the boat scraped against the stone quay. When he caught sight of the giant in the black cloak, though, he rolled onto his feet with a speed that startled even the Giovanni, who had expected it. "Piero," beamed Markus. "You're still with us."

"God willing, I'll outlive you, master," croaked the old man. With rheumatic, twisted fingers, he seized hold of the prow line and tied the gondola fast to the mooring-ring by his shoulder. "Is that the Egyptian we're expecting?" He clung to the rope with one hand and swung himself out over the boat, thrusting his head and neck down into the Setite's face. His weak eyes hunted for landmarks to know the stranger by, blinked when they found them and retreated. "Ah, it is. A moment, if you please, masters." Piero lifted a small, covered, metal lamp from the ground beside his watchful bed. He let the travelers see it— let them smell the hot oil and the hint of smoke that wafted from it—and hid it behind his cloak like a conjuror. While his body shielded the flame from their view, he opened the shutter that hooded the light. He stepped back and forth a few paces, lifted the lamp two times, then three, and gestured a great circle in the air.

Down the lane, across the campo, a second flame winked on and signaled an answer.

"That'll bring our men out to carry for you, sir. Raw lads, these new ones, but terribly strong, they are."

Before the men materialized to help unload the gondola, Markus turned to the Setite. "Can I persuade you to accept our hospitality, then? My grandfather would be glad to meet you, I think."

"I would be greatly honored, but I have other, very pressing business to attend to tonight—and I leave tomorrow," added

Andreas, forestalling the next suggestion.

"Well, consider the invitation open. Visit us when you come again to Venice."

"I shall," said the Setite, taking the hand offered him. "Keep me in mind should you or your kin need to travel or trade outside of your own territories."

Markus moved on and set foot on the lowest tread of his family's doorstep.

It was the extent of Andreas's contract. He bowed to the two he could see in the hall—and again toward the upper floors, where the elders might be watching—and set out across the city to make his next appointment.

Bianca de Geneve made a chill curtsy to her visitor. The hem of her golden gown dipped toward the floor, but not so deeply as to risk being soiled by the damp or torn on the rough floorboards. She looked down, inclining her neck as little as etiquette demanded, determined not to take her eyes off of the Egyptian envoy. In this, she was probably wise.

Andreas, for his part, returned her shallow reverence with a deep one. He had no fear of her, nor was he interested in playing games about status. His mind soared above the routine of the moment; he schemed, he calculated, and he laid plans for trouble, in case it found him. Andrew of Egypt's next commission, the great work Ankhesenaten anticipated, began at sunrise. It would be a long, almost an epic journey: the transport of a multitude—a city's worth of Cainites—*five* vampires—across almost the entire length of Europe. And with Markus safely home, Andreas felt he could indulge in a little further foresight.

"Welcome, and good evening," Bianca began. She settled herself regally into a throne-like chair.

"Good evening, and my thanks," answered Andreas. Bianca's lower lip stiffened in indignation. What was it? Oh, yes. "For the welcome, and for your time, my lady." She had been of some nobility, this *Franj* woman. She should have cast off such artificial strictures as class and title long ago, before she was ever brought to follow Set. Apparently, Aimery de Versey, her sire and tutor, had been ignorant of, or ignored, the need—Andreas suspected many of the *Franj* Followers were guilty of the same sin. Still, she sweetened when he addressed her "properly;" if he meant to finish here with any speed, he would have to flatter her. Later, when he had leisure, he would remember the lapse.

"I am all the more grateful in light of your great loss." De Versey was dead, destroyed by some unlucky Cainite childer. He and they had chanced into the machinery behind the great pilgrimage, and it had ground him fine as meal.

"I appreciate your sympathy," she returned haughtily. Condolences did her neither harm nor good. She didn't believe he meant them.

"You have some messages for me?" Best to get the matter over with, and leave.

"I do." She loosened the sash at her waist and freed a large ring of keys from it. The cabinet behind her had had its fastenings repaired, and strong iron straps cut through the original figured carving. Selecting the newest, most complicated key, she fitted it to the lock. "The couriers from Cordova came to me last week," she informed him dully, and then, with a meaning look (for no reason he could think of). "A girl delivered this package yesterday. She said she was just in from Cyprus, but I did not recognize her. I don't remember that Aimery ever dealt with her."

The papers were small and unlikely-looking—the senders hadn't bothered to seal them with anything but a little wax. The package, though, was promising. It was very heavy, swathed in linen, and tied with twisted strips of papyrus wax-sealed at the joins. On one end, beneath the wrapper, his fingers detected the shape of a keyhole. Andreas tucked it into a sack sewn into his inner robe and knotted it carefully into place.

Around his neck, he had a pocket book on a thong. The papers went inside that, and there were messages from Egypt to deliver here: two for his hostess, nine for other Followers whom someone expected to visit Venice.

He held the sheaf of papyrus out to her. She took them, still avoiding his gaze, and flung them into the iron-bound cabinet as desperately as if they were on fire. She slammed the doors shut and locked them just as quickly, then backed away. The lines around her mouth and the furrows (much deeper now) in her brow were very plain to read. Bianca de Geneve was terrified of him. She stood beside Aimery's throne, one hand holding to it tightly, the other laid across her heart—with an unpleasant, hopeless expression ruling her face.

Andreas discovered that he pitied her. The great gift given to her by de Versey was probably wasted on this unsuitable woman, but he wondered whether the original material had been good—whether she could have served Set well, if de Versey had not been her teacher, had understood better the tenets of the faith, or had lived to complete her education.

"Bianca."

She looked toward him, but not at his face.

"If there is anything you need—swords to avenge Aimery, servants to help you with your duties—you have only to ask Egypt for it. Even…" he slowed; this would be difficult to broach, since she so clearly suspected the truth, "even someone to advise you, or to complete your education…an older sister, perhaps…."

Bianca de Geneve made no reply. Andreas opened the door to the hall, the single candle guttered out, and he had to leave her trembling in the darkness.

Guilt and loathing drove him quickly out of her presence, through the warehouse's zigzag staircases, down to ground level. He opened the last door and looked out on to a bleak, dirty courtyard. There, a red-haired girl was waiting for him.

"Meribah."

"Hello," she said. "Take a walk with me out of earshot?"

"What do you want, Meribah?"

"Other than the pleasure of your company?" The *Franj* Setite scratched at her neck. "I need to go to Nicea."

"Nicea?" He was caught off guard, but not startled. It was strange, at first thought, that she should be traveling in the same direction as he planned himself—she seemed to be breaking in on his worries. Nicea was a long way from Adrianople, though, and there was no reason why she shouldn't have business in the wreckage of New Rome. Many irons were heating in that fire. Still, he was curious.

"So," said Meribah, breaking the awkward silence. "Can I persuade you to ferry me over that wine-dark sea?"

Andreas's hands rose in an apologetic gesture. He opened his mouth to say no. Meribah interrupted, anxiously.

"I know I don't have any goods to pay with. Nothing that you'd be interested in, at least—but I thought we could barter service for service." Her voice fell to a whisper. "I could steal something for you someday. You know I'm good at that. Remember Aleppo?"

"I remember." They and two others had broken down a Cainite truce—by blackmail, among other things—and Meribah had stolen, at great risk and difficulty, the letters that others had used to bargain with. Because she was *Franj*, no one trusted her to apply the pressure, or to speak, or to know the truth of the plot; but what she did, she did brilliantly. "And that would be a fair fee," admitted Andreas. He shook his head regretfully, but with decision. "But I still can't help you." All the ships he owned were in service already, carrying conquerors home from, sneaking refugees out of, or smuggling goods into the war zones in the east. The *Virtue* was all he had left, and he would not take Meribah on his personal vessel.

"I see," she replied, without concealing her disappointment. Determination spread slowly along her brows and jaw, and Andreas's curiosity grew with it.

"If you're on a mission for one of the temples, perhaps I could help you find another way...." Andreas trailed off, inviting her confidence. He was open to appeal on the grounds of duty to the faith, if she had any right to make it.

Meribah was an honest creature. He could find his answer on her face before she gave it words.

"No," she said, and her lips parted again, quickly, as if to add something—"I... no," she stuttered to a halt. "This is just a thing *I* do," she finished. "Just me." It wasn't what she had been going to say, he was sure of that, and it opened an awkward rift between them.

Andreas found himself intrigued, but he was running short of night and of distance. The harbor was very near—the first cluster of dockworkers, well-equipped with ears, was even closer.

"Well," said Andreas, "my prayers, and my people's, go with you."

To his surprise, she was delighted. Her strange, faint-blue eyes seemed to have stars caught in them. "Thank you," Meribah said gravely. "I—I'll do what I can for all of you, also."

The young *Franj* Setite gave the Egyptian a grim, somehow diminished smile, and abruptly bid him good night. She shed her great white cloak and wadded it up; she began to walk away with her arms full of dusty wool.

"What are you going to do, Meribah?"

She looked back over her shoulder. She didn't turn—her feet still pointed toward her goal.

"I need to find a man with a plantation," she sang, and seemed to think that finished the matter.

"What? Why? Aren't you going to Nicea?"

"Can't steal a horse on an island, Andreas," she explained, as if to a slow-witted child, and darted away without another word.

In the foremost cabin of the *Golden Virtue*, Willem the scribe toiled at a plank let down from the wall on rope hinges. At this rough desk, he wrote intently in a round and learned script. His inkpot nestled firmly in a hole carved to fit it; his candle was set, *very* securely, into a brass holder. Sheet brass had been tacked to the shelf all around it to protect the dry wood.

The master of the ship worked at another board by the window. Before him, there stood an elegant ebon writing box inlaid with silver and honeycombed with ivory partitions. Pen and ink lay untouched by his right hand. He sat with his left side to the window, and its shutters were propped open to let in the moonlight. There was no candle on this desk, and Willem knew to keep his own light well away—he had learned to leave his master in safe and comfortable shadow.

Andreas brought out his messages. The two letters could wait; he broke the seals on the package first. He unwound the long, thin linen tape carefully, rolled it into a neat round ball, and found a place for it beside his pens.

The box was small, narrow, and exquisite. The same hand

that had wrought the writing case had made this; on all four long faces, gold wire formed delicate lotus flowers. Each side showed a different stage of the plant's life: bud, new blossom, full blown, and graceful, falling-petal decay. The short, square faces held small keyholes. The lock within was horribly complicated. It was also, unnecessarily, beautiful.

Andreas reached out to the writing case and flicked open a tiny ivory drawer. Inside lay the key—electrum, in the shape of a papyrus blossom, with petals for wards.

This was the art of Gregory Lakeritos, the Wonder-Maker of New Rome. The gypsy tinker was the most important of the travelers waiting in Adrianople. Andreas plucked the tiny flower from its hiding place, fit it to the locks, and popped open the small square door.

Andreas unrolled the scroll and smoothed it out on the sanded board. He shifted a little in his chair, moved the papyrus closer to the light, and weighted it down at the corners with soft leather sandbags. Written in hieroglyphs, formally, in three colors of ink, it was the most elaborate missive his temple had ever sent him.

To our well-loved son, He-Lives-for-the-Sun-God, we offer greetings and send good news, the letter began.

We can confirm your earlier report that Gregory the Wonder-Maker did receive a commission from our unfortunate, unfaithful brother Khay'tall. We confirm that this commission was yet unfinished at the time Sarrasine attempted to devour our brother.

Attempted? Andreas blinked and read the passage again in disbelief. All the coteries of Constantinople had been sure (the gossips had chewed the matter over thoroughly) that Khay'tall had met his final death. The harpies of the court had quite enjoyed the drama of Sarrasine, Khay'tall's childe, crying out for vengeance on his murdered sire. Andreas's own spies were in a position to know better. Sarrasine had destroyed Khay'tall himself, to gain his blood, his strength, and his powers—and to shut his mouth. The old Setite knew too much about his offspring. He read on, wondering.

We confirm that Gregory refused to give up to Sarrasine that part or parts of the commission which he had completed, and that all the notes, drawings, communications regarding this construction remained with the Wonder-Maker.

How could they be so certain? Who would have known?

We commend your actions regarding Gregory. If he was building a secretary for Khay'tall's private palters, you have a valuable opportunity, and we pray that you shall recover them.

If?

However, we doubt our brother Khay'tall would take such exceptional measures solely to protect letters, poisons, or artifacts.

We have received your proofs of the treachery of Sarrasine and the weakness of Khay'tall. When presented this evidence, their ancestor felt moved to reveal that a greater prize may be in your grasp.

Search for the Scarab of Khay'tall.

"Lord of Deserts," whispered Andreas, "Khay'tall lives."

Pharaoh's scarabs guarded hearts; Khay'tall's scarab guarded his heart. Andreas had a quick, mad vision of Sarrasine in the tunnels beneath the Hippodrome, standing over the dry husk of his "father"—bloody-mouthed. His talons dug deep into lifeless flesh, and his mouth was buried in the withered neck. He tried desperately to drain the last drops—the essence remaining when all blood was gone—the Dark Water of the Afterlife and Khay'tall's soul along with it—in vain.

Ka, lifeblood, Water, had all been bound into his heart and removed. Hidden.

If Gregory does not have it, he will know something about its hiding place. The commission will have been designed to fit the cache.

Do not revive our brother yourself. We know you are skilled; this endeavor proves your worth. But he, though a fool, was a strong one.

A triple cartouche ended the formal message. The names of three elders were painted within it…the First Cantor of Thebes, a hierophant of great influence; a priest of Khay'tall's line, most likely the one who had revealed Khay'tall's secret; and an ancestor of his own.

There was a note below the cartouche in his sire's hasty, sprawling Greek.

Well done, Christian. You deserve a better name. I will craft one and make the temples confer it on you, immediately upon your return. Bring the good news to me, first, and we shall march on Luxor in triumph.

Mockery, decided Andreas. How like Sabine to offer balm for a wound that hurt only when she touched it. He suppressed a painful memory and moved on, trying not to think too much of her crueler humors. Andreas dashed the sandbags off the corners, and the scroll curled up and rolled off the desk.

"Master?" Willem sounded concerned. The slight breeze carried the smell of hot wax past the Setite. The scribe had snuffed the flame. "Are you all right?"

"It's nothing, Will." Andreas rubbed his beard wearily. "I was thinking, that's all." He reached down for the scroll, tucked it away into the writing chest, and opened the next message. "You can light the candle again."

"I don't really need it, master."

Andreas nodded, already reading. In the same clear hand that had penned the formal letter:

She tells me she has written something clever on the papyrus. Bear with her a little longer. There will come a change, or we will put an end to it. I need hardly advise you not to bring Khay'tall to her...but I will add my own concern. Do not try to deal with him yourself. Bring him to the temple and I shall see to it that the Dark Water flows to you, who most deserve it.

Interesting. Andreas's grandfather now wished to be his mentor.

The third message was routine: a cousin in Spain exchanging pleasantries to strengthen their connection.

Andreas filed them both away and set his mind on the new business. His crew had returned, the *Virtue's* hold was being filled (barrels thumped along the boards even now), her rigging checked, and the new men had been inspected.

It would soon be time to set sail.

Chapter Two

Ankhesenaten woke slowly. He lay half-conscious, meditating on the day's rest, hoping to find a dream drifting in his memory. There was none. It was Set's will, once again, not to reveal his will.

Without moving, he listened for many minutes to the sound of his people breathing. There were many waiting tonight. Someone large and calm inhaled deeply at the head of the bed—Goreb, the bodyguard, ever-relaxed and confident. Most took only short, shallow breaths, quietly. Eager and expectant as they were, none wished to wake him before his time.

When the Setite stirred at last, he heard cloth rustle, leather creak, and joints pop. Some stood straighter, some shuffled closer, some retreated respectfully—there seemed to be a great many of them. Alarmed, Andreas opened his eyes.

He was in the wrong place.

The ceiling was the right color, but it was too far away and the wood grain was different. Faces surrounded him; there ought to have been walls on three sides. Still, Goreb watched from his post by his head. After the first disorientation, Andreas realized what they had done. While he slept, his people had moved him from the alcove box-bed onto the pallet in the center of the wagon. It alarmed him—they would never venture to touch him unless the need were great. He sat up, looking to each of the culprits in their turn.

"Welcome home, Great One," Goreb intoned solemnly. With

his master fully roused and able, he stepped back and sheathed two great curved scimitars. Muscles rippled powerfully along his bare, brown-burnt arms. He wore no armor; he anointed himself with rare oils said to ward against all blades; his broad, bull-like breast and back bore powerful, serpentine tattoos—living amulets that gave him strength in battle. One long strip of linen wound round his waist and loins, and one thick, wide belt of red leather carried his paired swords.

On the cot's left side, Leiven the vintner stood with his wife and their youngest daughter. Magda and Leiven held each other close, but let the girl—nearly a woman herself, now—stand on her own. The family were short, sandy-haired, and fair-eyed; they had traveled with Andreas for three generations, and other branches of the mortal clan held office over his merchant business in Flanders. The Setite remembered a promise made to Leiven, that the girl should become one of the faithful with full rights on his return to the caravan—an important ceremony, and the family had claim to do this now, on his first waking. Yet it was not so heavy a matter to warrant moving his body by day, nor to justify such a crowd in his chamber.

On the right, Jacquy, master of the caravan—lean, wiry, black-polled, and willful. He was given to black scowls, even in good temper, even at his lord, and to sudden storms of joy and laughter, especially in times of trouble. On his weather-beaten, nut-brown face, a grim smile spread itself ominously wide. His three sons—Owain, Robert, and Carl—younger, progressively smaller versions of their father—were lined up behind him. Owain held back a disgraceful grin, Robert wore despair on his sleeve, and Carl seemed ready to fight and burst into sobs at the same time.

The old, white-haired midwife, Ljudumilu, sat on the cot's corner—the only one who dared be so close to him as he slept, and the only one so privileged that he would allow it. She held a piece of the blanket between her withered, gnarled fingers and worried its fraying edge.

Ljudumilu endured his long scrutiny without quailing, but her wise gray gaze grew grave.

Behind her stood a grandson, Dehaan the Rooster—absurdly

handsome, golden-locked, straight-limbed, strong. His hands held her shoulders; the old woman's flesh had begun to fail her, though her mind stayed strong. Dehaan adored her. He had left his parents at ten to follow her, insisting that he be allowed to serve wherever she went, to let his feet run where his grand-mother's failing steps could no longer take her—as ignorant of the reason as of the destination, but determined nevertheless. And Ljudumilu's son-in-law and daughter, faithful to Andreas's service, had let him go. The Rooster had other duties now, but as the end of Ljudumilu's life approached her, he still shared the burden her body had become. Andreas looked into his eyes as he had the old woman's, and Dehaan bore it as long, though not as well. Ljudumilu had taught him everything she knew of medicine and men, and he was beginning—soon now, he might be able—to share the burden of her heart.

And by the foot of the cot, hidden a little by the Rooster's bright green cloak, Willem knelt. His blond head was bowed, his deep-set, sorrowful brown eyes averted. The shy ex-novice had been merry enough at the port of Alexandropolis, and almost bold on the journey north. Tonight, he was as down-hearted as the rest. They had told him something; everyone knew.

Andreas burned to ask the secret, but the ceremony usurped all worldly considerations. His first duty was to the Lord of Storms and his eager worshipers. He signaled to Ljudumilu; she and Dehaan moved slowly to a rosewood cupboard. They brought it forward through the press of bodies and set it on the foot of the bed. Ankhesenaten's congregation moved aside to let them through, then knelt, sat, or backed away so all could see.

"Danica."

The vintner's child stepped forward, flushing brightly. Ankhesenaten took her by both hands and seated her before the little shrine.

"Open the doors, servant of Set."

Timidly, radiantly, she obeyed him. Within the case was a foot-high basalt statue, black as night, between three gilded panels. Ljudumilu and Dehaan lifted the top off the box and folded down the walls, and the idol stood alone.

Danica, resolute now that her goal was in sight, pulled

back her hair. She bared her neck—offered the blood coursing through that pearl-skin pillar—up to the creature beside her. Ankhesenaten kissed her on the forehead, as a father might. He kissed her neck and left the life intact within it. Then he picked up her hand, and he put a small knife in it. The girl grasped the hilt tightly and closed her eyes. She cut a tiny slit in the hollow of her wrist, gasping with the pain. Ankhesenaten braced himself against his hunger. Danica held the dripping slit above the statue, opened her eyes, and clenched her fist. A thin stream ran down the idol's outstretched arm, short hunting spear, his ears and mane, his broad chest and short linen skirt, and his thick, powerful legs.

When a small pool had formed around the statue's feet, the libation ended. Danica withdrew her hand. She offered the blood again to her lord.

Ankhesenaten seized it greedily. He brought it to his lips and drank, and the two froze together in ecstasy. For the girl's sake, he fed slowly, listening through the rapture for the flutter of her heart. Far too soon, the beating faltered. He fought his jaws open, and licked the wound clean and closed.

He released her—pale, slack-limbed, and trembling— into the arms of her parents.

Ljudumilu and her grandson closed up the shrine's sides again.

"Close the doors, daughter of Set."

Danica tapped them weakly. Dehaan had to latch them for her, but the ceremony was complete. Glowing proudly, Leiven and Magda lowered her onto the edge of the box-bed to rest, and Ljudumilu fetched out a cool damp cloth to bathe her temples.

Andreas waited.

"What is it?" he asked at last. He looked to the caravan chief, and demanded of him specifically, "What is wrong, Jacquy?"

"The Cainites have arrived, as you said they would, master." He licked his lips, and drew a deep breath. "But there are more than you expected. Many more. Lord Valerian was followed from Constantinople, somehow." Jacquy stopped altogether, looked his master in the eyes, and summoned his courage. "There are eleven, lord."

Andreas was startled into speech. "Eleven." Ljudumilu murmured mournfully, "Eleven."

"Lord Valerian asks the favor of an audience, as soon as you are settled in again," added Dehaan.

Magda picked up a robe from the bed behind her still-faint daughter. "Danica and I made this for you, master," she said, displaying scarlet cloth, golden embroidery, and carven lapis fastenings. "Richer than you wear on the road, I know, but when the hangers-on began to arrive, we thought—" she caught Dehaan's eye—"you might need to look..."

"Imperial," suggested the Rooster.

"Absolute," said his grandmother, with finality. Andreas shrugged into it, and let Magda adjust it to suit her taste.

"We have been attacked three times," Jacquy reported, as the costume went on and the gathering jostled toward an end. "One litter of half-grown Cainites, looking for an enemy among the guests. Valerian and one of the newcomers, Hadeon, faced the curs down. Ran them off. Then some bandits came in the name of the exiles. We bribed them, fed them meat and wine and your salt, and when bandits came in the name of Baldwin, the first lot dealt with them. We moved camp after that one; the fields were soggy with the blood, and the guests had a wild look to them once the wind brought scent of it. Done now, Maggie? Open the door, Carl. Let us out. A man can hardly breathe in here."

The caravan master's sons led the way and put the stairs in place; the vintner, his family, and Willem followed close behind. Ljudumilu's porter carried her down the three small steps—the Rooster crouching over the old woman to keep his golden head from striking the low lintel. Goreb ducked in his turn, and took his post beside the door, searching the night for foes.

"I found the men we needed, master—our choice of carpenters, another farrier, all the drovers and herdsmen a king could want. A few refugees came directly to us, knowing what you are, or who the guests were. I turned them away... I trust rightly?"

"Yes. Well done. This will be hard enough without inviting spies outright," Andreas answered, his hand on the doorjamb.

"Go on, now." The Setite waved his man ahead, and went forth to greet his people.

Later, with the waning moon rising behind them, Andreas and his followers walked east from their private enclave toward the larger refugee camp. Just outside the circle of their own tents and wagons, a pavilion stood: strong silk, striped brightly, pitched taut and secure against the wind. It was Andreas's own, given over to the use of his noble guest, Lord Valerian. Andreas and his inner circle approached, and the multitude settled themselves on benches and ground until the business were finished.

Goreb advanced on the curtained entrance, checked inside, and took up his station beside the fluttering door. Dehaan, head held high, preceded his master, and announced him to the prince within. Andreas left them waiting.

Under the canopy, by the braziers glowing red, there sat a husky, middle-aged man, unbending, on a long couch draped with clean fleeces. He had a lofty brow, an aquiline nose, and a titanic, clean-shaven chin. His iron-gray hair was cropped close in the classic Roman manner, and though his tunic and plain sandals were cut in the local Thracian style, he had belted and tied them in another, older fashion. He rose, and his bearing was kingly—

No, Andreas corrected himself, not regal. Patrician. Gnaeus Eligius Scaevola Valerian, senator of the Republic. And though the Ventrue lord's attempt to disguise himself was unskilled, unsuccessful, and even (for he looked in "poverty" like a lion hiding beneath an ass's skin) amusing, it was not unappreciated, or unlike the man. Valerian was no weakling, no fool. If Jacquy had not named the two who had run off the Cainite attack, Andreas could have guessed that Valerian was one of them. The senator had traveled with the caravan before, and had been the first of the five who sought his services after Constantinople fell.

"Lord Valerian," said Andreas in French, bowing low, sweeping the clean straw floor with his scarlet sleeves, "I understand you desired to speak with me. You do me great honor."

"Andrew, my friend. It is you who honor me." Valerian returned the courtesy.

"Let us speak, Andreas," said the Ventrue, switching to Greek as a compliment to his host, whom he believed to be a native speaker. The Setite crossed to the couch opposite his guest's, and they sat facing each other, upright, with their hands on their knees.

"My debts to you are legion. Let me discharge the first of them. I owe you an apology.

"One man, of my own kin, came to me seeking refuge. You know the code of my clan does not allow that request to be denied. My honor demanded an act of me, and though I feared that act might jeopardize you, I could not refuse it. I told him where I was to meet your men. I swore him to secrecy," Valerian emphasized, "but the oaths I extracted were not very great. I thought he understood my position, and yours, and that his word sufficed.

"That it did not, you may guess. The consequences of his indiscretion have more than justified my anxiety. My cousin betrayed my confidence; he allowed himself to be followed by a veritable horde."

Andreas nodded, but kept his peace, seeing that Valerian would say more.

"I have no excuse for myself, no solution to put forth, and no recourse against him. I can only tell you how sorry I am that I have put you in these straits…and offer to leave, myself, if you wish it."

"I do not. If you had done anything else, the deed would have lessened you. I cannot have that; you are my best client," the Setite admonished, smiling. Their eyes met, and the formality between them thawed. "Tell me about this mob, my lord."

"My cousin, Ewald Fairfax—he came south with the pilgrim knights because his sire was prince and refused him progeny. Ewald had something to do with the debacle in Venice, but not much. When the city fell, he joined the looters and found a girl to suit him, some manner of princess from the northeast, caught in the siege." The old senator rubbed his chin a moment, sighing. "Very beautiful, very royal, very frightened, utterly vulnerable.

Ewald claims he rescued her from the pack of French dogs who were ravaging her—in a church, of course—discovered she was wounded, dying, and so he Embraced her on the spot.

"He believes that his sire will accept this, because of the anarchy in the ruinous city: There were none to enforce the laws laid down by the Emperor Michael and his court, and no laws among the invading Cainites.

"I think he's a fool; his dam is a jealous bitch who brooks no rivals.

"He doesn't even speak her language. He took up with a woman who did: a Toreador from the lineage, by her own account, of Michael himself. She calls herself Galatea." Andreas knew the name. Galatea was a descendant of Paul Bathalos, Michael's "muse" of sculpture...a veritable high priest of art. She had spent much of her time in the caravanserai called the Silk Road—Khay'tall's honeytrap, where the high-minded court of New Rome went to sin, to drink drug-laced blood, and to learn new perversions from the snakes who ran it. Sarrasine had been, Andreas recalled, an intimate of this woman—but Galatea had also frequented the workshops of Petronius, another muse. Petronius was a good friend to Gregory, and Andreas had (almost) trusted him.

"It was through Galatea, who must have been Constantinople's town crier, that the two others found out." Andreas, still weighing the Toreador's character in his mind, asked absently, "Only two? There were three unaccounted for."

"Gregory's protégé is here as well. Zoë."

"She's not a vampire."

"She wasn't. She is now."

"Six."

"And the four you knew about."

"Eleven," said Andreas thoughtfully, chewing the words, "counting myself."

"It can't be done. I'll go."

"Let me talk to them first. You know my service; they do not. Some of the crowd may give up when they hear the conditions I impose."

The two rose from the benches together, and Andreas

turned toward the door. When Valerian would have followed, the Setite put him off, saying, "My men will gather you all together soon, and I will speak to everyone. Better that we come to the meeting separately." Andreas emerged into the pleasant darkness, and commanded his men:

"Bring them. I am ready."

Jacquy's sons and three other runners sprinted away, and the Rooster pointed down an aisle left clear between the tents, wagons, and rude huts. Andreas strode slowly along the narrow way, thinking through his problem, and his people fell into solemn, silent procession behind him.

Too many, ran his thoughts. Four—five, including himself—had been virtually an army of the dead, a nation. Most cities could not hold five without factions festering among them, divisions cracking open, and hatreds boiling beneath the civil surface. The mortals, too, grew more fractious as the darkness's numbers grew. Someone would be careless, hunting—too many murders would pile up at the Cainites' feet—the deaths would draw those who knew about fire, or stakes, or how to call the wolves.

Constantinople had held hundreds, but it was the greatest city in the world, with a mortal population only to be guessed at, supporting all those predators. And the Emperor Michael had inspired and aided much of its construction—laws and mores, as well as buildings—to suit his ideal, a heaven on earth for Cainites. It was made to hold all who believed in that dream, and Andreas believed—thought he knew for a fact—that even that paradise had rotted from the inside well before the invasion came.

His own plan, for the four, had been to attract the living refugees by the size and openness of the caravan. Whatever the risks for the undying, mortals were safer in numbers, and that herd would have fed and hid his passengers. Lord Valerian had elected to sleep, as well— he wished to wake only in specific cities. *How many can I persuade to slumber now?* He had selected his clients carefully, rejecting supplicants whose personalities would rasp against his own, the caravan crew, or accepted guests. Spite had destroyed entire cities of the dead in ages past.

Not least, there were politics to consider. Along his favorite route, the old Via Militaris of the Caesars, three wars smoldered among the living and two among the dead.

His known passengers posed difficulties: The emissaries—Valerian and the Tremere called Calleo—had enemies before them. The pilgrims—a Malkavian, and now Ewald—had enemies behind them. And the refugees—Gregory among them—had enemies everywhere.

Can I turn them out? Ankhesenaten asked his god. Would they tag along with us anyway? Would they pursue to avenge the insult?

Slowly, the priest and his procession mounted a gentle hill and descended into a small hollow at its crest. The customers were seated there in a semi-circle around a third of the depression—an audience in the natural amphitheater. Andreas cast a sidelong glance at the Rooster, and found the young man smiling at him.

"Wait here a moment, master. I'll pretend to talk to you, while you check them over," he said, winking. "Count the house before your performance."

Andreas shook his head, but inclined his head to listen, and to look.

Gregory Lakeritos sat on a bench at the far left of the invisible stage. He was a bearded, dark-haired man of thirty or forty—hard to tell, on a face so weary and sober, yet so merry around the eyes. His long robes hid misshapen legs and a twisted spine, but his arms were powerful and deft, and his hands long, thin-fingered, and the most dexterous Andreas had ever seen. One of the famous hands lay now, reassuringly, on the shoulder of the girl beside him. She was very young, this mortal protege of the Wonder-Maker. Zoë looked more like a Ravnos than her sire; her gypsy ancestry showed itself in dark, beautiful, coiling hair, an olive-brown tan, and thick, long, sooty-fringed lashes around deep brown eyes. Her face, naturally round and soft like a child's—like the child she had been, the last time Andreas saw her—was taut, drawn thin by worry, intense in grief. Both wore satin, gilded garments, much stained, torn, and patched. Andreas guessed that this was all they had. Their baggage would not be clothes.

Lord Valerian, next in the circle, had the only real chair provided, a courtesy of the caravan crew. They knew him.

By contrast, Ewald Fairfax had been given a long, low, rough crate. Someone's cape was thrown over it, no doubt not his, to keep his finery from being soiled or snagged. He was a very pretty young man, with long, sand-colored hair. His blond beard was trimmed in the fashion of a hundred years earlier, but his robes were fresh and fashionable, and his bearing self-possessed. Arrogant, thought Andreas. To look at, he amended, aware that he was reading into the man's countenance exactly what he expected to see. To Ewald's left, with a fiercer prettiness than the Saxon's, a young woman—the northern princess. She had green-gold eyes like bronze and ruddy-gold hair like copper, matched with the broad, smooth face of the eastern horse-tribes. She was haughty, refined, and bejeweled, but afraid. There was no contact between the two young Ventrue—no comfort. They were as clearly childe and sire as the Ravnos pair, but too proud to acknowledge it in public.

At the princess's left, leaning toward her solicitously, was Galatea. Andreas recognized her, though he could not have given her a name without Valerian's news. The Toreador whispered softly to the nobles, translating between them—sympathetic, respectful, and obsequious. If Zoë was lovely, and the Ventrue beautiful, she was as a goddess, otherworldly in her perfection. She wore a simple velvet gown and gossamer-thin wimple; her silver girdle bore an impractical, gem-encrusted dagger, a little pouch of tooled red leather, and, tellingly, a polished bronze mirror in an enameled golden frame. Andreas understood. Some Toreador were artists; she was one of those who made themselves the work of art.

The Setite, vaguely aware of the Rooster explaining a new dice game to him, moved on, looking to a ragged minstrel who was a mess of brightly colored rags, sewn to an ordinary tunic and leggings in makeshift motley. The cloth was dirty, the face clean—beardless, with bright hazel eyes and an eager, amiably intelligent expression. His chin was weak, and his hair thinning, but he possessed a distinguished, almost belligerent, nose.

If he had any weapons, they were hidden in the confusion of his clothes. He grasped a lute firmly between both hands, and his nervous fingers were fumbling through a fragment of a tune.

Next, Takouhi, the sole Malkavian he had agreed to transport. She was a plump, handsome lady, expansive in her gestures and her generosity, crowned by great coils of chestnut hair. Scattered strands of silver shot throughout it, but clustered thickest at her temples. Takouhi made the most of it. She wore no veil, but braided the gray by itself, wrapped in a silver circlet round the rest. She dressed much like Galatea, simply, but without jewels or adornments—the dagger on her belt, a brass-hilted, useful, used weapon, even sported a spiked silver pommel to wield against the wolves. The Malkavian was the last of the passengers he'd known about, and the one he had doubted most; she was supposed to be mad. Lunacy touched all her clan in some way, but her clear brown gaze, however ethereal, had always seemed to him fully rooted in this world. He had never seen or heard of her particular insanity, unless it were that she believed herself a Ventrue. Yet a sane Malkavian (could the common tales be wrong?) might well claim nobility, to escape the stigma of her kin—and the Ventrue might not even mind, provided the pretender never challenged their sovereignty. The madmen had a kind of fool's grace, able to take liberties without penalty. It might even be flattering to the aristocrats.

Another man, this one a stranger, lurked behind the enigma. He was the only one standing, and he did it well away, on the outer edge of the circle. His massive hands had blunt, opaque nails curling round their fingertips, and his bare feet—unmistakably clawed—were shorter from heel to toe than any human foot should be. Black, wiry hair sprouted from every inch of skin; only his palms and the sockets of his eyes were smooth. Andreas thought of bears, and knew the man was Gangrel. Yet that savage clan, who grew more like beasts the longer they existed, prided themselves on their independence, outside city walls. *A member of the outlanders, coming to me? He can't possibly need help traveling cross-country...can he?*

And last, on a stool of his own working, sat the sorcerer Abetorius Minor—called Calleo, the Knowing—returning from an abortive visit to Abetorius Major, the Tremere representative to New Rome. The hated Tremere, Andreas added parenthetically to himself. The wizards were guilty, one and all, of the worst crime the Europeans—the Cainites—could imagine: diablerie. This one looked the part; he had dark-blue robes, shoulder-length black hair, pale gray eyes, and a neatly clipped goatee. Calleo had contracted to travel with the caravan for protection, and brought his own wagon, reinforced and iron-banded.

"Enough, Dehaan," whispered Andreas, stepping into the open circle. He turned to face his guests, and began.

"Welcome," he said, his voice clear and soft, so that the audience must strain to hear it. "I am Andrew of Egypt."

He raised his voice slowly as he went on, in oratorical crescendo. "I am the prince of merchants, and the merchant of princes. My caravans and my ships carry goods from every corner of the earth to every corner of the earth. My name is known in countries that do not know each other—on the lips of kings who could not say where Egypt lies. My passengers number as the stars, and every one has left my custody in health and wealth, no matter the lands or seas we crossed," he said in perfect, if incomplete, honesty.

"I am the way across Europe," said Andreas, returning to confidential tones.

"You know me, or you know of me. I do not know all of you." His gaze flitted from the poor minstrel to Ewald's party to Gregory. The minstrel and Gregory had the grace to look abashed.

"Our purpose here tonight is the charter of a voyage. If there are any here for other reasons, make yourself known now, and I will speak with you." Andreas cocked an inquisitive eyebrow in the Gangrel's direction. The outlander folded his arms, dug his toes into the dirt, and rooted himself to the spot.

"Let me begin with our mutual problem.

"I have made this journey before, alone, many times. I have taken passengers along this route—one by one. I have carried two. I have carried three, once, at great risk." Andreas paused.

"You know you are too many," said Andreas, staring directly at Ewald Fairfax.

The boy flared into protest. "How dare you? I—I am not a—I am not willing to discuss my affairs before animals—mortals," he corrected himself, though not soon enough. The Gangrel growled warningly. "Before cattle," Ewald muttered viciously. "I would speak with you alone, Egyptian."

"You will not, until I have spoken here," Andreas replied. "Only the price is private; your business is with every member of the party. Overpopulation imperils all of you, those whose passage has already been promised, and those who have still to make their arrangements. And each of you who travel with me increases the difficulties all of us will share—even the 'cattle,' as you call them.

"You know you are too many," repeated the Setite, "but I am a man of business. I will turn no one away. However, I will be careful to state my terms. All such compacts—treaties between powers such as ourselves—should be considered carefully." He smiled without humor.

"If the *Franj* had specified *per capita* instead of *in toto*, none of us might have come to this pass."

He got blank looks from the Byzantine insiders, wry appreciation from Lord Valerian, and resentment from Ewald.

"So, let me say these things, not as a reflection on any of you whom I know—nor apprehension of any of you whom I merely know of—but as a man of business. It is possible that you may find my conditions harsher than you wish to endure. If so, I will do my best to help you find another route that will serve. Now I ask that you listen, all together, to the rules of my road.

"First, I expect peace from you. Make war along our road, and I will throw you on the mercy of the court in question. My obligation is to protect *bona fide* travelers, not to provide an armed force behind provocateurs. Be sure you understand the difference." Andreas paused, let the matter gain weight, and passed on. "There must also be peace between you. Make war amongst yourselves, and I will throw you out. Be wary of each other, for we are not safe neighbors...." He tapped his right index finger against a large domed ring on his left hand, thoughtfully. "There is a tradition among the Europeans I shall adopt for this journey. I shall convene a court to settle disputes, if any arise.

"Second, I expect any who travel awake to contribute to our mutual defense and mutual aid. Each shall defend the person of each, share havens in time of need, and alert the group to common dangers. Anyone who feeds as we go must assist in provisioning and defending the mortals, as well. This is not a market town," he explained, tapping on his ring again. "A living man killed or frightened away will not be replaced easily.

"I may also ask, and I regret the necessity, for your help in finding our road. It would be difficult to persuade the ruler of any domain that a dozen Cainites have come to his town merely to pass through it; I must climb that mountain at least ten times to reach Venice. I shall have to call in great favors to do this, and so I will welcome any help you can offer in getting through, and consider it partial payment for your passage." Andreas began to pace, slowly, drifting from one end of the gathering to the other.

"Third, you must acknowledge and respect each other's blood rights. As a large caravan, we will attract many hangers-on and camp followers. These are the common herd, available to all, and not to be wasted. There will probably be fewer than we need—small enough in number that they will sense they are being hunted if you are not careful. Consider them rations. I encourage you to provide a group for your own use—mendicants, tinkers, refugees, returning crusaders—people who will feel grateful for your protection, and not wander even if we travel very slowly. I will lay in supplies to feed whomever you gather around yourself.

"Fourth, you may create no progeny. This is absolute.

"Fifth, we travel incognito. Do not reveal yourselves or each other to mortals unless you have their tongues in check. You may make yourselves known to the courts we travel through if you are sure of your reception—do not reveal others, under any circumstances. They can do that themselves if they so choose.

"Sixth, some of you must sleep. Several of you who came to me originally had planned to spend the trip in torpor," said Andreas, stretching two to 'several.' "I am forced to ask that others join them. Remember that if you sleep, you need not fear thirst, nor defend the caravan, nor risk being recognized, nor endure the boredom of the journey. If you are concerned for your safety—"

"If they doubt you, they can come to me," put in Lord Valerian, "It is my choice of passage, and I have confidence in your methods."

"My thanks, lord," Andreas answered, relieved that the Ventrue had decided to lead in the matter.

For the last commandment (he felt, as he always did when giving this speech, as though he should provide tablets of stone for the hearers to carve upon), the Setite ceased all motion, standing in the center of them all—mortal and immortal—and his voice soared again.

"There is another, ultimate law you must agree to. For the first six, you must obey or be exiled—obey or be hunted down by your fellow travelers. For the seventh, the penalty is mine, and I will take it.

"My people are sacrosanct. You may not feed from them. You may not bind them with your blood or magics. You may not slay them."

Andreas held up his hand, waiting. Jacquy sprang to his feet, slipped out of his chemise, and stretched out his knotted, sinewy arm. In the paler, hairless skin under the shoulder, a raised and darkened sigil marked him—a snake coiled around the hieroglyphs for thunder. The caravan master marched down the line of Cainites, showing each the symbol, and not moving on until he was satisfied that the guest knew it, and would remember it. If they could not see it—not all of the undying could see in the dark as well as his master—he seized their hand and rubbed the chill fingers over the deep-ridged scar.

"Know them by this, my mark, and learn their faces as well. They are under my protection, and their word is enough to shield anyone—there are others, not privy to our nature, or too young to be branded, who are essential to our progress. Do not assume that we shall answer an attack only with retribution. I have taught them all what they need to know to protect you from your enemies. They know to use the same weapons to defend themselves from you—they will not submit without leaving a sign for my vengeance to find."

Jacquy finished the exhibition and took his place again. Andreas rubbed his hands together, steepled them, and pressed

the two index fingers together, to his lips, and then out in a con-
cluding gesture. "I am not paid in gold," he explained. "Think
on that, and think on your reasons for travel. If there are any
among you who are not certain of your welcome, I suggest you
reconsider."

"As for our contract: If you cannot bear my terms, walk
away now. If you begin the journey with me, you accept my
terms, and you are witnesses to each other's agreement."

The Setite smiled, finally, and bowed.

"I've had my say. Thank you for your patience. When you
have decided whether you will make one of the party, send
for me, and I will visit you. We won't leave until I have had a
chance to meet with everyone." He bowed again, gathered his
men about him, and swept back down the hill, evading the bur-
geoning questions.

"You sent for me, my lord?" Andreas asked the question as he
entered the Ventrue's borrowed silk pavilion. He stopped just
inside the curtain—Valerian was not alone. Ewald, the princess,
and Galatea sat, huddled, and reclined, respectively, on the
couches provided.

"Yes, Andreas. As you know, I have chosen to sleep between
cities. You have my list of the places I would like to see, if our
route goes through them. My cousin and his retinue will take
the same course," he said, and reluctantly went on, "and I make
myself responsible for his debts."

"No." The Setite's tone left no room for argument, and he
was pleased to see Valerian's eyes relax. If the obligation of hospitality compelled the Ventrue to make the offer, he had nevertheless not wished to make it, and was relieved, not offended,
by Andreas's refusal.

"No?" said Valerian, mildly.

"Show respect for the Lord Valerian," Ewald commanded.
In French, he added, "Damned filthy serpent." Andreas understood it perfectly, but gave no sign. "He is a most puissant
prince, though he holds no city. His treasury can pay a dozen
times your fee, and his honor is beyond reproach."

"Of this I have no doubt, sir, but it will do me no good if

something happens to him along the way. If he were assassinated, God forbid, or wounded to insensibility for centuries, or slept, unharmed, too deeply to be waked, I would go unpaid for all four of you." He shook his head, decisively. "This I cannot do."

"I tried, my son," Valerian said, sighing. "Go now, while I finish this with our host."

They waited for the others to leave, watching them. Ewald fumed out. The princess looked utterly bewildered by it all, for Galatea had not translated anything after no, and Galatea herself had only a perfect, marble-hard, mysterious smile.

"Goreb."

"Great One?" The bodyguard thrust his head through the curtains.

"Have the children see that no one overhears us."

In a few minutes, the sound of young things laughing surrounded the tent, punctuated by the brushy thud of a leather ball scraping along the packed ground.

"Where will I be?" Valerian inquired.

"In a wine barrel."

"In vinegar."

"Eventually." The Egyptian grinned.

"Do you know what you want of me?"

"You are the prime ambassador of King Alexander and Queen Saviarre at the Grand Court in Paris."

"Yes," confirmed the Ventrue warily.

"I would like to be the prime, chartered, and endorsed carrier for their emissaries."

"In return for my safe passage, you have my word that I will exert myself on your behalf." Valerian smiled. "If you can carry off this enterprise, you will more than deserve the honor."

The Gangrel lurked outside the wagon town, off the road, on the edge of a grove of stunted trees. He stepped out to meet Andreas, but kept his distance. Goreb sidled closer to his lord, hand on hilt. The runners faded into the background, watching as best they could around the corners of a safe, solid barrel-cart.

"Andreas Aegyptus, I have a proposal for you."

"I am listening."

"You are traveling in my direction, and I in yours, whether we like it or not. I have no need for your wagons or your slack-armed guards," said Hadeon, with rumbling contempt for those who did, "but give me hunting rights among the refugees you plan to fatten for the city maggots, and when I kill game I'll bring the carcasses in for your herd to feed upon. I'll scout for you—keep an eye on wolves and blood beasts—and you'll tell me if any of these fops antagonize the local gentry. If you are attacked, I'll fight for you, and if I am attacked, I can come into your wheeled fortress to lick my wounds."

Andreas studied the outlander for a long moment. "That's all I'm going to take from you, serpent, and all I'm going to give. No gold. No 'price,' whatever it is you drag out of the others."

"Of course not." The Setite scratched his jaw thoughtfully. "I accept your proposal. I am only trying to decide whether I should designate a wagon for you—even though we will hope you never need it—and find six or seven fugitives to keep for you, exclusively."

"Do as you like, Egyptian," said Hadeon, disappearing under the trees. "I don't care."

Calleo stood inside his own iron-banded wagon. Its door was split in two, and he leaned both elbows on the ledge formed by the closed lower half. When Andreas approached, the Tremere remained where he was. They spoke across the steps.

"Ah, Andrew," said Calleo, as if he had only just noticed his host. "Let's get this over with. You will accept the fee we discussed before?" They had settled on a magic, a ritual which could trace the lineage of an immortal. The price had been easy to fix; Andreas knew he would have a much harder time deciding on whom to use it.

"I accept."

"That's that, then. Good night." Calleo swung the top door closed abruptly and shot the bolts noisily across it.

Galatea reclined on a silk-draped litter. Her velvet dress molded itself to the curves of her body; the nap shone in the moonlight, outlining the crests of breasts, belly, and thighs. The moon threw her profile into sharp relief, and her stark perfection was breathtaking.

Andreas had no breath.

"I am here, madam."

She smiled, slowly, and her eyes explored him thoroughly.

Andreas inhaled. He used the breath to speak, immediately, to conceal it—to be rid of the effect she was having on him.

"What will you give me in return for your passage?"

"You should have been an actor," she told him. "Your voice is wasted on trade."

His lips parted, but he said nothing.

"I admired your performance earlier. Very good," she assured him, sitting up. "Very masterful. I liked that in you; I had expected something…boot-licking." Her bare toes curled. "Gold-hungry." She leaned toward him. "Grasping." Galatea's smooth hands twined tightly in the silk scarves she sat on.

Andreas watched her move, and his fingers itched to touch her.

"What will you give me," he repeated, "in return for your passage?"

The Toreador lowered her eyes, and whispered. "You have heard of the Secret History of the Emperor Justinian? The intrigues of the Empress Theodora? The corruption of the racing Blues and Greens? The lusts of Belisarius's wife?"

"Yes. I already have a complete set of Procopius's works, if that is what you are aiming at."

She shook her head, and fixed her eyes on him again. "No, no. I have another work; a Secret History of the Emperor Michael."

"Who wrote it?"

"A Nosferatu of his own faction. Malachite charged him with recording Michael's madness, and this man—my friend—wrote them down. When I discovered it, I persuaded him to make a copy—there would have been another for Malachite, somewhere. My friend hasn't been seen since the first fire, and the third fire burned out his home." She arched her neck, challenging him. "Do you want my little book, or something else?"

"I will take the book, madam." He clenched his fists so hard

the joints popped, and he hoped her ears had missed it. "I will
take the book now," he decided. "Go and get it."

Galatea rose with one motion: an undulating flexion of every
muscle, ending arm's length from the Egyptian. She bent over
the litter, reached under it, and drew forth a compact, blocky
journal, four inches thick. Handing it to him, she tried to make
their fingers touch; Andreas took great pains to see that she
failed. He opened the book, read a few sentences on the first
page, flipped randomly through six or seven others, and studied
the final entry carefully. It seemed genuine. He would have to
assume it was mainly lies, cover to cover—the proverbial ounce
of wheat in a ton of chaff. Unless the author were slavishly
enthralled to the Toreador—a possibility worth considering—he
would have written only truths that Galatea was already known
to know, and told Malachite exactly what he was doing.

If one could find out whether the Nosferatu had been her
slave... Andreas determined he would have the book, at least,
and make what he could from it.

"I accept."

"Good." Galatea smiled again, and the sun shone. "I will
follow Lord Valerian's lead, and wake where he does." She sank
gracefully to her silken bed, and composed herself. "What do
we do now?"

"I—I have others still to see." *Pathetic*, he thought. *I sound like
Willem talking to the blacksmith's daughters. Thank Set, the boys will
pack her away in the morning.*

"Pity."

"You go into your casket in the morning," Andreas said, as
quickly as possible. "My men will wake you in Sofia." He fled.

"Andreas, love. Come along and have a seat." Takouhi threw
wide the doors of her wagon, plunked two little chairs on the
ground in front of it, and flung thick sheepskins onto the seats
as cushions. Then she pulled out an awning and tied it to two
posts, saying, "Here. We'll hide from the stars. Just because they
always look down, doesn't mean they have to see anything."

The Setite settled into the nearer chair, and Takouhi lowered
herself gingerly into the other.

"Not as young as I used to be," she confided. "Now. Let me solve one of your problems. I'm not going with you."

"What?"

"You have too many. You said it yourself. And I hate to sleep. I will make my own running; I usually do, one way or another."

"But, my lady," Andreas cleared his throat. "You have already paid for your passage."

"I know. I was there. Did it work, by the way? Yes."

"Distance? Color? Hearing? Can you smell who I had for dinner?"

"Yes," the Setite answered patiently.

"Good. As I told you, my chick—it's nothing, once you know it can be done."

He sighed. "It is a very great thing, and I am in your debt, unless you travel with me."

Takouhi shrugged. "So, you owe me. I look into the future... and I see that we will settle our score soon enough." Andreas began to laugh, and shut his mouth just in time. She was serious; she was telling the truth—whether the premonition itself were true or false, she had seen it. Who knew better than he, her pupil, that she had Sight?

"Do you see anything else?"

"You want something from the Ravnos tinker. He will not give it to you; you will get it from the girl.

"You should trust the red-headed child, but not her words." Here she faltered—focused on the sky between horizon and the canvas's edge—spoke again:

"Boleslaus. There is a doom on him I do not understand, but it is inevitable."

"Boleslaus?"

"What? Why?"

Concerned, Andreas searched her eyes. No one looked out of them. "Takouhi?" he asked softly, and touched her sleeve.

"Yes. What were we talking about the minstrel for?"

"Nothing."

"Don't worry, my chick. You can owe me for your seeing lessons." There was a tall walking-stick leaning against the wheel beside her; she put her weight upon it and heaved herself out of the chair. A packed rucksack lay on the ground near Andreas's feet; she pointed at it with the ferrule of her staff, and obediently, he lifted it to her hack. Takouhi whistled, and two hefty bearers came at her call. Their packs were larger than hers. "I'll be fine. See you in Paris, I hope."

"Be careful."

"And you, my chick."

Ewald's messenger found Andreas as he watched Takouhi walk away.

"They're ready for you, master. Over there," pointed the little girl, skipping off in that direction. She danced back, caught his hand, and towed him along behind her.

"Slow down, Chiara. I don't skip." She grinned knowingly up at him. "In front of customers," he amended. "It's bad for business." They continued at the stately speed of an arthritic tortoise, in dignified silence. Chiara bowed Goreb solemnly into Fairfax's tent, and held the curtains for Andreas as prettily as any queen's pageboy.

Ewald and the princess rose to greet their host.

"Pleased I meet you," the girl ventured in Greek, delivering the line like a lesson learned. Ewald nodded encouragingly at her effort. She went on, in very cultured, but strongly accented Turkish, "Good stranger, I beg of you, if you understand me, make some sign."

Andreas, much intrigued, looked to Ewald as if for a translation. The Saxon shook his head.

"Is she from 'I understand'?" asked the Setite, putting the last two words in Turkish. "I once heard speech like hers, from an old man in 'you what.' No one could tell what he was saying except a merchant from 'do you want,' and he died before anyone else who knew the language came to the city."

The princess held out her hands. Andreas took them, assuming an expression of polite incomprehension.

"This barbarian has kidnapped me and stolen my soul. Can you help me?"

Andreas bowed over her hands, and released them. "Later,"

he murmured, "that was the name of the old man. Strange how one remembers these things."

"Andrew," said Ewald, in a calm, level tone unlike anything the Setite had heard from him before, "I must apologize. I have been ill-mannered, and I well know it. I can only try to explain my conduct. I am...helpless...in this place, and...I am not bearing it well. It is difficult to be gracious in a position of weakness, and intolerable to be reliant on my elders, no matter how much I admire them.

"May we start our association anew?"

Despite himself, the Setite softened toward the young man. Fairfax possessed more mettle than he had displayed before Valerian, to be sure, and Andreas had felt the thumb of an elder pressing upon his own independence many times before. For the time being, he would ignore the insult he had heard in French.

"On a blank slate," he answered.

Ewald gestured toward a bench, and the two men sat at opposite ends of it. The girl threw together a stack of cushions, and perched anxiously atop them.

"I have nothing to pay you with, Andrew."

"I see."

"We have gold, and Tsarika brought jewelry to wear to the Byzantine court. It is very fine—workmanship like it has never been known in the world before—but I understand mere treasure holds no interest for you."

"No, it does not."

"All I can offer is my word. I will not rest until you have fair exchange for your services to myself and to Tsarika. My honor would depend upon it—but I understand that my word holds no interest for you, either."

"No," Andreas replied, "it does. I will accept your oath, on one condition: You must render my fee before we reach your sire's domain—if indeed you choose to go back to her." The young Cainite's deliberation rolled visibly across his face, but the thoughts underlying the expression could not be identified, though the Setite did his utmost to decode them.

"I will make recompense before we enter Normandy," Ewald told him at last. "This I vow."

Boleslaus was waiting when Andreas returned to his own door. The poor Toreador had come alone, unwilling to let anyone carry his bag, and evidently unused to being served. His errand-boy walked far behind him, whistling a snatch of song. It was the one the minstrel had tried out on Raedan.

"Andreas, sir." Boleslaus came up to his host shyly. "You wanted to see us all. I thought I'd come myself. I'm sleeping rough, you see. I'd be ashamed for you to see it." He set the lute and satchel on the running-board of the closest wagon. Andreas studied him intently. Takouhi claimed this unlucky creature was marked for death, and the Setite found himself fascinated by the idea. The temptation to bring him along, even if (as Andreas suspected) he had no means to pay, plucked at the Setite's curiosity.

"If you let me come with you, I don't want to sleep. I can't stand the thought of it, and my music goes sour if I let it alone for long. Awake, you know, I practice a lot.... I thought I could entertain your people, along the road. Play dances, sing ballads, tell stories. That kind of thing."

"We would be glad to hear you," Andreas assured him. "The wagons are very slow over mountains, and we will be weeks between settlements."

Boleslaus grinned painfully. "Now, I don't have any things—valuable things—with me. I've never had any, really. My audiences don't have them, and if I try to better myself, the real artists—the courtly ones, anyway—turn their patrons away from newcomers, you know? They'll listen to me themselves and take my songs, but there's no getting past them.

"I'm hoping, though, that you'll let me come with you if I tell you a few things." His eyes shifted side to side, checking for eavesdroppers. "Secrets," he said, almost inaudibly.

When Andreas was slow in answering, the Toreador persisted. "I know I don't look or sound like a man carrying anything important in his head. A ragged troubadour with a lute that falls out of tune like a man from the gallows, who's just told you he never sees the great men, the powerful places. But I play for the peasants and the slaves. They hear more than you could imagine." Boleslaus darted forward, until his mouth was inches from the Setite's ear. Goreb seized him by the arm, but he had time to whisper: "I performed in the sewers, my lord. Would you like to know who destroyed Michael's Heaven, and why?"

"You know?"

The Toreador picked himself up from the ground where Goreb had thrown him. "I know."

"I accept your offer," said Andreas, though he didn't believe the man. The story would make good listening in the mountains, when the rains came and mired the caravan in—and the temptation to test Takouhi's prophecy was a delicacy he would not resist.

Boleslaus, in astonished gratitude, threw himself at the Setite's feet. "You will not regret this, my lord."

"Enough," Andreas commanded, embarrassed by the pitiful gesture. "Get up. Carl!"

"Master?"

"A wagon for our guest."

"You do not want to hear the tale tonight?"

"I have other business to attend to. Save it for the road, when I can better attend to it."

As Andreas approached the Ravnos wagon, he related his results to Jacquy, and the latter ticked them off on his fingers.

"One gone, four to sleep except in cities—"

"A few cities."

"A few cities," repeated the caravan master. "One who says he won't come into camp unless his life depends on it, one awake and singing for his supper, and one who intends to hole up in his own wagon the entire way."

"Yes."

"Speaking of him…have you thought about the weight of the thing? Its wheels sink half-an-inch deeper into the ground than anything we have. I'm not looking forward to hauling it up the Danube in the spring thaw."

Andreas said nothing, though he doubted the caravan would take the relatively gentle riverside route. *Enough time to tell him when we reach Sofia; the court there will know how the Bulgars and voivode will receive travelers. If my fears come to* nothing, he will rest easier, never having known.

"These two—sleepers?"

"No. At least, I hope not."

"If they slept, you could go through his things—find what you are looking for, and have done with it."

Sighing (for the thought had occurred to him, as well), Andreas rejected the advice. "No. We don't know what we are looking for, nor how to open it, and Gregory is too good an ally to offend on such a slender chance." Images of Greek-fire traps and holy-water atomizers flashed across his imagination, and he became doubly determined not to risk a brute-force approach.

Jacquy, unconvinced but utterly obedient, nodded his head in agreement. "Four awake, then, master." He trotted off to find Willem, to make the boy do the arithmetic of wagons, men, and beasts.

Their door was closed. Goreb raised a massive fist and knocked, not over-softly, and Andreas heard someone jump inside. He waved the bodyguard around the corner, out of plain view, and called softly.

"Gregory?"

The door opened a crack, and Lakeritos peered out.

"Andreas, my friend." In a whisper, "Come, Zoë."

Gregory pushed the door wide and descended the steps, limping slightly. The girl crept stealthily after him. She managed a deferential bow, though it appeared she did not want to finish it—that she would have preferred to stay hunched over, staring at the ground, and clinging to her sire's arm with both white-knuckled hands.

"Andreas, this is my childe, Zoë. You have met before, I think, when you visited three years ago."

"I remember," said the Setite kindly. "You were much younger then, Zoë. How tall you've grown, and how pretty."

His effort was wasted; she gave him the look the lamb gives the butcher.

"Shall we talk business?" Gregory let the girl slide out of sight behind him, but kept hold of her sleeve, preventing her crawling back into the wagon. "We will stay awake, I think."

The girl shuddered in the background, and Andreas deduced that she loathed the prospect of sleeping for years. "I am still not sure what I can offer you," he confessed, "but if you are still prepared to take me—to take us, now—on faith—"

"I am."

"Few would trust one of our clan this much, Andreas."

"I know you."

The tinker smiled. "Let me pledge it." He spit in his palm and shook hands with the Setite, then dragged the girl out.

"Swear, Zoë. You will keep his rules and pay him back."

Reluctantly, she obeyed. Her hand touched his for the least possible time, and she flinched away immediately. Gregory saw it, and bundled her into the wagon quickly.

"Excuse us for a moment, please," he called around the closing door. He was absent ten minutes, and Andreas wondered whether the two would emerge again before the sun caught them all. The tinker came out alone, and young, trembling fingers shut the door on his heels.

"Forgive her, my friend." Gregory stroked his beard, glanced over his shoulder to the wagon's shuttered windows, and fumbled for a crutch-handled stick propped against the front left wheel spokes. "She is…well, she is frightened, as you see." He began to walk, quickly, but with a very lop-sided gait, away from the girl and their home. Andreas fell into step beside him.

"I did not know," the Ravnos explained, "until she told me just now, but Sarrasine had been to see her before he left New Rome. You know him, I think?"

"Unfortunately."

"Ah. I am of your opinion. The man was vile, and he tried to force my Zoë to give him something she…" Gregory paused, and Andreas held his hopes in check. Surely, Sarrasine had come to the Ravnos's workshop for the scarab—how much easier his task would be if the Wonder-Maker told him, himself, that the heart's cache existed. "Well, she was a very young girl…too young for that kind of thing, whatever the courtesans do at that age."

This was disappointing, but Andreas made sounds of sympathy.

"She knows," Gregory continued, "that you and he—and Khay'tall, whom neither of us like—are cousins. Her experience with Setites is limited, and universally bad—a limited set of data, but overwhelming, and...well, she has our curse to contend with, too."

"Curse?" Andreas was startled. For some reason he had assumed that the Ravnos—foreigners, drifting in from lands he did not know—were free of the guilty fears of the Cainites. The Christian immortals claimed Caine, son of Adam, had been given endless half-life as punishment for the first murder, and it crippled their thinking.

"I know, I know," said Gregory, although his next words proved he had no inkling of Andreas's real opinions, "How could I pass it on to her? I feel the sin of that; it rides my back like the Beast itself." He turned to his friend. Grief filled his eyes, and weariness shadowed his face. "It was a moment of anger. I will not speak of it.

"You, my friend—have you passed our evil on to any mortals? Have you any advice in helping so young a creature come to terms with the taint?"

Internally, Andreas bristled. He had not and would not create childer. He was the eleventh of his line, abysmally weak, and resentful of his own sire's selfishness in performing the rite herself, when a greater Follower could have granted the gift. Moreover, the dark waters of Duat—these were a blessing, not an evil, and he detested hearing them spoken of with shame. He mastered himself, and answered, "No," without elaboration.

"Can you do something for me, though? I think it may help her, and it will make my task an easier one."

"How can I aid you?"

Gregory flushed, mortified to ask it. "Leave her—leave us— alone. Don't come where she can see you."

Andreas listened to his plans crumbling. If he could not see them, speak with them, he could hardly persuade them to hand over Khay'tall's heart. Yet there was no polite way out; if he terrified the girl despite Gregory's request, the tinker would take offense, justifiably, and the prize would slip even farther away.

"I cannot promise," the Setite began cautiously. "The

business of running the caravan may take me through your territory from time to time, if the need is urgent. But I will do my best." He groped for another way out, and found one. "I will miss our talks, though... and I was looking forward to playing backgammon with you again. Will you come to see me, when you have the time?"

The Ravnos grinned through tired eyes. "Of course, of course." He clasped Andreas's hand, held it tightly, let it go. "Often. As often as I can." They turned back toward his wagon together, and Gregory left his host at the last corner out of sight of the shuttered windows. "Thank you, my friend." He shuffled forward, and the Setite listened to him pound a special knock on the barred and bolted door.

Hinges creaked, and Gregory murmured something to the girl inside, but the last thing Andreas heard—what he took to his bed with him at dawn and woke to as the next night fell—was the sound of Zoë's hopeless, tireless sobs.

Chapter Three

Into Byzantine Thrace on the Via Militaris
June, 1205

Andreas walked into the clearing a little after midnight. Young people and children swarmed around it, dancing, and the tall grass, beaten down by their feet, smelled like a hayrick…warm, damp, and green. Older refugees, and those still too stricken by memories of their city sacked—they sat in clumps around the circle of festivity, talking, gaming, or just listening to the music.

Boleslaus had joined the band, he saw, and was leading them in a quick and simple tune. Andreas wandered through the crowd, nodding, smiling, and greeting his own people, the hired men outside his flock, and the refugees whose names he had already begun to learn.

Once he found Dehaan and Ljudumilu, he and Goreb passed the time with them, visited often by his other followers and once by Boleslaus resting his fingers. Andreas had arrived when the crowd was at its peak—as he sat with the Rooster and the midwife, the dancers, and the ring around them trickled away. There were miles to go tomorrow; there were oxen to harness and cows to milk at dawn. Only a rough third of the refugees were left when the horn sounded the alarm.

The commoners didn't recognize it—there were horns in the little troupe round the minstrel. It was the wrong tone, and distant, and its message had naught to do with entertainment.

"Someone's coming," Dehaan said, in the voice his grandmother could hear best. "Willem!"

The scribe had left his place in the dance already, and his line descended into chaos before he reached the tree under which they sat. Some of the other followers—Carl, a tired Jozef, Danica—abandoned their partners and dashed to join their leader.

"Take her home for me?" Dehaan surrendered Ljudumilu into Willem's arms, and ran off to join the guards in camp. Andreas followed, more sedately, confident that the warriors knew their business. Willem and the others—none of them fighters—took their time, for the old woman's sake, but without delay.

Andreas was still in the clearing when Robert came riding up with the news. Another group of dancers stopped in their paces—most of the refugees the Setite could see had risen to their feet. The festivities had died, though the music played on.

"A rider from the east, master. Hadeon heard it—the horn call was his. The horse gallops; it will be here in minutes," he said, and turned his mount back to the eastward edge of camp. More mortals scurried away after him, seeking their own blankets and firesides. Boleslaus's lute struck a wrong note and clanged through another. Andreas looked to him, saw his face set into a fiercely frightened mask, and heard him find the tune again, defiantly loud and strong.

Gregory opened his door, a question on his lips, and let it lie unasked. A small round face peeked around his shoulder, saw the Setite, and withdrew. Andreas heard the dogs complaining vociferously. They whined as well as barked; the rider was a dead one. Gregory nodded, and sat on the steps to wait.

Andreas climbed up the side of his own wagon, peering east, along the road. He could not stretch his vision. His men had built—as they should have done, and he was glad—a bonfire by the roadside, and the glare was painful to the crypt-adapted sight of Setites. With Goreb towering beside him, he squatted on the edge of the roof, closed his eyes, and listened. As the alarm spread, even the mortal refugees caught it. A hush fell over the entire encampment, and Andreas found that he could stretch his ears, instead.

"Here he comes." Jacquy speaking, low and wary.

Hoofbeats. A horse in heart-bursting gallop. Closer...breaking gait...slowing...pulling up short, the rhythm confused, using every step to break their momentum.

"Hello," someone called in high-pitched Greek. It was a woman's voice, or a girl's.

"Hello?" echoed Dehaan, sotto voce, puzzled.

If Jacquy were surprised, it had no effect on his speech. "Ride around," he said firmly. "My master's camp lies across this road, and you may not enter."

"Oh," answered the rider, and Andreas recognized the voice. "You have that kind of master," said Meribah. Her tone matched the caravan master's exactly. "I see. I'll go." Iron shoes clattered on the gravel. "Who is he?"

"I cannot say," said Jacquy, guardedly.

"No. Well, I won't give you my name, either." She sounded vexed. "I don't see the point; this road has only two ends. I'll see you all in Philippopolis—" Andreas determined then that she would certainly not— "and I'll know you when I do, sir."

No one answered her.

Meribah cried shrilly to her mount, and it whinnied in low harmony. From a standing start, the horse sprang into motion. They sped out into the darkness, and turned, and cantered off to the left. Andreas followed the hoofbeats throughout their arc. Alone in Macedonia, he thought, praying against rabbit holes, ditches, and other leg-breaking obstacles. He clambered off his high perch and walked around the square. "It's over," he announced.

"What was it?" asked Gregory.

"Nothing. A girl by herself," explained his host. "She's gone." Clothes rustled in the darkness behind the tinker, and Zoë slipped across Andreas's line of sight. They would have been of an age, realized the Setite, fourteen, fifteen summers....

Suddenly he decided Meribah would find him in Philippopolis, after all.

Chapter Four

Philippopolis, On the Bulgar-Byzantine Frontier
June, 1205

Prince George of Philippopolis decided to use Andreas's visit to humiliate an errant childe. His theatrics went on for hours, involved half-a-dozen other players, and ended with the staking of the young one. The old Cainite delivered a lengthy, incoherent lecture on obedience directly into the ears of his paralyzed progeny, ordered the body thrown into a rat-infested tomb— "You'll go free, boy, when the vermin gnaw the wood out of your heart, and not a night sooner"—and finally turned his attention to the guest. His mood was excellent. He remembered Andrew of Egypt's previous expeditions along the Roman road and their prior good dealings without dissembling, and the Setite's participation in the drama weighed greatly in the caravan's favor. Andreas emerged from the stage of power with the grant to bring his clients within the walls, permission to hunt in the surrounding territory, an offer of mortal provisions and planking on good terms, and a feeling of considerable satisfaction.

He gave Jacquy the contract for food and wood, Willem the written grant, Dehaan the good news for the waking passengers, and Goreb his liberty. They took their leave, lit their torches (well away from their lord), and picked the least beggar-lined corner of the square to leave by.

Andreas stood alone on the lowest step of the prince's elysian hall, watching them go. He waited there until his men were no longer in sight. He used the time to pray—a brief devotion in thanksgiving, with his eyes and ears wide open. Then he walked after them, at the same careless pace they had affected.

There were seven little shapes curled up along the northeast side of the square—wretches who had arrived too late or were too timid to fight for the cleaner, straw-bedded places under Prince George's eaves, where the alms were given. Seven piles of threadbare rags, seven sets of calloused feet, seven pairs of grimy hands holding seven pathetic bundles tightly in their sleep, and seven hollow faces dreaming deep—but of dark, dusty heads, only six.

"Get up, Meribah."

The last urchin in line opened her eyes, and fear glimmered in the clear, shallow blue.

"Take a walk with me out of earshot?" he asked, in the exact words she had used in Venice. Meribah seemed to relax at last. Her smile deepened and grew roots.

"I thought you were going to Nicea, Meribah."

"I did go."

"That's traveling fast. You found your landed horse-breeder?"

"Even better," she replied, "I found a sea-going horse trader. Fast ship, fast horses, very nice." After a pause, "What gave me away?"

"Your hair," he said truthfully.

"It always does, under torchlight. Did you do that on purpose?"

"Yes." He had, though he had seen the red before his men passed by her—their light was provided to explain his keen eyes away, to let his men find her, and to dazzle lookers-on who hoped to follow them. His men had split off, their fires extinguished, once out of sight of the prince's hall and the hidden girl. Now they slipped through the darkened alleys on either side of their master, far enough away to conceal their movements. Each had a torch, a coal-pot, and a sword—Andreas had no fear of Meribah, but the prince's humor was notoriously mercurial.

"I didn't know he was protecting you, you know, and I wouldn't have hurt him. I'm not a person who can afford to feud."

"It's all right, Meribah."

"You're not mad?"

"No. I would have done the same—or sent my men to do it, instead. It's wise to investigate whomever you've met."

She stopped suddenly. "Then what do you want?"

Andreas wasn't ready—he had planned to lead gradually into his proposal. "I beg your pardon?"

"If you're not mad, and you knew I was going to be there— your guards would have told you I crossed paths with them— then why are you talking to me?"

He laughed. "That was quick," he said, patting her shoulder and walking on, "and right, too—I do want something. Are you still on your own project?"

"Mm-hmm."

"Could you set it aside for a while?"

"I guess so...."

"I am on a mission for the faith," whispered Andreas, close beside her ear, "and I am in need of services only you can provide."

Meribah grinned in incredulous surprise. "Me? I haven't been asked to do anything for the temples since—well, it's a long time, anyway. What can I do?"

"Travel with me. Bring your belongings to the camp, in three nights' time. Look for the man you spoke to on the highway. His name is Jacquy; he is the caravan master. He will tell you the rules under which I accept passengers, show you where to sleep, and bring you to Ljudumilu, who will help you. You will pretend to my guests that you are a paying customer, and you will not claim kinship between us. You won't deny it, if asked, but it isn't a thing for telling.

"All I want you to do...first...is to make friends with someone. I want to talk to her and her sire, but I can't go near them. Our kin in Constantinople have blackened our name in her eyes. She won't know you, and you look—"

"Harmless?" Meribah sounded discouraged.

"Non-threatening," he temporized. "You look like an innocent, no matter how dark your past, Meribah. It's an asset. I think you can get to her, and persuade her that I am—"

"Harmless?" The girl was mocking, now.

"Her sire's protector," Andreas continued, "and deserving of her trust. Which I am," he stated solemnly.

"Why?"

Why ask Meribah for help? Why protect Gregory? Why persuade Zoë? Or why do I deserve Zoë's trust? This one poses questions like a child or an idiot, Andreas said to himself, irritated. *Or a philosopher,* he added, and was even less pleased by that comparison.

"There are too many ears in this city," he declared, "and too little noise to fill them." The Egyptian stopped, met his *Franj* cousin's eyes, and asked, "Will you do me this favor, in Set's name, Meribah my sister?"

Meribah stared back in silence. She seemed transfixed, though there was nothing new in his question. *What's the matter with the girl?* Andreas checked himself—no, he hadn't used the eyes of Set to stun her—he hadn't called on his god's power at all. Her trouble was in her own mind....

"I will," she replied, like a prisoner consenting to her execution.

And suddenly, with her mind made up, she was the Meribah he remembered, cheerful, eager to go. "I will," she repeated, like a village girl agreeing to her marriage. "I'll help you," she promised, beaming.

After Andreas had made his farewells and the street grew silent, Meribah stood where he had left her. "And then you can help me," she murmured sadly, "in the name of Set, Ankhesenaten my brother."

Chapter Five

Into Bulgaria on the Via Militaris
July, 1205

Zoë sat nervously on the edge of the seatboard, uncertain whether she was hoping to see the new girl or not. When the hoofbeats came up beside her, she turned her head only very slowly. There was the enormous, dun-colored horse, and there was the dirty white cloak, and there was the rider, leaning so far forward that she almost lay along the beast's neck. She gave Zoë a wide, secret smile.

"Hello."

"Hello," Zoë answered shyly.

"Nice night," began the stranger.

"Yes?" said the Ravnos, with the kind of polite disbelief the seasick give sailors who talk of calm waters.

The stranger's eyes darted up and around the four points of the horizon, examining the heavens. "Nice," she confirmed after a moment. "Why, what's wrong with it?" She seemed to really want to know—as if Zoë might be right, and the sky playing tricks on her own senses.

"Maybe it's just me," answered the gypsy girl. She twisted her hands in her lap and watched them move. The stranger stared into the mane of her horse, embarrassed by the other's silent sorrows.

"Are you Zoë?" she asked at last.

"Yes." Zoë sounded grateful—and wary. She didn't add anything else.

The stranger grinned. "I'm Meribah." She clucked to her

horse, and he doubled his step for a few paces—enough to bring her head, not his, in line with Zoë's. "I heard about you from Boleslaus," she said.

"I don't know him."

"He didn't say that he knew you. He just said that…well, that you were very pretty," and Meribah let a wistful, admiring glance escape her, "awfully shy, that you didn't come out of the wagon much, that you didn't talk to anybody, and that you were…new."

"New," repeated the fledgling Cainite. She tried out the sentence for herself, as if speaking another language. "I am new."

"And I met your—I met Gregory the other night."

Zoë nodded, but said nothing.

"He seems very nice," Meribah decided. She waited a little while before she said it, and even longer afterwards, trying to get the Ravnos to say something. While the pause stretched into outright break, she clucked at the horse again, swung her left leg over his bag, and rearranged herself sidesaddle.

"Is he yours?"

Meribah looked up, and Zoë's face held real interest. "He's mine," she answered, nodding happily.

"What's his name?"

"Eureka."

"You found him?"

"Sort of." Meribah looked from her own hose-clad legs to Zoë's full skirts, considering. "Would you like a ride?" It was a sacrifice, but she was prepared to make it. If her quarry loved horses, that would be an opening easy to get through. She felt she could talk for hours—maybe whole nights—about Eureka and the adventures they'd had galloping across Greece and Nicea.

The other girl looked doubtful.

"You can ride, can't you?" Meribah didn't mean to sound scornful—she was thinking about her conversational gambit, watching it crumble in that vacillating expression.

"Of course I can ride," Zoë snapped out, and Meribah was sure that she could not. Zoë realized it, too, but wouldn't or couldn't back down. "Where I come from, we use saddles and bridles," she said haughtily.

"Oh." Meribah scooted over, straddling the horse's hips.

"Then you sit in front, and hold onto his mane, and I'll give him the guides from back here." When Zoë hesitated, she offered, "Since you'll have a handhold, would you mind if I held onto you?"

Zoë gathered up her skirts and stepped onto the horse's shoulders.

"Steady, boy, steady," whispered Meribah, as the animal winced under the ill-placed weight. "One leg each side, there you go...ready? Hup!"

When Meribah and Zoë returned, there was hay in the gypsy's hair and mud on her dress. The *Franj* had added grass stains to her white cloak, and dust rained from her tangled curls with every step. The stallion's coat was slick with sweat, and there were burrs buried in his feathers.

Meribah dismounted with bounding grace. Zoë slid down Eureka's flank—a controlled fall, better than she had fared earlier. She landed on two feet, and both girls burst into giggles, remembering how the hay got in her hair. Once the laughter had burned through, and there were only occasional sparking fits of it, Meribah reached out and brushed the straw out of Zoë's hair and the mud—the dried patches, at least—off of her dress. Zoë tried to do the same for her new friend, but it was hard to tell which stains on the cloak were new, and there seemed to be more dirt on Meribah than on the road.

"Oh, never mind it...I'm going to get messier still, cleaning him up," said the *Franj* girl, patting Eureka's filthy hide affectionately. "Best to do it soon, too, before it cakes in." She scrubbed the skin beneath his eyes very lightly with her little finger, and threw an arm around his neck. "We'll be off, now, I guess." She jumped and pulled herself up. Straddling the horse, she asked, a little shyly, "Come again tomorrow?"

"Please," said Zoë, smiling back.

"I'll see if I can find a bridle for him—if he'll take it," Meribah finished. "Bridle," she said, and Eureka's ears twitched alarmingly. "Good night," she called out over her shoulder. "You used to wear a bridle," Zoë heard her argue, as they trotted off toward the corral.

Gregory hurried away from the window to bend over his desk, pretending to study from a diagram of his own making. He turned to face the door as she came in, and his hands were full of ivory, wood, and glue.

"Been out?" he inquired amiably.

She was defiant. "Yes."

His eyebrows rose, but he said nothing. He held out the work for her to take from him, and she did. He picked up the drawing, and they walked together to the second wagon, their workshop. There were several workbenches set up outdoors, where Andreas's servants placed them every night. Inside, Gregory had installed all the tools and half-finished projects salvaged from their house in New Rome. One end, near two windows left open in good weather, he had lined with clamps and vises. While she kept pressure on the setting glue, he fixed a clamp and padding to hold it steady. Each opened a window, to let in the air—and the sun, by day, when they slept in the light-sealed house wagon.

"You're not going to tell me not to see her," said Zoë darkly. It was an order and a question, and full of reproach.

"Should I?" he asked mildly. This confused her, and she showed it. "If I had a reason, my dear child, perhaps I would. I don't. In fact, I have a reason to have some faith in her, but it's not a reason that you would like."

"What do you mean?"

Gregory sank onto a stool, sighing. "In Adrianople, Andreas had to take everyone who asked, to avoid slighting them or having them follow along in the mob, without agreeing to his rules. This girl joined the caravan in Philippopolis, not Adrianople." He studied his pupil. "Do you deduce nothing from that?"

"He didn't have to let her travel with us."

"Correct. Ergo, she is a person whom he is willing to trust even in these crowded, irregular conditions. And because I trust him in certain circumstances, I trust her, within a smaller set of those limitations." He let her digest this a moment, and then, "I would like to suggest that you be careful. I may be wrong in my judgment of him, as you think. And he may be wrong in his judgment of her. Keep in mind what she is, and what you...

have become," he continued painfully, "and consider that we do not know who she is, where she comes from, or what she might want."

"I am going to go with her again tomorrow," Zoë told him sullenly.

"Good," said Gregory, without apparent concern. He smiled beneath his whiskers, where his childe would not see. "I hope that you have a very pleasant time."

One week later, the riding lessons had become a nightly routine. Meribah begged a horse for Zoë from Ljudumilu, and Andreas arranged for the grooms to provide it. The Ravnos spoke to the stable boy once and to Carl twice, and had been seen on the fringes of the crowd at one of Boleslaus's story-tellings. Andreas and Gregory met more often, and for longer, and tonight they had hopes of playing chess as well as backgammon. They sat on either side of one of the tinker's tables, out-of-doors, and the two boards were set out between them. In the second gammon, while Gregory considered his sixth move at chess, the muted thunder of girls on horses passed by.

Gregory made his move, and punctuated it with conversation. "Will they be all right, do you think?"

Andreas looked up, trying to read behind the question. "They stay within the guarded cordon," he began.

"Meribah is the most carefree creature I know, but not a careless one."

"She's a very interesting girl—unusual. Wherever did you meet her?"

"Antioch," answered the Setite truthfully, aware of the pitfalls now. "A few years before Richard and Philip broke the truce."

"She's old, then."

"Not yet a century, I believe," replied Andreas. "Older than Zoë, of course, but a child still, beside old men like us."

"What does she do?"

"What do you mean, do?"

"I tinker, you move men and goods, she...?"

"She wanders, I think."

"Only that?"

"When I met her, her mentor had plans and friends and grudges and all the rest of the usual agendas. She followed his lead," explained Andreas, tapping a pawn significantly. "He was killed shortly after I left them. I haven't heard of her doing anything meaningful since then, but she does travel far and often."

"An orphan," mused Gregory. The Setite nudged the pawn into the next square, where it threatened nothing, but allowed the king's bishop freedom to move. "Of what clan?"

"My clan—and by that I mean mine, not Khay'tall's or Sarrasine's." He felt no qualms in describing the little *Franj* this way. She was no Egyptian, and hardly a paragon of Set's virtues—but she was no decadent, no heretic, no blasphemer. He was as sure of that as he was of his name. "Is that reassuring?"

Andreas grinned. "I think so."

The Ravnos nodded. "Let's not tell Zoë, though."

"But you don't mind?"

"No, not at all." Gregory rubbed his chin, and his smile was wide enough to show through the beard. "It's good for her to get out…to be taken out of herself. She's been very low, and I remind her too much of what happened." He picked up the dice, clinking them together in a loose fist. "Of what she's lost," he murmured, and Andreas wondered how morbid the instruction must be that he gave her—guilt-ridden, curse-burdened, soul-staining, wrong.

"Do you know what happened last week, for the first time in months—when Meribah came?"

"No," said Andreas. "What?"

"Zoë laughed."

Meribah sprang up the steps of the midwife's wagon, but knocked quietly on the doorjamb.

"Come in, Blessed One."

Meribah squirmed—she had been to see the old woman almost every night for three weeks, and Ljudumilu had called her by that title every time. The girl recognized in the matriarch wisdom, cunning, endurance, and a will greater than her own.

Yet the matriarch revered her—literally worshipped the blood flowing through her veins—and treated the Setite in a manner she was certain she could never deserve. Meribah entered the wagon, knelt by the old woman's bed, and took her hand.

"Granddame," said the girl.

"I am ready to serve you, Beata," said Ljudumilu, sitting up.

"Please, lie still...don't tire yourself. I'll only be here a moment."

"As you wish." Ljudumilu lay back again. She half-closed her eyes.

Meribah tried to remember what she had wanted to say before respect threw her off. It took a moment while she looked for the answer in the floorboards. The midwife, unobserved, observed a great deal.

"Animals," said Meribah. "You remember I thought Zoë liked horses, and then she didn't? She likes animals. She says she used to make animals....I don't understand that, because I asked if they were sculptures, and she said no. Her birds sang, and her cats walked around and hunted mice, but they don't work anymore—she's very upset about that. But I thought she might like to hear birds...if someone has a pet bird, you know... or see real cats." The young Setite spread her hands wide. "I only know horses, you see, and dogs, because the grooms keep some of those, too. Are there cats?"

Ljudumilu nodded yes. "Magda keeps cats to protect the grain, Beata. They patrol the cook wagons."

"Where the fires are," said Meribah, discouraged.

"I will ask if there are kittens, Beata." replied the midwife. "There are almost always kittens. Magda can bring some to me, and you might take them to your friend."

"She is my friend, now."

"Very good, Beata. I will tell my master that you have suc-ceeded so far, and we will give thanks to our Lord."

Meribah kept silence.

"Is there anything else I may do for you, Beata?"

"I wish—" the Setite looked up into the old woman's line-graced, mother's face, then quickly back at her own bare toes. "I wish you would call me Meribah, or—or girl, or—or 'hey, you.'"

Ljudumilu's eyes opened wide, and she turned their piercing gaze on the Child of Set beside her, fearing to see what expression the little goddess would display next. "And why should you wish that?"

Before the answer could come, brisk steps sounded outside, and a confident knock—a signal, rather than a request—burst from the door. Dehaan was already inside before he noticed his grandmother's visitor. He stopped immediately, aghast.

"Forgive me, Granddam," he murmured, though the words were very clear. "I didn't know you had a guest." He backed away, putting his hand on the wooden lintel, ready to duck under it and out.

Meribah sprang to her feet. "No—" The mortal man turned again, alarmed. "No," she said less violently, though still in a kind of humiliated panic. "I was just leaving, really." She could feel the old woman staring at her, and felt the gray eyes groping through her secrets. The man—she had seen him, she had heard a little about the Rooster—backed away. His eyes were curious, and friendly, and even sympathetic

But whatever the red-haired girl thought as she slipped out of Ljudumilu's domain, the midwife was not watching her go. She was looking at her grandson instead, and what she saw disturbed her deeply.

"A pretty mystery goes walking there," whispered the Rooster to himself.

"Is she?" The old woman's hearing was as sharp as her sight. Dehaan broke his reverie. "Is she what, Grandma?"

"Pretty."

The young man seemed genuinely confused. "I haven't thought about her body, Grandma." He closed the door behind him, shaking his head. "The mystery is what I admire."

"What mystery.7"

He laughed. "Now you are joking." Her robe and shawl hung from pegs beside her bed, and he took them down, turning the sleeves right-side-out. "You must know how much she is wondered about, amongst ourselves." Dehaan pulled the blankets down to his grandmother's waist, assisted her to sit up, and helped her slip the heavy wool on over her thin linen chemise.

When she was dressed for the cold night air, he crouched down beside her, his young hands on her withered shoulders.

"Why did he…acquire…this girl7 Why haven't they spoken since we left Philippopolis?"

Ljudumilu waved away the supporting arms and struggled to her feet herself. "Our lord, Dehaan, he does not tell me everything, but I can guess." She sighed, and the sound made the young man old.

"What do you guess, Grandma.7" He dreaded the knowledge.

"I do not tell you everything, Dehaan," said the matriarch, with an affectionately sinister chuckle. "Trust in Set and our lord. Be content. And do not become too fond of our pretty young guest, or you may regret it."

Chapter Six

Sofia, Bulgarian Empire
July and August, 1205

Ankhesenaten intoned the final words of the prayer for aid in counsel, and closed the case around the presence of his god, careful not to spill the libation pooled around the statue's feet. He had given of his own divine ichor, and five of his worshippers had felt moved to offer their lifeblood. His and theirs mingled in hope of requital. *Lord, answer us. Give us safe haven in this changed domain.*

Tonight, he would petition for formal entry to the city. Bela Rusenko, the prince, was a newcomer to the town and title. Andreas had hoped to find the predictable tyranny of Prince Basilio awaiting him as it had on every previous journey into the city, News had come to him, however, that Basilio had left with the last Byzantine officials several years ago and this young Cappadocian Bela had managed to replace him. Such transitions were rarely peaceful and Andreas could only hope the new prince would understand the advantages of giving fair shelter to traders and envoys hailing from across Europe.

Andreas stepped out of his wagon, and found the women preparing his heralds for their mission. Dehaan would go to speak. Willem carried letters and the roll of names and lineages seeking hospitality of Bela. Magda and Danica finished adjusting the men's livery and turned to Ljudumilu for approval. The midwife had seen the Setite emerge from his haven, though, and deferred to her lord.

"Very good," he said proudly. "You shall do us credit."

Andreas sent them off on their embassy, and let himself be fussed over in turn.

They dressed him in the scarlet robe he had worn in Adrianople. When he was costumed to their satisfaction, they seized the reluctant Goreb and wrapped him in cloth-of-gold and white linen. Then they waited, all together, for word to arrive.

Prince Bela's herald brought permission for the audience within the hour. Andreas began his march to the city gates, bodyguard in tow, and picked up his guests as he walked.

"Hold still, Gregory." Meribah tried to fold the cuffs of the tinker's sleeves to hide the fraying edges. "Give me the pin…there. How does he look?"

"Better, I guess." Zoë wrinkled her nose, thinking. "We need to do something about the burn marks, though. Can we cut up my vest to patch it?"

"You need your vest. You keep it," ordered her sire. "You look very pretty in it," he added more softly. "Besides, I don't think we have time for this, girls." The Wonder-Maker was tired, and he felt his patience ebbing. He appealed to the fourth member of their party, the minstrel Boleslaus. "Didn't you say the heralds had already gone in?"

"Yes. Not long after sunset." The Toreador cocked his head to one side, considering the girls' efforts. "But I'd say to keep working, up until the last minute. Basilio kept a formal court, and I doubt his successor has completely dispensed with formalities."

"Master Lakeritos?" Magda stood on the edge of the Ravnos's territory. "My lord sends his compliments, and desires that you should join him." She cast a glance over the darned hems, the pinned sleeves, and the scraps of cloth in Zoë's hands. "He sends you these, as well—" Danica crossed to the Wonder-Maker, and placed emerald-colored samite in his unresisting hands. There was a leaf-green gown for Zoë, a parti-colored tunic for the minstrel, and an outfit in turquoise satin to set off Meribah's hair.

"Please return my thanks to your master, madam. We shall

attend upon him presently."

"Thank you," said Meribah to Danica, and the mortal laughed nervously.

"If you want to thank us, Bea—" she caught herself— "be as careful as you can in them, and save us scrubbing out the bloodstains."

Prince Bela held court, where his predecessor had, in the belly of Serdica Castle. The procession made its way toward the great fortress and then underground into the rooms now reserved for the undead. Roman-era columns bore iron sconces driven deep into the stone. There were four to a column, all too high to reach without a ladder, and set at the quarter points like a compass rose. Each sconce was filled with a torch, and the ceiling was of hammered gold. Bronze and steel shields hung from the walls, polished to mirror finish. The light was very bright, and Andreas had to force himself not to look up or at the walls. Bright lights were no friends to the Followers of Set and he wondered whether this new prince knew that.

No, he quickly concluded, *Prince Basilio was a master of shadow-magics. Bela guards against his predecessor's return—or that of his kinsmen.* His eyes stung, but he endured and led the way forward through the hall. His passengers trailed after him.

When Zoë entered the golden room, she stood on the threshold entranced. Not since the terrible night she had died had she seen light—real light, like the day, not feeble candles, pale lamps, or distant, ruddy fires. She forgot her troubles, staring up at the gleaming ceiling—then into the beautiful lights themselves. Fear and wonder mounted in her, fighting for power over her feet. Through the rising panic, she felt Gregory's hand tugging her forward. The spell broke and she walked on, trembling.

Meribah came in last, behind Boleslaus. He was taller than she, and blocked her view of the hall until she was inside it. Stung by the glare, she became confused by it—felt sure someone must be holding fire in their path—sought out the source— and blinded herself looking at the nearest torch.

"Hell," she muttered. Boleslaus took her hand and guided her through the colonnade. "Thank you," whispered Meribah.

His arm felt strange under her fingers, and she thought how different people seemed when you could not see them.

After a long and stumbling walk, the texture of the flagstones changed. By the sound, this room was smaller, though still large enough to echo. Boleslaus turned, moved on, and then halted. Meribah felt a pressure behind her knees, guessed, and sat. The Toreador took his place beside her. As she listened, she heard someone speaking Latin. It was Andreas, apparently finishing a lengthy speech.

"...For in this new era for Sofia and all Bulgaria, I know we will find a wise and forward-thinking ruler."

"In the name of all Sofia," intoned another, rather gruffly, "I welcome you and yours. Your reputation in this city is a good one, Andreas Aegyptus. You are granted your rights here as you have had them before. I trust it shall not be the last occasion. I extend our welcome to your guests, and make them my own for your sake."

"My thanks, Bela Rusenko," said Andreas, and Meribah thought she could see a dark red shape bow to further darkness, "though I believe you will find my guests more than worthy of their own welcomes."

"I am sure of that."

Lord Valerian stood and stepped forward.

"Gnaeus Eligius Scaevola, you are most welcome in our city, which many still call Serdica, so named by your own ancestors," said the prince. "The vicissitudes of time have not yet come close to erasing their legacy and I am eager to hear tidings of the Grand Court."

"You honor me, Prince Bela. I hope you will favor me with news of your neighbors." The Ventrue emissary returned to his seat, and the next guest presented himself.

"Milord, I am Ewald Fairfax, Ventrue childe of Anne, childe of—"

Bela, long haired and pale skinned, waved the recital off impatiently, and his courtly manners cracked a little. "I have that, boy—" He tapped the scroll on his knee for emphasis. "As much of it as I want. It's a man's achievements that make him great, not his kin or clan. I'm happy to have you here, and your lady. There have been reports of truly vile acts in Byzantium and I would hear the truth of it."

Galatea rose next, and the movement made her the most important creature in the room. Andreas stared, rather pleased at how well his guest compared to Sofia's beauties. He could hardly keep his attention on the prince, and when he managed to concentrate on the man, he felt a jealous pain. As Galatea spoke her name—softly, in that deep, musical voice—Bela's eyes traveled down the perfect body, lingered, and climbed slowly up again. Something of a waif himself, and devoid of even the mockery of living warmth most Cainites possessed, the prince seemed like a pauper before a mound of gold, to gaze on such beauty. He read her ravishing face, as if to memorize it forever. His lips parted, and the new lord of Sofia revealed his quality.

"Stow it, bitch."

Galatea's radiance snuffed out like a candle. The body was perfect still, the eyes almost as bewitching—but only mortally so, and her real beauty was marred by hollow fear. A low hiss sprang up among the courtiers. She paled, and Andreas suspected she was close to frenzy. She would fly at Bela and be slaughtered, or bolt and kill someone else and be hunted out of the city.

"Thank you," said the prince, as though she had complied with an ordinary request. The tension parted. "I understand that you must be frightened, so far from home, but you will need no weapons here." Galatea took the opening he had left for her.

"I...I am sorry. We have been through so much...."

"Of course," answered Bela shortly. She could save face, but he would not pretend sympathy for her. Andreas had none either—he strove to hide his wrath with her, while he searched his memory for the signs of magic. *There must be some way to tell when she is doing that,* he told himself. *If Bela had not seen through it, I might have begun to believe in her.* There was, of course, a deeper question: How had Bela seen through—and resisted—her charms?

"Abetorius Minor," said Calleo. He retreated immediately, and the prince showed no desire to stop him.

"I am Gregory Lakeritos." The Ravnos gestured to his apprentice, who made an anxious courtesy to the large, rough man on the ivory throne. "My childe, Zoë."

"Welcome," Bela said casually with little attention. He didn't, it seemed, recognize the Wonder-Maker of Constantinople.

"I'm Meribah," said Meribah, feeling silly.

"Boleslaus, at your service, my lord."

"A minstrel, I understand? Perhaps you will favor us with a song, later." Bela released the Toreador from his scrutiny, and settled himself to address them all.

"I grant you hospitality," he announced. "But because you are visitors, residents of the city are forbidden you for blood. You shall be given hunting rights only among the traveling kine."

And that simply, the audience, as such, was over. Prince Bela descended from his oversized dais. The courtiers left their places to meet the guests. Conversation simmered.

"And now, my friend, a word for our ears alone." The prince sat his guest down at a long oaken table. It was meant to hold forty, lengthwise, but they faced each other across the shorter dimension.

"Thank you."

There were a warm, fragrant jug and two goblets between them, and Bela poured generous draughts for them both. "Unless you would rather not?"

Andreas shook his head, smiling, and took an eager sip. "Before I grill you for news of Constantinople," began the prince, "for you must know that I am not satisfied with the tales your clients spun me the other night, and before I pick you quite clean of information on my dear neighbors in Venice—is there anything I can tell you?" The Setite nodded, and his face was grim. "Tell me anything you know about the road ahead. Are there wolves?"

"Not lately. Something strange seems to have come up the high road with you, though. Some kind of bear?"

"A Gangrel. He wouldn't come in to see you, though he sends his respects." That wasn't exactly what Hadeon had done, but it was a lie Andreas felt confident about.

"No matter. So long as the wolves haven't found a bear to join them."

Andreas shuddered. "There aren't such things, Prince Bela."

The prince laughed nervously. "No, thank god, that's truly a legend." He took a long, steadying drink from his goblet. "As far as the mortals go, the land is unsettled, and you might find yourselves attacked by bandits making use of the chaos, or by an army determined to capture loot and provisions. You've come through worse, I think...you could marshal your forces and do it again. Our benighted cousins are less active, but more hostile. Your connections are good, and I think you would have no trouble, except for one thing."

"Calleo."

"Yes. I did what I could to keep that mummery the other night short and to the point, but he doesn't hide what he is. After this, he'll be known to be traveling with you—since the city has become fully Bulgarian, there's no telling just how many Tzimisce spies live here among us. I don't have to tell you how many hate your Tremere.

The wizard will make you a target, no matter what friends you had last time you took the Military Road. He could be an excuse for attacks against you. He will be something to make—" the ashen prince grimaced in detestation, "politics around."

Andreas thought for a moment. "What news of the road west?" he asked at last.

"To Skopje? Wolves. The mountains grow them like trees. I'm afraid that my predecessor did not take very many precautions to keep them in check. In that direction, the land is theirs. The road itself is rough going. There's good Roman stone for the first half, slippery under the mud and rain, but solid. After you cross the river Struma, it's just a wide cart-path. If the rains hold off, you might get through without much trouble. If the rains come early, you'll be lucky to make two miles a day, and you'll certainly have to winter in Skopje."

The prince paused and did not seem to notice a fly that landed on his cheek. "On the other hand," he continued, "Count Tomislav would certainly welcome you. The beasts press very hard on him, particularly in bad weather. The whoresons seem to thrive in it. If you promised your men and yourselves—those of you who can fight—to defend his domain, he'd probably throw open the gates for you himself."

Bela studied his guest's countenance and found doubt. "I can send a courier ahead," he offered. "Tell him to expect you. Tomislav and I are on good terms."

"No," Andreas said, and continued slowly. "I am not sure yet. Let me think on it a while."

"Very well. Tell me before you leave, and I will send whatever message you like." Bela refilled their cups, drank again, settled himself comfortably in his chair, and grinned. "Now. Perhaps you have some tales to tell me...."

The first one came dressed as a monk, and there was nothing ominous about him. He begged entrance to Prince Bela's court reasonably enough and made a blasphemous speech about the Christian Messiah which was well tolerated, but not really listened to.

The second came in the guise of a nun two nights later. She proclaimed the blessings of Christ on some who were present, and condemned others—Andreas, in particular—as enforcers of lies. This tried the prince's patience and the city's resources a little further, but troubled no one. Most assumed that the two were mad and not worth resenting.

The third wore bloodstained rags and a cross of human bone on a thong around his neck. His petition for entry came during the gathering meant to wish the caravan well on its journey north.

Andreas and Valerian had been speaking with the prince about sin and statehood—basic principles of right and wrong in murder, execution, and war. It was a topic of conversation the new prince seemed anxious to gather opinions on, and the problems interested the Setite as well.

As the petitioner shuffled into the chamber, the courtiers and caravan travelers drew aside to give him room, though not so far back that they would miss the spectacle. The monk advanced, clasped the newcomer's hands, and called to the madwoman to join them. Bela let the three confer for several minutes. No one else spoke.

"My lord," said the monk. "Our brother brings news of great joy."

"Does he really?" The prince's voice was dry as salt.

"I know you do not believe the glorious truths we have discovered," began the monk.

"I think it fair to say I do not understand them. Until just now, I didn't even realize that you and that woman were talking of the same thing. This man shares your—what is it, exactly, that you share?"

"Faith," cried out the ragged one.

"I see." Bela no longer sounded interested.

"Yes. We have a new understanding of the message of our Lord."

"You are welcome in my city for one week," decreed the prince. "After that, you must move on, all three of you."

"My lord—" entreated the madwoman, piteously. "The north road is—" began the monk, deeply concerned. "Prince Bela," said the ragged man, turning to the dais. "There are miracles happening among us. We wake by day and see angels in our sepulchers. We meet by night, and the patriarchs walk amongst us. And I have seen a vision, milord. Caine himself came to me in a dream, and told me that you would believe, and grant us sanctuary, and make a freehold for our church—"

"Enough, Appius." The prince looked ill. "You have a week, preacher. You and these others must move on before the seventh sun rises." Bela rose, bowed to his guests, and headed for the door of his private exit.

Andreas walked a short way with him, in respectful silence. He had no idea who this Appius was, but he was known to the prince, and Bela seemed to be dismayed by his zeal. The Setite made his footsteps a little louder, and his host stayed his hand on the door's latch, and looked back.

"I go to Skopje," said Andreas quickly.

Bela nodded once, and walked wearily away.

Chapter Seven

Through Bulgar Macedonia toward Skopje
August and September, 1205

Meribah hopped into Ljudumilu's wagon with a resolute smile on her face. She was determined not to be intimidated this time, no matter how reverent the old woman might be. "Thank you for the kittens," she sang without looking.

"You're welcome," said Andreas, coolly.

The redhead stopped short. Ljudumilu was not in bed; she wasn't there at all. "Hello," Meribah answered in confusion.

"I felt that we should meet face-to-face again."

"All right."

"Have a seat."

"Sure." Meribah plopped into a tiny chair by the door and looked receptive.

"You've made a great deal of progress. I'm impressed." Meribah turned a little pink, shrugged, and let him keep talking. "I realize that you have your own project to work on, and if you need to leave, I am prepared to accommodate you."

"It'll keep," mumbled the *Franj*, looking away. Andreas said nothing, hoping that the silence would goad her into speech. He still had no idea what her personal mission was, and his curiosity was quite a gadfly. Meribah sat in sphinxlike calm, and he gave up.

"You are willing to continue?"

She sighed in exasperation. "Yes. So, get on with it."

"I think you should tell her your clan."

"She won't like it."

"Perhaps not, but she saw enough of Cainite society in Sofia to want to know. Better that you answer the question before she asks it."

Meribah nodded, considering.

"So," Andreas changed tacks. "What do you think of her?" Meribah scowled. "She's nice. Really nice—kind of sweet, you know? Innocent...." The young Setite said it pityingly, and trailed off. Andreas couldn't tell what she was thinking. She went on, "There's something she's hiding, and it's horrible." The red head waggled, and then, "At least, she thinks it's horrible. Not the same thing."

"She's sneaky. She slips away from Gregory all the time. She even does it when he would have let her go anyway. She's really proud of being able to do that. If he questions her, she gets very touchy. Defiant, I think I mean."

Andreas murmured encouragingly. "Has he objected to you at all?"

"No." The girl's eyes opened wide. "Good god, they both seem so relieved when I show up. I get the impression that they don't say much to each other when I'm not there. I've listened a few times when they didn't know I was around. It's bizarre."

"Interesting," put in Andreas, who felt that Gregory's "curse" lay at the bottom of that mystery. "Helpful to us, I think. Well, tell her you follow Set, and see how she takes it. Looking in from outside, she seems to trust you enough to weather the shock. Remember that my goal here is to get closer to them both. Try her on the idea of meeting me."

"I will."

The older Setite rubbed his jaw, weighing Meribah's performance in his mind. He decided to take a chance. "While you are doing this," he told her, "Zoë may mention Khay'tall or Sarrasine. They did the damage in the first place," he explained, "and their actions—the reasons underlying their actions—intrigue me."

"Ugh," said Meribah.

Andreas's hand left his chin, and his brows rose in mock astonishment.

Meribah made a face. "They don't intrigue me," she declared. "They're awful. Ever go to the Silk Road? Well, I went once." She put her hands on her knees and leaned toward him. "Now, I see nothing wrong in eating well. And there's nothing wrong with a little self-indulgence. I like to feel full. But the kinds of things those addle-brained fools got up to in there—"

"You disapprove of orgies?"

"I hate to see good blood wasted, that's all. And if you dope up the poor mortal before you drink, they can't enjoy it. There's definitely something wrong with people who need their vitae laced with hashish, iced in cut-glass vessels, and served on the corpse. It spoils the hunt," she said defensively. "Ruins the smell. Weakens the herd." Meribah looked up at her elder. "Are you going to say anything, or are you going to just sit there and let me rant?"

"Why interfere with such a flawless argument?"

"Now I know you're laughing at me," complained Meribah. She gave him a playful shove and headed out the door.

Meribah waited too long.

"So, what are you?" asked Zoë, casually enough. They were lying on top of the lead wagon. From here they could watch the guards tend the fire, and they often did. It was a safely thrilling little hobby, and very good for their nerve.

"What do you mean?" said the Setite, rolling onto her elbow to look the Ravnos in the face.

"What are you? What clan?" Zoë propped herself up, too, and met her friend's jittery eye. "You've never said." It was almost, not quite, an accusation.

"You won't like it," Meribah told her, in the same tone she had used telling Andreas. "Look," she started over, "it was a long time ago, and I'm not exactly a paragon of my family's virtues."

"What?"

"I was…raised…Setite."

Green dread filled the younger girl's face. She scuttled away until she was sitting in the farthest corner of the wagon roof, where her heels had been, with her arms wrapped around her knees. Dark eyes watched Meribah suspiciously, and she asked, "Why?"

"You think I had a choice? Did you get a choice?!"

"Yes." Zoë said it proudly, lifting her head. Meribah looked hard at her. "No," whispered the Ravnos, and then, "maybe."

"He picked me because of my hair. That's why," explained the Setite. "And I said yes because I didn't know what would happen if I said no." Meribah sat up herself, leaning forward imploringly. "It was a long time ago," she said. "And he's dead." She shook her head.

"Why didn't you tell me? Nobody told me," whispered Zoë.

Why *does she think I didn't tell her? You got your wish, Merrie-girl—you terrify somebody. Good lord, if she backs up any more, she's going to fall off the roof.* "I was afraid to tell you, Zoë." Meribah straightened, trying to give the younger girl more room to cringe in. "I knew you didn't...you didn't like...my kind."

"How did you know? Who told you?"

"No one told me," protested the Setite. "No one needed to tell me. The whole camp knows how—"

"How what?"

She's gotten over me, thought Meribah, *or she'd be off the roof and running. She'd guessed already. Now just keep talking, and give her time to admit it.* She thought about her next move, and her face set. "How rude you are to Andreas."

The dark eyes widened in indignant surprise.

"Oh, come on. You're under his protection here—we all are. And yet you treat him like a leper. Worse, 'cause I think you'd treat a poor leper pretty well." She let her lower lip quiver just a bit. "And now you're going to treat me like that."

"No," said Zoë earnestly, coming out of her defensive curl a little. "You're different."

Meribah snorted. "How do you know?"

The Ravnos looked alarmed.

"I don't mean that I'm bad. I mean, how do you know that Andreas isn't just as different as I am? And who am I different from? How did you get to hate us—fear us—anyway?"

Very soft sounds emerged from Zoë. Meribah couldn't understand what they were. She caught a whiff of blood, and saw light gleam darkly on the skin below Zoë's eyes. Then she realized that her friend wept. Awe struck her; she had never seen the dead cry. Also, she was hungry, and ashamed that the smell of the tears had made her so. She crept slowly across the roof and put her arm over the sobbing childe.

"I'm sorry," she said. "I'm sorry." Zoë huddled into Meribah's side, and the older girl rocked the younger back and forth like a very small child. "I didn't know," said the Setite, and she still didn't. They stayed there for a very long time—one minute, one hour—Meribah hardly knew what she thought while she waited. She only held tight, hoping that she could somehow hold her friend together.

At the end of the time, Zoë shook away the circling arms, gently, insistently, but not without gratitude. "I'm all right. I'll be all right." She wiped her eyes, saw the color of the tears, and shuddered.

"You want to know what happened?"

Zoë squinted up the inside of a tiny brass tube, filing the burr off of a fresh cut. When she heard the knock at the door, she set down her tools. The day servants were sleeping. The night servant was busy in the kitchen. It was a bother, going to the door, but not onerous. She was accustomed to seeing visitors for Gregory's business and never afraid to do things herself. This would be a delivery of supplies—a merchant aware of whom he dealt with, willing to come by night—or a client newly arrived in town, hoping to see the artist himself but unsure where to find him.

She left the workshop, crossed the atrium, and opened the little hatch beside the door. No torch burned there—Gregory wouldn't have one by his own door, and the man waiting brought none—but there was a light upstairs for her to see by.

He had a dark-ashen, bloodless face. She didn't recognize him at first, but knew he was a dead man, like her foster father.

"Good evening, sir. May I help you?"

"I've come to see Lakeritos. Let me in."

It was a hard voice. She placed it immediately: Khay'tall's son, the Saracen. Sarrasine had come here once, long ago. Khay'tall she knew well. He came often, and recently—the night before, in fact.

Gregory hadn't been here then, either. She had let the Setite in, when he insisted, and though he'd been poor company, he'd been no trouble. Granted, he had pushed by her, dashing into the workshop, and meddled with things there. Zoë hadn't liked that, but the only thing he had touched—she'd kept a very careful eye on him—was the piece he had commissioned himself. She supposed that he had a right to do that. Naturally, she had inspected the bench, tools, and half-finished artifact as soon as he had gone. Nothing had changed. That set her at ease, and she decided that the strange man had simply been nervy. He had been absurdly anxious about the peculiar construction all along.

Nevertheless, she didn't want to let this one in. There was no special project here for him—no legitimate business.

"Master Lakeritos cannot see you now," she said politely.

Low laughter came through the little window. Her arms prickled, and she started to close the hatch. There was a rushing noise outside, a face close to the opening, and golden eyes where brown had been. She froze with her mouth open, feeling dull and stupid.

"Open the door."

Her hand fell to the latch and pulled it. The door swung free on its hinges, it was pushed open, touched her hip and shoulder, and broke the spell.

Zoë ran.

She ran inside, where there were hammers, tongs, hot coals…fire. She had only the vaguest idea what to do with them, born from the knowledge that Gregory disliked them. She made a hurried grab for a lamp and rushed to light the torches and her brazier.

He pursued, entering the room as she lit her third weapon— another lamp, springing to life almost as he reached her. She saw him clearly—tall, muscular, glistening with perfumed oil, wrapped in damask brocades. He had thick-braided hair, dyed red. It was rust-colored, not hennaed, and there were dark stains on his shoulders.

He hunted her down. He seized her wrists. The flame poured onto the floor and soaked in. The flagstones were on fire.

He kicked the legs out from under the quenching trough and drowned the light. He picked her up and carried her under his arm to the center of the room. He paid no attention to her—she was just something to be kept out of the way. Zoë hung uncomfortably over the invader's elbow. She struck and bit, wriggled to get hold of his fingers and bend them—he tightened his arm, and she could not breathe.

Now Sarrasine turned slowly, surveying the vast, vaulted chamber. From this vantage point he could see every part of it, and very little. There were scrolls, books, and row upon row of shelves to hold them. There were great tables crammed full of alchemical apparatus, racks of beakers and pots suspended from the ceiling, and desks loaded with paper. The walls were lined with benches, riven by pegs and small sconces, and hollowed out to store small things—precious stone, metal, gems—rare woods, ivory, shell. The great forge in the center was cold—Gregory never used it himself, and there were crates and barrels piled on top and all around. And everywhere, in all stages of completion, lay the Wonder-Maker's works.

Sarrasine took his prisoner's wrists again, and stood her up. His fingers were like iron bracelets. They didn't hurt unless she tried to move. He waited for her to realize this. Her resistance subsided, but she wouldn't meet his eyes. She had learned her lesson at the door.

"Look at me."

He twisted his grip, taking both arms in one hand. He used the other to wrench her head up to face him. The golden stare pierced her and paralyzed her body.

"Surrender," he commanded. "Yield to me."

The glowing eyes were two torches, moving toward her. They passed through her own and into her skull. They burned along paths in her memory, looking for something. Zoë resolved that they would find nothing. She made the paths circles without understanding how she did so. She willed that he would walk on—was he walking, holding the torches?—through the same uneventful night, over and over. The image failed her suddenly. The circle was meaningless. She tried to remember what her own feet looked like.

The monster grunted, in what she hoped was frustration. She prayed it was.

His eyes relented and returned to their own sockets.

"*Khay'tall was here. I know it. What did he come for?*" He demanded—*she must obey.*

"*I don't know,*" she said weakly. *It was true.*

"*He came inside. What did he do?*"

"*He asked to see my master.*" *Another truth. She had no difficulty saying it. It was hard to keep from volunteering the rest of what she knew, but she could resist if she tried.*

"*Why did he want to see him?*"

"*I don't know,*" answered Zoë, *and the miracle went on. All his questions were the kind she could answer without betraying Gregory. They went on for hours, but she found a way around, over, or under them all.*

At last, the interrogation stopped. Zoë's relief was almost more than she could bear. She sagged into her captor's arms, heart-sore. He dragged her, not roughly, to the closest workbench and sat her on it.

"*I am not fooled,*" hissed Sarrasine. "*I know that you are keeping something from me.*"

And the pain began.

He left no marks.

She told him nothing.

She passed out.

When he brought her around, he gave her wine to drink. She felt far better—almost grateful. He was powerful, and he had let her live.

"*I was not here,*" he said.

Zoë felt pressure on her heart and fought it off. She nodded obediently, trying to placate his furies.

"*You will say nothing about our talk to Gregory. You will not remember it. You will not remember me. You worked, you answered the door, no one was there.*"

"*No one was there,*" she repeated softly.

"*You returned to your duties. You fell asleep. You never saw me. You will not remember me when I leave. You do not know who I am now.*"

She made her face a blank, and he smiled.

"And then Gregory came home," whispered Zoë, shivering, "and we..." She stopped quickly. "I told him," she finished. Meribah stared at the younger girl in awe.

"You fought off Sarrasine?"

Zoë turned her red-rimmed eyes to her friend, confused.

"You didn't tell him what he wanted to know?" Meribah felt light-headed.

Zoë shook her head no, vigorously.

Meribah sank onto her haunches. "Zoë, when you fought off Sarrasine, you bested an elder vampire in a contest of wills. He used powers I didn't even know Set granted, and you won anyway. I couldn't have done that. I always—I'd cave in first thing. I'd have rolled over and done tricks for him. I'd bet Boleslaus— Andreas—Gregory—maybe even Valerian—couldn't have held out against all that."

"Really?" The young Ravnos brightened fearfully.

"Didn't Gregory tell you?"

"No." Zoë wiped her eyes again. What Gregory had said to her—what he'd done when he came home—she still couldn't talk about, but she listened eagerly to her friend's admiration.

"Look, I'm a nobody. I can't do that kind of magic. But I've seen Andreas—" she regretted the example as soon as she spoke, but didn't stop, for fear of calling attention to it— "push around a papal legate with his eyes, and soldiers, and guild masters. Strong mortals. And you were just a little girl."

"Zoë," said the Setite solemnly. "I am so sorry that this happened to you, and I don't blame you for hating Sarrasine. Now that I've heard, I hate him too. And when Andreas hears it, he'll be just as mad as you are."

Zoë shook her head. "Don't you tell him anything about me. I don't know what Sarrasine wanted, and I don't want any more of those monsters to think I know it—I don't want anyone else to come after me."

"He wouldn't do that. He's very important in the clan. He could protect you, and nobody else would dare—"

"No!" Zoë scooted off the side of the wagon and fell to her feet. Meribah stuck her head over the edge and looked down. "I don't want him. I don't trust him. I trusted you—" she gasped for breath to speak with, cooled a little, and went on— "I think I still trust you. Please don't tell him. Just understand that there's a reason why I'm frightened of him, and don't ask me to pretend there isn't."

She ran off. Meribah climbed slowly down. Though she had, now, a great deal to tell Andreas, she walked in the other direction. That meeting could wait for another night.

Zoë avoided her for a full week. Meribah kept well away from the Ravnos wagons, hunted among a different band of refugees, and tried to be patient. She spent most nights sitting on the forward wagon, watching with the guards. Occasionally the horn cry went up, sending everyone into desperate readiness for wolves. Nothing came from the alarms but excitement. She did learn to know the armed men by name, though. When Jacquy saw that she could fight, he found a sharp silver cap for the butt end of her broken spear.

Meribah was listening to the punch line of a very old joke when she heard a noise from the back of the wagon. She half rolled, half crawled to the edge and peered down. Zoë stood where Meribah had last seen her, looking up.

"Is there room for one more up there?"

"There's room." Meribah dropped her spear shaft and extended a hand to help the gypsy scramble up.

"You haven't told him?"

"I haven't told anybody."

They smiled sheepishly at each other. Zoë broke away first. She caught sight of the new cap on the spear, reached for it, and subjected it to a serious examination.

"Silver," said Meribah.

Zoë nodded and set the weapon down. The two girls stretched out along the rooftop to watch the watchers, and they said no more about it.

Another night on the first wagon. Meribah lay flat, staring into the darkness, thinking about the talk she still hadn't had with Andreas. She wasn't even trying to dodge it anymore—the man simply never had time to see her. Zoë kept herself a little better amused—she had brought along a little chisel and hammer, and was busily decorating Meribah's silver spear-cap with scrolling vines and what she said was an amulet of protection.

The horn called out. Zoë took her tools off the staff, and Meribah seized it. "Go home, stay inside until it's over." She was firm and Zoë nervous, but each hopped off the roof calmly enough. They had done this twice the night before and ten times in the last week.

Meribah trotted up to the guards, near to hand, but far from the light. The horn blew again.

"He's come in," muttered Jacquy, meaning Hadeon.

More signals sang out: *Wolf. Many. South. West.* Jacquy pulled out his own horn and blew, then looked to Andreas.

"Run ahead, Carl," said their lord, "and tell the west guards we will exchange with them, in two groups. Send Robert and Ton Wheelwright first. You will remember? And I want you to come back with them to man the road post. Dehaan stays here for you."

Carl nodded and dashed off. Andreas and Goreb followed him slowly. After several minutes, Robert and Ton loped in. Meribah and Jacquy set out to join the flank guards, and crossed paths with Ern the blacksmith and his eldest daughter Annemie halfway between the stations. The caravan master and the *Franj* Setite joined the others, and spoke by horn to the other posts. Answers came in, and time passed.

"Get ready," said Andreas. "We'll start changing places again in a minute. I don't want them to see us roosting."

The attack came to the heart—along the broad west side, as they expected, but northerly, to their left. Meribah raced along, fiercely frightened, with the rest.

She ran through screams, barking dogs, kicking horses, stamping oxen, and wild men. The pilgrims were rioting. She caught sight of a face, white in the moonlight, touched by madness. The woman reached out to her, and was pushed away by the pressure of the mob. Meribah recognized two of the men-at-arms from the north-road post among the terrified, mindless horde. A sword fell to the ground at her feet. She ran on, smelt blood, and knew that someone had walked barefoot on the blade. The scent moved on—no one stopped. The crowd would run forever.

At last she saw it—bigger than an ox and taller than a wagon, it still moved faster than anything had the right to. She only caught clear sight of it because it stopped to bellow a terrible lupine war-cry. It was, as far as she could tell, a huge wolf, although it seemed to rear up on its hind quarters like a horse and stay there. Its maw was huge, filled with fangs and dripping with blood-tinged foamy spittle. The smell of piss and blood was strong in the air.

Goreb stood before the beast, and Andreas slithered on its back. Slithered, because he had invoked the blessings of the god and taken on scaly, shining skin. Tougher and more agile than the undead human flesh of the vampire, this holy form gave him a chance in combat against such a beast. Meribah, not for the first time, wished her fool of a sire had seen fit to teach her such use-ful tricks.

The wolf lurched toward her and she jabbed at it with the silvered end of her staff. She felt it connect, and was thrown to the ground by the back of the monster's hand. A man stepped on her. He reeked of horses—Owain. Meribah waited until he was finished before she tried to rise, then sprang up to poke again at the beast. It tossed Andreas into the air and trampled Jacquy. Goreb darted in with both swords, and nearly missed carving into Meribah herself. The creature turned on the bodyguard, dripping five kinds of blood. Meribah caught the savory scent, and decided to go mad. She abandoned her spear, sank her claws into the wolfs matted hide, and buried her teeth under its ear. It bucked, and she flew through the air. Her landing broke the wheel of a wagon, her leg, and both arms. The hub cracked her skull. Stars burst in front of her, and the daze brought her out of her frenzy.

It was gone—almost everyone was gone. The pilgrims had finished fleeing, and the wolf-beast was nowhere in sight. Only Goreb stood. Jacquy lay prone, drinking of Andreas's arm. In sec-onds, he was up again, his wounds mending fast enough to bear. His master, now wearing the smooth skin of a man again, had already moved on. He bent over Owain with the gash still open in his wrist.

Meribah fixed her leg and one arm and struggled to her feet. Even she could see that the young man was far worse wounded than his father. She was surprised he still breathed, but he was strong enough to speak and move. He batted away the offered hand and bubbled a few words through the blood. He spoke a dialect she had trouble following. Flemish, realized the little *Franj*, wondering when she learned it. She limped forward, healed the other arm, and listened. She was very hungry.

"Let me go," whispered Owain. Andreas knelt beside him. The father was already there. The young man spoke to both. "I can hear my mother's voice."

"He's delirious," cried Jacquy. "Stay with us, son."

"I am too near the gates to turn back. You know that. And—we cannot outfight wolves, father," Owain insisted, and Meribah had seldom heard a man sound so sane. "My mother calls from Duat, to tell you this. Let me go, and we will plead together before the Lord of Storms. He can save us."

"She can go alone," urged Jacquy.

"She has been alone for a long time, father." His voice faded. "Let me go."

The caravan master said nothing, but he took his son's hand with tears in his eyes. Andreas sealed up the gash on his own arm.

"So be it," he declared. Andreas began to chant softly, in the young man's own language, preparing him for the journey.

It did not take long. The pale fingers grew paler, then lax. The father gripped tighter. He raised the dying hand to his lips.

The horns called again. Meribah scrambled for the gleam of silver and found her broken spear. Goreb caught her eye and put her on watch without speaking. He stepped over to the fallen man, leaned over, and kissed Owain's forehead.

"Go well and quickly, O blessed martyr."

Goreb was up again and alert. He looked expectantly at Meribah.

She crossed to the body hesitantly, not sure what to say. Hoping for inspiration, she bent and kissed the cold forehead. The crash came behind her.

The monster was back—or a different one. Meribah heard a

roar, and it was her own. She plunged the spear into its thigh. Jacquy dropped under its feet again, and it took an enormous bite out of Andreas. Then it pulled on the spear shaft and brought her in. Claws raked her side, and her belly was gone. She fell beside the caravan master, and watched the fight from underneath.

Andreas came in again. The creature lunged for him. Growls filled her ears like thunder. Suddenly the beast was twice as big—no—two of them, fighting above her. Their claws tore into her newly mended leg. A piece of fur landed on her face, and the battle moved away. She could see it only in the corner of one eye, then not at all. Noises wandered farther off.

Jacquy rose painfully and followed the sounds. Andreas appeared above her, holding a body. He dropped it on her and disappeared from view. The corpse was no one she knew, dead of a cut across the eyes. She fed herself and did what she could for her mutilated flesh. It wasn't much. The wolf wounds would take weeks to heal.

Meribah stood miserably.

Andreas held Owain in both arms and offered him to his cousin. She could hardly carry him over a shoulder—she just managed it.

"Take him to his brothers," he asked.

She nodded.

Jacquy charged back in sight, and Andreas went to meet him. As she walked away, she heard the Egyptian begin his plans. "Move us at first light. We don't stop again, day or night, until we're through the city gates."

Chapter Eight

Skopje, On the Bulgar-Serb Frontier
Over the Winter of 1205 and 1206

The caravan rolled into town in the last hour before dawn, but all of Skopje was awake to welcome them. Armed men on horseback escorted their column, and Andreas's men were relieved to let others share the strain of watching. Hay wains lumbered along to pick up the footsore refugees and pilgrims. Count Tomislav himself, with all three of his Cainite subjects and the mortal rulers of the town, stood in state to receive them. The gates were open wide behind him, covered in bright-colored silk banners—Tomislav's own, Skopje's, and a strange device, quartered, bearing a sphinx rampant, the eye of Horus, a papyrus blossom, and a snake coiled to strike. Andreas felt flattered. He walked out alone, ahead of the wagon train, and met his host.

"Andrew of Egypt!" exclaimed Count Tomislav. The crowd behind him began to cheer. Their lord ran to embrace the Setite, and the two men kissed each other's cheeks twice. The mortal lord did the same. "Welcome, welcome, noble Egyptian. Skopje is eternally grateful for the battle you have fought in its cause! I make you free of the city!"

The serfs cheered again. A path opened through their midst, and Andreas waved to his drivers. The wagons, beasts, mortals, and Cainites moved up as fast as exhaustion would allow. With the people's attention diverted to the caravan itself, the count drew his guest aside.

"Your shoulder?" asked Tomislav anxiously. "Your leg?"

The robes could not hide the missing pieces. Wherever the wolf had bit, the cloth sagged in. "Are the others in as bad a state?"

"Some of them. I have not healed very much." Andreas had fed often, but almost every drop of the dark waters had gone to save the wounded caravan crew. "Here they come, my lord. You may see for yourself."

Hadeon looked more like a bear than ever. His tunic and hose hung in shreds from neck and waist. Under the cloth, matching scars marred his hide. Sullenly, he approached them.

"Hospitality," he muttered.

"Granted," said the startled count. "Seneschal! A bed for this warrior." The Gangrel passed into the care of a pageboy, and hurried off into the town.

Gregory, Meribah, and Zoë came in together. Zoë walked between the other two. The Wonder-Maker leaned on her right shoulder and his cane, and the Setite leaned on her left and a crutch. Andreas swore—he hadn't seen his little ally's wounds since the night of the battle, and he hadn't really looked at them then. Meribah's neck bore claw-marks that disappeared beneath her clothes, and her dress hung so loosely about her waist that he knew almost all of the flesh was gone. He bounded forward and picked her up in both arms—for once Zoë didn't seem to mind his presence; she looked grateful—and presented her to the count.

"Meribah of Antioch, my lord. A cousin of my own." Meribah smiled and started quoting Homer on the blessings of a good host—Andreas paid little attention. He caught the Rooster's eye and brought the mortal running with a jerk of his head.

"I am honored," said the count, when the recitation was finished. "Seneschal!"

"Near my own quarters," suggested Andreas to his host, and relinquished the girl to Dehaan and the guiding page.

"Gregory Lakeritos, Wonder-Maker, and his childe Zoë, my lord."

"Not warriors, I see. You are welcome nonetheless. Seneschal!"

Last, and much later than the rest, came Boleslaus. He had to be wheeled up to the lord of Skopje in a barrow—the wolves had taken his legs. The people cheered louder for him than for anyone yet, and the poor minstrel looked completely embarrassed. He tried to make Ern, his porter for the night, go on past the count and Andreas without stopping. The smith laughed indulgently, but pushed him right to them regardless.

"What a fool I look," complained the Toreador. He pulled the hood of his cloak up to hide his face. "Being torn apart is nothing brave. Hadeon fought," said Boleslaus. "Hadeon was wonderful. I was just—dog's meat. I didn't do anything special."

"That isn't what Hadeon says," Andreas told him. To the count, "He held his post on the north side of the camp. Until they cut his feet out from under him, he gave not an inch to the beasts."

"Valiant and humble," Tomislav said happily. "We shall have to make you a knight." He bent down to clasp the cripple's hand—

And Andreas saw—thought he saw—blue skin, wrinkled and blistered, on a limb so twisted that the fingers curled up instead of down. He blinked, and Boleslaus's hand was a true hand again, scarred and grubby, whole and sound. Andreas felt the minstrel watching him.

"Seneschal!" hollered the count, oblivious to his guests' darkened moods. Ern and a page pushed on.

"He was the last," said Andreas.

"I thought you had more—Bela said—"

"Calleo has not left his wagon since the night of the attack. He is well, but unwilling to see any of us," explained the Setite, keeping his suspicions to himself. There had been stories—mad tales, gleaned from the mortal pilgrims—of a holocaust, a wolf on fire, and a creature made of stone setting the woods ablaze. Andreas believed very little of that, but hadn't made up his mind which parts he put faith in. "We have others too wounded to move," he went on, feeling that the sleepers would be safest in Skopje as heroes of the battle. "My men will look after them, if you can set aside a place no one else may enter."

"It will be my pleasure."

Andreas crept into Meribah's sitting room quietly. He expected to find her lying down or still sleeping. She was sitting by the window, staring down at the town with a curious, wistful smile. Her clothes fit again, and they were new.

"You're looking better."

Meribah turned without surprise. "So are you."

"I thought you'd be in bed. They told me you weren't quite well yet."

"Oh, Gregory and Zoë treat me like I'm made of glass. Fragile, you know. I think he knows better, but she—well, she doesn't really understand. Thinks I'm going to get an infection and go belly-up. Suffer a relapse. Need a leech instead of be one." Meribah sighed. "I tried to tell her you can't get worse than dead, and she's a smart girl—she just doesn't believe it yet."

Andreas laughed.

"Well, come in," said Meribah, rising. She hopped over to a low chair and pulled it toward her window. "Sit down. Tell me about the world beyond my bed of pain."

"Our mortal fellow travelers have started coming in. The Genoese group arrived this morning."

"That's good. I felt awful abandoning them out there."

"We brought as many as we could. We left almost all the food and water for the rest. More than enough."

"Half of them weren't sane, Andreas."

"They've recovered." He shook his head. "They weren't attacked again once we left. I think the wolves wanted us, and only us."

"Paranoid."

"Maybe." The conversation died off. "I spoke to Tomislav," Andreas said at last, with strange reluctance, "about the wolves. He tells me the wolves seem to be at war with each other. Have been for months."

Meribah sat up straight, horrified. "What about Owain?"

"What about him?" responded Andreas, bitterly. "No, I know what you mean. His father isn't speaking to me. I prefer to think he and his mother intervened for us just in time. The second wolf was the tool of Set's will. But...I wish you hadn't asked the question. You give me doubts...your faith doesn't lead you to my same belief?"

"I—I hadn't thought of it that way."

"Ljudumilu did. Immediately. She is preaching the miracle to my flock. Jacquy isn't speaking to her, either, and she refuses to see him."

The *Franj* Setite twined her fingers round her right knee, studied the interlocking pattern, and thought of Ljudumilu's displeasure.

"I talked to Zoë," she offered, to change the subject. "On the road from Sofia. I have the information you wanted about Khay'tall and Sarrasine."

The Egyptian's dark eyes flashed his interest. "Good. Very good..."

"But?"

"But I'm going to have to ask you to hold onto it for another night or two." He rose, tight-lipped. "You're not the only person up and walking again. There's one I need to talk to before he can run."

Andreas did knock, shortly, and then pushed the door open without further ceremony. Boleslaus was lying propped against soft cushions in a high featherbed, tucked in amid fine wool and linen. Two crutch-handled sticks lay by his side. He looked up at his visitor and reached for the canes as if to rise. Andreas gave him a glance with no friendship, closed the door, and barred the heavy portal fast behind him.

"I have seen through you," said the Setite. "You are a liar and an impostor. These are not sins, in my eyes, but you have taken advantage of me and my caravan. You have exposed me to greater risk than you can imagine. Explain, now, why I should let you live."

"I'm sorry," began the man in the bed. "I am accustomed to travel in disguise; I always hide my face, one way or another, to save the mortals the pain of beholding me. I know—I knew before we'd gone ten miles together—that I could have and should have told you. But I didn't dare show my face or travel under own name in Adrianople. My life was in danger. Constantinople was full of spies and assassins come to hunt out...my group. And I was followed from the city to our rendezvous in the suburbs—I dared not reveal myself. By the time I knew that the pursuit had been left behind, I knew you were not the man to forgive my deception."

Andreas considered this. "Who are you?"

The man in the bed hesitated, and the Setite countered with relentless patience.

At last, "Boleslaus" pulled off his nightcap and pushed down the blankets. He struggled a little further up, got comfortable, and closed his eyes. His skin began to fade. The ashen-cream became an all-over, venous blue with a texture like pleated leather. There were blisters on most of what Andreas could see—clear, small vesicles—not the worst Nosferatu hide Andreas had ever come across. It was rather pleasant, compared to the leprous corrosion or gangrenous pustules of many. Where the man in the bed suffered most was in the form of the body itself. It was so deformed that the anatomy was hard to decipher. Unless the arms themselves were wrong-ways-round, his fingers sprouted from the wrong sides of his palms. The shape of his skull was painful to look upon.

"My name is Vaclav," said the Nosferatu.

Andreas raised an eyebrow. "One of Malachite's brood?" he asked skeptically.

"I have that honor."

The Setite pursed his lips, reevaluating his counterfeit guest. As a Toreador, Boleslaus had offered secrets in exchange for his passage, and as a Toreador, those secrets had been of only moderate interest. What Boleslaus claimed to be true might or might not have been—the artist clan could confuse good intelligence with good storytelling, easily, and in all innocence. The Nosferatu, permanent outsiders because of their deformities, experts in espionage because of their powers of disguise— even invisibility—made secrets their business. Vaclav could be believed where Boleslaus left doubts.

There was a prophecy to consider, as well. Andreas felt rather gratified—he knew something that Takouhi did not. The mysterious doom hanging over the minstrel was revealed: He was another man, a hunted fugitive, and a witness to the vortex of destruction that had been Constantinople's last nights. An important witness, if his claim of descent from Malachite, advisor and confidant of the vampiric Patriarch of Constantinople, was truthful.

"When we spoke in Adrianople, you told me that you knew who killed Michael's Heaven. Do you still wish to tell me that to pay your passage?"

"It is a secret that should be known to you, among others."

Andreas frowned, unsure of what the man could mean. "You may live," he pronounced. "No prince pierced your disguise and took umbrage; I suffered no loss through your deception. If you jeopardized us on the road, you also defended us. My people were saved with your aid, and you have lightened the hearts of the pilgrims with your music.

"If you wish to continue with us, you may. I will accept you on our original terms and keep your secret. Disguise yourself as you like."

"Thank you." The image of Boleslaus began to spread across Vaclav's hideous form.

"And now," decided Andreas, "I believe it is past time for you to tell me that secret."

The face of his guest—half-blue, half-cream—tried to smile, and the misshapen skull wobbled back and forth.

"It is time," he replied, and commenced his narration.

Four nights later, Andreas listened to Meribah finish a different story—the story of a mortal girl facing down the worst snake in Byzantium. Meribah made a very exciting thing of it. She ran with Zoë to the workshop. She heaved the girl under her arm to stand like Sarrasine, with an evil expression. She bent over the huddled body of the child, trembling as she imagined Gregory would have done, finding his girl in such a state. In that pose, she stopped, backed a step away, and stood up.

"She didn't tell me any more. I don't know what he did; I think it upset her." Meribah scrambled onto her window seat and looked earnestly at her cousin. "It wouldn't have taken much to upset her just then."

"Not much," agreed Andreas, visibly disturbed.

"I think—" Meribah hesitated— "I don't think that Zoë is

going to be ready to talk to you—to see you at all— for a very, very long time. That scar runs deep, and it's not the only one."

Andreas's hand rose to his beard. He stroked the gold-beaded braid slowly, considering what his *Franj* accomplice had brought him. Sarrasine, yes—and Khay'tall, too, visiting the workshop—going to his cache—shortly before his murder. Did he come to take the scarab from Gregory's house and hide it, or bring the scarab to hide it with the Ravnos? The possibility was slim. Why not stay to see Gregory, if he wanted to hide the heart with him? And how was it that the girl saw no change in the—whatever it is—when Khay'tall left?

"I'm sorry I couldn't persuade her for you," continued Meribah. "I tried my best, but—she's not very logical."

Her cousin laughed. "And you are?"

"Of course I am! At least, I know enough to recognize a fallacy when I see one. Zoë thinks, 'Sarrasine is a right bastard. Sarrasine is a Setite. Therefore, all Setites are right bastards.' Fallacy. Pure and sweet."

"Where did you learn that?"

"That one is easy; the bloody crusaders taught it me. 'Turks don't speak French. These villagers don't speak French. These villagers are Turks.' And then they killed them all."

Andreas grinned appreciatively, though he wondered who had actually instructed her. The *Franj* invaders had little love of learning, and Meribah's sire had had no use for philosophy or critical thought. Sutekhankharen played his games by instinct, primitive guile, and base seduction; Meribah quoted from the classic poets and rendered phobias into postulates.

"Don't be sorry," he answered at last. "You did very well; you brought me almost all I needed. I need time to think about these things," he went on, standing to leave. "But I believe I will have something else for you to do very soon, if you are willing.

Gregory caught Zoë at the door of their shared chambers. She was startled to see him there—he had come in the other way—and flushed guiltily.

"Where are you going?" demanded the sire of his childe.

Zoë glared up at him, angered to the verge of tears.

"I came," he said softly, "to take you out to hunt. Every third night, we hunt. You know this."

"I'm going by myself."

"I cannot allow that," began the Wonder-Maker sternly. "You are too young and inexperienced." His voice changed. He pleaded with her. "It isn't safe for you go alone."

"Isn't safe?" she cried, laughing bitterly. "I'm safer with you?" Gregory flinched. She pushed him out of her way ruthlessly—his twisted legs weren't steady enough to hold him, and he fell against the doorjamb.

When she had done it, she gasped. In an instant, she was beside him, helping him up. "I'm sorry," whispered Zoë. "I didn't mean to...." She found his cane and gave it to him.

"It's all right," Gregory assured her, enchanted by the sight of her face, filled with concern for him. "No harm done. Now, let's go."

The round and gentle face furrowed and darkened. Zoë drew back. "No!" she shouted, and then more softly, "No." She looked away, fearful. When she met his gaze again, an inspired light struck the dark eyes. "I'll go with Meribah," she offered. "I won't hunt without her, I promise."

Neither satisfied nor happy, he had yet no objections to make. She took the silence for an answer and left him without looking back.

The first snows fell on All-Hallows Eve. Meribah stood on top of the city-side battlements, where the guards were fewest, and watched the white shroud descend on Skopje. She wore her dirty-white cloak to keep the snow from her borrowed clothes, but left the hood down and wore no wimple. Snowflakes caught in her red curls and landed on her face without melting; she had been outside long enough that the house-warmth was gone from her.

Andreas found her there, saw her eyes delight in the snow, and bided his time. Long ago, in Palestine, he had been as dazzled by the frozen sky—a desert child stopping in green Jerusalem, camped with his tribe on the hills above the city. It had snowed then and turned the silver frost white—stung his cheeks and eyelids with the cold—and vanished before the sun could rise to see it.

Meribah turned to look at the palisade beside her. Thick, feather-light caps covered the wood. She slid her hands beneath the snow, lifted the crust off the palisade, and crushed it between her hands.

He ducked too late; the snowball missed his face, but hit him square on the forehead.

"Serves you right, sneaking up on a poor girl like that," lectured Meribah, grinning. Andreas brushed the snow from his eyebrows and nodded his head ruefully. Sobering, she searched his face—something caught her attention, and she brushed herself briskly off. "What is it?" she asked seriously.

"Have a seat." Together they cleared the archers' ledge and hunkered down on it. Andreas checked the flagstones around them—theirs were the only footprints, and no one was in sight.

"I have another task for you." He leaned his head on his doubled fists, looking earnestly into her eyes. "I want something from the Ravnos—that which Gregory was building for Khay'tall. I need to obtain it."

Meribah's face fell. "The thing that Zoë was afraid of people coming after? You want it?"

"Yes. I suppose that justifies some of her fears of me—and I understand if you would rather not involve yourself any further. However, this is a temple matter, Meribah, and very important to me. My mission hinges on the possession of Khay'tall's secret cache. I believe that in my hands it will advance the cause of Set in the living world. And I desire, above all things, to keep the prize from falling into Sarrasine's bloody hands.

"I also believe that Gregory, and Zoë too, are in danger as long as they control Khay'tall's secret. Sarrasine knew that they had it; I think that they brought it with them—that is why I called you in, in the first place—and others may know. Sarrasine will kill them for it, if they cross his path again. He has no reputation with Michael's court now, nothing to lose by a direct attack. And Gregory does not travel in secret. He is famous for his craft. I keep our route to myself until we leave each city, but it may be guessed easily."

His cousin thought for a long time. Eventually, she asked, "What do you want me to do?"

"I would like Gregory to put the prize in my hands, as a favor between friends."

Meribah looked relieved.

Andreas smiled. "It is possible that the cache was left behind in New Rome. If that is the case, I need to know, but I suspect that they took it with them when they fled the city. Gregory believes that Khay'tall lives—"

"He doesn't?"

"He most certainly does not. Sarrasine murdered him." Andreas pressed on. "Gregory and Zoë owe me a boon in exchange for their passage, but the form it takes is for them to decide. The Wonder-Maker has many things he could give me that would equal our debt—what I need is someone to put the idea in his head that Khay'tall's cache should be the gift he makes." He paused. "If that doesn't work, I will wait until we reach Paris and he has left my protection, and then..."

"And then?"

"You are the best thief I know, Meribah."

"Oh," answered the girl, pleased. "Thanks."

"While you sow the seeds for a fair exchange," Andreas went on, "feel around for Khay'tall's secret project. I suspect it may be an unfinished piece, with a quantity of letters and drawings concerning its construction. Discover what it looks like, and where it is hidden, but make no move toward it. Then we will be prepared for either tactic.

"If you're willing?" he inquired. "If your own project can wait?"

"Oh, that—no. I've lost track of it, really. It'll keep."

Andreas licked his lips, tempted again. He gave in.

"May one ask what you were working on?"

"No," answered Meribah dreamily, staring out at the snow again. "No, I don't think you can."

"Evenin', Gregory." Meribah stuck her head in the Ravnos's door, beaming. The tinker held an enormous book across his knees, absorbed in his studies. "Zoë home?"

Gregory looked up, alarmed. "Isn't she hunting with you?" He shut the book. "This is your usual night—"

What? Oh, Lord—what's she done? The Setite kept her smile in place, nodding, "Sure. We were supposed to meet at the stairs," she covered, as casually as she could, "but I'm early. Thought she might be in here." Meribah shrugged with her hands. "I just popped in on the hope—if she's not in her room, I expect she's gone 'round the back way. Sit! Stay put—I'll do the looking. Both of us barge in there, she'll think the sky is falling...."

Zoë's room was empty.

"Nope, not in," sang Meribah. "And now I'm late to meet her. Bet you a penny she'll be waiting for me, now, and making cracks about my punctuality."

Laughing, the Ravnos turned to his page again, and Meribah disappeared at something like a run.

Tomislav had set aside two workshops for his artisan guest: a large room, ordinarily the castle laundries, full of cauldrons, sturdy tables, and brass boilers, and a smaller, ell-shaped cell with large windows, an old bread oven, and some solid kitchen vessels. Gregory used very little of the large room. His wagonload of tools and material hardly filled a corner of it, and the clutter he enjoyed eluded him. He never left his work out when he went to bed each morning. The second room, provided as storage space by an over-optimistic count, was turned over to Zoë for her own.

More happened there; the girl threw herself into her work in a way Gregory had had no stomach for since the sack of New Rome. Zoë spent most of her time in the workshop, playing with Magda's cats, drawing diagrams of them, and tinkering—futilely, as far as Meribah could understand—with the bronze cat sculptures she claimed she used to animate. There was a miniature clockwork horse in the making, one that Meribah suspected she wasn't supposed to know about yet.

Meribah had come here first, looking for Zoë. When her knock wasn't answered, the room was dark, and no one replied to her calling, she had gone on upstairs. She found a long-poled torch, lit it by the kitchen fire, and wound her way through the keep back to Zoë's room.

In a spirit of hope, she knocked again before entering. All was silent within; she pushed the door open.

"Zoë?"

Meribah stepped on something soft, just inside the room. It felt like one of the kittens Magda had provided to keep Zoë company. Meribah picked her foot up again right away, aghast, but heard no mewing. She reached into the corridor and brought the torch in. The cat was dead—cold dead.

She set the torch against the wall and moved farther in. Small things rustled on the table—rats, clustered around a platter. Some of the vermin were dead, too. On the platter, a meal lay scattered: raw meat, bread, an apple, and a wedge of cheese. Everything had been torn around the edges by the rats, but there were human bites out of most of it as well. Pieces of food lay on the floor close by, chewed but undigested. Past it all, in the corner made by the join of wall and oven, she found Zoë, curled into a wretched ball.

"Zoë."

The ball didn't move—Meribah circled it, found a point from which she could see into the girl's face, and stopped cold. Her eyes were wild. Little drops of blood, so dry they had begun to flake away, smeared Zoë's mouth. *She cried to eat food. She must be mad*, thought Meribah, kneeling down beside her. She took hold of an unresisting hand.

"Zoë?"

The girl uncurled a little. "My cats..." She could barely speak around her sobs. "You gave them to me, and I..."

"What happened?"

"I was so hungry."

Oh, god. She told Gregory she was hunting with me. She told me she was hunting with Gregory. How long has she gone without feeding? Meribah backed away, aware that the starving creature before her bore little relation to the peaceful friend she knew. "When did you feed last, Zoë?"

"I don't know. I can't remember. A long time."

"Why are you doing this? You have to feed."

"I don't want to. Mustn't drink."

"In God's name, why?"

"In God's name…I want to stop. I want to go back. Stop this."

"You can't go back. Starving yourself won't change that. It only makes the hunger worse—much worse. You don't know—you might kill somebody." Meribah looked down at a dead, dry cat, and shuddered. She stepped further back, thinking about the awful problem Zoë had made for her. *How in hell are we going to feed her?* Tomislav's people were like Andreas's—look, don't touch. Meribah couldn't smuggle anyone past the guards—they would want to know why, and the poor creature would die the moment Zoë smelled him. Or her. If she tried to take Zoë past the guards, she might snap and devour the count's own soldiers. She might snap now. *God, I wish I were stronger. I could never hold her by myself.*

"You need help," she said at last. "I'm going to get Gregory."

"No!" Zoë's sobs started anew. "Don't tell him."

"I'll get Andreas."

Even in her pitiable state, Zoë had room for fear. Her eyes showed white all around the iris. Meribah stood stock still, sure that the hunger would win control of the young Cainite.

"Boleslaus, then."

Zoë rolled over, but said nothing.

"I'll be back very soon. Don't leave this room. Don't try to do anything until I get back."

Meribah took a halt at the top of the stairs. "Are you sure two is enough?"

Boleslaus glanced back at her. His hands were full of wool, the wool was on the heads of sheep, and the sheep were skittering away at every opportunity. "Two," said the minstrel, "will hold her until you can get her into the town. Catch that one—easy does it—down, now."

They bundled the animals along the hallway and up to Zoë's door. Meribah, leading again, looked her helper in the eyes. "Promise you won't tell?"

"It's your private party, Meribah. Just—don't spoil the meat. Cook expects them slaughtered, bled, and butchered by sunup."

Meribah opened the door. Her torch still burned; the Ravnos still huddled in her corner.

"Bring in the first one," whispered the Setite. Boleslaus hauled the sheep in by the scruff of its neck. Together they prodded it toward the starving childe. "Here you go, Zoë. Drink."

The gypsy shook her head in misery. "No," she begged.

"Drink, you silly girl," ordered Boleslaus.

Meribah flicked out her claws. Carefully, she sliced into the sheep's neck, just above the vein—and jumped out of the way as Zoë lunged for the blood. She finished it in seconds and sniffed the air for more. Boleslaus shoved the second sheep forward. Zoë sank her fangs into its neck. As quickly as the first, she drained it dry and was up again.

Meribah was closest.

Zoë leapt for Meribah's throat.

Boleslaus caught her arm and yanked—she tried for his neck, and Meribah seized her other arm. They held her down until she stopped struggling. After a long time, the fight left her eyes, as well. A little later, someone they could recognize returned to the body.

"Zoë?"

"I'm sorry. I tried to—"

"That's all right." Meribah let her up, smiling weakly. "We expected you to. When you starve, you lose control. Easy. Happens to the best of us."

"Not in a friendly city, it doesn't," muttered Boleslaus in French. He released his hold, and Zoë rose to her feet, pale and stricken. He threw the mutton across his shoulders and walked toward the door. Meribah went with him.

"She talks sanely enough," Boleslaus said softly. "She ought to be able to hunt without murder, now." Meribah adjusted the legs of the sheep on his left side, finished, and found the minstrel watching her keenly. "Where's Gregory?" he asked.

"He doesn't know."

"What's wrong with him? He ought to teach her better—it's his responsibility if she kills."

"I know."

Boleslaus searched the Setite's worried face. "Poor kid," he said to Meribah.

"Yeah," said the redhead, looking over her shoulder. Zoë

hadn't moved since they left her. "She tried to eat food, for God's sake."

Boleslaus shook his head in sympathy; under his skin, Vaclav smiled at Meribah's preoccupied humility. "Let me know," he told the little serpent, "if there's anything else I can do to help."

"Just don't tell anybody."

"You have my word," he promised, and hiked off to find the butcher.

"And then I took her to Gregory's workshop and cleaned her up," finished Meribah, slumping over the table between herself and Andreas. "I took her into the poor quarter to hunt, and she behaved herself. She has ever since—I take her twice a week, and I watch to make sure she actually feeds. I've never seen anyone so—so repulsed by drinking blood. She's disgusted by it—ashamed of having to do it." Meribah wrinkled her nose in exasperation. "She keeps this up, she'll end as a blasted Gnostic—no food, no wine, no sex, no love, no flesh, no fun. Bad enough spending one lifetime like that. She'll be mortifying herself for eternity. Unless she goes mad and gets put down." She buried her head in her arms.

"Gnostic?"

"Bogomil? I lose track, sometimes… one of the heresies that didn't believe Christ existed in the body, anyway. Ethereal dissenters," she mumbled through her sleeve.

Andreas let it lie, and Meribah moped in silence.

"I wasn't going to tell you," she said in time. "It doesn't have anything to do with your mission, I guess. But I like her, and that's your fault. She's a good person—good enough for me—and she doesn't deserve what she's doing to herself." Meribah raised her head, peeking up at her cousin. "I want to help her, but I've run out of ideas. You're older than I am—you lead people—you believe in things. Can you—think of something?"

"She's Gregory's problem," Andreas began, a trifle disturbed by the way the little *Franj* emphasized *believe*.

"He's as messed up as she is."

"Yet he is her sire, and the laws of Cainites give him dominion over her until he sets her free."

"Since when do you worry about any laws but your own?"

"I need something from Gregory. I will not jeopardize that."

"If she falls by the roadside, how tractable do you think he'll be?"

Andreas tugged on his beard, frustrated. He pitied the girl himself. He had since the first moment Gregory mentioned his "curse." Still, he was among those Cainites who observed the letter of the law, and dare not risk offending the tinker. While he pulled his hair out, Meribah mused aloud.

"Thank god she isn't logical, after all. She sins to live; she would sin in suicide; she'd have to cease to exist in a cloud of base particles. Atomized. Returned to the Word."

"Be quiet. Let me think."

Meribah settled down immediately.

"Poisons," Andreas opined, "spring from a single source, and spread throughout the mind. What you tell me, and what I see, indicates that the poison crippling Zoë was sown there by her father. Sarrasine prepared the soil, perhaps. Find out what passed between them after he left, and before Adrianople. If you can get her to talk about that, perhaps—and I promise nothing—that will give us a handle to pull her up by."

Meribah waited until Gregory had left for the library. She slipped into the Ravnos apartments by the back way.

"Zoë?"

"In here," said the gypsy from her room.

"I brought your dress. I had it washed. It faded a little, but the stains are gone."

With a pained grace, Zoë accepted the little bundle. "I'll never wear it again, I'm afraid."

"Thanks," snapped Meribah. "I'm glad I took the trouble, then." She ran a hand through her red curls. "If you don't wear it, he's going to ask what happened to it."

"He won't," murmured Zoë. She withdrew into her chamber, and Meribah trailed along behind.

"He will. Zoë, he notices everything you do. Almost everything," said the Setite, looking blackly at the newly washed dress. "He loves you."

The gypsy laughed bitterly at that. She sat on the edge of the bed, smiling like a corpse.

"Zoë, I don't understand you. I'm here—I'm willing to help. You know that. But if I have to steal more sheep, or pull you off Boleslaus again, I want to know why." Meribah found a chair in a corner and sank into it. "Tell me what happened to you?" she pleaded. "Tell me why you're—punishing yourself like this. Why do you think you have to—"

The Ravnos merely shook her head. "It's awful," she whispered. "What I've done."

Behind a sympathetic smile, Meribah ground her teeth. "Whatever you've done, Zoë—whatever's been done to you—I swear to you I've seen worse. I've done worse, too, I expect."

The bitter laugh rang out again. "What have you done?"

Bloody arrogant, thought Meribah. *Like she's the worst creature ever to walk the green hills of earth. Well, she asked for it.* "What, me?" asked the Setite innocently. "Starting from the beginning?" She crossed her legs, tailor-fashion, and leaned back. "Oh, Original Sin. That came first. It's the birthright of every sad Christian soul, isn't it? And then there was this Israelite who died for me, about twelve hundred years ago. That's a terrible thing to hold over a child. On the other hand, no one ever expected much of me because of it."

"Be serious," groaned Zoë.

"I will, but only if you make a deal with me. Promise," said the serpent earnestly, "that if my story is more horrible than yours, you'll tell me what's bothering you."

If," said Zoë. "If."

Meribah grinned. "Fine.

"I was born on the first great pilgrimage to Jerusalem. My mother was a pious woman who followed Peter the Hermit and his Blessed Donkey south from some barbarian wasteland called Hibernia—Iberia—Bern—I don't know exactly.

"If she was ever married, she was an adulteress, and God sent her belly-proof of her shame. Her first confinement delayed her in Constantinople while the Hermit and his followers marched on to be massacred. So that was lucky.

"She had a stillborn boy, and the priests told her that she

had sinned against our Savior by sleeping with men on pilgrimage. As a penance, she continued her journey to Jerusalem. She joined one of the real armies bound for Antioch. You may know that the armies suffered horribly, crossing Anatolia. They starved, they thirsted, they fought, they were ambushed. To live, she needed protection, and so she commenced relations with one—or more, maybe, because when I asked about my father, she certainly never told me the same name twice—of the holy knights.

"She was thrown out with the other women during the sieges, and she took time during one of these rest stops to be delivered of her second child. Me. I was a bastard, and the daughter of a whore, and so born into even more sin than most.

"They called me Meribah, because I was born beside a well near a battlefield. The priest who baptized me had to use stale water with blood seeping into it, and the women wailed because their Messiah had led them into suffering. I am named for discord; for the waters of strife.

"We pushed on to Antioch, eventually. I don't remember it, but my mother said I was walking by then, and an excellent beggar. I called all men my father, and shamed the ones who had known her into providing for our keep. We besieged the city. The knights failed every sally and blamed the women for their weakness in battle. Sin sapped the righteous strength needed for pillage, I suppose. They did penance for the lewd living in the camp, and the knights threw us out again.

"But when the crusaders took the city, the camp followers entered it with them. They celebrated their salvation with more loose living and a lot of looting. My mother gathered coins from the pockets of dead men, and sent me crawling down holes after corpses she couldn't reach. That's theft, a cardinal sin—one of my favorites."

Zoë only stared at her. "Are you joking?"

"No.

"We moved on from there. There wasn't any food inside the walls at all, and we had to fight to break out again. There's a madness of mortal hunger, too, you know. The people walked in delirium. The papal legate had visions and died of them. And when the knights rode out to meet the Saracens, the angels, the saints, and their own dead comrades fought beside them. Or at least, that's what they said, later.

"So, we broke free of Antioch and marched out for Jerusalem, an army for Christ. It warred amongst itself, when no one else was handy, and small bands branched off to capture cities on either side of the route.

"My mother took up with one of the real fanatics—a beast who could kill an entire Christian Annenian family as the poor things knelt before an altar to his own God, just because he couldn't understand the words, they begged him for mercy in."

Zoë closed her eyes.

"It's true," said Meribah quietly. "It's true. They did this. They still do this. You saw Constantinople. It's true."

"So this man, her lover, lusted for glory, as well. He left the main armies behind and struck out on his own. He and his men found a place—very small, not too strongly defended—and sacked it, hoping to find provisions. There wasn't any food there, either—

"And so, they killed their captives like cattle, spitted them over fires, and ate them.

"My mother cooked the villagers for the knights. She dressed the adults like deer and the babies like suckling pigs.

"I was weaned at Ma'arat. The first solid food I tasted was the flesh of another child—"

"Stop," said the Ravnos.

"And so merely drinking the blood of the living was a step up for me, really."

"Stop!"

Sarrasine was gone. Gregory had come home. Everything would be all right, now. Zoë fell into her foster-father's arms and told her story around her tears. He patted her head; he smoothed her hair; he made soothing noises; he held her too tight.

Zoë raised her head to tell him he was hurting her, and she couldn't find his face. Where the Wonder-Maker's soft brown eyes should have been, there were bloodshot fires, staring into space like those of a statue.

Sharp teeth—the fangs she knew he possessed, but had never, until now, been allowed to see—showed between his parted lips, and the hands which held her bore inch-long talons, rough, black, and very sharp. She buried her head against his chest. It hurt to breathe.

"Stay here," growled the Wonder-Maker, releasing her.

Zoë sat, frightened, on the stack of crates in the great forge. There were shouts in the courtyard—their men-at-arms protested, but she couldn't make out the words. She heard armor rattle and creak in the atrium. When Gregory returned, his face was his own again, and he carried a tray of food—the dinner she hadn't eaten. He fed her hot soup and cold juice, then packed her off to bed.

He was in her room the next night almost before the twilight faded.

"I'm going out. I've set the guards to watch over the house."

"What if he comes back?" asked Zoë, clutching at her blankets.

"He won't."

"How do you know?"

Gregory hesitated, thinking of the great scene played out in Elysium the night before. Sarrasine had burst in on the gathered Cainite court, crying for vengeance. His father was dead—murdered, said the son, foully by some unknown hand. He bore a blanket full of ash and charred cloth, all that could be found of Khay'tall. He brought the tale of the slaughter in his elder's house. After the serpent had spoken his piece, he swore an oath against the killer, then disappeared to track him down. Gregory knew, now, that he had done no such thing. He had left the crowd of sympathetic, outraged courtiers and come here to torture a little girl. Gregory no longer credited Sarrasine's story. He suspected the snakes had fought each other, and the more the son railed against the killing of his father, the less the Raimos believed Khay'tall was dead.

Gregory resolved to ferret out the truth about the snakes' private war. The crime against Zoë, terrible as it was, was no crime by Cainite standards, just bad manners. But if Sarrasine had lied to the court, or his lies touched the life of the city, Gregory could call in the guardians to punish and avenge. Sarrasine surely flouted every law the Triumvirate had ever passed. A few nights' investigation would uncover enough to bring to Malachite as evidence. Best not to tell the girl any of this.

She wouldn't grasp the politics of it; she would feel far worse if she understood the status of a mortal girl in Michael's golden city. And the Wonder-Maker had always shielded his adopted daughter from the coils of other Cainites. She was the one bright thing he could turn to when the evils of the night dwellers overwhelmed him, and the light he focused his meditations upon.

"Where will you be?" asked his beacon.

"Hunting him." Gregory sat on the edge of the bed. "I will have justice for what he did to you," he promised, trying to stroke her cheek. She evaded his affection—she remembered the monster—and his gentle brown eyes grew very sad.

"Stay here, Zoë. Stay inside our walls until I've brought the matter before the court and settled it. Promise me?"

"Be careful," said the girl, putting her hand over his. He smiled, kissed her forehead, and set out for the seamy side of his city.

Weeks went by without a trace of Khay'tall's fate. Proof of Sarrasine's treachery was harder to sieve from rumor than Gregory had thought. He spent less time in his house and more in the underbelly of Hew Rome, the Silk Road, and the great hidden library that housed the records of the necropolis. His meditations grew few and brief, and his visits to the mystics of the Dream Circle—to all his friends, unless he had hopes of aid from them—ceased entirely.

Zoë spent a few obedient nights at home.

The pilgrims from Venice settled in around the emperors they had established. The ashes of the early fires cooled. Franj wandered the city, awed by its grandeur. Their leaders pressed their young imperial ally for payment. Gregory and Zoë paid little heed. He had his vendetta, she some fascinating friends in the poorest bazaar. When the riot began and the third fire, the great fire, coursed through their wealthy borough—when the knights from the west put the city to the sword for their money—neither of them were in the villa.

Gregory escaped the Library of the Forgotten with burns on both hands. He raced home and found the living quarters afire but the workshop untouched. Relieved and giving thanks, he threw open the doors of the house.

Zoë wasn't there.

The servants had to restrain him from plunging into the fire to find her. She was gone, they told him. A kind soul suggested she had left to look for him. A neighbor thought the girl had traveled north with a dark-skinned family, easterners who looked much like her, to find safety in the suburbs.

The Ravnos decided to leave, then. His city had been destroyed. His dreams were over. His girl was gone. The Franj Canutes could have Constantinople; they would not have him.

Gregory set his four guards, three maids, two grooms, and the cook to clear the wood and lath away from the workshop. He gave his guards their mail, the maids the linen they had saved from the blaze, the grooms his horses, and his cook every rock of salt, pinch of spice, and jar of honey. Then he piled all he could carry into a donkey cart and fled with the populace into the less-harrowed north.

Every face was hers. He had to stop and look at each of them. When a woman, a girl, a young boy spoke, it was her voice, and he had to listen carefully to know better. If he went quickly, he knew she was behind him, and if he slowed down, felt sure she was just over the horizon.

Near dawn, he reached a nameless town, swarming with refugees already. Its little inn was overwhelmed by the migration. Gregory realized he had nowhere to sleep—no refuge from the merciless sun. Climbing down off the cart, he decided to abandon it. In the hills he could look for a cave, a burrow, or a barn. This town had been an outpost of the old empire—there might be an aqueduct, or a tunnel.

They hailed him from a window of the crowded inn. Lord Valerian led the shouts, recognizing the master craftsman of New Rome. They bustled him inside as the eastern sky turned to indigo from black.

It was a gathering of travelers—the Ventrue ambassador, a wizard, and a friend, Andreas Aegyptus. Through the fog of shock, they spoke to him. We go west. Come with us. *Valerian offered patronage,* Andreas, protection. *Gregory agreed, though he was not thinking of Paris. All his hopes lay in Constantinople, looking for him—fled north, even now, with a family who looked like her—in ashes, under the soles of Franj invaders—or huddled in the darkened workshop, waiting for him to come home.*

He slept, and suffered nightmares.

At sunset, he unloaded his cart and drove his poor beast south again. He had told Valerian that he would go to the workshop and bring back more tools, and he did that, as well. He found three servants standing guard over the shop. None of them had been guards, before now; the armed men were gone. No one had seen Zoë. With their help, he filled the cart with the rest of what mattered—his books, unfinished works, more tools, Zoë's own things—all that was precious and portable. He made a gift of everything else, from ambergris to alabaster, copper kettles to bronze ingots, to the cook, the maid, and the groom who had stayed. Their fortunes were made, if they lived.

Gregory set the cart in motion with half the night to spare. He let the donkey follow its nose. Searching was useless. The city was vast, the girl small.

On the street dividing the bazaar from the sinful quarter, a three-story house stood, safe, amid a waste of charred wood, stone, and plaster. It was the only building untouched by the holocaust. Curiosity steered the Ravnos toward it. As the cart rolled by the miracle, there was another—he heard her beloved voice. He sprang from the buckboard and sprinted for the door of the—inn? tavern? a shop?

A curtain of dull red, homespun linen covered the entrance. Gregory reached out to draw it aside, and could not touch it. An unreasonable fear grew on him. He was sure that the fabric had been dyed in blood, but had no idea how it could have this effect on him. He shouted.

"Zoë!"

Inside, Zoë leapt up, unbelieving. Her hostess rose with her, alarmed.

"Don't go, child. Stay here, while I see whether it is your Gregory..."

The girl hurtled past Layla Madeer, unheeding. Zoë was simply too young for that kind of caution. She rushed out to him, her face filled with joy—he was safe. They embraced, and her happy chatter ran over him.

"I was so afraid, Gregory. I went home and it was on fire—the whole city was on fire. You're safe. Oh, God, it was horrible. But you're safe. I prayed all day that you would come back. We sent a man tonight and you weren't there. But you're here! Oh, I was so frightened. Where have you been?" Zoë pulled away, looking at her foster-father. He stared past her—he was staring at the house. "Come inside. It's safe here. Layla wouldn't let it burn, she has wards and amulets to protect the house from fires."

"You've been here before?" he asked slowly.

"Yes," prattled Zoë. Gregory's eyes sharpened. She realized what she had said, and tried to minimize her admission. "A few times. Once or twice..."

"When?" His voice rang with suspicion. "Have you come here since I told you to stay home? Since Sarrasine—"

"Yes," confessed the girl reluctantly.

"This is where you were when the fire started last night, instead of in the workshop—in our home—where you should have been? Where I came looking for you?"

She whispered, on the verge of tears, "Yes."

Gregory glared at the female form behind the curtain. The fabric parted, and a pair of coal-black eyes challenged his, unafraid. They had a hatred for him, those eyes, and a personal interest in his girl—a motherly concern, perhaps. Jealousy stabbed at him. His relief for Zoë's safety faded, and the gratitude he should have felt for her protector evaporated. This was the woman responsible for luring Zoë away. He took a long look, with all the eyes his blood, the years, and meditations had given him.

Her aura shone black, somehow intensely bright, tangled in a pattern of deeper veins. A heat shimmer rose from her feet. Sparks rose from unseen flames. She walked in hellfire.

"Get into the cart," he ordered his ward.

Gregory came no nearer the house. He climbed into his seat as if to leave, but focused his will on the ground before the demon-worshipper. Without sound, the cobbles erupted—a shining, silver-white claw pushed the stones aside. The witch looked down in horror. Jewel-scaled *talons snatched at her feet—the clawing becoming audible, as the Ravnos concentrated his powers. Madeer staggered back. The dragon slithered under the magic curtain and into the evil house. His illusion might not last long against the darker powers, but he felt good about giving the hag a scare.*

Gregory cracked his whip above the donkey, and the cart rolled on.

"And so, he took me to the little inn that night, and told me we were going on the next evening to Adrianople. He scolded me all the way—he was so angry with me for sneaking out, as if it were my fault that he was never home anymore—and then he'd act as if it were his fault, because he'd left me alone so much. That's when he explained about the court and Khay'tall's murder, and—his son—and everything."

Zoë hesitated. "We were in the cellar. He was going to sleep on the floor. There was a cot for me, and a little lamp. I said—I said I didn't want to go with him. I had friends in the city, I said, and I could stay with them.

"And Gregory—he told me I would go whether I wanted to or not. He called poor Layla a witch! She knew a few charms—she'd taught me a little—but she wasn't what he said. And then he told me what he'd done to her, when we left.

"I hadn't seen anything. I called him a liar.

"So, he made a little bird, to show me he could do what he said...and I knew he'd done it. Maybe she was dead...maybe just injured. I started to leave. I was going back to find her, to see if she was all right. I picked up the lamp.

"He shouted at me. He ordered me—ordered me—to stay. I told him he couldn't stop me leaving, once the sun rose. He took his belt off. He threatened to tie me up with it. His eyes were just like when he came home, after Sarrasine had been there...."

She trailed off, and the Setite said nothing. Zoë's voice had grown flatter, less animated, more numb, as the story spun on. Meribah didn't so much as move, for fear of breaking the spell.

"I swung the lamp at him. The flame was in his face, and I was screaming. I remember his hands on my neck...and the taste of blood...and at sunset, the next night, knowing I was dead."

Zoë sat in listless stupor. Meribah, frightened by her friend's absolute apathy, spoke up.

"Not dead, Zoë. Not really."

"Worse, then," murmured the stricken girl. "Cursed. He passed his curse on to me."

"What curse?" the question escaped an honestly astonished Meribah.

"This—this horror," explained Zoë, returning a little from her trance. "Death in life. Drinking blood..."

"It's not a curse," insisted Meribah confidently. "It's a blessing."

Zoë's face gained more expression—astonishment of her own. "You're mad."

"Oh, no. Now listen: You're young, pretty, strong, and talented. You're going to be like that forever. I've only lived a hundred years, but I've already gone to places you've never dreamed of—learned things one life isn't enough time for—met kings and poets and—and an angel.

"And you...you have something I never did, much better than any of that."

Zoë gazed at her, uncomprehending. The words in her ears were in another language, forming ideas from another world. "What?"

"Well...you have Gregory. He loves you. You and he can, you know, stay together. Forever."

"He doesn't love me. He never did."

"The hell he doesn't," Meribah almost shouted. "He adores you. A blind man could see it."

"If he loved me, how could he do this?"

"So, he hurt you. Lots of fathers do that. He got mad. If he'd been a mortal, he'd have smacked you. If he'd been a brute, he might have used his fist. But you said it yourself—you put the fire in his face. You know what the sight of fire can do to us. You know how the panic takes over. Instead of locking you in your room, he went for your throat. So, you made a mistake, with the lamp, and he made a mistake, losing control at the wrong time. So, it's over. Stop punishing yourself—and him."

Meribah ran out of anger. "He's miserable," she continued,

very quietly, "because he sees that you're unhappy, and thinks it is a curse." She brushed her hair out of her face, embarrassed. "Trust me. This is love. I've seen enough of the other thing."

"It's been some time since we spoke," Andreas began.

"And you want to know what happened?" Meribah hopped onto the table again and let her legs dangle off the edge. "I didn't think you were that interested. I seem to remember having to persuade you to let me meddle."

"Just tell me."

"Well, I told Zoë the sad, sad story of my life. And she cracked open like an egg, and spilled the riches of her history at my feet. I told her Gregory loved her, and she went off to talk to him. The next night, he's at my door, practically falling over himself with gratitude. She's giggly-pleased with him. Joy," said Meribah dryly, "and rapture unconfined...jubilation. And now they're inseparable, which I guess you know, or you wouldn't be so curious. And where I used to be all that kept them together— the center of every bloody conversation—now I can't get a word in edgewise. Hence the books. Couldn't stand the..." her lower lip trembled a little, giving her the lie— "blasted gushing."

He let her go, found a chair, and dragged it beside her. Reclining, at ease, with his feet on the table, he grinned up at his cousin. "Now, tell me again what happened, and spare me no details. I want to hear how you performed this miracle."

When the recitation had ended, his question surprised her. "What other thing?"

"Oh. That isn't love? Just the other. The opposite. The antithesis of the platonic ideal of agape, if you like," she declaimed with a flourish. He recognized the ploy—it was what Meribah did when she wanted to avoid further inquiry.

"When did you see enough of that?"

"Before," evaded the girl.

Images of Sutekhankharen, heavy-handed and unfeeling, appeared in his memory. "How did you ever come to be one of us, Meribah?"

"What kind of a question is that?" She laughed bitterly. "I have red hair, remember?"

He said nothing, and for once, silence drew her out. "Mamma sold me," Meribah told him, matter-of-factly. "After Acre. She said we were prisoners, and that we were both on the block...but they gave her the money. I saw her leave the souk with my price in her hand."

She cleared her throat, but her voice remained bright— removed, decided Andreas, was the word for it. "Somebody was picking up slaves who spoke French, for the Damascus market. They wanted children. Little minds they could raise to be loyal to the Seljuks—teach us Arabic and Turkish so that we could translate for the wars against Christendom. For Christendom's war against them, at least.

"They set the sale for morning, and the Suti came, with some other deathless, to look us over before the mortals got a crack at us. I was very expensive," explained the little serpent, not without pride. "I had red hair, white skin, and green eyes. I spoke the *langue d'oc* of Toulouse and Provence, the *langue d'oil* of northern France, and some other things—learned from my many 'fathers,' I suppose. The Suti saw my hair, and would have no other child but me, despite the cost."

Meribah stopped there, and Andreas probed no further. Hatred of false law was a pillar of his faith, but hatred of the laws of bondage had fallen out of...fashion...among the Followers outside of Egypt. Sutekhankharen had been dealt with. But Khay'tall, in Constantinople, had taught mortals and Cainites that slavery was natural, the result of superior power in the master. Sarrasine spent his nights finding new means of shackling souls without mastering them, and dignified this laziness by the name seduction. Even Bianca, on her own in Venice, used drugs to control guards she could neither endear to her person nor hold by awe.

"What about you?" Meribah cut across his thoughts.

"What about me?" Andreas was quite thoroughly lost.

"How did you end up a soldier for Set?"

"I was a priest—a Christian priest—many years ago, in Palestine, and in Assyria."

"When?"

"During the reign of the Imperial Justinian and Theodora,"

he intoned solemnly. "I was what they deemed a Monophysite. The only safe haven, in all the Empire, lay in Egypt. I fled there, and when the fiends in Constantinople—" again he spoke more fiercely than he meant— "sent their puppet bishop to Alexandria, I fled down the Nile. Thebes needed village priests. New ones. I followed the call to a little cluster of a hundred souls. All but twenty had turned to older gods, by the time I arrived. Apollo-Amon the Sun, Nut-Demeter for their crops, and Set-Asclepius—a healing god, yet mighty to defend his people. A storm against the laws of Justinian—a vengeful god, like my own, but one who was willing to act. He would never watch his priests be slaughtered, never demand that they love their oppressors.

"There was a priestess of Asclepius, adorned with gold and adders…." *Sabine*, he thought, *mistress of my own chains*. "I chose Set over the Jealous God, very quickly, and do not look back."

Meribah searched his eyes, silently, and if she doubted his profession, she made no comment. They sat together over the Christian chapel until nearly dawn, but nothing more would be said between them until the caravan moved on in spring.

Chapter Nine

South toward Thessalonica, along to Vardar River Valley
April, 1206

Count Tomislav, resplendent in silks given him by the caravan, had seen them off shortly before dawn. They had chosen a difficult night, with no moon, at his behest. Dark skies were most auspicious for traveling through wolves, he informed them, and none could contradict his experience. The long line of wagons threaded through the city gates—they were strung along the road already, in position to roll as soon as there was light. Andreas's people, happy to be moving again, shouted gaily from one to another. Even the beasts seemed glad to go.

Meribah dawdled on horseback, close by and downwind from Ravnos wagons. Eureka grazed on fresh spring greens; she lay on his back, watching the stars—and also, eavesdropping.

"Shall we begin?" Gregory asked pleasantly.

"What?" Zoë sounded distracted.

"It is time for our meditations, if you are ready."

"Oh...well, just let me finish carving these molds."

"And how long will that take you?"

A pause. "A few hours."

"Leave them, then. You can do your handwork after your lesson."

"Gregory...I really don't think the meditations are helping me."

"That is because you don't concentrate, child."

"I do concentrate," insisted Zoë, in a wounded tone. "I just don't think it's ever going to work."

The Wonder-Maker gave a patient sigh. "I know you are frustrated. You are young. You have seen little of our baser nature. But trust me. It is better that you learn to overcome your faults this way, before you experience the frenzy or the fear that come with our...condition."

In the obstinate silence, the serpent imagined her friend's stubborn jaw pushing forward. Zoë had experienced them. She wasn't likely to forget that night with the sheep. But she could hardly tell her sire that—and the meditations Gregory put such faith in hadn't prevented him killing his ward.

Meribah was sitting on the first wagon, when Zoë found her. "It's been a while," observed the serpent, but they settled in, side by side, as if it had been no time at all.

"Meribah," the gypsy whispered. "Did you ever...well, how do you overcome the Beast?"

"The what?"

"That's what Gregory calls the hunger. Fire-fear. Pride."

Meribah blinked. "I...I don't know. I don't so much overcome it...just, when I'm hungry, I drink. When there's fire, I let myself run." She poked a finger through the knife-hole in her palm. "Why not? So long as I don't hurt anybody, I don't mind doing what 'it' wants. And if there's someone I'd rather not feed from or run through, it's easier to tell—the Beast—that I'll make it happy later if it knows that I mean that." *So far, so good,* thought the Setite, mystified by Zoë's—Gregory's—identification of pride with their Beast. *But who's proud?*

Zoë, with a very worn-out, strained look, rested her chin on her crossed arms. She stared out at the southward road. "Tell me again how this is a blessing, Meribah. Tell me some more."

A gentle fog drifted through the sleeping caravan, and Meribah drifted with it. She slipped between the wheels and awnings like a ghost, making for Andreas's wagon. Feeling nervous, for she had never before gone to see him in camp.

"Come inside," said Andreas to his ally when he saw her, dismissing his men with a glance. The Norman scribe hurried after the blacksmith's daughter, but Meribah felt the Fleming's attention on her, as he left—the younger Setite scuttled indoors, out of sight, as quick as she could.

With the windows shut, the wagon was dark. She could barely see the low-backed stool Andreas offered her. She sat down, gingerly, and pushed the chair against the wallboards. Her host closed the door, and his lair became utterly lightless, airless, and close. Covertly, Meribah's fingers explored her sur-roundings—sought the sharp corners, overhead shelves, loose wood—and found smooth edges, ample headroom, and secure joinery. Andreas enjoyed a cozy, comfortable darkness, and she felt at home.

"It's about Zoë," opened Meribah. "She came to me last night. Gregory has taken over her education in earnest."

"I'm glad to hear it," he answered, though it was no news to him. The Ravnos had set out on the south road with a new strategy on the chessboard and a new confidence in himself. As a refugee and an unwitting sire, Gregory had lost his direc-tion. With Zoë's education to strive for and responsibilities to be worthy of, his star was rising and his hand steady on the tiller. Whatever Andreas himself might think of the course his friend had set, the effect on the Wonder-Maker's morale brooked no doubt. "An improvement, surely. We haven't enough sheep to spare."

"You think you're funny," scolded Meribah, "but we're going to need them, if he keeps on training her this way. He's talking about dreams—"

The little *Franj* paused, thinking she heard a small noise from the other side of their table. Andreas said nothing, and so she went on:

"—telling her to sit still and say magic words—not prayers— for hours and hours. He told her that the dreams and the medi-tations can overcome this curse he thinks he's under—her too, of course—and let him go without blood. Learn to not want it, is what she thinks he said. Zoë hasn't told him yet how she tried doing that over the winter, but she's determined not to let him make her try it again. She's afraid of being hungry, and she's crumbling under the guilt—curse-guilt. I don't think she minds keeping secrets from him.

"I wouldn't like any of this, but I wouldn't take it up with her. I had enough of meddling in Skopje. But this time, she came to me, Andreas. She wants to learn...and I don't know what to tell her."

The Egyptian leaned back and studied his accomplice. Meribah could not see him; he watched her eyes track aimlessly across the empty air. He wondered whether he gained through his advantage. He could read nothing in that ice-blue expression. In her voice, in her words—the key was there. *I don't know what to tell her*, thought Andreas. *No flourish. No quotations from the poets. Meribah comes to me, to inform me of this development, without any agenda of her own. In Skopje, she pleaded for permission to help the girl out of her despair; she asked me to help the girl. Now...this reluctance... no zest to proselytize Zoë, no eagerness for the rescue. A report. Dry. Devoid of responsibility.* The silence aged between them. Meribah, growing restless, reached into her chemise and drew forth a little pendant charm. It was a cross—protective camouflage, he assumed, until he recognized the workmanship. One of Zoë's trinkets. The sight reassured him. Meribah's strength, the genuine, friendly nature she used to influence others—it was also a weakness. She felt real affection for Zoë, and would naturally shy from manipulating her unless the cause were perfectly just.

As for the proposition, it intrigued him. Zoë craved the truth—she needed what Set taught of the next world and the freedoms of this one—he could lift the curse Gregory had laid on the girl, simply by showing her the lies that wrapped the world. And his quest for the heart might be easier with the Wonder-Maker's apprentice on his side. If the cache were disguised, she would know it. If it were trapped, she could disarm it. If it had been left in Constantinople, she might know where it had been hidden, and she could certainly persuade Gregory to reveal it if not.

"Tell her," Ankhesenaten said at last, "about the Road of the Serpent. Start her on the lessons of the First Pillar."

Meribah blinked in stubborn surprise. "I say meditation won't work for her—I feel that—but she's not going to want to worship Set, either, Andreas."

"No, perhaps not. But our discipline, our methods—she admires them in you. The lessons of the First Pillar can be taught to anyone without compromising their faith, or ours, if you omit the prayers and the Great Name."

Meribah fidgeted, ticking her claws into the wooden stool legs. They made the same sound she had heard from across the table, earlier. Before she had time to consider her discovery—if it merited the term—Andreas continued:

"If she is worthy, then, later, we may decide to let her approach the Lord of Storms."

"And...of the First Pillar—if you leave out the prayers—what parts would you consider that you had left over?"

Andreas found the question curiously obtuse, coming from the theologian of Skopje. "The necessities of survival. How to remain sane despite existing in both this world and Duat. The justness of sating basic hungers. Gaining control, though the indulgence of its urges, of the physical soul—the *ba*," he concluded, testing her.

"The *ka*," she corrected him, and quoted, "O *ka*, who art my starving soul, I feed thee from the life of the living. O *ba*, who art my soaring soul, I send thee to drink from the River of Duat. O *ahk*, who art my shining soul, I beseech thee pray from the court of Set for I his sla—servant."

"Of course," agreed Andreas, "you are right. Teach Zoë to feed the *ka*."

Chapter Ten

Thessalonica, Latin Empire of Byzantium
May, 1206

A ndreas's caravan entered the ancient port city Thessalonica
without ceremony. This was the busy season on the water.
Mortal traders swarmed through the markets and the trade
quarters. Its main road—the Via Egnatia, built by Rome as the
prime artery between East and West—teemed with great hordes
of Constantinopolitan refugees and returning crusaders. The
Setite's camp blossomed beside the other itinerant tent-cities and
awaited the pleasure of the prince, a Norman Ventrue who had
used the recent crusade to take the city.

His highness made no haste. An immaculately liveried herald arrived on the third night, thrust a short and unornamented
parchment into the hands of the first caravan guard he came
across, and rode off without asking for a reply.

The writ, in essence, read: "Camp outside my walls. Feed off
travelers. Stay out of my way."

Valerian, on hearing of their welcome, snorted with annoyed
laughter. He called for quill and ink and wrote a message of his
own on the hair-side of the sheepskin. He did not offer to let
Andreas see it, and Willem, who had brought all his tools with
the pen, melted wax to seal the letter. Dehaan delivered it—and
returned at the head of a veritable embassy.

In seven colors of ink, at great length, Prince Thibald extended
his invitation to the Ventrue emissary and whomever traveled
with him (and was vouched for by him) to visit the city, to hunt
within the walls, and to dine at his stronghold the very next night.

Valerian, smug, turned to his host. "You'll come, Andreas?"

Only six attended the feast. Valerian and Andreas led the way, mounted; Ewald, Galatea, and the Tsarika rode a cart behind them. Calleo followed on foot. The Ravnos pair and Meribah begged off the obligation. Gregory intimated, in Andreas's private ear, that Ewald had let slip news of the libertine habits of this prince, who was known to him. Boleslaus disappeared, presumably to find his Nosferatu cousins in the city catacombs and sewers. Meribah claimed to have caught word of something more pressing that interested her. Hadeon, of course, had refused to enter even the suburbs of degenerate civilization.

Thibald's idea of dinner nauseated Andreas. The prince presented blood as a spectacle—a circus feast, staged in a great, vaulted hall. From chains spiked into the arches dangled countless cages of prisoners, slaves, and captive beasts. He arranged his forest-thick victims in rows and columns according to some complicated scheme of his own imagining—gradations from pale skin to black skin—from sanguine-humored to phlegmatic—from powerful, able-bodied men to helplessly crippled lepers—from pygmy to giant—every variety of mankind the Mediterranean slave markets could bring him. There were freaks, as well—pinheads, hydrocephalics, twins of one body, and monkeys dressed as mortals. Thibald entertained his visitors with guessing games. From what land had this race of mankind sprung? What was the nature of this beast or that? And, most popular of all, could they identify from which fleshly vessel each draught of blood had come?

Andreas, inured to such scenes among the Cainite lords—and a few, if truth be told, among his own, less devout, more decadent kin—suppressed his own opinion and amused himself by observing the other guests. His five were not the entire party; the sea, the road and the wars brought many voyagers to Thibald's realm.

Faced with the banqueting hall, some guests turned back, horrified or frightened. Some rushed forward, delighted by the delicacies. Most walked forward, smiling with polished faces, to meet their host. He pressed all to join him—to play his

games—and the jovial cruelty of his demeanor was very per-
suasive. Most partook of his bounty, and many participated in
the game—feverishly. When in Rome, thought Andreas, you
dance to Nero's tune, or pay for it. He thought of Thessalonica
in exactly that way, as a city on the verge of conflagration. The
Bulgar and Greek armies would probably retake the city and
he imagined the native Cainites—who were notably absent
tonight—would dispose of Thibald's petty princedom soon
thereafter.

Valerian avoided drinking, adroitly, to the admiration of
Andreas. Calleo fed without apparent fear or pleasure, and soon
lost himself in the mingled guests. Galatea drank and played
enthusiastically. This prince made no objection, or did not see
through her heavenly beauty. She outshone all other women
present, and she was very good at guessing the "vintage" of
vitae. Thibald fawned over her. Ewald nodded curtly to the
prince and took a token sip of one goblet, the blood of a woman.
Andreas noted the characteristics of the victim. Ventrue were
notoriously particular as to whose blood they would drink—it
might one day be useful, to know from what kind of mortal
Ewald, so limited in choice, might feed. The Tsarika appeared
shocked to immobility by the perversions of this feast. Ewald
treated her kindly—less remote, in public, than he had been.
He guided her gently from point to point, kept his hand on her
arm, and talked to her continuously. If the words meant nothing to her, the tone seemed to penetrate. She trailed docilely
behind him as he made his rounds.

Andreas began his own circuit of the hall. In the archway
ahead of him, a small group of Cainites bearing the crosses,
shells, and other insignia of pilgrims parted suddenly. A familiar form bustled through: Takouhi, dressed as a lay sister.
"Andreas, love—it is you!"

"My lady," hailed the Setite, making a low bow. "What a
pleasure it is to see you again."

"And for me. An unexpected pleasure. I thought you meant
to travel north, my chick, on the easy road."

"I did—" Andreas thought to explain the visit of the evange-
lists to Sofia, and decided, without quite understanding why, to

leave the mendicants out of his story—"but I decided to winter in Skopje instead of Nis; I feared Petar might find his fief too small to host so large a group as mine. How have you found your own road, my lady?"

"Smooth and even," she replied, "with fine company and good weather. I wintered in Peritheorion."

The Setite shook his head. "I'm afraid I don't know the town...."

"You wouldn't know it, my chick—it's a very small place. Mind you, we had a very fruitful season preaching there."

"Preaching?"

"Andreas, love, I found something on the road from Constantinople that I have been seeking for a very long time. I heard the gospel of a new apostle...a pure soul, with a revelation to deliver." She gazed intently into his eyes. "A truth to tell, about the Christ, that explains all his mysteries—resolves the paradoxes—and lights a new path, for us, his children, to follow.

"We sent a missionary up your way, early in the summer. A very enlightened spirit."

"Appius," he remembered, and regretted that Takouhi had converted to the new heresy.

"Appius," echoed the Malkavian seer.

"He was turned away in Sofia," Andreas informed her.

"Was he?" Takouhi smiled as she asked, and sounded as if she knew something he didn't. She humored him, and it galled. "I can see you're upset," she said, after a moment, turning to view the room instead of him. "We'll let it lie, my chick."

Andreas looked with her, curious to see what interested her. She was looking at the four courtiers of his party. Lord Valerian sat next to the prince, talking with him. Galatea cooed over his shoulder. She favored Thibald with her eyes, but her hands rested carelessly on the senator's forearm and knee. The Tsarika, on silken cushions beside Galatea, smiled sweetly on her. All the while, Ewald scowled over his princess's shoulder, watching her watch the Toreador.

Takouhi strode off without a word to Andreas. She snatched Galatea and Ewald up from their couch and promenaded them around the room, one per arm, irresistible in her conversation.

She seemed to have a great deal to say to them, of urgent import—but when the Setite strained his ears to hear her, her monologue had most to do with trees. While she, for whatever reason, probed their opinions of laurel, myrtle, and wormwood, Andreas made haste to the princess, left alone in their wake.

"Your highness," he murmured in Turkic. "At last, I am free to speak with you."

The Tsarika looked up in bright anxiety. "Is it safe?"

"Come with me," answered the serpent, taking her hand. Obediently, she followed him into a side chamber. No guests lurked here, and the cages swaying overhead held no living souls. Andreas scouted out a dry chair for the girl and a stone bench for himself.

"Thank you, my friend," said the Tsarika. "I had lost hope, when you said nothing in Sofia."

"I had no opportunities there." The Setite pondered his intertwined fingers for a moment, then ventured on. "I must warn you, my lady, that you should place no hopes upon me. I am a businessman. I make my way through this dark life by interfering with the schemes of the powerful as little as possible. I try not to get involved."

"But you are here," she pointed out. "And you are listening to me."

"I have sympathies, my lady." As he said this, his expression left no doubt—his sympathies lay with her. "I confess to curiosity, as well. I do not even know your name."

She spoke proudly, aware of the effect her words should have: "My name is Theodora Anna Romanovych, Tsarika of Galicia-Volhynia, and I am the great-granddaughter of Iaroslav the Wise, Emperor of all the Kievan Rus'. But you, who are my friend, may call me Sascha.

"I came to these Greeks to contract for my marriage. My father wished to make alliance between our house and these Angeli. I was to be empress—a Theodora. I would be the most powerful woman in this world, and my father's grandson would wear the purple. Our agent bargained with Alexius the Third, that I should wed his son, and I came south.

"When this miserable, blind Isaac Angelus returned to

power, Papa's agent made a new alliance, with Alexius Ducas Mourtzouphlus, protovestiarius of the Angelus household. I was to marry Alexius Angelus and rule with him. When this fool Alexius the Fourth crumbled beneath the weight of the *Franj* army, we contracted with Mourtzouphlus, and I and my entourage moved into the Great Palace.

"When this Fifth Alexius abandoned his throne, my father's agent agreed to an offer from Constantine Lascaris. My father's agent said that Lascaris would be emperor-elect, and so he was. He ordered these Varangian Guard to go—to battle these damned *Franj*. They went to make war, and I moved into Hagia Sophia for sanctuary.

"But when this Constantine rode out to call the people to fight for him and for their city, they did nothing. This Lascaris returned to his Great Palace and rowed away in his little ship for the provinces.

"I will say this for my Constantine. He did not abandon me, as Mourtzouphlus had done. When I woke in the morning, there were guards waiting to escort me to a ship.

"Now, my friend, understand: If I had been able to leave the city with him, he would have returned before now. I would have made it so," she promised savagely. "My father's troops would have ridden south to his aid…there would have been one, united Empire, and New Rome would still bear her crown, as the greatest city in Christendom."

Andreas listened with reservations. Ex-emperors spawned from Byzantium like worms from cheese; an ex-empress was not rare. They grew old in other courts, scavenging crumbs of patronage from more potent monarchs. Some raised armies to regain their thrones—Alexius the Fourth had raised the *Franj* forces which destroyed him and his prize together. Theodora's claims, so far as they went, were impressive—

"But these doubly-damned and stinking barbarian *Franj*— three times already they had denied me my throne, and they would do it again. When the city fathers—the holy patriarch— they went to the *Franj* to offer the crown to this Boniface of Montferrat, they knew not what they did. These *Franj* are animals. New Rome was theirs to rule—a city freely given—a bride for their own emperor-elect—and they ravished her.

"These barbarians took the palace as I ran for my ship. My people and I fled for our lives to sanctuary, to the most holy Hagia Sophia. There, beside the sacred relics—beside the Veil of Veronica, the true icon of Christ's own face—I hid, like a rabbit, in fear—I, descendant of Iaroslav, and consort-elect.

"And that night, these barbarians stormed even the great church. They sacrificed men on the altar of the Lord. They spilled the virgin-blood of my maids before the mandala of the Virgin herself. My father's agent was killed at the sacristy, and his body mingled with the body of Christ. And they took me—on the floor, in the chapel of the martyred St. Domnina, and I prayed that she might strike me dead, so I should not live with my shame. She put the dagger in my hand—I took it from the belt of the man who...I took it from his belt, and I plunged it deep in my naked belly.

"These *Franj*, they shouted at me for this. And the shouts brought more barbarians, to see what I had done. One of them was this cursed Fairfax, of the yellow hair. He drew his sword, and he killed his own men. I could see through the darkness in my eyes. I thought, at last, here was a man of honor. But when the knights lay dead around me, and I knew that I would follow, he picked me up. He carried me into deeper shadows, and he gave me an evil potion to drink.

"He stole my soul, this monster. He has it still, and without my soul, I cannot bear the sun. I cannot eat the food of men. Tell me, my friend, how can I conquer him, and regain it?"

Andreas licked his lips, hesitating. "There is no way to undo what has been done to you."

"You do not know a way."

He nodded. "I do not. And I know many who have sought to undo this...bewitchment. Most achieve only their own undoing."

"I will not be empress, after all. I must find something else," resolved the girl, staring into the distance. She faced southeast, realized Andreas; she was looking past the walls to Nicea, where Constantine had founded his new Empire.

Andreas decided, suddenly, to do as much for Theodora as he had had Meribah do for Zoë. "My lady—Sascha—I do not know what Ewald and Galatea have told you of your new existence, but he is no magician. The potion you drank was his own blood, and your soul was not stolen. They may say to you that this is a curse, and you are damned. I believe myself that when you died—" Her head snapped up. She had not known.

"You did die. Your suicide—your martyrdom, to preserve you family's honor—you were successful. And when you died, your soul flew away to the place of judgment." Ankhesenaten struggled a moment to find a Christian mask for the truth. "Purgatory, you may call it. When Ewald gave you his blood, he called back a portion of your immortal soul, and it is that which animates you now. The other part abides in eternity, and its presence in Heaven is the font of your life and power."

"Power?"

"You wished to be empress, Sascha—to be immortal, in the memory of men. You are immortal in fact. There are things you cannot do, it is true, but there are also powers granted you, if you learn how to use them."

"You will teach me," said the Tsarika.

"You must learn from your own family. You are still the descendant of Iaroslav—but now you are also the childe of a dynasty far older. Ewald is the scion of a great house in the West, a clan of kings, called Ventrue."

She absorbed this silently.

"Sascha—you were to marry into the imperial families of the Greeks. Do you not speak Greek?"

The Tsarika smiled thinly. "More than they know."

"You call me friend. Let me advise you. Go to Ewald, and talk to him. He can tell you more of your new lineage than I can. He can teach you the magics coursing through your blood. And...he is more powerful, in some ways, than your husband would have been."

"Over others," asked Theodora sharply, "or over me?"

"Both."

"I am property?" She realized, her voice suddenly frail. "The spoils of war?"

He gave a regretful nod. "A childe is ruled by her sire until he releases her."

"I see."

Chapter Eleven

Into the Despotate Epirus, Along the Via Egnatia
May and June, 1206

Meribah took Zoë away from the caravan for her lessons. They left their horses behind. The Setite feared for the animals if her teaching went awry. On a bare hill overlooking the road, she bade Zoë halt. The place was perfect. Sheep grazed the slopes beneath them, but the children who tended them had left to gawk at the horde of travelers and to sleep. Only a few adults and dogs kept watch tonight. Meribah had gone to great pains to find the strongest, healthiest shepherd in Achaia—out of sight now, and safe if things went well—able to resist, if things went poorly.

"The First Pillar is Anima," said Meribah, leaning against a boulder. "Instinct. The will to live. It drives you to eat when you are hungry, fight when you are cornered, and run when you are in danger. It is very powerful, and you must obey it—but you must also be powerful, and learn to make it obey you. It can be ridden, as you ride a horse. And like a horse, if it feels that you waver—if something you are not expecting startles you—it will run away with you. When this happens, you must be ready to ride with it and to guide it, not fight it, until you can calm it down." Meribah cocked her head to one side, grinning. "Got that?"

Zoë nodded.

"Good. Lecture over." The *Franj* shrugged, grinning, apparently quite pleased with herself. "You hungry?" she asked, as if the lesson were finished—this was simply chat.

"Not really," said Zoë, blushing.

"When did you feed last?"

The Ravnos looked away to find the answer. "A couple of nights ago. Three, I think."

"Five," corrected Meribah. "I've kept track, even if you haven't. And I want to know why you haven't done anything about it."

"We've—we've been in the caravan the whole time. I don't like to—"

"Horsefeathers. You love it. You can't help but love it. It's food and drink and the nectar of the gods. You just don't like to think that you love it. I'm telling you, you have to learn to like liking it, or you'll go mad—or you'll fast again, and kill someone."

Zoë stood still as marble, staring at the ground without expression.

Meribah took the gypsy girl by the arm and dragged her up the side of the great rock. "There." Beneath them lay the scrubby pasture and several dozen woolly clusters. "You're ashamed of drinking blood? God made it so. He gave you this hunger. He gave you the power to use it as you choose. You feel guilty, drinking from mortals? You're afraid to hurt them? Drink from animals, if you can stand the taste. There's half-a-hundred sheep there. Go!"

Zoë, strongly stubborn, closed her eyes.

"Why don't you?" whispered Meribah. "Think, Zoë. We go back to the caravan and Chiara runs up to us. She trips and falls and scrapes her knee. The blood seeps out. The smell of it runs right down your throat. How do you resist that, if your belly's empty? If you want to do right, you must learn to feed often—as often as your instinct tells you you should—so that you are not weak when the real hunger gnaws at you. It's your responsibility. Go."

At last Zoë jumped off the boulder and into the field. Meribah hopped down after her. The Ravnos took longer to sate her hungers than the Setite, flitting from animal to animal, leaving each after only a sip or two. The red-haired creature, from long practice, knew how much she could take from a beast without weakening it, and followed her own advice—she fed every night without fail, and enjoyed it very much. While Zoë finished, Meribah clambered up the next ridge. The dark movement on the cobbles preyed upon her caution; she wanted a better view. Her hair whipped into her eyes and her cloak snapped in the wind—but she could see.

No campfires, she realized. *That was what had nagged at her. It can't be a caravan, then, or pilgrims. An army would have watch lights. Herd animals would be sleeping now. Wild animals—there couldn't be so many, together, on the road. Who travels without light?* she asked herself, knowing full well the answer.

Zoë scrambled up beside her. She smiled weakly, wiping her mouth with a double handful of leaves. "What is it?"

"I don't know yet," said Meribah. "But I smell trouble." She unclasped her cloak and started peeling off layers. "Lesson's over. You'd better get along home."

Meribah led Ankhesenaten into the hills early the next night. The earth was rougher here, and the wind, dried by the salt it carried, blew strong as the tides themselves. To climb the ridge was to fight the sea, and the horses' sides were quickly soaked in sweat. Halfway up they stopped to rest. Their own camp lay behind them—a string of golden beads, glowing cheerfully even in its fire-free center. The wind, turning perversely for a moment, brought Boleslaus's rich voice with it, singing a ballad of Charlemagne. He came to a chorus, and others joined in—bright and sleepy together, harmonious and off-key, in good *langue d'oc* and in nonsense words guessed by Greeks. The scent of mutton, basil, and onion settled around the Setites for an instant. When the wind changed again, Egyptian and *Franj* set off along the ridge, and only the sea blew with them.

The dark camp lay a day's march behind them, but two riders on blood-fed horses could cut cross-country much faster. The strangers' wagons and tents—coming down, not going up for the night—came into view only an hour after the ride began. Andreas left Meribah to tie up their mounts on the lee slope while he crawled down the windward; they had a land-breeze now, blowing straight from the encampment. He could hear and smell better than he could see, and he stopped just below the ridgeline. Any closer, he decided, and he could be seen himself. *No fires,* thought Andreas, *but I smell smoke.* Even with the sight Takouhi had taught him, he found not even a single glowing coal—yet the smoke rose thick and black enough to hide the stars overhead. Oily smuts drifted on the wind, and now his heightened senses caught the smell of burning fat. Andreas feared he recognized the scent. *Meribah knows it. She was right to fear these pilgrims.*

His cousin slid into place beside him, subdued, serious, and silent. She waited patiently for him to move or speak, and he stretched his hearing once again.

Creaking leather. Animals restless in harness. Crying children...a singing child...the consecration of the Eucharist, performed by a priest in the Latin rite. Moans. A woman in rage... or passion...or pain...and then her death rattle. The transfiguration continued, as if the dead woman had read part of the mass, and her last breath were only the cue for the congregation to respond. Many feet stirred—the faithful took communion, and a woman gasped, loudly.

Meribah rustled in the brush like thunder to his straining ears. "Can you tell anything from here? They had a—a cross— on the center wagon last night. They were...crucifying a mortal. Is she—"

A booming voice from the valley interrupted her. Even mortal ears could hear it from here, with the wind to help them. Meribah settled down, and the two Setites listened to the sermon being preached to the darkness.

It told of Caine, and the First Murder.

It said of blood, "It is written in the scriptures that the life is in the blood, and therefore mortal men are forbidden to eat meat with the blood still in it," and Andreas recognized the law of Genesis.

It spoke of Abraham and Isaac, of Joseph and his brothers, of Pharaoh and the slaughter of the first-born sons of Egypt, and of Moses and Aaron. It warped every story to show the favor of the Lord upon the firstborn and on the youngest son, and used the twisted scripture to hoist the first son of Adam ever higher in the heavens. Meribah, learned in heresy, could barely recognize the forms of this one—no cult she had ever known taught like this.

Then the voice went on to interpret the gospels. It related to the faithful a new story of the miracle which changed the water into wine. It explained how it came to be that Christ raised Lazarus from the dead. And it revealed, as a marvelous mystery, how a man hung upon a cross could leave his tomb three nights later. A son of Caine, said this river-deep voice, had been nailed to that tree. First son, first choice of the Lord, first savior of mankind.

Meribah shuddered and hid her face in her hands. Andreas's arm closed round her shoulders. He led her back to the horses. In that sheltered hollow, the wind carried no anathema her ears could catch. He held her there while she wept, listening to the darkness. The crucified woman had been freed; he could hear her feeding on the mortal pilgrims. The pitiful souls prayed to her to take them and make them one with the miracle, and the priest raved on about the angels drinking blood.

Andreas swung into the saddle and made ready. The younger Setite, as ever on horseback, recovered her wits and bravado. She galloped down the hill without waiting for him, and he was hard pressed to catch her. With miles between the Cainite heretics and herself, Meribah let Eureka set his own pace. As their horses walked wearily side-by-side, Andreas mused aloud, so her mind should not dwell on the abominable sermon.

"They travel by night, we by day—by dawn they must be almost within sight of our refugees. Thank the Destroyer, none of our mortals have seen theirs yet...it's a risk. They proselytize among the Cainites. I expect they evangelize as fervently among the 'Children of Seth.' If their sacraments include torture, death, and the Embrace, they must replenish their congregation at every opportunity, or devour their childer...which they may do.... We will have to avoid them."

Meribah glanced at him, disturbed by the unfinished thought. "How will you keep them away?"

Andreas scratched at the base of his beard. "We could travel faster, to outdistance them, or move aside for one night, to let them pass."

"Leaving the road would be easiest on the animals and the foot-borne," observed the veteran pilgrim at his side.

"I think we will go faster, though. Days are longer than nights. If Jacquy makes an effort, we can put another mile or two between us at every march, but if we let them get ahead, we will have to go at the pace they choose, and we will reach every new city after they have already entered it." Andreas urged his horse to a trot. "We'd best make haste. Jacquy will need all the time we can give him, and I shall have to signal Hadeon to come in for council."

The Egyptian sped to a canter, and Meribah rode along as in a dream. Andreas, she realized, had discussed this important decision with her first, not the crew.

They stopped at Ohrid for only one night. Hirelings and tag-alongs hurried into town to make the most of their time; the caravan crew drew back to their camp, far outside the city walls, as soon as the provisioning was complete. Magda and Isabelle laid out a feast for the mortals. Later still, Ton Wheelwright and Riki brought forth pipe and strings while Jozef thumped a barrel-head to give them a beat. Meribah, feeling out of place, reached for her cloak, not looking. Her fingers touched something soft and warm instead of wool.

Meribah whirled round. Dehaan stood on the green, his hand on her cloak pins.

"Come down," invited the Rooster. "Dance with me, Beata."

"I don't know how."

"You should learn the art, Beata. You find out more about a person in one dance than in twenty days of talking."

"I can dance," protested Meribah. "I just don't know *Franj* dances."

"Flemish. We're going west; you'll need them. Let me teach you, Beata."

The redhead tumbled off the seat. "All right. Teach me. Just don't call me Blessed while we're doing it."

He led her through the steps three times in the shadows.

She knew the pattern the second time through; on the third rep-
etition, they kept up with the tune. Dehaan brought her into the
gathered circle, and when the lines formed again, Meribah took
her place with the rest. She was light, quick, and graceful, and
she shed her troubles in the music. A happy girl met him at the
top of their set; her eyes were as bright as any mortal's. When
the musicians rested again, she followed him happily behind
the wagon for another lesson.

She smelled it before she could see.

"Yours, Beata," whispered Dehaan, offering his bared arm.

She drew breath, frozen. The moon whitened his skin almost
as much as hers; the single black dot glistened on his wrist like
jet. *Absurd*, she thought dizzily. *Yeshua and Lucifer on a high place
above the kingdom...Zoë and Meribah on the rocks above the flocks of
Achaia...Meribah and this mortal, in the shadows below the shrine...
how beautiful is Dehaan, son of the morning...I am losing my mind.*

The spark approached her lips—she swayed backwards to
escape it.

"No." She could look at nothing else, but— "No. Thank you.
Not hungry."

The Rooster laughed at her. His fingers grazed her temple.
Her head turned of itself, curving into his hand, following the
smell. "You're always hungry."

"A-a-a-Andreas. I-I-I-I promised."

His callused palm brushed along her cheek and lips. She
shut her eyes tight—shook violently away—darted behind the
corner of the wagon. Her feet would take her no farther. Gravel
scuffed toward her—peeking, she watched Dehaan lick his
wrist and heal the pinprick. The smell died on the wind, and
the knot in her throat began to loosen.

"What kind of goddess are you, Beata?"

Meribah slid down the footboards and sat crumpled in the
dirt. "A loyal one," she mumbled weakly, "guest in your master's domain."

Chapter Twelve

Durazzo, Despotate of Epirus
June, 1206

Brujah clansmen welcome Ventrue nobles as battle-hardened mercenaries welcome raw, untested, princely knights: civilly, with neither insult nor deference to their theoretically higher state. The warrior-sage Geseric welcomed Lord Valerian thus; to Andreas he gave warm, heart-felt greetings. The *Golden Virtue* and her trading sisters frequented the safe harbor of Durazzo. Years of favors granted and repaid bound fief lord and merchant tightly, and the Setite had only rarely felt the lash of the Brujah clan's infamous temper.

At their court meeting, Geseric professed himself astonished to see Andreas traveling by road. Almost apologetically, he informed his guest that neither the *Virtue* nor any other vessel was in port. The Egyptian thanked him for his concern, but offered no explanations. The Brujah could count; he would deduce Andreas's reasons. He might not even be surprised when the caravan turned north from here, shunning the easy summer sea for the tortuous coast of Dalmatia.

Andreas left his passengers to their own devices. The Cainites here were almost as populous and half as savage as Thessalonica's. Everyone but Hadeon and Calleo would find conversations or common interests with the courtiers. He had business of his own here, vastly more important than any immortal gossips.

Andrew of Egypt kept a warehouse by the docks, not far from the first temple he had helped to found in Europe. He and

Goreb hastened from Geseric's threshold to their own, as fast as their horses would take them. All the crew had crammed inside the complex; a reunion feast weighted down the tables of the counting-room and sanctuary. His clanmate Sebehlsenkare— known as Sybil in Durazzo—and the townsfolk who prayed in her shrine embraced him fondly; the Flemings stationed here clustered round their patron and sought his blessings. Sebehlsenkare and Ankhesenaten performed the cult of their god together, before both images, and then took a room apiece, at the center of their own tables, and watched the mortals eat and drink their fill.

After the feast, there were messages from Thebes, letters from his men at home, and news of the fleet to hear. The crew presented their concerns for the next leg of the journey. Ton needed wood and iron. Jacquy gave his opinion, not good, of the oxen, horses, and mule-teams that had survived the trip from Sofia. Andreas arranged for materials and replacements. Funds came out of the trading-house accounts; the trade-goods Willem and Dehaan had acquired along the route went into the stores. A few of the crew requested leave to stay, to go to sea, or to travel home, and some of the locals asked to join the wagons on the road. Andreas judged each request on its merits, suggested other paths, and finally allowed everyone to follow their hearts.

Only one man failed to obtain his desire, and he had not expected to have it granted: Dehaan pled with his lord on behalf of Ljudumilu's health.

"The road is killing her, master."

The old priestess was not too ill to object to this; Ankhesenaten laid a hand on her arm to quiet her until her grandson had finished speaking.

"I ask that you leave us here to go home on the next ship. My mother—all my kin—would wish to see her before the end. I know she herself would never think to leave you, but I have to ask, for their sake."

Andreas turned to Ljudumilu. "Will you go?" Unrelenting gray eyes held his. "You need the boy," declared the matriarch.

"Will you go alone?"

The corners of her mouth twitched. "If you command it, Great One."

"I give you no orders. You are a free woman, not a slave."

"I stay."

"So be it," decreed Ankhesenaten, and it was so.

Meribah made her haven in the guest-chamber of the temple. Two nights before their departure, Andreas found her alone before the image of Set. She crouched on the floor before it, gazing up at the god. She wore her turquoise finery; Geseric held audience tonight, the last before they left. Trying not to disturb her prayers, Andreas walked softly into the shrine. He sat down on the bench behind her and waited for her devotions to end; they could go to the Brujah manse together.

"Andreas?"

"I am here."

"I'm starting Zoë on the Second Pillar as soon as we're on the road again." Courage was the Second Pillar. Meribah had prepared herself to teach it—bought tools to make the lessons safer and practiced lighting torches in the stone-walled, uninflammable safety of her quarters—but the courage she needed was of a different breed. She could turn around, this minute, and tell her cousin what his servant Dehaan had dared in Ohrid. Surely it was as forbidden for the crew to seduce the passengers as for the passengers to seduce the crew. If Andreas had used the Rooster to test her loyalty, as she more than half suspected, the final hurdle must be to reveal this "betrayal" to him. On the other hand, if Dehaan had come to her on his own, he might suffer if it were known. He would keep silence, in that case, and her secrets were safe until she told them.

Meribah hid her guilty face from her cousin, and felt a coward, but she said nothing about Dehaan, the rule of the caravan, or the boon she craved.

"I am glad Zoë has progressed so far," said Andreas, encouragingly, "but have you had any success with the more important matter?"

The red head shook: No. "Gregory doesn't come out of the wagons much, anymore. He teaches Zoë, then he holes up in the

workshop by himself for the rest of the night. She only sees him
for lessons and dawn."

Andreas considered this. Turned around, it meant that
Gregory saw his daughter only for her lessons and when she
came home to bed. To Meribah, if Zoë felt ashamed of neglect-
ing her sire, the girl would portray the choice as his, but if the
Wonder-Maker neglected her, wouldn't her youthful pride drive
her to say she had left him? The Setite resolved to talk to the
lonely Wonder-Maker and discover if his truth were the mirror
of the girl's. "Don't forget that the cache is what we are here for."

"I won't." Meribah rocked back on her heels, but did not
rise. She stayed there, looking at the floor, and asked again,
"Andreas?"

"Yes?"

"When I get to the Third Pillar…well, I've never taught
anyone…faith…before."

"You hadn't taught the first two pillars before now, but you
seem to do that readily and well."

"They're easier. I knew how to say those concepts in Greek."
She swallowed, audibly, and her sharp nails bit into the wooden
floor. "The Suti—he taught me in Arabic, you know…and he
was…" Meribah trailed off, rallied, and struck out once more.
"The Suti was slightly unorthodox, in his interpretations. I
think…I need…your help." A long pause. "To get the words
right."

Andreas tapped knucklebone on ring, amused by Meribah's
understatement. Sutekhankharen, in his later years, had gone
far beyond "orthodox" worship of the Lord of Storms. His
strength lay always in the act of corruption itself. He could turn
anyone to commit any crime. Al-Suti's wisdom and imagination failed him whenever the time came to use the tools he had
created to work Set's will. He taught, at last, that the act of corruption was more important than any other worship. He had
voiced this revelation with his fellows in Antioch, eager to share
the dream with others less enlightened.

It had brought about his fall.

Thebes had been confident, however, that when
Sutekhankharen had initiated and taught his childe, Meribah,

he had had a true, if brutal, vision. Tested in Antioch—without being told of the test—she had been letter-perfect in both ritual and creed. She never flinched at any task. Though she was *Franj*, untrusted by the hierarchy, no real suspicion attached to her. Sutekhankharen simply hadn't seemed to care enough about her to lead her astray.

A slow smile crept across the Egyptian's face. Meribah perceived the shaky foundation her sire had laid for her.

She sought guidance though she hardly needed it. She was the first *Franj* he had ever known to ask. "We have no time for debate tonight, my sister." He rose and offered his hand. "But when we return to the road, I promise, I will help you prepare the Third Pillar—for your friend."

Geseric's Elysium swirled with bright color. Though he himself had no love for spectacle, he stood willing to let his favorite childe create the scene. Herleva had her pick of fabrics, incense, and musicians. She alloyed the raucous gaiety of the Norman Sicilies, papal pageantry, local vitality, Greek sophistication, Arab learning, and Turkish lavishness—all the cultures pressing on Durazzo's interests, and all the friends hiding daggers up their sleeves. The mortal city had become a possession of Epirus, but Geseric's own loyalty lay with vanished Vandal tribes and dead cities and his private sympathies inclined toward the isolated kingdoms to the northeast. The blend made Geseric's politics tortuous, but it shone brilliantly in his hostess's hands. Galatea and the Tsarika, close by, stood side by side watching Persian dancers. The women held a goblet each—red wine, not blood. Many living attended the festival tonight; all the dead carried on as though they drank the weaker draughts.

Andreas strode impressively through the buzz of the reception. He passed under the center, north portico into white-plastered pillars hung with saffron gauze. The space had been furnished with soft satin divans. Gregory and the girls sat here with Boleslaus, Calleo, and even Hadeon in a group together, surrounded by admiring quick and dead. The minstrel was telling the story of their battle with the wolves, in Greek. Meribah translated for the Latins and French—often jumping up to act out parts with the storyteller. Hadeon stood with his back to the wall; the Gangrel resented being commanded to attend the fete, but he seemed to be enjoying the tale.

Valerian collected Andreas and brought him to the prince's couch. They spoke of the road ahead. Ragusa, revealed the lord and lady, was friendly to them, and would remember the Egyptian's fleet's many visits. Valerian expressed his pleasure; he looked forward to the visit. In Split, the three men—the lady concurred—anticipated possible trouble. Split belonged to a Lasombra prince, as infamously haughty as any of that clan, and less discreet than most in his uses of their shadow-power. In the many small settlements, walled or undefended, Geseric warned of continued mortal movements. For three years now, the battle fleets had traveled up and down all the Adriatic coast, pacifying or liberating the Venetian conquests. Andreas broached, carefully, the subject of the heretics swarming up the Via Egnatia. Geseric listened without alarm; he had faced Bogomil uprisings, Orthodox pogroms, and Roman repression in the past. Durazzo would survive.

While the Brujah made his point, Andreas listened attentively—but his gaze was drawn to Galatea, gliding along the inner wall like a vision. He looked away immediately, and found two light-haired merrymakers to focus on—Ewald and the Tsarika stood in the open together, enjoying the night and music. The Tsarika laughed sharply, jostling the cup in her hands. Two beads of red sloshed up, glistened, and dropped back into the bowl—

Ewald seized the princess's wrist. He pulled her hands, still holding the goblet, to his nose. Carefully, he sniffed it; gently, he wrested it from her resisting fingers. Savagely, he hunted with his eyes—found his quarry flattering her betters by the prince's couch.

"Galatea!" Fairfax bellowed. He stalked furiously forward, his fangs and talons unsheathed. The crowd parted, awed, before the thunder-mad Ventrue; Ewald's jaw twitched with bloodlust. The Tsarika, helpless, baffled, fearful, trailed helplessly after him. "Galatea, you see the sun this morning! I swear it!"

Andreas stepped forward, concerned for his passengers. He was tardy; the prince beat him to the floor.

"Why do you disturb my peace?" challenged Geseric. He reached his guest; he was shorter than the Norman, older in body, and less imposing, but he checked the young noble's progress. "Do not start this here, Ventrue. Do not give me a reason for rage, or you will regret it."

"My...apologies, my lord. I forgot myself." Ewald bowed his head—briefly. "My wrongs overcame me. Let me ask, now, that my grievance against this—woman—Galatea, be heard."

Geseric mounted the steps with dignity and assumed his seat. Ewald followed heavily, his hand in the Tsarika's.

"Princes—" hailed the young noble. "I come before you seeking justice." He bowed to Geseric and to Lord Valerian. Belatedly, he made a small obeisance to the Setite as well. "The Toreador Galatea has trapped my childe into the blood oath." Rage coursed through his voice for a moment only, as he said this. "I present my evidence." He offered the goblet—dented and bent by his bare hands—to Geseric, who smelt of it, frowned, and passed it to Lord Valerian. The Ventrue emissary shook his head, deferring to Andreas.

"The Egyptian is prince over all three of us." Andreas sniffed the dark fluid gingerly. It was deathless blood. No one could argue this. He beckoned to Galatea—silent since the first shout went up. He flicked a claw delicately across her thumb. The scent...intoxicating...matched that of the goblet exactly. He passed her arm, as an object, to Valerian and the Brujah.

"Tsarika," called out Andreas in Greek. "Is this your goblet?"

"Yes."

"I love her," whispered Galatea. She found courage and voice, going on: "She loves me. And she hates him. He is Norman; he conquered my city and her hopes." This, Andreas felt, was true, and the Toreador hated the Ventrue as well. Galatea lifted her shapely head, near tears. "I did not wish to...bind her...at first. She persuaded me." Something fond and rueful lifted her lips, then vanished. "And I was glad of her...." The Toreador raised her hands toward the princess, who smiled uncertainly in return. "How many drinks?" pursued Andreas.

"Only one," Galatea, cried, indignantly. "I would never give more…it wouldn't have been right. The Tsarika is still a childe."

Geseric looked to Andreas, one eyebrow aloft at this display of virtuous restraint.

"Privacy?" asked the Egyptian.

Geseric gestured to the door behind his couch.

"Sascha—come. I must question you, your highness." Andreas said it in Turkic, and had the pleasure of seeing Galatea flinch.

"What is this, my friend?"

"You never spoke to Ewald, did you?"

The high-held head turned away. "No. I will not give him this victory over me. I speak no good Greek."

"Did Galatea tell you anything of the blood-powers? Healing, holding mortals to you, enthralling those who drink it?" He found only faint recognition in her eyes. "The blood oath, Sascha. Did you know about it?" The girl shook her head. "Then you were not willing to take the blood oath to Galatea?"

Enlightenment flashed upon her. "I? Swear fealty to a barbarian?! Never."

Andreas rubbed his aching brow. "But you have, Sascha, and more. Immortal blood bears worse than fealty with it. How many times have you drunk of Galatea?" Soundlessly: "Twice. Sofia."

He nodded, thinking how best to explain her peril. "Do you remember, Sascha, when we first met. You appealed to me to save you from barbarians—two of them. In Thessalonica, you feared only Ewald. The first drink endeared her to you. The second—you love her—it took a wound to your pride to make her a barbarian again in your eyes. The third drink would tie you to her, eternally, against your will."

"This can be undone," insisted the Tsarika, hopefully.

"With much time and a strong will, two drinks can be overcome. The true oath is almost impossible to break—" *Without a death*, he added to himself. "You must guard against her, if you feel inclined to drink again."

Theodora clenched her teeth. She would not be tempted.

Until she sees her love again, remembered Andreas. *That is the test.*

"Now, Sascha, let me advise you. I admire your pride more than I can say. You have never surrendered to your captor, but I tell you, you must go to him and make peace. Until you know more about this existence, you are a babe in arms, helpless. He is your protector and your nurse, as well as your jailor. Learn from him, or you may not survive to be free of him."

Andrew of Egypt spoke from the top step. Valerian sat to his left, Geseric to his right. "The crime is not complete."

Ewald, relieved, sought his princess's hand. Galatea stooped a little.

"The offence is two drinks. Two drinks shall be the penalty."

Ewald nodded, satisfied, clearly looking forward to a Toreador near-thrall. Galatea, frightened, opened her mouth to object.

"Because the evil was done unto a childe, I will not levy the fine in full. Galatea shall drink only once from Ewald Fairfax— she shall take the other sip from the childe she would have enslaved."

Now the Ventrue found fault with the judgment—he would have liked the offender bound to him in punishment. He stopped short of argument, however. He slashed his wrist and poured blood into the battered goblet. Galatea swallowed it with poor grace. Very tenderly, the Tsarika took the cup and filled it. Her affections were obvious; Galatea sipped from her less bitterly.

Lord Valerian leant to reach the Setite ear. "Don't bother to wake me and these brats in Ragusa," he whispered. "You need a rest."

Chapter Thirteen

Up the Dalmatian Coast to Spalato
Summer, 1206

From the wagons, only the torch itself was visible. One had to walk through a belt of trees and into the high grass to see what it shone upon: One form, bright in the firelight, stood alone beneath the great oak. Zoë, tall, slim, and wearing her skirt kilted up above her knees, waited.

Another, darker figure, easier to find by hearing than by sight, dangled from the thick branches, dancing with the flame. Meribah hung by her knees from mossy limbs, shaking leaf and light together. The torch rose to her hand. She took aim, released it, and watched it plummet toward Zoë's head.

The fire fell short. Strong chains tethered it; it could not quite touch the Cainite on the ground. Zoë quivered like a plucked string—but she held her ground.

Meribah hauled up her missile, fussed with it, and without warning, at a different angle, it dropped again.

Zoë ran.

A whistle pierced from the tree. The serpent somersaulted down from her perch, narrowly missing the swaying torch. Eureka loped up to her signal, let her mount, and hurtled off in the direction of the Ravnos's flight.

Minutes passed. At last, beating hooves, returning—Eureka, carrying both girls on his back. At the tree, there was a bloody apple for the horse. He trotted off to his post of his own volition; his mistress clambered barefoot up the trunk. Zoë turned her back on tree, torch, and Temptation—beautifully poised.

From his place in the high grass, Dehaan could hear as well as see them—Meribah's cracked-wit wisdom and encouraging yelps—Zoë's ever-more confident answers. Now a closer sound disturbed him. Turning only his head, he looked for the source and found it. A solid darkness, moving away from him and from the girls, had trodden on dry leaves instead of green shoots. The Rooster couldn't see the face but knew the man by his limping walk. Gregory the Wonder-Maker knew where his girl had been.

Meribah stuck her head around the corner of Andreas's door. They worked on the Third Pillar for the rest of the night: "I know *ba*, *ka*, and *akh*. But how do I explain them to a Christian?"

"Don't. Leave it be. Tell her that her soul is in two halves. Part in heaven, part in her body. Call the *akh* destiny. That's close enough."

"It is the duty of the gangs of *Sth* to use *hqa* to *ketmyt maat*. *Sth* is Set—I'm not calling him Typhon unless you make me—but Zoë won't need to know that—but how do I translate *hqa!*"

"Blood-power."

"Not magic?"

"Too easily misunderstood."

"Ketmyt!"

"'Corrupt.'"

Meribah sat up straight. "'Corrupt'? Not 'disrupt'?"

"Yes." Andreas paused, looking at her troubled face. "'Breaking together.' Is there a problem?"

"Um. In Constantinopolitan Greek, I think so—in Latin, I know so. Corrupt is vile—it denotes festering, as well as destruction."

"No...no, I don't remember that it takes that meaning."

"It's new, I think. It doesn't mean that everywhere. I heard it first in Venice, after Aimery set up shop, and then in the Genoese quarter of New Rome."

"Next to Khay'tall's district?"

"Mm-hm. And Zoë speaks Byzantine dialect."

Andreas tugged at his beard in frustration. Mortals delighted in changing tongues faster than he could learn them. "Damn. Call it disruption, then."

"And *maat*?"

"Order."

"Order? Not good?"

Andreas tugged at his beard again. Meribah delighted in splitting hairs faster than he could mend them. "'Good' is also correct. I don't suggest it, however. To a Christian, so many of the things necessary to 'break-together' 'order' are 'evil'—forbidden acts—'sins'—they have difficulty accepting them. And the word—" He sat up, throwing the window open. The eastern sky grew blue; dawn was coming. "It is hard to explain, even in the old language, that things can be good without obeying laws, and lawful without being good."

Taps and bangs echoed around the Ravnos's workshop wagon, drowning out Meribah's hearty knocks. "We're almost finished," shouted Zoë. "Come inside."

"Are you sure?"

The door swung open. Meribah compromised; she sat on their steps. A very complicated, metallic tangle took up nearly all their table space. Zoë crouched at one end with her tiny brass hammer; the Wonder-Maker loomed above the other wielding a large rawhide mallet. Two minutes later, the cacophony died off. Gregory inspected his apprentice's work, approved it, and patted her head fondly.

"Help me take it outside. This wants testing." The three of them maneuvered the contraption—marvelously light— through the narrow doorway. "Clean up, please, Zoë. Then you may do what you like." Meribah's ears burned; he was looking at her. Gregory headed into the camp and she dodged into the caravan for cover.

Zoë sat at her bench and tinkered with the clockwork of her miniature horse. She made no move to welcome her friend, nor did she set upon the cluttering tools and debris. "There's a stool under his desk," she volunteered, without turning around.

Meribah wiped the metal shavings off the seat and took it. After a while, in growing boredom, she reached for the nearest rag.

"Not that one," cautioned the gypsy. "That's only for

polishing. The dust cloths are under a loose board at your feet."
The *Franj*, feeling snookered, found the loose board and the
right rag and waged war on the dirty floor and counter. When
she had won, she considered the tools. "Where do these hammers go?"
"Give me the little one." Zoë slid it into a rack above her
head and kept her eyes on her clockwork. "His hammers go into
a rack like this. Files go in the drawer, punches in the cabinets.
It's very organized."
The Setite stowed the hammer. When she came to the files
and rasps, she opened all the drawers, just to be sure she had
the right one, and found them bursting-full of tools. She had
to hunt, honestly, through all the layers to find the gaps where
the used ones should go. When that was done, she looked at
the cabinets. There were dozens, making the most of every corner and hollow the wagon offered—and as she was doing Zoë's
chores for her, she felt no compunction whatsoever in searching
them, lightly, so long as she was here.
Pliers—brass ingots—wooden blocks. "What kind of wood
is that?" she asked aloud.
"What color?"
"Sort of purple."
"African."
More wood, ebony, and things. A box of...*I suppose they're
animal teeth.* Vises. Some kind of golden tube. "What's this gold
cylinder thing?"
"Unfinished scroll case."
Rocks—someone should tell Jacquy he's hauling rocks up
all these mountains. Ink—charcoal—parchment. Punches...*I'd
better put some away now and leave the rest for after I'm finished.*
Colored stones. "What's this big green stone?"
"Malachite."
"I like the gold flecks."
"Lapis, then... blue. The candlelight just makes it look
green." Zoë spoke in the very patient tones of someone who
will not remain that way much longer.
Oh—good lord, that's pretty. "What's this caskety thing?"
"Don't touch those."

"Oh. Oh! It wasn't one of these that Sarrasine came to see you about?!" Meribah dropped the jeweled box like a burning brand.

Zoë whirled round. "What?" She glanced first at one of the closed cabinets, then at the Setite and the open shelves. Everything lay where it should; Meribah had dropped the box only a careful half an inch. "No."

"Good," said Meribah, in a small voice. She smiled foolishly. "I guess you wouldn't have brought that all this way with you, anyway."

Zoë returned to her work, distracted again and annoyed. "No—actually, he did bring it. It's small enough, and very valuable, even if Khay'tall never comes to claim it."

"Gold?"

The Ravnos sighed. "Not everything valuable is made of gold, Meribah. Silver is precious, too." She herself was not yet allowed to work in gold, the Setite knew. "And the carved stone is very rare. Something sort of green from the Silk Road."

Meribah put away the rest of the punches. She marked in her memory the cabinet that Zoë had checked in her panic, but opened one as far from it as possible. "What are these white stringy things?"

"I'm finished," Zoë decided suddenly. "Let's go."

"It's 'small enough,' not simply small. And it's probably silver, or mostly silver, instead of gold. I think it's completely Gregory's work, or she would have mentioned the part she had done on it—very proud, you know—and the stone is so rare that she didn't have a name for it." Meribah hesitated, scrunching up her face. "Or she may have known what it's called, but been so sure that I wouldn't know that she didn't bother. And it's only 'sort of' green."

Andreas waited with his pen over his last note. "Anything else?"

"It may be in the workshop. She looked right at one of the cabinets when I riled her...but I've been thinking, since, and Gregory usually sits just there. It might have been habit, to look to that spot in conversation."

"Well done." The Egyptian pushed the parchment scrap into one of the writing-box's pigeonholes.

"I've been thinking about the locks I saw in the shop. I could pick about half of them—the ones on the drawers, the supply cabinets, and the base-metal stores. I might be able to get through a few of the rest, but it would take a long time for each one. He doesn't build them any way I'm used to."

"He is exceptional." Andreas rummaged around in his desk, seeking the suede-wrapped, lotus message-case. "This is one of his." The keys were tied to a corner of the protective leather; he held them and the box for his ally to take. "See if you can open it with the key, first."

The little thief took the challenge eagerly, but without careless haste. Settling herself at Willem's board, she began by feeling all around the polished case. *She cannot see it*, realized Andreas, and he lit a candle for her.

"Dehaan tells me Gregory saw you teaching Zoë."

"That's what Dehaan says."

"Has Gregory said anything to you?"

"Nothing. I saw him last night, and he told her she might go with me... he could have made an issue then..." She brushed her hair out of her eyes. "I need a hint, or something to write with. Both keys work in all four tumblers...at different depths. It must be a sequence lock." Andreas provided chalk and slate, and she scratched away earnestly. "Assuming he wouldn't make the owner sit up all night unlocking it, he might use, say, four movements—choice of four holes, two keys, two directions to move the tumblers—4,096 possible combinations. Fewer if he keeps it symmetrical and doesn't reuse an option—right. Only 384. Much smaller."

"He called that a simple lock."

"He's a bloody genius. I'd bet that half of this mechanism relocks the other half whenever it's tampered with." Meribah held it as close to the candle as she dared. "Unless I'd picked scores of his work before and he uses some consistent logic, which I doubt—I couldn't get through this in a night without a miracle." She turned to face him, demonstrating. "The springs feel the same all the way through. I can't tell what's happening inside."

"If you had time?"

She grinned. "With time, I can do anything. Disassemble the blasted case, if need be."

"Good. Keep looking for the cache. Know how to reach it if I ask you." He thought of her searching through the Ravnos wagon with a candle, and disliked the picture. Bare hands would be worse still. The Wonder-Maker gave his roses thorns. Andreas reached into his desk again. "Let me give you something, Meribah, to pay back what I owe you thus far."

"Oh—no, you don't have to do that."

"A small thing."

Meribah took the tiny object in surprise. "A mirror," she said flatly.

"Sight." He gestured peremptorily. "Look, and tell me what color your eyes are."

"They're green," she answered, without obeying.

"Look, Meribah."

"They're still green."

"They're blue. Day-colored. Didn't you know? Keep looking at that mirror, every night, until you can see the blue by candle-light, and then you won't need the candle anymore."

Chapter Fourteen

Spalato, Dalmatia
The autumn and winter of 1206

When the caravan entered the Lasombra Principality of Spalato—or "Split" in the tongue of the Croats who held suzerainty over the port city—Andreas stopped it on that border. As a precaution, he sent his heralds ahead before approaching the city itself. Prince Ignatius Jacobi required the utmost in skillful handling. He was quite capable of demanding homage, seizing a toll, or denying passage through his lands. The Setite sent gifts with his messages and prayed.

Jacobi took his time. Nights passed without an answer, forcibly conveying the possibility of refusal. Andreas bore the delay patiently, Lord Valerian with effort, and Ewald with poor temper. At long last, a civil greeting arrived and summoned them to the seat of government. They rolled forward, making excruciating preparations for their procession. No honors due their host could be omitted. No compliment they could pay him dare be overlooked. The Ventrue, jealous of their own status, took pains to display it. Andreas directed Magda to costume the common travelers even more lavishly than she had for other cities, and Dehaan raised the banner Tomislav had given the Egyptian.

Their welcome was surprisingly warm. Prince Jacobi directed his guards to bring them to his own palace, the heart of the city. It had been built by the Emperor Diocletian, ruined, restored, and added to continuously for a thousand years. The prince's captains, smartly liveried, escorted them through the great north gate, along the impressive central peristyle

colonnade, past Diocletian's crypt and the temple of Jupiter—
now a cathedral—and into the Great Hall, Jacobi's throne room.
Only the Lasombra himself awaited them, resplendent in black
robes and a thin golden crown. No other Cainites attended the
audience. There were mortal guards lining the upper galleries,
but their lord ignored them; they did not exist.

Andreas strode forward fearlessly, made a sharp, deep
obeisance, and waited to be addressed.

"Andreas Aegyptus." The Lasombra smiled—he had a
mild, genial face, beneficent and unlined as a child's. "I bid
you welcome in my domain."

The Setite bowed again. "You honor me with your welcome, my prince."

"You are not unexpected. I have prepared rooms in the
west wall for you and your…retinue."

Andreas could not see the Ventrue behind him. He didn't
need to—their rage filled the hall like steam.

"The southwest tower, I reserve for our most distinguished
mutual guest." The Lasombra descended from his lofty seat.
"Master Lakeritos—it is a true pleasure to have you here in
Spalato." He gave his hand to the artist, who bowed low. "I
am something of a collector of your unique work. I trust you
will favor me with a demonstration of your talents. I have furnished a workshop and the finest materials for your use."

"Thank you, my prince." Gregory gestured to the girl
beside him. "My apprentice, Zoë."

"Delighted," declared Jacobi. His eyes slid over the other
commoners. He spun abruptly to face the Ventrue.

"Gnaeus Eligius Valerian Scaevola, I salute you. May our
meeting prove fortunate for both our houses. If you will inform
me when you are ready to discuss the Hohenstaufen treaty,
I will await your convenience—in that matter." Neither man
bent their head; neither gave an inch. "Your quarters are above
the west council chamber, by the emperor's sepulcher—the
best Spalato can offer. How many of your coterie shall share
them?" Jacobi's mild gaze flicked across Ewald, the princess
and the Toreador lovely. "Only I travel on the Grand Court's
business."

"I see. I'm sure my seneschal can find someplace to put the others."

"It's the oxen," explained Jacquy. "Three of them have died in the last week."

"Can't you buy replacements?"

"Yes, but there are twelve more ill. Something's hit the entire herd. The market here knows already. Prices are going up."

Andreas sighed.

"This prince's drovers tell me the disease is common here. The chief herdsman can physic the beasts, if his lord allows and we buy the medicines."

"I'll ask tonight."

"It will take time for a complete recovery, master. Nearly a month."

"Can we trade them these, one-for-one, if this treatment is so effective? A month's stay here will have us wintering too far south to reach the passes this spring."

"I suggested it to the drovers. No chance."

"Very well. Valerian wants a week, regardless. We will gift him with four."

The official reception was a chilly affair. Like all Lasombra, the prince surrounded himself with shadows thick and dark. Some of his cousins could ameliorate the blackness with laughter and music. Prince Jacobi had lost that talent. His minstrels made quiet, dry polyphony without words. Mortal guests, power-ful men, and ladies of the living city, drifted dully through the dimness. Andreas recognized this blankness. The Lasombra had worn down their wills, leaving their bodies empty vessels.

All the Cainites here were relatives or toadies of the prince, imperfect reflections of his personality. They circulated through the crowd, engaging the guests in conversation—bright, sin-ister, scholarly, or simple, as befit the perceived nature of the visitor. Andreas, as his fifth host passed politely on, realized he had heard identical opinions and answered the same questions for each one. He fought the urge to yawn, avoided the eye of the sixth native, and watched, slightly sickened, as the proud

Tsarika made herself agreeable to her Norman lord. *He's bound her now, I suppose. A pity, though I suspect she will be less unhappy this way.*

The Setite swallowed his own pride and paid his respects to Jacobi. Of course, the herdsman could be spared to tend the caravan beasts—and the prince would provide, from his own gardens, the special herbs to treat them. The delay was unfortunate, they agreed, but the Lasombra would be happy to let them stay on in Spalato. And now, if Andreas would excuse him, he would tell Valerian and Gregory the news himself.

The oxen were not well in four weeks. They were not well in eight, either, and the caravan was forced to winter in Spalato. Prince Jacobi gave another fete to console the travelers and to celebrate his own, unlooked-for, marvelous luck. This party was still less festive than the first; the caravan guests were disinclined to mingle. Jacobi's gray hospitality wore thin. It was Andreas's suspicion, shared with his lieutenants and Meribah, that the beasts' illness sprang from feed provided by the prince. He did not tell his passengers—such words would have amounted to an accusation, and he could prove nothing—but they, too, were restless. They clustered together whenever courtesy allowed. Even Calleo sought company, and Andreas found Galatea on his arm.

"Let me walk with you," she suggested, in confident, public tones. These were the first words she had spoken to him since the judgment in Durazzo. "I am afraid of the shadows," she whispered, and he did not reject her.

Meribah slipped past the high, heavy doors into Andreas's suite of rooms. The guards smiled to acknowledge her—they were caravan men, not Jacobi's drones—and waved her through to their master's presence. His bedroom—purely nominal, not slept in by the priest himself—was an ell-shaped chamber. The outer door opened on a kind of sitting room; the other leg of the ell held a canopied bed, hidden from view from the entrance. Andreas looked up, interested, as his cousin barreled in, triumphant. "They're blue," exclaimed the red-haired girl.

"Very good," Andreas said. "I'm glad you've had time to train your eyes. Gregory has been asking for you, and he had to come here to do it. He and Zoë haven't seen much of you since we arrived."

"It's not my fault," she protested. "They're always working—and when they're working, the guards won't let me in to disturb them."

"I've had the same problem." Andreas shrugged. "Not his idea, apparently. Jacobi's reverence for him overreaches itself. He left here determined to see the captain immediately. I don't think we'll have any difficulties in the future." The Egyptian smiled, thinking of the gentle artist's indignation unleashed on the guardsmen. He thought to share the image with his cousin, looked up, and found her staring at him. "I think Gregory wants you to teach him the *langue d'oil*," he explained instead. "Zoë too, of course. Will you go?"

Meribah smiled uncertainly. "Sure," she told him, and hopped off the wall. "I'll go tonight." She seemed lighthearted again—almost careless—but he knew she harbored doubts.

Andreas unbolted the door and held it open for her. He realized he felt rather touched by her worries. His *Franj* cousin cared; she had wanted to save him. She acted in her own interests, no doubt, but she had rushed to protect his free will—his soul, in fact—with an unexpected, fiery intent. He watched her walk out, through the shrine (without a sign to the two mortals), hurry past the bedroom (ignoring the Toreador woman entirely), and sidle through the great door. A half-smile curled his lips.

Ljudumilu moved, very slightly. Andreas caught sight of her face, and there was that in her eyes which disturbed him. Dehaan rose to adjust the pillows behind her back, obscuring the Setite's view. When he moved away again, the gray eyes had not changed. They held Andreas's own, relentlessly.

The next night, Andreas woke in his ironbound casket, turned the key with his teeth, and pushed the hatch aside. He slithered out the tiny opening, stood up, and cursed Jacobi. The traveling box was a cramped, unlovely little thing. It had many virtues.

It would protect against stakes, crushing, and (for a very short time) fire. It was peg-built, and the pegs could be removed from the inside to free the occupant instantly. And it did not look like a coffin; no mortal could worm their way inside its narrow mouth. But Ton had made it as small as it could be and still hold his master. It was uncomfortable, even for the dead. It was meant for short stays in untrustworthy lodgings. Andreas had slept inside it every day since coming to Spalato, and loathed it.

Goreb, seeing his lord afoot, rolled off of the beautiful, curtained bed and took his post by the outer door. He bowed, but said nothing—he glanced deferentially to his left, to the sitting room Andreas could not yet see. The Setite stepped forward cautiously, wondering who could be present in his own chamber, unasked, and what the matter might be.

Ljudumilu was waiting for him. Dehaan sat, uncharacteristically quietly, in the small chair beside her couch.

"Blessed lord. I greet you waking," croaked the old priestess. "We must speak about the red-haired child."

Andreas approached her slowly. "Say your piece."

"Last night, lord, I heard the *Franj* speaking with you. I beg you forgive my eavesdropping." This was a matter of form; she begged him for nothing. "She disapproves of your congress with the muse woman. She denies the joys of the blood. She scorns desire."

The Egyptian shook his head. "Meribah was concerned for the consequences of the blood, not the pleasures of it."

The wrinkled face twisted with pity for his naivete. "You do not see. You turn a blind eye to the child's sins. I tell you, milord, I know. I offered her my grandson." A withered hand shook toward the young man. "Dehaan tested her, and she failed. She is not a true follower. Her presence defiles the shrine of Set. You know the penalty. We must cleanse her error by sacrifice to the Destroyer."

Ankhesenaten gazed down upon his priestess. "I am the judge here, not you, priestess, and I have not lost my sight. Meribah is no perfect Follower, I know, but I do not think she is a heretic. Dehaan—tell me what you have done, testing my sister."

The Rooster spun his tale obediently, looking now at his grandmother, now at his master, in equal turns. His words were few—he began and ended each scene with the offer, keeping the details to himself—and uncolored. He made no argument for Ljudumilu's side, nor Andreas's. If he had an opinion of his own, if he longed to hack the *Franj* impostor's head from her body or would rather shield the girl from his grandmother's uncompromising faith, the signs were buried deep and the Setite could not read them.

Ankhesenaten stood still for many minutes. No one else dared speak.

"I compliment you on your zeal, Ljudumilu. You are a wise woman indeed; there is none other like you."

In the old language, which Dehaan did not yet understand, he then went on heatedly: "Old fool. If she takes offense, my mission is at risk. I need her, no matter what her sins. And your jealousy put the boy in needless danger. What would you have done if she had killed him?"

"I watched from a distance. You were nearby. Had he fallen, I would have sent for you, and made you choose."

"I will not make that decision in haste, and I will not condemn Meribah based on your savage prejudices. Do not presume to measure the chosen until you join them."

Ankhesenaten returned to the Rooster's own dialect. "Where you find blasphemy, however, I see an exceptional instinct tempered by fine guile. Meribah wants a favor. She has no wish to jeopardize her ultimate desires for immediate ones." He turned to the boy directly. "Dehaan, I would have you try again, if you are willing. I will explain to my sister that I ordered you to make this test, and that there is no ban remaining upon her actions. We will see what she does."

Four of them rode out to look at the north road together: Jacquy, Goreb, Meribah and Andreas, making plans for the spring. The weather was fine and the earth dry under the horses' hooves. Brightly shone the moon, and white pebbles glowed on the ground beneath her. In the free air of the country, the travelers relaxed. The distance between the horses grew, and the

Egyptian managed to have words with his men away from the prince's many ears.

Goreb and the caravan master fell behind, going up one hill, and the two Setites stopped to wait for them. Jacquy dismounted and felt the animal's forefoot. Andreas sidled closer to the girl. "The mare's picked up a stone, I think."

"Looks like it," sighed Meribah. "Should we ride back down?"

Andreas's horse pushed forward restlessly, but he said, "Not yet," and turned his steed until he and the *Franj* were face to face and nearly leg to leg. "I have something I want to say to you, first."

Her brow furrowed. "What is it?"

"I want to thank you for your loyalty—and your restraint. For fasting, my sister."

The girl said nothing. Doubt danced in her eyes.

She must know what I mean, and whom. Why not answer? "It's all right, Meribah. I know that the Rooster offered you blood."

She blinked at this.

I see. Suddenly, she speaks less Greek than the Tsarika. "It was a trial, sister." Andreas found himself speaking slowly, as to an infant. "I have tested you through my servant, Dehaan, and you have proven loyal and trustworthy where the lives of my people are concerned. You fought men for them, faced the wolves for them, and you denied even your own desires for their sake, and for mine." He stretched a hand over the men below them, and further, to the city in the distance. "I make you free of them. You may hunt among my own people when the need presses, and you may feed them, if you like and can spare the blood." He dropped out of his grandiloquent declamation. "Next time we're in a scrap, you can help me heal the wounded. I felt like a public fountain after the wolves' attack."

Meribah stared down the hill thoughtfully. "Thank you," she murmured uncertainly. Her gaze met his. She seemed pleased, although a little embarrassed. Her hand crept down to stroke Eureka's neck. "A test. I suppose I should have expected it from you. You only knew me the one year...and Al-Suti wasn't...you might well doubt me. I'm glad I passed."

Andreas relaxed, only a little, and only on his own behalf. She would not leave the caravan in umbrage. He could still use her to find the heart of Khay'tall. But she lacked the arrogance he would like to see in his kin. This time he was grateful, but someday he might be made to act.

The little *Franj* grinned broadly, laughing. "A test." There were bitter notes within the words. "Of course it was."

He saw it then: Meribah had her pride—as much as Thebes could ask for—and it stung her. Andreas knew the Rooster. He could guess that the mortal hadn't merely opened his wrist beneath her nose. He remembered how Spartan the young man's account of their meetings had been, and how quietly Dehaan had listened as his grandmother passed sentence on the little *Franj*.

Interesting.

Meribah wasn't looking for anyone. She visited the caravan crew to gossip with Carl and Robert, not the Rooster. She walked through Andreas's rooms to get to the shrine, not to him. She hunted in the east quarter because there were crowds there, not because he frequented the Iron Gate ale-house. But when she was finished there, and had run out of places in which to avoid him, she felt worse. Her feet turned toward the stables and Eureka. She was a meteor, falling—if she rode like one, she might be able to catch up with herself.

At the end of the colonnade, a figure was waiting. Meribah could see the edge of its garments snapping in the wind, before she glimpsed the face. She walked on, fighting the gale, watching the silhouette flesh out. It was a man, leaning against the last arch before the stable door. He was too tall for a groom, too slender for a guard, his hair too long for a friar, his cloak too green for a priest. When she came nearer, he turned, and his dull-gold hair whipped into his face.

Dehaan's eyes were grave, his expression serious. Meribah stopped where she was.

"Aren't you finished?" she accosted him, more sharply than she wished.

"What do you mean?"

"The test. Isn't it over?"

"It is," lied the Rooster. "I wanted to see you, myself, to apologize."

"Why apologize? You played your part very well."

"I'm ashamed of it. I would never treat a girl that way."

"I'm not a girl. I'm as old as your grandmother."

"You're a girl, and I threatened you."

She shrugged. "Not much."

"I tried to blackmail you."

"It didn't work."

"You've been hurt."

"By someone who threatened and blackmailed me?" Meribah tried a smile. It cracked in half.

"I led you to believe I meant something else."

"You think I believed it?"

"I don't know. But I want to tell you I did mean it." His hands rose toward her, rather helplessly.

Meribah took one of them and bit into the palm. Blood—rich-scented red gold—spilled into her mouth and trickled down her throat. The mortal sagged against the ancient pillar, closing his eyes in ecstasy. She released him, licked the wound, and stood by while he recovered.

"There," she said quietly. "You have what you wanted. You don't have to mean anything."

"Damn you," he spat, panting, his chin low and outthrust, his eyes angry. "If you breathed, girl—"

"What?"

His hand shot out and seized her wrist. He pulled her in and held her against him, vise-tight and unyielding. Meribah didn't struggle. His cloak wound round them both; she was out of the wind; he fought it for both of them. He was a rock. He could shield her.

Meribah realized her rock was shaking. Dehaan's heart beat hard enough to move his body. Mortals are never still. She pushed away, searching his eyes. *He's bound to Andreas—to Ankhesenaten. I can't believe him.* He leaned down to kiss her, and she let him. All at once, she didn't care whether he lied or not. It was nice to be held. She curled both of her hands around one of his. The skin paled immediately—her flesh was as cold as the ice on the troughs. She snatched her fingers back.

"Come to me," she whispered. "Tomorrow night, after moonrise?"

"Yes."

Meribah's room was in the undercroft beneath the west wall, among the servants' quarters, close by a busy staircase. Dehaan evaded maids and weary footmen, and rapped lightly on the door. No one answered, but there were metallic footsteps behind the suitor—he pushed the door open and escaped the prowling guards. He would wait inside; he would see if she were within, and had not heard his first, embarrassingly timid knock.

She didn't seem to be there. A candle guttered in a small niche by the door. Dehaan picked it up and stepped forward. There was the bed with curtains drawn—a stone-topped table, laden with a smoking brazier, covered dish, and steaming wine. A spark sprang up in a corner, as he walked nearer. He saw the washbowl, a jug of water, and the light—Andreas's tiny mirror, reflecting his own flame. Dehaan moved on to the wardrobe. Here was the templar cloak on its hook, the broken spear shaft with its silver spike, and the dresses Danica and Magda had sewn for her, laid out carefully on the top three shelves.

Below them, three to a shelf, lay a dozen neatly folded small, dirty bundles. They were gray, dun, yellowed and white, with reddish-brown stains. Some bore embroidery, others had been stitched onto newer cloth. Dehaan guessed they were old—he was sure they were not meant to be worn.

He would have touched one, had not Meribah's voice, high and alarmed, rung out behind him: "Dehaan?"

She was sitting in a thin, sheer shift at the top of the bed steps, with the curtains framing her on either side. Heated air wafted through the gap; he could see linen- wrapped warming stones piled on the foot of the bed. Meribah held out a fever-hot hand.

The Rooster raised a wry brow. "Food, wine and warmth?"

She blushed, rose-cheeked and shy. "For you." She disappeared behind the curtains and left them open. Dehaan set down his candle, quickly, and followed her into the bed.

Ljudumilu waited impatiently as her grandson made his offerings at the shrine. She spoke almost before his fingertips left the
silk-smooth rosewood case.

"You have seen the girl? Spoken to her? What of the test?"
Her eyes devoured the Rooster's image. He turned to face her;
the steely gaze softened as she beheld his satisfied expression.
"Good, my son, I bless you." The matriarch, relieved, lay back
on her couch. "She fell. We will be rid of her."

"Granddam..." Dehaan hastened to kneel by her bed, smiling, shaking his head. "Granddam, I spent the night with her.
All the night." The young Fleming leaned over to kiss the old
upon the cheek. "She is holy, Granddam, and she is an excellent
spirit of Set."

Ljudumilu s withered hand curled around his wrist and
tightened painfully. Suddenly she let go and reached for his
chin. "Tell me," ordered the priestess.

The Rooster laughed mildly. "I offered blood once more, and
this time Meribah took it." Memories caught at him. "I spent
the night," he said again, looking into the shadows beyond the
shrine. Ljudumilu's gaze raked across him, keen for detail. Her
silence demanded more—but the Rooster's secrets were not
forthcoming. He had revealed nothing of the templar crosses,
when he saw those—nothing of how the mention of Meribah's
boon broke her down—and he would not talk about his red-
haired lover now.

The thin, dry nails of Ljudumilu's fingers rasped down his
unshaven jaw. Mournful lines crept across her brow, and her
mouth puckered in weariness. "I sent you into danger...I am
sorry, my child." A strange sound, part chuckle, part cough,
escaped her. "And I thought you were immune, Rooster-mine."

He looked on her again, indulgently. "You don't believe me,
dear heart?"

"I do not." She watched him still. "You will not see the girl
again," she decided.

Dehaan's jaw set, and he shook away her hand. "Why?

She is not chosen—and now she makes a fool of you." The

Rooster frowned. "Who speaks? The priestess of our Lord, or my Granddam?"

Neither priestess nor grandmother answered.

"I see." Dehaan kissed the old woman a second time. He rose, added fuel to the brazier, and stirred the coals.

"You're leaving?"

"I promised to help Ton with the lumber. Do you need anything?" he asked fondly, returning to her side. Ljudumilu handed him her comb. Gently, he brushed the thin gray hair, plaited it, and covered it with her kerchief.

"Ram's fleece," said the priestess. "For the ritual."

Dehaan fetched the dark brown wool obediently.

"Are you comfortable?" A brief nod rewarded him, and he picked up his cloak. "Tell our master what I have done, and assure him I will come back to report after the moon rises."

"Why?" demanded his grandmother anxiously. "Will you not be here when he wakes?"

"Meribah. I want to be there when she wakes up."

"What is she? The village virgin?"

Her acid tones bit him at last; he flushed, then paled, and blinked. "I will ask Magda to come sit with you, Granddam. Good night."

Chapter Fifteen

Spalato, Dalmatia
The Spring of 1207

Spring brought sweet breezes to Spalato. The salt winter wind gave way to the freshness of green grass on the hills and budding trees overhead. Dawn lay in wait below the horizon; already the sky was blue, not black, in the east.

Andreas rode up the line of wagons and inspected his caravan with pleasure and relief. *It has been too long,* he thought. Damn Prince Jacobi. The crew's preparations had been made, at his own order, only by daylight, without the "help" of the prince's people. To foil the Lasombra's spies, Andreas had stayed away from the back yard and the stables; this was the first time he had seen his kingdom in months.

All of the trail-damaged wains had been repaired. The women—except for Annemie, who forged axles as the snow fell—had used the long nights to clean and renovate the house wagons. The delay had given Ton time, too, and the carpenter had used it to try a few improvements to wheel, hitch, and harness.

The oxen were fit to travel once more, and eager to be moving. For an entire month, they had eaten only grain and hay bought in secret by the Rooster, hauled to Spalato by Jacquy, and smuggled into the stables by the children. The subterfuge might have been unnecessary; the prince's herdsman had predicted the animals' recovery by spring. Willem doubted whether the traveling treasury could stand the strain, and Andreas wondered whether he had overreacted to the Lasombra's eager, solicitous hospitality.

Ahead of the wagons, the road was not empty: The mortal

refugees' ranks had swollen in Spalato. There were towns-folk among them now, desperate to leave the Lasombra's rule behind. Already, the most adventurous, fearful, or impatient had begun to walk or roll north on their own. Andreas spoke encouragement to such of these as he knew, then turned the horse's head back toward the city.

The prince, his brood and the caravan guests were assembled by the city gates. Jacobi hailed Andreas courteously.

"All is in order, I trust?"

Andreas dismounted. "Entirely. I thank you for your concern." He turned to his passengers. "If you have said your good-byes, you should take your places."

Valerian began to lead his coterie toward their berths. Andreas turned to follow them.

"Not yet, Egyptian. We have business to discuss before any of you leave. It is time to pay the toll."

The Setite turned slowly. "What toll is this, Jacobi?"

"Entry into my domain is free, from the south," explained the Lasombra. "On the north road, to pay for its defense, I am forced to exact a fee." The serene, amiable face smiled deprecatingly. "A tithe of all cargo which travels along my highway."

Andreas scowled. "You might have mentioned this before now," he complained. "Jacquy! Unload the tenth part of the wine and spices. We leave it here, for his highness." Sullen murmurs emanated from the crew, and the Cainites stopped moving. Valerian and Boleslaus drew near to listen.

"No need," assured the Lasombra kindly. "I have no interest in that trash you carry by the bale. I levy my tax on your true cargo."

The Setite understood immediately. Hoping he had heard wrong—calculated the prince's mood in error—he asked the question: "My true cargo?"

Jacobi's smile widened. "You trade in the transport of Cainites, Egyptian. You have ten. I will take one."

"You have no right," said Valerian.

"You did not challenge my rights when you thought I wanted only mortal merchandise."

"We are not chattel," returned the Ventrue.

Andreas stepped back with one foot only. He still faced Jacobi, but now could see the crew and train. Jacquy and the men were watching closely, their hands casually close to swords and staves. Magda, behind their line, caught his eye. She tucked a stray braid beneath her wimple, then used the hand to point, inconspicuously, up the road. Andreas took his line from her, and saw what she saw.

The escorts provided by Jacobi—introduced as an honor guard, arranged as a show of respect for the senator and the Egyptian—lined the road with spears held high. They had spread out since Andreas had ridden by, and their spacing was irregular—two near Willem and his wife, four where Gertje and her daughters awaited Ton, one enduring Chiara's teasing with a stony grin. There was a soldier within spear's length of every mortal in his congregation.

"You are not chattel; you are far more valuable." Calleo spoke. "We are not slaves, Lasombra, to be sold or traded."

Meribah sidled up on Andreas's left. In Turkish, softly: "If you have to, leave me. I'll get away—I'll catch you before the Alps."

"Oh, no, young lady," intervened Jacobi in the same tongue. He returned to Latin to declare, "I choose my portion."

"Who?" asked Boleslaus.

"I claim Lakeritos," said the prince.

"No!" It was Zoë, and she screamed the word. Gregory put an arm around her, quieting her. Meribah left Andreas to stand by the tinkers. The column of refugees slowed, and some of the families from Constantinople, the old-timers, stopped in their tracks.

"You go too far, Jacobi," warned Valerian. "I will assume that this is a parting jest, and not mention it in the courts."

"I never jest, Senator." All around the prince, the shadows began to thicken. Andreas looked down, and found a dull black pool at his feet. Rivulets of darkness streamed out to each of the passengers; coils rose from the ground, plucking—as yet, only lightly—at the hems of skirts and robes. The threat could not be clearer, and the Setite knew how the battle would play out. By himself, Jacobi could hurt them all, and the wounds would be deep. He would not, perhaps, destroy them. Some would fall, some flee. Valerian, Ewald, Boleslaus, Meribah, and Andreas would attack their enemy, possibly drag him down. If Hadeon were close enough, he might join in. Together, they could possibly send Prince Jacobi back to his long-delayed grave, but his childer would undoubtedly rescue him, guard him, and seal the gates against the outsiders. The caravan's survivors, few or many, would then be burnt by the sun. If they fled into the wagons, their sanctuaries would be hewn open by the prince's troops.

And Andreas's own people, his flock, would be slaughtered before the battle even began.

"We leave no one behind, Jacobi." The Setite's arm rose, signaling to Jacquy: *Roll wagons.* And then he pointed, calmly, their direction: *Take them south, into the town.*

"All of us will leave you," continued Andreas, with a humble kind of confidence, "together." His eyes rose to meet the Lasombra's. "But it seems that we shall not go tonight."

They met in Diocletian's tomb the very next night: passengers and crew, as one group, for the first time since Adrianople. Hadeon growled away the lone priest in the sham chapel—a creature of Jacobi's, weak-willed, and sharp-eared. The older children sat in the portico and on the windowsills. They faced the night; they would listen to the debate, but watch for eavesdroppers. The rest of the travelers settled in amid the ruins of the imperial sarcophagus.

Andreas stood in the narrowest length of the room, waited until all had found seats or perches, and began his speech. "You are all aware of our predicament. We cannot leave with Gregory. We will not leave without Gregory. There is another matter, unknown to most of you. We were delayed last autumn by the illness of the oxen. I told you then what Jacobi's people told mine, that a disease brought the beasts low. I suspected poison; I said nothing. One does not accuse lords lightly, without evidence.

"I have no more proof of this treachery tonight than I did then, but I harbor no doubts. I tell you this that you may understand—this latest outrage is no whim, no sudden decision. I now believe that Jacobi intended this from the moment we came within his walls. He never intended to let Gregory go, and no mere words will free us. I bring you together that we may concentrate our ingenuity. I await your suggestions."

After a moment's pause, Valerian, as befit his station, went first.

"What influence I have in court and country, I will readily exert against this tyrant. I have nearly finished a letter, already, to my own King Alexander and Queen Saviarre, asking their aid. Andreas, I know you have connections and debts to collect among the noble clans, the Cappadocians, the Giovanni traders in Venice, and your own family. Ewald, your lady wishes your return, I trust, and would send her assistance. And surely, all of you among the, well, freemen, there must be allies you can call on, even here."

From the back of the room, huskily, spoke Hadeon: "If he'd said peasant, I'd have torn his throat out."

To Gregory, but too loudly for the echoing, amplifying stone chamber, Zoë whispered, "What makes a clan noble?"

Hadeon's mouth opened to reply, but Meribah piped up before him. "Noble clans' blood magics are good for raising armies. Freemen fight one-on-one."

"Enough," interposed Andreas, though the strife was already fading. The red-haired girl's judiciously vague definition could include any clan who pretended to the upper echelon—and could, if stretched, exclude any clan disliked by the pretender. As such, it was the only definition that was in any sense true.

Calleo broke the next silence. "Lord Valerian," he began, "do you honestly believe that your letters will change anything?"

The senator frowned like thunder, but he listened very attentively.

The Tremere went on. "Can you even get these messages out of Spalato?"

Jacquy stood a moment. "If he writes them, we will get them through." More quietly, to his master, he added, "Sybil could send them on from Durazzo."

Calleo bowed to the caravan master. "No doubt you would succeed... in time. But how long can we wait? It is a year or more to Paris—months to Cappadocia or Egypt—weeks to the Norman Sicilies. And what will your allies do about the matter, when these letters arrive? Send armies? I doubt we could fight our way out during a siege. Censure Jacobi? Less likely still that he would care how infamous his name became, half the world away. I have never heard that Lasombra give a damn about Ventrue disapproval. Set up an embargo and stop trade, perhaps? Do these foreign princes hold anything he desires more than the Wonder-Maker?"

Hadeon lumbered forward, glowering. "We should leave. Just get up and go, one at a time. Let Gregory and Zoë be the first. You would have to abandon your wagons—fend for yourselves, all of you—but you would be free. Andreas and his people could leave safely enough, I think, once Jacobi has nothing to gain by keeping them.

"No." All heads turned; the voice was unknown to most. The Tsarika stood for them to see. "Not this one. He is cold-blooded, this man, but no less the tyrant. He would not let it happen. If these Ravnos escaped, despite him, he would be forced to punish us all, to maintain his own power over his subjects. We would all pay. I see this." Ewald watched his princess resume her seat in silence—he had said nothing yet, and that was unusual. Andreas caught the young man's eyes and raised his own brows in invitation. The Norman had nothing, it seemed, to say.

"There is another option," began the Wonder-Maker slowly. "Something which none of you, strangely, have considered. I could stay."

Zoë grabbed his hand as if there were gates between them already. "No! I won't let you," she said ferociously. "Don't let him," she demanded the gathering.

Meribah shook her head. "We can't do that, Gregory. I've heard you talk about his interference—prying into your workshop, trying to tell you what to make and how to design it. He would destroy you, given time. He'd make you like his childer—flat-souled and dull."

"I refuse to allow you—or any of my clients—to imprison yourself here." Andreas's lip twitched. "Jacobi doesn't deserve you," he added, earning a look of true and unreserved gratitude from the gypsy girl.

"It would set a dangerous precedent, Lakeritos." Valerian rose, took the floor, and addressed the Ravnos where he sat. "If a prince can kidnap any Cainite who passes through his fief, how shall any of us travel? If Jacobi can 'tax' you, the lord of Zara can take Zoë, the bishop of Aquileia will keep Boleslaus— no one will reach Paris but the oxen and the dogs."

After the meeting, the travelers moved their quarters. Valerian accepted Ewald and the Tsarika into his suite, Calleo abandoned his fine corner apartment for a hole in the wall near Boleslaus's own, Galatea took the tiny closet across from Andreas, and Meribah terrorized the maids into giving up the room above her own, adjacent to Gregory's staircase.

The empty room behind Ankhesenaten's shrine was given over to Gertje, who made beds there for every child old enough to leave their mother yet too young to fight. Magda and Danica came to live with Ljudumilu by the shrine. Jacquy, the single men, and the few fighting women filled in the empty chambers between the tomb, the tower, and their master. The party was stretched very thin, but their territory was unbroken.

The letters tore south in Robert's saddlebags. Valerian had high hopes of them. Calleo had come in conference, twice, to explain what he knew of Assamites and their uses—a long study, born of loathing and the principle of knowing one's enemy. Hadeon roamed the countryside, Boleslaus the city, seeking the means to bring down the Lasombra prince. Andreas haunted Jacobi's presence, hoping for an opportunity to reveal itself. He made offerings at every dusk and every dawn.

And Meribah, ever-cheerful, spent most of her time putting heart into the caravan guards or the cloistered tinkers. The guards were easy; they had faith in their leader and his powers, but to comfort the Ravnos was a struggle.

Zoë could be reached; she had as much pride and indignation as Valerian himself. On the road, given time to think about herself, she had collapsed inward around that pride. Now, with someone else to loathe, she became a fighter.

Gregory, however, sank low. He would not hear of plans on his behalf, of messages delivered, greetings sent, or advances made. His work slowed. He seemed afraid to finish the commissions given him by the Lasombra. He spoke, one night in May, when Zoë had left them, of Daedalus and Icarus on the shore. Wings, thought Meribah, and the death of the inventor's child.

The next evening, she hunted out *The Odyssey* from its place in the wagon. It had been left there, still packed away for the caravan's departure—Gregory had not taken it back into the tower after his imprisonment. Meribah tried to read aloud the hero's escapes from overeager men, gods, and monsters. The Wonder-Maker forbade it, and sent the girls away to give him peace.

Meribah took Zoë out to the tavern where Dehaan, Willem, and the other men passed their time. None of the crew were there, so she gave her charge a tour of the narrow streets. All winter long, the Ravnos had not left the palace, and the city was delightfully new to her. The Setite, however, had learned it well—well enough to hide from Zoë that they were being followed. Jacobi's men clung most tightly to the Wonder-Maker himself, but the apprentice's talents had not escaped the prince's notice either. Meribah led her friend and their escort back through the gates and into the stables. There they found Dehaan and Leopold the drover just tightening their horses' girths. She liberated Eureka and one of Andreas's saddle-horses, and gave the soldiers a winning smile.

"We're off to the hills, sergeants. Would you mind, very much, coming along with us, for safety's sake?" The cold-eyed swordsman smiled uncertainly. "Do you have horses? You can get horses, can't you?" Meribah grinned. "Get good horses; ours are very fast." She trailed along behind the men and inspected their mounts. "Not sound enough," she told them each time they chose a steed. "Just look at his knees, you couldn't have a real gallop on that one." They ended their search with the finest stallions in the prince's stables, and watchers set off with watched as a happy party of eight.

They rode along the east road and out into the country-side—through fields, beside woods, and between ruins of the Romans, starkly beautiful and sharp by moonlight. The caravan four held a race around one desolate foundation. The soldiers, at their ease outside their lord's long shadow, marked out the course and played judge of the games. With the moon newly risen behind them, the little band turned for home and a fine gallop in the straight, gentle verges west.

As they approached the city, a bizarre spectacle greeted them. A horde of pilgrims were streaming into the south gate, encamping around the walls, and trampling down the pastures between town and farm. The mob overflowed the road from Ragusa and were spilling up toward the east gate and the road by the time the riders reached them.

"They have no fires," observed the leader of the escort, "and they travel by night. Who can they be?"

"I know who they are," Meribah said grimly. "Ride through," she ordered the others, taking point herself. "Say nothing to them, and don't listen to anything they may say. Don't let them touch you, and do not dismount."

She rode on at a fast walk because the crowd permitted nothing faster. They had the pinched faces of mortals drained too often. They recognized the nature of the girls at once. Meribah—snow-white and rose-red—became an object of adoration. Eureka's gait slowed, and they moved at the speed of a feast-day procession. Plucking fingers reached for her templar cloak, and pale, peeling lips kissed her bare feet. There were tonsures, graybeards, and babes-in-arms among them, along with plowmen, townsfolk, mothers, and children. And beside the ill and weak, healthy faces gleamed like blisters—too red, with hungry expressions. They were ghouls, fed on the afterlife, like Dehaan, Goreb and her own horse, but with a difference—these creatures had no reverence, no loyalty. They would take any blood. Meribah feared them. They would drag her and Zoë off the horses and devour them, if they thought it possible; they would drink the blood of Dehaan and the drover as well, for the traces of Andreas inside their veins.

Meribah let Eureka make his own path, without regard

for the jostling bodies. She glanced back and found the others' horses near bolting from the unnatural crowd. Zoë's animal showed white all around its eyes, and the high-strung Spalato stallions quivered with panic.

The troop neared a tent—one of the first ones raised, apparently, for it occupied a choice plot between two towers. The owner's wagon had been pulled into the lee of a ruined, transverse wall a short distance away, and the space enclosed was almost empty.

"Zoë?" A woman in nun's robes rose beside this privileged tent, calling to the riders. "Dehaan? Is that you?" The Ravnos looked to the Rooster, shaking her head. Meribah glanced over her shoulder again, inquiringly. The crowd split before them; Eureka was making for the clearing by the tent—it was the best way through the crush. The troop reined in. They had reached the wall; they must turn north to gain the gate.

Dehaan waved Leopold on. "Tell our master." He drew up beside Zoë and Meribah. "In Adrianople, remember, miss?" he said softly to the gypsy girl. "Takouhi. She was to have traveled with us."

The guards on the gate began yelling to the Ravnos's escort. The soldiers left with Leiven, and the five had little difficulty getting through without the deathless children. "We don't stop," insisted Meribah. "Come on." Takouhi already stood between Zoë's stirrups and Dehaan's. "How are you, girl? How fares your sire?" Concern and affection colored her voice.

"We do very well, thank you, ma'am."

"And how is the Rooster? Lost your heart yet?" The Malkavian examined the mortal kindly. "Not as carefree, these days... Is your grandmother...?"

"More ill than when last you saw her, my lady."

"I see." She patted his arm consolingly. Her fingers strayed to the horse's neck. The beast quieted immediately. "Poor thing," she murmured to it. "Poor thing." She reached for Zoë's mount and calmed the mare as well. "And how is my noble friend, Andreas? What troubles him that troubles you?"

The Fleming grimaced, but held his tongue. Takouhi waved a hand. "Back, my ducks, back away now. You press my guests too close for courtesy." The pilgrims shuffled off to a respectful distance, but Meribah eyed them warily. The space was welcome, but the new circle was too thick to charge through without a fight. "Is that better, boy? What binds your master?"

Dehaan gestured vaguely. "The troubles of the road, common to all travelers."

The Malkavian smiled, giving him the lie. He seemed embarrassed, and she let it go. She looked to Zoë, then to Meribah, who had remained quiet. She regarded this silent stranger with interest.

"Stay, my chicks," she invited the three, "and when I finish preaching, we will talk." She indicated seats by her own.

"No." Meribah said it firmly, but her knuckles coiled cracking-tight in Eureka's mane. She remembered the last heretic sermon she had heard and would spare her fragile friend that horror. "Stay on your horse, Zoë. We're leaving."

"The red-headed child," murmured Takouhi. "I'm afraid they will stay until my little lesson is finished. Are you going to ride them down?" She resumed her place and began to speak.

"Repentance," she began. This surprised Meribah—no word of sin or atonement had drifted up from the Via Egnatia the night she and Andreas had listened. "Repentance is the key to the gates of Heaven, children. Take it. Use it. You live, my loves, and with that life you have been given a marvelous gift. God's special gift to the living to redeem yourselves from sin: fear.

"Lucifer sinned without repentance. He was deathless. He had no fear, no humility. But the fear of death made Adam and his Eve humble. They asked for forgiveness from the Lord, and they received it. Any of you, my dears, can do this. I tell you, do this tonight. Do it before you ask my brothers for a new existence. Do it before you seek to join my kind." The congregation stirred uneasily, but Takouhi ignored them. "It is most blessed to repent before your death, children." Some pilgrims scowled at this, others smiled. A few seemed thoughtful, and the rest hung on the words most expectantly, without seeming to grasp them.

"To some," Takouhi continued, "some few, not so blessed— more sinful, perhaps, than our brothers and sisters—or in greater need of salvation—there is given a second life, an opportunity to atone, to do penance for the sins of the first."

Meribah looked quickly to Zoë. The Ravnos's lips were parted, her eyes wide and brimming with crimson tears.

"Have you sinned, daughter?" the Malkavian inquired gently.

Zoë, trembling, nodded.

"Do you wish to be free of your sin?"

Meribah jabbed her heels into Eureka's sides. "That's it," she said. "Move." Carefully, the great dun-colored horse picked his way into the first row. "Tell them to move, sister, or I will ride them down."

Takouhi gestured, and a path opened. Dehaan took Zoë's mare by the bridle and led her away.

The Setite felt something touch her knee. It was the Malkavian. Somehow the serene and stately woman had reached the edge of the clearing instantly, and without a sound. Her soft brown eyes gazed into Meribah's, studying her. "Have you never sinned, Beata?"

This name, from a Cainite, shocked the serpent into stillness.

"A shroud lies across your path, child. Choose soon."

Meribah, trembling, shook her head.

A crowing whistle came from the gate. Eureka started forward, obeying the Rooster's call, taking his mistress away from the seer and into the city.

Dehaan saw the horses into the grooms' sure hands, the Ravnos safely into the tower, and the Setite into her stolen maid's room. He held her there, stroking her hair, searching for a reason. "What's this shroud? Was she threatening you? What else did she say to you?"

Meribah gave no answers; she buried her head in his shoulder, whispering questions of her own. "If something happens— if I have to leave—will you remember me? Will you forgive me?"

The mortal took the news to his master, and they sequestered the caravan passengers, the crew, the remaining refugees who had journeyed there with them. Andreas warned Jacobi, and the Lasombra listened. Hoping to drive the heretics north, he forbade them the city, but the weeks dragged on, and the pilgrims did not leave. There were conversions, disappearances—denunciations by and recruitment of the local priests.

A month passed, and the heretics finally moved on, but the caravan still waited.

Ignatius Jacobi walked up and down Diocletian's seaside arcade. His offspring trailed along behind him like baby ducks. Andreas paid quiet attendance upon him from a respectful distance, to the side, as an equal, and Jacobi played no games with speed or step to widen the gap. He simply paced up and down the southern loggia, back and forth, all night long.

At first, the Setite had thought that the prince searched the sea—that he feared a threat from across the waters. He believed this no longer. There were guards, a watchtower, and a harbormaster to do this for Jacobi, and the prince rarely turned his eyes toward the waves. Nevertheless, the patrol was his habit, and he walked more slowly going west, toward the Adriatic, than when he faced the mainland.

Occasionally some city official, captain of guardsmen or cleric would arrive and bring news to his liege. Invariably, the matters were trivial. Jacobi insisted on being informed and consulted about the pettiest facets of his domain, and he dealt with the decisions in a predictable pattern. The mortal would report; the prince would listen. Andreas listened, too, for chance or Set to bring him something. Eventually Jacobi would speak and his subject would listen. As a chorus, in order of rank, the Lasombra's children would concur, and they never, ever, expressed a thought of their own. The night's third suppliant, a timid monk, was just leaving. The young Lasombra toadies radiated smug approval. Andreas stifled a yawn, and then it happened.

A shout came from the watchtower, and a bell began ringing. Jacobi rushed to the arcade and leaned over the balustrade. Andreas followed him. One ship rose over the horizon, clear in the cloudless, mistless night. With effort and his blood-brightened eyes, the Setite identified it: a light roundship, fast and maneuverable, its colors Venetian, its banners papal. He let his extra senses go; the bells pained him.

Andreas examined his host, surreptitiously. At first, he thought Jacobi as passive as ever—he might have seen an albatross on the water, not a man-of-war—but a gritty noise, on the lower fringe of hearing, attracted his attention. The Lasombra's claws were showing, and they dug into the gray ash rock as if it were clay.

The oldest childe gasped. "What shall we do, father?" The Egyptian fought down his surprise. What can one ship—or twenty—do to a prince of shadows and this obedient, well-ordered city? He remembered the ship's banners. He cannot fear the Church. He has the priests of Spalato tamed, and his kin weave nets about the pope. Narses, the Venetian prince, is Lasombra. Who sails against Jacobi?

"*We* will fight, you fool," snapped Jacobi.

"My lord?" Andreas inquired as courteously as he could. "This ship troubles you?"

The Lasombra turned on his guest. "This fleet troubles me—and you, as well. You do not know... you have not been to Zara since the Crusaders passed through it." He stalked off toward the western wall, scanning the waters for more vessels.

Andreas hastened to the prince's side. War beckoned; this was a gift from the Destroyer. "If I eliminate this fleet for you, will you let us leave?"

Jacobi made a bizarre sound—laughter. "Where are your ships, merchant? Where are your armies?" He shook his head, amused by the madman. "If you remove this thorn from my paw, mouse, you and yours can go."

And so Ankhesenaten went to pray the Lord of Storms to send a tempest.

"It will be a miracle," the priest explained to his congregation. All the caravan were there, crammed into the rooms about the shrine, and Meribah sat among them. "Miracles require sacrifice."

Goreb, Hand of the Destroyer, stepped forth. "I will find an orphan child, Great One. There are many miserable souls in

Spalato who would be eager to leave the Jealous God for Set."

Ankhesenaten shook his head. "This is not an apology, to be sent by a three-day convert. Our need is great; our sacrifice must match it. We will have to send one of our own. I need a believer who can speak for us before Him of the Northern Deserts."

Seconds passed, and no one spoke. Meribah could hear a hundred heartbeats racing.

"I will go," said a high, cracked voice. Carl stood and repeated himself. "I will go."

His father seized the boy's wrist. "The hell you will. I lost Owain to this madness already."

"Madness, Jacquy? Have you no faith?" croaked Ljudumilu.

Ankhesenaten placed a hand on Carl's head. "You are brave, and you will be favored by our Lord. But I cannot let you go."

"Send me," volunteered a hidden child. Jozef wriggled his way into the shrine from the bedroom, his parents, very pale, close behind.

The Setite looked on Ton and Isabelle. "You would allow him to make this sacrifice?"

Ton nodded.

"Isabelle?"

"I…I would."

Ankhesenaten searched the mother's face. "With a willing heart?"

Isabelle faltered. One arm crept about the boy's shoulder, and her eyes brimmed with tears. "I…"

"Mother!" Jozef shrugged out of her embrace. "I could save us."

The priest knelt before the child. "You mean this offer. I see that. So can our Lord. But you cannot go, for the same reason Carl cannot. There are places in Duat, on the way to the Blessed Realms, where the soul is tested. There is a lintel, above the Door of the West, where the traveler is asked his mother's heart's secret name. It is something you can never know in life—even she and I do not know it. When a man dies, and his mother has gone before him, the name is there for him to know. When a child dies, he must wait for his mother to come and speak to the lintel for him, or for her heart to let him pass on. There is a second door, for fathers. It is a terrible thing, for a parent to send their child ahead into Duat—far worse to do so knowingly. Hold your head up, and know that your mother loves you, and never be ashamed that she would not let you go. Be proud."

Jozef's hand slipped slowly into Isabelle's. Ton picked the boy up, and the family returned to the bedroom locked together. Ankhesenaten turned, and saw that Carl, too—older, not to be spoken to as a child—had taken the words to heart, as the Setite intended, and sat leaning into his father's burly chest.

"No more." Ljudumilu said it softly. "You do not deserve it, any of you." She tried to raise herself, coughed, and reached for Magda's hands. "Your children have more faith than you do." The vintner's wife helped the priestess sit up, and the priestess continued. "I am going."

There were gasps, and some of the women began to weep. Dehaan left his place beside his master and fell to his knees at his grandmother's feet. He took her hands in his.

"Not you," whispered the Rooster.

"Stay," pleaded Magda. "We need you. No one can replace you. I—I know so little."

Ljudumilu ignored them. She spoke only to Ankhesenaten. "There is no one who can present your petition before the Destroyer so well as I can."

He nodded.

"I am an old woman, so old that no one listens to me. They say I am wise, you say I am wise, yet my warnings go unheeded." Dehaan bent his head over her hands, and one sob escaped him.

In the old language, still to her god, the priestess spoke: "I am a greedy old hag, Lord. I want my reward a good deal sooner than you will have yours."

"I have no doubt you will be a queen in Duat."

"I want my dynasty in this world. Give me your promise."

"I said before, I will not make this decision in haste, or by your order, priestess."

Hoarse laughter answered him. "Promise."

"I will make him one of the blessed, Ljudumilu. I will do

this because Set desires it, not because you bargain with your soul."

"Promise me you will save him from this girl, too, my lord."

"She can hear you, Ljudumilu."

"She does not speak this tongue."

Ankhesenaten glanced, briefly, to Meribah. She showed no sign of comprehension, but she had had time to dissemble, if she wished. "Sister," he said, not looking at her. "Tell me, did you ever visit the House of the Traveler in Hut-nesut-of-the-Eighteenth-Nome?"

The little *Franj* said nothing.

"Sister," he asked again, now in Hebrew, "did you ever visit the temple of Khonsu at Sharuna?"

"What?" Meribah answered in confusion. "No. I run errands for Thebes. I've never gone farther south than Karnak. Why?"

"A question of ritual—nothing—we will proceed without that prayer."

Ljudumilu smiled. "Think of that, when I have left you, Great One."

"I will," promised Ankhesenaten.

"Up," ordered the priestess. Dehaan stood and offered his arm to raise her, and Magda hastened to pull the heavy blankets off the old woman's legs. Her feet touched the ground for the first time in a year, though she leaned heavily on her grandson's shoulder. They walked—he carried her, but upright, with dignity—to the shrine. Magda brought a cushion for her knees, then opened the rosewood doors.

Ankhesenaten approached the idol from the west, where his *ka* had flown. He offered his own blood to the basalt portal of their god. When he had finished, Ljudumilu knelt. She raised a hand to Dehaan, tracing the path of tears down his cheek. She pulled him down to her, kissed his forehead, and turned away.

She prayed, silently, and that was all.

With her eyes closed and her hands folded, she fell, very slowly, onto her left side, facing west.

Dehaan paled. Magda closed the doors of the shrine.

Ankhesenaten dropped his knife, knowing he would not need it. He reached for one frail, blue wrist. No life dwelt within—no pulse. The priestess was gone. Her grandson gathered her into his arms, to wait for dawn.

Ankhesenaten emerged onto Diocletian's arcade and searched the sky. No clouds softened its awful clarity—but there was wind, and the storm-priest had hopes of that. He stepped out onto the great balcony.

Lord Valerian followed, glancing upward with apprehension. The Ventrue, like the other Cainites, had been told of the deal made with Jacobi. He had listened with interest and formed plans of his own while the Setite told of the bargain; he had listened in skeptic disbelief as Andrew of Egypt, mercenary merchant-prince, explained that he would destroy the fleet by conjuring a storm. The senator's doubts ran deep, but he said nothing. Their position would be no worse if this first plan failed. He could try his own hand in war next, if need be, and in the meantime, he would watch, respectfully, the weather-magics of ancient Egypt.

Meribah trailed after the great men quietly, uncomfortable in her fine, delicate, awkward court clothes. The formal dress had been a courtesy to Jacobi—a token of respect, to gain a poor girl's admittance to court and arcade—a voluntary humiliation, because she was unwilling to watch from a lesser vantage point. She tugged her voluminous skirts out of the doorway with a short and bitter curse. She had not needed the costume, because the Lasombra had not bothered to come. The humiliation was Andreas's, and Meribah felt it for him.

Jacobi sat in his Great Hall now, meeting with the town's priests, guildmasters, burghers, and guardsmen. He planned for negotiation, for siege, and for defense. When told of the storm, he had looked on the clear heavens coldly, and returned to the civil matters without interest or hope. Ewald, the Tsarika, Galatea and Boleslaus remained with him, listening to the preparations and trying to watch the skies through the tiny windows in the bricked-up arches. Calleo, Gregory, Zoë, and the crew waited in the workshop tower, where they would have the best view of all.

Ankhesenaten stretched out his arms, and the sleeves of

his scarlet robes snapped loudly with the force of the wind. He let a handful of streamers—red silk, dark-spotted, embroidered with purest silver thread—whip away into the night one by one. The gale snatched them to itself, and clouds developed over the western sea.

A grayness drifted across the water. Slowly, it blocked out the moon; the stars disappeared behind it. The wind strengthened.

Meribah moved closer to the balustrade and looked out. At the edge of sight, the ships of the papal fleet weighed anchor and fought for sea room. The mists enveloped them as she watched. Sounds reached her from the harbor. Sailors and shoremen, sleepy in their alarm, prepared, hastily, to defend against a storm instead of ships. Now waves crashed against the hulls of the boats at dock. Lightning struck, and Meribah looked quickly toward it. She hoped the flash would show her how fared the fleet—but it struck again, and the small scout, anchored nearer than its fellows, was all that she could see.

It had been less than half an hour since Andreas offered the streamers.

The door of the emperor's apartments opened behind the travelers. Meribah turned and saw two of the prince's childer looking out, curious and round-eyed, at the change. One darted back inside almost instantly, and his running footsteps echoed from the stone corridor. The other remained, awed, her mouth agape.

Spray filled the air around the observers, but there was as yet no rain. It was all on the water, and the scout ship had disappeared. Meribah saw no horizon—it was long gone and now nothing separated sky and falling water, rain, and tumbled surf. It was impossible to discern how close the cataract had come.

Prince Ignatius Jacobi emerged from his palace. No one turned to greet him. All eyes feasted on the storm.

The violence drew steadily closer to the city. It moved less quickly than the wind blew, and that was strange. The prince and the other Cainites retreated to the safety of the covered arches, but Meribah fought forward. Lashing gusts drove tiny stinging droplets into her skin. Her fine dress sagged and tore. Her wimple blew off, stolen by the wind, but she gained the balcony, and her hand crept into the Egyptian's.

Minutes passed. The tempest became a wall before them; it swallowed up everything outside the harbor jetties.

Something bumped hollowly against the seawall far below the Setites. Meribah craned over the balustrade to find the cause. It was a keel—only the keel—torn from a roundship. Other debris drifted in to join it. Slowly, the noise and angry air subsided. The gray curtain fell away; there was moonlight behind it, a clear sky, and the bodies of the drowned.

Meribah covered her eyes.

Jacobi settled himself placidly upon his marble throne. "What bargain do you speak of, Egyptian?" He blinked his gentle eyes innocently. "I do not remember making any such agreement with you."

Andreas and Valerian exchanged dark glances.

"On the loggia," Andreas reminded the monarch, "the night before last, when the crusader ships first hove into sight."

Benign blankness answered this.

Andreas, fighting down his rage, said nothing, and the pause grew long. He could hear his passengers restless behind him, shocked by this fresh treachery. The few crewmen in the delegation—Jacquy, Goreb, and Dehaan—stood stock-still; he could not hear their feet, only the hard, heavy breaths of living anger.

"I remember, Father," a woman offered timidly. It was one of the Lasombra childer, the woman who had remained on the arcade to watch the miracle. "You did give your word to him, that he and his should leave freely if he dispatched your enemies."

Jacobi turned his head to look upon the rebel—his eyes half-closed, his mouth half-open, no human emotion on his face. The childe quailed, and her siblings moved away from her.

"You did nothing, Egyptian. You thought to reap the credit for the luck of nature? For the judgment of Christ on the sinful pilgrims of Venice?" Jacobi shook his head. "You did nothing," he repeated. "Did you truly believe that I would abrogate my rights because of a freak of the weather?"

A choking protest broke out behind Andreas. He whirled round in alarm, and found himself staring at an altered Gregory. The fury of the tinker had made him incoherent, almost unrecognizable. Zoë, who'd been clinging to him, startled away to stand with Meribah. This was the face which had frightened her in Constantinople—the wondrous wrath of the Wonder-Maker.

Jacobi, merely amused, dismissed the embassy. The next night, the guards on the tower rooms were doubled.

Gregory was no longer permitted to roam.

Zoë leaned over her workbench, pretending to bend wire around a form, watching her sire at his desk. Meribah lay on her back in a window-ledge, her legs straight up against the embrasure, playing with green and blue gemstones. She was talking nonsense in the *langue d'oil*—funny stories for the Ravnos to practice on, because they would need the language as soon as they reached Paris. Which would be in just a year or two, of course—damn Jacobi. And had they heard the one about how the fox got into the wine barrel?

"Meribah. Be quiet."

Zoë stopped fiddling with her wire. Meribah held her colored stones and her tongue. Gregory sat static, stagnant, still— the girls were motionless. His words held no hope, but the tone had been sharp, even annoyed. This was more animation than the Wonder-Maker had shown in the weeks since the great storm.

Slowly, one twisted arm reached out for a parchment, its fellow for a quill. They wrote—quickly—dashed off two notes, and held them out to Meribah with the ink yet wet.

"Take this one to your cousin, Meribah. Then take this one to the prince, with my compliments. This has gone on long enough." He turned to Zoë. "Pack your things."

Fear and questions flew from Zoë's eyes to the serpent's, but Meribah had a mission, and no answers, and neither girl dared ask the Wonder-Maker his mind.

When Andreas emerged from the workshop, he found Meribah waiting for him, curious and concerned.

"Sister-mine," he said in Syrian, "do you understand this?"

"I understand it," answered the *Franj* in Greek, "but I never learned to speak it."

"Can you change your skin?"

"Say that again?" Meribah listened intently. "Oh...no...the Suti never taught me, and no one has bothered since."

Her cousin nodded. "Why?"

"Forget that I asked." Footsteps echoed down the hall. It was Dehaan; Andreas resumed his thought. "Do me this favor. Find a set of laborer's clothes for me—my height and build, and not new—a dozen torches, and some ration animals. Small ones."

Dehaan passed by her without a glance, but her eyes followed him down the corridor. "Rabbits?" she said, still staring at the mortal's back.

"They'll do. Be secret, little thief."

"My am yes," she ventured.

A smile crossed Andreas's face, then faded. "Meribah—do you speak no Egyptian?"

Wrinkling her face, she shrugged. "I can say the prayers. I know the rituals by heart. You remember," she added defensively. "You were there when they tested me."

"The chosen of Set should understand the old language."

Meribah looked at her feet. "Al-Suti was killed before he could teach me."

"It should have been the first thing you learned, before ever you were dedicated to Set."

"Oh." A pause. "You could teach me."

"Yes," admitted Ankhesenaten. "I could. When we reach Paris, and my goal is won or lost—there will be time for other things." He heard the Rooster's steady steps falter, then move on. "Stay with the caravan," he invited the little *Franj*, "and come to Flanders, and we will speak of this again."

They made their goodbyes in the workshop. The prince would not permit Gregory to see them off from the gate. The Wonder-Maker acquiesced, but forbade Jacobi to come anywhere near them that night. He demanded privacy for his parting. He lit the dozen torches and drove the shadows out of his tower, yet he was forced to suffer a brace of guardsmen and one of the Lasombra childer looking on from the next room.

Zoë's belongings and most of his own were gone. Everything, in fact, except what Jacobi had given him was on the wagons already—packed by Meribah, unpacked, in a fury, by his ward, packed by the Setite again, and carried away.

Gregory's farewells were never made. His apprentice, sulky, refused to accept them.

"I won't go," persisted Zoë. "I'm not leaving you."

"It's for the best."

"It is not! He doesn't deserve you!"

"He deserves two of us still less, my dear."

"I won't go. I can't believe you want me to and I won't stay with him," she shouted, pointing at Andreas. "How can you leave him? You swore we would go together!" Gregory sighed; the argument grew stale, and the caravan was waiting. "You must trust me, child. Obey, this one time. Promise me—" the tinker stopped short— "No. Don't promise. We...we have not done well with those, you and I. Listen to me." He took her hands in his. "There are things, dear heart, which I know, and you do not. There are things which I can do, and you cannot... and things which I shall endure, that you must not. Obey me. Go with Meribah, and do exactly what she says, and all will be well, in the end." He embraced his childe once more, then brought her to the door. The red-haired girl reached for her friend. "Take care of her for me."

"I will," promised the little *Franj*.

Andreas stepped aside. "We'll all look after her, Lakeritos. Be well."

The Ravnos only nodded, and the two Setites led Zoë stumbling down the stairs. Men from the caravan hoisted the few remaining bundles in the antechamber and shoved past the soldiers roughly. With an apologetic, shallow expression, the Lasombra bowed and followed them.

"Wait," Gregory called to the last crewman on the steps. The mortal turned, and the Lasombra resumed her post. "There is one other box, a small one, for my girl. Will you take it?"

"Of course, sir."

"Come in. No—not you, my lady—I will not have you prying into my last gift—my legacy—to my girl. Get out of my sight," he said, and slammed the door on the Lasombra. Little bells hung on the inside jangled, rang, and chimed. They would go on for several minutes.

"Quick," Gregory ordered, digging mirror and razor from a drawer. "Give me the clothes."

The "mortal" stripped to his skin; the tinker shaved off his own beard and mustache, then cut his hair to match his accomplice. Finishing first, he rose to shed his own outer robe. As the other struggled out of chemise and breeches, Gregory took them up and donned them.

"Who are you?" he asked, lacing his boots.

"An old friend," replied the crewman. His skin melted into the face of Boleslaus.

Gregory laughed. "I always thought you were a poor musician—for a Toreador—"

Boleslaus grinned and became Vaclav. "Thanks. Shall I be you, now?" A blue claw hooked the robe where it lay between them.

"Leave it. You go out the window," explained the Ravnos, straightening his belt. He stepped back, studied the desk for a moment, and pulled out the chair. "Or the door, if you can pass unseen," he added, absently.

Vaclav kilted a strip of linen around his waist. "What will you do?"

"Hush," mouthed the Wonder-Maker, and suddenly there were two of him to say it.

The shaved and disguised one looked his twin over, critically, circling him to see from every angle.

Vaclav, for his part, stared in awe. "The stories of Ravnos illusions," he muttered, "I had assumed...you are a magician...."

The newcomer, nude, looked down on himself with an expression identical to his creator's. He spoke, frowned, and pointed to his mouth.

"I said, give me a voice. Thank you," the *doppelganger* said in Gregory's voice. "Might I ask you to reconsider these hips? I'm afraid the articulation is all wrong—surely, you can't move the left one so far as this? Ah. Much better. And perhaps the legs? Shouldn't the right one twist back a little more? I'll have to have your limp just right." The two Gregories nodded in unison, satisfied at the same moment. Vaclav picked up the robe and held it for the new man to slip into.

"It bears weight," he whispered. "It thinks."

Gregory ignored him; his every thought poured into the apparition. "Remember, be seen as little as possible. Forbid it entirely, for as long as you can. There are rabbits in the bedroom. Make them your excuse for not hunting. I've left some small things for you to feign work on—"

"I know, I know. I'm a dream, not an idiot. Pick up your box and get going, before that creature knocks on the door."

Under the north walls, the caravan was already underway. The baggage carts and trade goods snaked up the road. Pilgrims and refugees—some original fugitives from Byzantium who had stayed with their patrons during the delay, others escaped from the heretics, and more townsfolk looking for a life outside the shadow—plodded steadily along beside them. The city watchmen held their place by the gates. No Lasombra were there to wish them well. The tax had been paid, and nothing else interested Jacobi.

The ox-teams pulled the Cainites into the convoy. One by one, the Ventrue's, Galatea's and Boleslaus's wagons rolled away, then Calleo's strongbox and the Setite girl's tiny, empty haven. The Ravnos workshop-wagon started with a jerk, and Meribah thanked any god who might be listening. She sat on the workshop floor with her arms crossed and her back to the door. She was meant to be consoling Zoë; the resulting quarrel had devolved into a battle for the exit and this staring contest. Meribah had it won from the start—she cheated. The door was barred from the outside, by her request. She hadn't told Zoë, and wasn't looking forward to her friend's finding out.

Hours went—very slowly—by. The light through the shutters gleamed indigo now, not black. Just a little longer, thought the Setite. Just over the next hill, maybe. Then my own bed, and dawn, and sleep. She wondered how well Zoë would sleep, and whether she would need to be locked in again. *I hope this plan of Gregory's—whatever it is—starts soon. How many more nights are we going to have to do this? Maybe we can tell her about it tonight....*

A knock jarred her shoulder blades.

Meribah put her mouth to the crack under the door and yelled through it. "Who?"

"Boleslaus."

"All right." She shot back the iron bolt loudly, masking the sound of the lifting bar.

The minstrel, naked to the waist, loped alongside the rolling house. Meribah offered him her hand and hauled him up.

"He's not here yet?" Boleslaus hunted about in surprise.

"What?" Both girls said it.

"Damn. Wait a moment."

The Setite lay full length on the boards, craning her head to look out. Boleslaus stood over her, clinging to the lintel. Zoë clambered in at waist-height, her left foot and right knee digging into the *Franj* girl's kidneys. Meribah had her revenge—her magic eyes saw it first: a horse bearing two riders. The caravan crawled, but the over-burdened mount wasn't much faster. She pointed to them, was rewarded by a little scream from Zoë, and wriggled out from the bottom of the pile half-deaf.

Meribah plopped down on the master's workbench. She watched Boleslaus watch Zoë watching the riders. This occupation palled quickly, her attention wandered, and she tried the locked cabinet, just in case. The gypsy hurtled out joyfully, Boleslaus abandoned the door for a stool, and the Setite, balked by the bolts, looked innocent.

"He's had a rough time," the minstrel told her. "That limp—his legs—it pains him to walk normally. He couldn't drop the act until the guards left us, and that was only half an hour ago."

"Is that Andreas, bringing him?"

"Yes."

Meribah nodded. After a moment's pause, she slipped off her perch and out. The minstrel tracked her with his eyes, followed on foot, and found her walking in the opposite direction from Gregory and his childe.

"They won't need us," she explained, as he fell into step

beside her. "Not tonight. I'll see him in the evening." Boleslaus put an arm around her, and they set off to spread the news to the others.

Chapter Sixteen

On the Dalmatian Coastal Road, toward Zara
March, 1207

The meadow was perfect: round, and greener than emeralds. It crowned a hilltop ringed by tall, stately trees. Jacquy's road passed through it, transecting the circle well west of its center. He brought the caravan to a halt here, making camp early. Tonight would be the first full moon outside Ignatius Jacobi's domain, and Andreas had ordained a celebration. The caravan women spread a feast for mortals beneath the sheltering north pines. Level ground made good dancing in the east, and Boleslaus's band chose a hillock between food and flat—the children kept their ale-mugs full and their trenchers high. On the south side, closest to Spalato, the living were less inclined to linger, and the waking dead gathered there soon after dark to hear the tale of Gregory's escape.

Boleslaus made little of the adventure. Such hints as he had given Meribah the first night—a miracle, a walking dream— faded into simple shadow play. Gregory had made a figure to walk around the workshop and to sleep in his bed of nights, a noise of hammers, and a voice to tell the Lasombra to leave him be. The Wonder-Maker had come to the minstrel early, pleading for silence, and Boleslaus had promised readily. Andreas knew, and Zoë. Calleo and Hadeon must not hear the truth. Meribah would have to believe that he was impressed by a simple illusion.

She laughed as the story ended. "I'd love to see Jacobi's face when he realizes he's been...no, on second thought, I wouldn't."

Gregory nodded. "He will not examine the chimeras closely for some time. We have had a week; we might have another. A voice, a noise, and a shadow…they will not last forever." This was true of the walking dream, as well. It might buy a month, a year, a decade—or a single night. "We must hurry."

"We will," promised Andreas. "Jacquy will not stop again in daylight until we reach Zara. The Venetians hold what is left of that port and Jacobi fears the Venetians. We will be safe there."

He had the last word. The Cainites' nights in Spalato had been long and anxious, confining and—for all but Hadeon—crowded. Now each seemed more grateful than the next to leave the others. Gregory and Zoë made their farewells with haste and thanks. Calleo stalked toward his wagon with grim pleasure. Boleslaus grinned at the warlock's speed, then bettered it, joining the band. Hadeon, watching the minstrel, found a girl looking hopefully at him. The Gangrel had spent months in the wilds alone, waiting for the caravan; he jerked his head at the young woman, and they plunged into the dance without speaking.

Andreas, with his cousin tagging along behind him, wound his way through the crowd to his crew's own plot. The children, unrestrained, ambushed him. He let them cling while he found his seat, and he settled down with two tots in his arms, a half-grown boy on each leg, and Chiara wrapped around his neck from behind. Mothers and older siblings rescued the demigod so assaulted, and his lieutenants took their places to hear his will.

"Go, Jacquy," said the Setite lord. "All of you—go and have a good time." His hands waved away the Rooster, Leopold, Leiven. "You have earned a night of your own. We will talk of business tomorrow." More slowly than the Cainites, the crew seized their new liberty, and only Willem and a few children remained. Andreas's gaze swept the gathering, but his voice was pitched for the scribe alone.

"Tell me, Will. How much did it cost us to maintain our followers in Spalato?"

The scribe took up a stick and began to scratch figures in the earth before them. "Including room and board—alms—cloth for new tents—"

Andreas raised a hand to stop the list—he had caught sight

of the red-headed thief standing where the fringes of the family had been. "Go on," he urged his cousin. "Dance. Enjoy yourself. I must finish with Willem before his wife comes to fetch him."

Smiling at the thought of Annemie raising a hand against either priest or husband, Meribah faded obediently away. She turned north to follow the crew. Dehaan stood behind the food, breaking bread into small portions and laughing with Danica. He heaved a kettle off its jack, poured soup into lighter vessels and filled cups for children. Eventually, as he reached for an empty trug, he looked beyond the line of feasting pilgrims to Meribah.

When their eyes met, she found no sign in his—the lively, expressive face moved not at all. Danica chattered across the Rooster's silence without noticing it. Her mother, more observant, laid a hand on Dehaan's arm and filled a wine bowl for him. He drank it off in one go, and did not look Meribah's way again.

The little *Franj* wandered away, without destination. She followed the ring of trees around the circle with as little thought and memory as possible. Boleslaus smiled as she padded by, but kept playing. Hadeon whirled past, intent on the girl who had found him. Andreas sat in council. Calleo's windows were shut. Chiara and Jozef led a pack of children in games. They hid in the blue-white moon-dark, but she could see through Stygian blackness and the game thus held no fun for her. Girls flirted with their beaus beneath the pines, but she could marry no one. Young mothers cradled babes in their arms and showed them proudly, but she would have none. Old women sat and talked, content with warm stew, cool beer, soft grass, and wise company, but Meribah would never grow old.

Her steps brought her to the caravan's corral. Here the oxen stood dozing after a long day's labor. Eureka slept among them, weary himself—Jacquy had pressed him into service, hauling with the teams up the harsh hills of Dalmatia. The stallion whinnied in his sleep, and Meribah smiled. He knew her, even now. He woke, and nuzzled her wrist. She threw her arms around his neck and buried her head in his mane. Eureka arched his neck to reach her—blew softly into her hair—found her wrist again, and bit it.

"I see," said the serpent, laughing suddenly. "You're hungry...and that's all." *Serves you right, Merrie-girl.* She slit her wrist, fed the beast, and walked briskly up the road to complete her circuit. *Now go back and get the kids to change their game—or sit with Boleslaus until story time, take all the good parts, and steal his thunder...he's holding out on you—*

Gregory and Zoë sat beneath a low-branched fir, the tree closest to the wagons and to the young Setite's path. Luxuriously, the sire leaned against its bole; the childe lay with her head on his shoulder and her arms around his chest. With a small nod of acknowledgment, the intruder changed her course to give them privacy—but the Wonder-Maker, seeing her veer off, beckoned.

"I don't want to impose," began Meribah.

"Not at all. We were looking for you earlier. Please, sit down." Gregory radiated kindness and welcome; Zoë beamed up from the crook of his arm, including her friend in their special circle. Meribah cast off her cloak and sprawled across it, facing the pair.

"I want to thank you," Gregory informed her, "for everything you did to help me in Spalato. Andreas tells me that you were all that kept my girl from charging back into the city to my rescue." All three smiled at this, and he went on. "I want to thank you for that, and for keeping our spirits up. I know it was no easy task."

Meribah shrugged. "It was nothing, a pleasure."

"Most of all, Meribah, I want to thank you for all that you have done for Zoë—"

The little *Franj* felt the elder Ravnos's dark eyes settle upon her. Instinctively, she looked away—looked, as it happened, at the gypsy girl. The too-smooth innocence of her friend's countenance warned her. Afraid to accept the compliment, she let it hang in the air between them.

"—for all your help," Gregory resumed. "For... tutoring... my girl."

Zoë's olive face shone as guiltless as the day. Meribah felt her still heart jump. *How much does he know? It can't be only the one time he saw us. What has she told him?*

"Please, child, don't try to hide your good works. I have seen you teaching her. I have heard you instructing her. I am not angry," he stressed, "I am grateful.

"I had never planned to have a childe, and at first, I was not prepared to train her. There were lessons—physical things— for which it was good that the teacher be swift, agile, strong-limbed—qualities I do not possess. It was necessary for Zoë to learn them. I tried to teach them to her from inside the wagon. She could not learn them there; she learned them from you, and I am glad of it."

His voice fell sincerely on the Setite's ears. She met his gaze and found it forgiving.

"But, now that you have given Zoë the basic skills, she needs to survive the external, material wants and threats, I feel I must insist that you leave her education to me. She has higher things to learn, powers to develop, and curses to master." Behind the black beard, the Wonder-Maker smiled. "I must be the one to guide her down her new path, Meribah, but I invite you to join us as we walk it. Come to our wagon whenever you like. Meditate with us. And—" Gregory's tone lightened "—if you wish to teach anything else to Zoë, you may do it in the open, where I can aid you." The last words, however airily delivered, fell flat. His last invitation had delivered an order: Get out. This one bore an ultimatum: She could come or not, exactly as she wished, but there must be no more secret lessons.

Meribah noticed the invasion soon enough—she had a message from the north guard-post to deliver to Andreas. He was play-ing chess with Gregory, and from their vantage point she could see that her windows were open. She knew she had left them closed. Her cousin and the Wonder-Maker noticed her con-sternation. Could they help? Did she expect an enemy within? Meribah declined the offers—perhaps she had forgotten the shutters, this one night—but she entered her wagon very slowly, staff in hand, claws extended, and prepared to holler for armed assistance.

"Good," said Zoë. "You've come."

The Setite shut the door behind her. "What are you doing here?"

The Ravnos smirked. "I've come for my lesson."

"Meribah?" A man's shout, Gregory's.

"Meribah?" Andreas, this time.

She thrust her head through the front window. "It's all right. One of the kids must have done it. They left a—a frog in my bed. Just a prank. Thank you."

"A frog?" complained Zoë.

Meribah set down her pike and wiped her brow. "A frog. Why not? Chiara and Jozef get together, anything can happen. If those kids marry, the result will— When I saw the windows open, Zoë, I thought... Well, it might have been anyone."

"I'm sorry."

"It's all right." Meribah reached for the coverlet and folded it. "What lesson?" she asked, looking down at her friend.

"The Third Pillar," said Zoë. "Teach me." Her dark hair fell into her face, and the brown eyes twinkled conspiratorially through the veil. "I didn't tell him anything, Meribah. He saw us once, and he guessed a little more—things I'd learned about hunting that he hadn't taught me—but I never said a word. I was so afraid you were going to tell him, the night of the feast. He thought if he acted like he knew, then you would confess to it all." The gypsy laughed, enjoying her secrets.

Meribah regarded the rebel thoughtfully. "I've been warned off, you know. He has plans for you. Good plans, I think... Gregory—"

"Doesn't know everything," Zoë finished for her. The tone held no doubts. Sardonic, certain eyes gazed levelly into Meribah's. "Tell me," she demanded.

Meribah sat heavily on the edge of the bed. "The Third Pillar," she revealed, "is faith."

"Faith," repeated Zoë.

"Yes. Faith. A belief in something. The thing that can stir you from sleep...besides hunger."

"But what faith?"

Meribah threw up her hands. "Anything. Christ. Mohammed. Yahweh. A goddess. A dream. Precisely what doesn't matter." She paused there, and the pause became a silence.

"That's all?"

"That's a lot."

"Yes…but…you had so much more to say about instinct and courage."

"They're easy."

Zoë stared at Meribah, and Meribah stared back.

Chapter Seventeen

Zara, Dalmatia
April, 1207

No formalities barred entry to the walls of Zara, because Zara had no walls.

The warrior pilgrims and their Venetian allies had sacked it on their way to Constantinople. In the four years since, the survivors and the conquering colonists had built a raw-wood, mushroom town upon its bones. Fresh mortar and fresh mortals stacked the old Roman stones into new shapes, but the church of St. Donatus, intact in Zara's center, bore three smoke-scars like the cavities of a skull, and the streets around her teemed with heretics.

No Cainite prince dwelt within the ruins. A Malkavian named Gari had called himself prince, but he had fallen to a witch-hunter soon after crusaders arrived on his doorstep. Now, a Nosferatu loyal to Venice, one Octavia, watched over the city for her liege-lords. Powerless to forbid the heretics the city, she had acquiesced, and to the caravan she extended a warm and eager welcome. She offered her own ramshackle villa to house her guests. When this proved inadequate—two rooms and a cellar, one acre of land—she interceded with the monastery. Would the reverend abbot give the newcomers leave to camp within the brothers' grounds? The abbot hesitated. Appealed to by the Egyptian—would the reverend abbot grant this, so Andreas's people might have distance, fields, and hedges between themselves and the heretic swarm?—the abbot relented.

The crew roused the sleepers, and the messages went

out. *We have escaped Spalato; we have fought free; we need no aid.*
Andreas, peering at Caine-cultists through cracks in Octavia's
fortified villa, wondered if this were true.

Two camp-followers were found dead in the alleys near St.
Donatus, and Andreas gave orders to the crew to stay inside
the monastery grounds. Hadeon patrolled the countryside and
Boleslaus the city, seeking signs of death, danger, riot, or if they
were lucky, migration.

Answers came swift from Venice and the Sicilies—brought
by hand, and the hands were noble. Valerian, a princeling of
Lasombra, and a Cappadocian knight retired to confer together.
They took three nights. Andreas kept the wagons packed.

The Sicilian envoys made the adieus and took ship. Fourteen
of the Byzantine refugees disappeared into the heretic encampment. Riki, fetching water from the abbey well, went missing.
He limped home at dawn with nail wounds on hands and feet.
The crew built fires, doubled the guard, and went to their beds
armed and armored. The Cappadocian sailed for home. Jacquy
readied wine barrels to receive Cainite cargo, and Andreas
found Takouhi waiting on his doorstep, holding a mandolin.

She sat under the broad blue awning with a sack at her feet,
her staff by her right hand. She had shed her pilgrim's robes and
wore the clothes in which she had walked out of Adrianople. Her
face had descended from the celestial heights of Thessalonica.
It was careworn, tired, and quite simply sad. Dehaan, in attendance on the visitor, faded away as his master approached. The
Malkavian rose, starlight full in her eyes, and blinked past the
glare.

"My lady," bowed the Egyptian. "How may I be of servi—"
He recognized the mandolin—Boleslaus's instrument. "Be of
service," he finished, in pale tones.

"Andreas, love—I fear I have—" Takouhi broke off, lowered herself to sit on the step once more, and began again, her
voice quite different. "I have slain the idolater Vaclav, Andreas.
I hunted him from Constantinople to Hadrian's city, and I lost
track of him there, waiting for you to return from Venice. I found
him, unlooked-for, tonight in the crypts beneath the forum. I
fell on him, and destroyed him, and dragged his remains into

the light. He carried this, which your passenger, the minstrel, played the night I left you." She swallowed, an uncharacteristic act. "Have I killed Boleslaus, as well?"

Andreas nodded without expression.

"I am sorry. I liked him, as a Toreador, and I would not wittingly cause you harm or offense." She set the mandolin gently down. "I could have walked on, love. Perhaps I should have done. But I didn't like to think of you trying to find him among the pilgrims—losing men to the mob—so I came to apologize, and to tell you, I am in your debt, now."

The Setite nodded again. His hands came together, twisting his signet ring. "Not I alone, my lady. All those in this caravan are sworn to protect each other."

Takouhi's hands closed on her walking stick. "Take me to them, love."

"No. This judgment is my own to make. They have not sworn vengeance. That duty falls to me." In the hush behind his words, he heard a small noise—scraping wood—the sound of Takouhi's claws sliding slowly from their sheaths, forcing her fingers up off the carven staff. His own emerged in readiness.

"It was a mistake. I believe that," said Andreas. "That being so, I am not sure that the retribution must be a killing matter. I do not know what it is, and therefore I defer it. It is more important to me to see my remaining charges to their destinations. Let the penalty wait until then...but give me something now."

"I can teach you other tricks of the sight," she offered. "There are ways to see that do not involve eyes or ears, you know."

"I want nothing for myself." Andreas stroked his braided beard, thinking. "You will stay with these pilgrims? You can influence them?"

"I can stay with them a little longer, if you want."

"We winter in Aquileia. Lead your people anywhere else."

"I will." She gained her feet, leaning heavily on door and staff. "Andreas—I am sorry. Had I known—"

It was true that the serene, placid glow of the pilgrim no longer spread across her face; it was tightly compressed, concentrated in the cores of otherwise kindly eyes. Andreas had seen that light before, and that look, in the priest who had led

Justinian's soldiers to his home. *Had she known, she would have followed Boleslaus until he left my protection, and killed him then.*

Takouhi straightened. The moon shone into her face, and now Andreas was equally certain that the vision had been his imagination. In better light, with clearer sight, the zealot's fire—which never leaves one it burns—was gone, and he felt better about letting her go.

"By now, what I have to say will already have reached your ears. Boleslaus is dead." Andreas stood in the center of the ring of Cainites and watched their faces. He had surprised no one. "I spoke tonight with Takouhi, whom I believe is known to you all. She travels with the heretics, and she discovered the crime." That much was true, and he must tell no outright lies to his passengers. Galatea's acute senses might enable her to smell a falsehood. Valerian could probably see them. "She brought me the news, and these."

He held up Boleslaus's clothes—blood-stained, scorched, and full of fine ash.

Valerian reached for and was given them. Amid stark silence, the Ventrue fingered the tears and gashes, the marks of claws or steel. The motley and the mandolin passed to Gregory, then on around the circle, with the reverence due saint's relics.

Death among the deathless, thought Andreas. *Have they seen it before? You hear of it; you know it happens—how often do you hold it in your hands?* The rags arrived to Meribah, who took them with quiet wonder. Leopold, the drover, received them from her and took them away. He offered to relieve her of the mandolin, but the red head shook no.

Her arms cradled the instrument. Andreas was not long looking at her—he didn't wish to see her face—any of their faces.

"In Adrianople," he resumed, "you agreed to act in aid of all. To defend each other. It is too late for that, now." His gaze flickered over the left arc of the circle, and caught sight of Zoë. Her head lay pillowed on Gregory's shoulder, but her eyes were on Andreas, himself. "In any other fief…" Ewald held the Tsarika's hand. Their expressions were serious and concerned, but detached. *They hardly knew him,* thought the Setite. *While*

Boleslaus fought wolves, they slept. "In any other fief, I would present the evidence of the murder to the local lord and demand justice. Seize it, if the lord were lawless." *We could not have escaped Spalato without him.* "There is no lord in Zara."

The Nosferatu Octavia stirred slightly—the movement served to remind her guests that Venice claimed Zara, however empty it seemed. Andreas took no notice. Among vampires, a fief could not be ruled across a sea.

"We are nine. We could stop here. Call a blood hunt against the killer. Avenge Boleslaus." He stared up at the stars. "But we would need a name, and proof. It would keep us here, perhaps for months. We have been two years on this road already. And whoever has done this, I feel they travel with the pilgrims. They will hide behind them, use them as a living shield."

"Why," asked Octavia, "do you assume a Cainite has done this? Kine have killed Cainites on this ground ere now. Mortal hands slew the court of Zara and toppled Byzantium."

"Nevertheless, the guilty sleep beside the innocent. I have no heart to slaughter the one to reach the other; I have decided what I and my people will do. We will press on to France. I leave the killer to time and God's justice."

"Boleslaus deserves better from you, Andreas." Galatea spoke bitterly.

Hadeon scowled his agreement. "If one of the nobles—if Valerian—were dead, you would not leave his blood unanswered. But a lowly Toreador dies, and you do nothing."

Gregory, softly, corrected him. "He was not a Toreador. He was a Nosferatu. I saw his face once, in Spalato." Now surprise rippled through them. Angry eyes flew to their host.

"Did you know this, Egyptian?" Calleo demanded.

"I knew." Andreas met the warlock's gaze without evasion. "He asked me to keep his secret. He feared for his life."

"Rightly so," mused Valerian.

"Boleslaus...or rather Vaclav—" one or two of Andreas's listeners looked up, hearing the name, and Galatea closed her eyes— "thought he would be safer traveling incognito." *But why drop* his *masquerade here,* the Setite asked himself, *where he must have known Takouhi had come?* "And because of that, I know, at least, that none of you betrayed him." *Yet I don't know that. Anyone might have seen through the disguise. He knew many secrets; anyone might have sought his silence, and told the Malkavian who he was.*

"You may feel that I am shirking my duty toward our late companion, and perhaps I am, but I must look to the safety of the rest. If anyone wishes to leave the caravan, I will understand. I can try to arrange a ship for you, if you are willing to wait for the summer trading fleets to sail." Valerian raised his hand, waving away the suggestion. "The ocean holds its own perils. I trust your abilities."

"I'm staying with you," said Meribah loyally.

Calleo snorted. "I leave at Aquileia, in any case." Hadeon, his lip curling, stood to go. "I'll be waiting on the east road, when you're ready."

Gregory held Zoë close. "I have faith in you, Andreas." Galatea said nothing. She looked to Fairfax and his princess, awaiting the Norman's answer. Ewald, uncertain, glanced first to the Tsarika, then to his host. "We accept your judgment, Egyptian. We will not stay in Zara another night."

Chapter Eighteen

The caravan traveled the north road grimly. Roman legions had built it through the easiest, flattest, broadest land available, but the mountains here were rooted in the sea. At sunset, the peaks cast shadows over the little cart track that the highway had become. The hills broke the backs of the beasts in harness; the rocks invaded their feet and hampered the pour souls who were on foot. Clearings were rare and needed for the animals' pasture. The caravan often camped in single file on the road wherever the daylight left them.

Cainite tempers sharpened with every mile. Gregory chided his apprentice gently, holding forth lessons in illusion as a bribe to curb her willfulness. Zoë studied the new magics eagerly, but she never ceased nagging her other teacher for the secrets of the Third Pillar, which she was convinced her friend was holding back. Meribah began to hide from Ravnos, from Andreas, and from the crew. The guards saw her sometimes, roaming the hills beside Hadeon.

The crew grew fractious. They had traveled this part of the coast before; they expected wolves from the crags and heretics from behind. Jacquy and Leopold drove men and beasts without mercy. Magda's patience shortened. Her duty as priestess was a heavy, chafing burden, and her god had no time to instruct her. She could not perform the hidden rites; she could not pray in the old language. Dehaan was told to teach her what he knew, but he had become distracted and withdrawn. The

Rooster made the battle up the hills his excuse to leave her. He joined the ox teams and was welcomed. Eureka was biddable only in his hands.

Meribah woke to angry voices and bellowing oxen. The sun had barely set. Opening a window revealed a turquoise-lavender sky, a light strong enough to burn her skin, and a section of countryside that was hauntingly familiar. *We haven't moved all day,* she thought, snatching up her heavy cloak. The thick felt of Edessa could protect her from the dying sun, so she was the first of the immortals to reach the chaos on the hilltop.

Through the bright, rain-fresh air, she saw the men—every man of the crew save the guards and Willem—clustered around a single wagon. When she drew closer, she recognized it as Calleo's iron-banded strongbox. It had slipped out of the ancient ruts. *No,* realized Meribah, *it has forced the stones themselves off the road.* Its wheels were mired hub-deep in the mudslide it had caused.

Willem and his master walked past her then. Fuming, Jacquy and Leopold hastened to Andreas.

"At dawn," said the drover, "first thing. Ten feet forward, and off she goes."

"It's too heavy," Jacquy clarified. "We've harnessed every damned animal in the line to this one wagon, and we can't shift it. All that iron—"

"Not just the iron," spat Leopold.

The caravan master agreed. "Whatever he has inside must be at least as heavy as the wagon itself. We'll have to unload it, take the door and shutters off, maybe take apart the roof. We'd have done it already, but we didn't know how he sleeps, and Dehaan thinks diose marks—" Jacquy pointed to whitish lines stamped into wood and metal—"are some sort of ward."

Andreas studied the canted strongbox. "I see. I will ask Master Abetorius to lighten his load," he proposed at last, trudging through the mud to the warlock's door. The top half of it opened as he approached, and the Tremere peered querulously out.

"Egyptian," he said curtly.

"My lord," Andreas replied. "I trust you slept well."

"I did not. I woke on the floor. I see why, now. What are you going to do about this?"

"We will have to unload your wagon, my lord."

"That cannot be done," declared the wizard. "No one may cross the threshold but myself. Your men will have to pull it out."

"They have tried, my lord. All day long, they tell me. Your wagon is too heavy for the animals to move. It must be emptied. It may have to be disassembled. You can see, yourself, how deep the wheels have sunk."

Calleo leaned over the half-door and looked. Furrows spread across his forehead, and his jaw thrust obstinately forward. "Impossible."

"As you wish." Andreas turned to the waiting crew. "Unhitch the oxen. We shall leave Master Abetorius where he is, and move on."

"No!"

One brow arched politely, the Egyptian gave his attention to his passenger. "Perhaps you could bring things to the door yourself, my lord, and let the men take them from there."

"Very well," said the Tremere.

The crew brought baskets and a small cart that had been emptied on the downward face of the hill to the wizard's wagon to carry the goods across the summit.

First came robes, then a bundle of linen. An armful of parchment, then another, and three great piles of books took their place in the driest, cleanest corner of the cart. One square, gold-heavy casket chinked in beside them. Then came a basketful of small stone jars—two baskets—three. Meribah smelled blood and slipped through the crowd to investigate.

The jar she picked up was a cube the size of her fist, as like the next as peas in a pod. A tight-ground stopper of the same stone closed it. A ring of soft wax had once sealed it, and a rich redness stained it now.

Another basket landed on the boards at her feet. Lieven emptied it out and went back for more. Seven loads later, the cart was full. Carl fetched another, but he had trouble maneuvering through the multitude—Gregory, Zoë, and Hadeon had all come to see the fun—and the crew had been joined by scores of refugees and pilgrims. Glaring, Jacquy ordered the onlookers back. His face was purple, and some unfortunate children chose to tell him so, to the laughter of the crowd. Meribah had to hide a smile herself, thinking of the poor man hauling the load up every hill until this one. The flow of baskets showed no sign of ever stopping, though the jars in them now had unbroken seals. A fourth cart rolled into place, to the cheers of the pilgrims.

It broke upon her suddenly. Andreas's and Hadeon's expressions were dark enough—they had understood it far earlier—and Meribah felt a fool. *He hunts with the rest of us, but those... rations, there are hundreds—maybe a thousand—and enough empties to feed a Cainite all the way from Adrianople.*

There's someone else inside that wagon.

When the fifth cart was only half filled, the stream of baskets slowed. Lieven set the last load, still in its basket, on top of four neatly stacked layers of jars, and Carl drove them away.

Leopold and Jacquy urged the ox-teams forward. Other men stood by with boards and rocks to wedge under the wheels of Calleo's wagon. Slowly, the mud gave way, and the iron rims rolled up the makeshift ramps inch by inch. Men among the spectators rushed up to lend their shoulders. Children skipped beside the laborers, and someone began to sing one of Boleslaus's favorite tunes. The warlock watched it all, nervously, from his half-open door. The drovers made their effort a single, sustained pull, and neither man nor beast ceased to strain against the ropes until the climb was finished. Jacquy called a halt on the hill's crest, and the refugees cheered again. Leopold and his men started unhitching oxen, and the basket line took their places. In half an hour, they had returned to Calleo all his chattels, and the crowd drifted away to supper and slumber bereft of spectacle.

Meribah watched Andreas and Hadeon walk up the hill in war-like tread. The crew gave way before them, and Meribah decided not to trail too close behind them. Eureka, still wet and lathered in his harness, gave her an excuse for staying. She made a wide circle around the wagon, the better to avoid her cousin and the Gangrel, and slipped under the yoke and strapping. She took a rag from the closest crewman and began wiping down her horse. All the while, her eyes remained on the two men who were knocking on Calleo's door.

"Abetorius Minor," Andreas called, "we must talk."

Hinges creaked, and the Tremere appeared. "What is the matter? I have no time for talk. I am very busy undoing the damage this little incident has caused me."

Hadeon snarled. "You know what we come for."

"Does this animal speak for you, Egyptian?" sneered the wizard.

"No. But this Gangrel has an interest in the welfare of my caravan." The Setite moved closer to the wagon steps. Though Meribah could not see his face, his words were clear. "We can discuss this inside or out, but we will settle it tonight."

"I'm not going to talk before him. I won't come out."

"Then I come in," Andreas declared, reaching for the doorknob.

"There's a ward," warned Calleo.

"Will it kill me?"

"No."

Andreas mounted the steps and vanished—with a small, pained grunt—into the warlock's den.

"Ears, girl," snapped Hadeon.

Meribah darted forward to listen at the keyhole. She caught one word—*is*—disjointed, without meaning. A moment later, *stone* and *creature*, then *wolves*, and she began to weave these snatches into whole cloth. "This is the stone creature," Andreas had said, and probably, "who fought so hard against the wolves," or "whom the guards saw the night of the wolves."

Hadeon prodded his eavesdropper to speak. Meribah gave up trying to understand the fragments and gave what she heard directly to the Gangrel.

"'Yes.' That's Calleo. Andreas now, saying something about a stowaway. Calleo answers, 'Yes.' Now Andreas again: 'idea… danger…on the Danube…worst…violation of our agreement. Inexcusable.' The wizard again: 'My secret. A small thing…not a proper Cainite…impossible to bring it to a conclave such as your oath-making...independent will...this is a creation...my possession.'"

Andreas's voice rose. Hadeon could hear the Egyptian himself now, so he shushed his spy.

"Your possession? You talk like Jacobi," accused the Setite. "You do not understand."

"I think I do," growled Andreas. "This is your slave."

A third speaker grated low. It seemed as if the earth itself echoed. "Slave? What is a slave, master?"

"My god, warlock." Andreas' disgust carried through wood and iron. "I would never have given you passage with—with this—"

Calleo cut him off. "Spare me your virtues, serpent. What will you do?"

"I am thinking," said the Egyptian. "I am thinking, and I am sorely tempted to drag you into the light and let the caravan judge you."

"You promised me passage. If you are going to keep that promise, you must keep my secret."

"Must I? You lied."

"I told no lies. Am I at fault, because you neglected to ask me questions?"

"Do not make light of this," hissed the Setite, "I am not obliged to carry you a foot further. I am not obliged to protect you. You were obliged to reveal any particular threats you brought to my haven, and you will make amends for your transgression."

"Vaclav paid no penalty," insinuated Calleo.

"He did, Abetorius, and he paid it with far more grace than you."

Silence reigned within. Without, the Gangrel knelt on the steps beside the keyhole, and Meribah pulled her skirts in under her knees.

"You must pay its—his—passage," declared Andreas, "and a forfeit."

"What forfeit?"

"You have gone to a great deal of trouble to conceal him—her. I have not overlooked your planning. I appreciate that you intended, for your own reasons, to avoid the double drain upon my resources."

"He has been no drain, Egyptian."

"Your wagon is filled with stone, Abetorius, and your—he is not small. Animals have gone lame hauling this box of rocks up the Balkans. Three oxen died getting it through the Sars, and seven men have been injured trying to break its descents. I will take a ransom for this stowaway." He named an amount, and Meribah blinked.

"I don't have that much."

Hellfire. Kings don't have that much, thought Meribah.

"You can get it from your kin in Aquileia," suggested Andreas, "or this poor creature stays with me."

"And to pay his passage?"

"You can lay a rumor to rest for me. Tell me, what goes into the creation of such a one as your—possession?"

"That is a secret, Egyptian," and Calleo's tone was all arrogance, "not to be revealed to outsiders." A minute died, and the silence bent the warlock's voice. More humbly, he temporized, "It is forbidden."

"It would hardly be worth my trouble, if it were not." Andreas laughed. "Tell me, or I will have no reason not to tell, say, Hadeon, Octavia, or the Tzimisce of Aquileia, exactly whom you have here."

The warlock's answer was too soft to hear. Meribah pressed her ear to the keyhole again, but the Gangrel shoved her gently away.

"Little girls shouldn't hear that wickedness, Merrie-lass. Go and play. I'll keep this vigil alone."

Chapter Nineteen

Principality of Aquileia
Over the Winter of 1207 and 1208

"Andreas, you devil, how have you been?" Titus Brutus Caesar, Prince of Aquileia, threw his arms around the Egyptian. There was nothing formal about Titus. Ancient, he wore his body's youth easily. Noble, he refused decorous distance. Powerful, he scorned ceremony and homage. The image was of a ruler so much the master of his city that he needed none of these. Yet Andreas thought he saw deeper currents behind the illusion.

Mortal Aquileia lay on the frontier between Frankish West and Greco-Slavic East. The Lasombra and Cappadocians fought each other to the south. The Tremere, Tzimisce and Ventrue warred to the north. Both halves of the empire, ten kingdoms and five clans used the Eastern Marks as their chessboard. More spies and intrigues traveled through and festered inside Aquileia than in any other Adriatic port, and the prince could trust no one. He used his high position to speak with everyone, even his enemies, whisper-close and neighbor-friendly. Listening with seductive interest, he learned more himself than lackeys could have brought him.

"You look well, Andreas, prosperous even. By Jove, I am glad to see you!" He stepped back, his hands on the Egyptian's shoulders, and laughed. "What is it I heard about you and Jacobi? You blackened his eye, I think. Well done, Follower of Set!"

Andreas smiled, bowed, and made a note to tell Gregory that his chimera had perished.

"You will winter with me, I hope?"

"Gladly, my lord, and gratefully."

Titus grinned wickedly. "I can't wait to hear the tale of your travels, Setite." He passed on to Valerian, and Andreas followed him down the line of guests, listening. "Scaevola! Well met, you rascal!"

"Caesar, you have not changed," said the senator, and the two elder Romans fell into some ancient dialect the Egyptian could not quite wrap his ears around. It cleared up one mystery for him, at least—the master of the Eagle-city was old enough to remember the Republic; he spoke the Latin and Greek of that time. Of the Caesars, Andreas reasoned, of the clan, even if he was not of the purple himself. Outside the Marks, it was rumored that Titus was no patrician, and that his name was not Caesar. Another tale gave him the right to the name, but claimed that a crucial part of it had gone missing over the centuries—Titus had not been a Caesar, but a freed slave of one. Most often, the gossips cast doubt on his Cainite past. He was an odd-looking, long-faced youth with a weak chin and high forehead, and his manner was eccentric. More than one Tzimisce *voivode* called him mad.

In the south, letters to Alexander's Grand Court in Paris asked, deferentially, whether Titus were Ventrue at all. There had been madness among the Caesars, after all, and perhaps a Malkavian had fancied the young Titus. Would Alexander send a lineage? Would not Paris feel safer with Aquileia in more steady hands? Paris, whatever doubts it might harbor, seemed broad-minded. Titus served the Grand Court's interests, in a difficult place, with skill and relish.

"But we are being rude, old friend," Titus said. "We must continue this another night. Andreas, introduce me to this fine young couple."

"Ewald Fairfax, Ventrue childe of the Lady Anne. I think you met his grandsire, years ago."

"During Charlemagne? That pup survived the wars? Well, well. What an unexpected world it is." He turned to Fairfax's companion. "But you, my dear, you're no Frank. You're not Greek, either, I know those eyes."

"My childe, Tsarika, Caesar."

The prince laughed. "Tsarika isn't a name, whelp, it's a title." The Tsarika smiled at this, and Ewald flinched as if struck. Titus ignored him ever after. "What is your name, lady?"

"Theodora Anna Romanovych."

Titus clapped his hands. "I know your uncle—great-uncle—Danylo."

"I have a younger brother Danylo," the princess said uncertainly.

"Probably named for my friend. You are young? Recently sired? Then you would not have known him. Probably you have visited his tomb, sung a prayer for his soul? He writes me often. He has such a marvelous humor—he goes to the family chapel himself to listen!" With thoughtful eyes, Theodora let her cousin kiss her cheek. Standing a little behind and to the right of Titus, the Egyptian could see the next girl's lips forming words.

"Galatea, a Toreador of Constantinople, my lord."

"Radiant," whispered Titus. "Exquisite."

"You flatter me," the girl protested demurely.

"Yes," agreed the prince. "I do, but not much, and I enjoy it. We shall know each other better before spring," he promised. Galatea returned his bow without flirtation. Andreas began to guess what had happened to her, and when.

"Now, these are a pretty pair, Andreas. Where in Jove's name did you find such girls?" Meribah blushed for the prince and looked at her feet; Zoë met his gaze with wary confidence. "Beautiful," murmured Titus, kissing first the gypsy, then the Frank. "So young," he whispered, holding one hand of each. "So spirited. Whose heart was so cold as to stop yours, little girls ?"

Now Meribah's eyes fixed on the prince and Zoë's dropped. Gregory, beyond them both, raised his hands to his head and turned away. Andreas witnessed the ruination of years of his and his cousin's hard work. For a moment, not one of the three moved; the master mourned, the apprentice remembered, and their friend's face burned as red as her hair.

"Yours is warm, is it?" Meribah yanked her hand out of his. "My sire was a whoreson, sure enough, but he warned me about old men like you."

Andreas cringed, but the prince was laughing. He released Zoë politely, and he seemed pleased with the fighting Frank. "What are your names, children?"

Andreas hastened to provide them. "This is Meribah, a relative of my own." His tone was enough of a warning. She grinned apologetically up at the Caesar. Titus took her hand again, kissed it, and let her go. "Zoë, a Ravnos—the ward of the Wonder-Maker."

"Ah," said the prince. "I see I have offended everyone. I am sorry. No insult was intended. Forgive me, Lakeritos, and be my guest this winter."

Gregory bowed, but said nothing.

The Setite guided his host forward. "Hadeon of the Gangrel," he explained.

Titus looked down his nose at the bearlike traveler. Here were skillful shades of deference and lordship, realized the watching Setite. Hadeon's tunic was earth-stained and rain-spotted, but Titus laid his clean hand on its threadbare shoulder. Wordlessly, he accepted the outlander as a guest, and his glance was not patronizing. The Gangrel allowed the contact with neither submission nor defiance. The prince nodded as though receiving the most profound honor, and the two parted equably.

They had reached the end of the line, but Titus stepped forward, pausing where the last man ought to have been. All he said was, "Andreas?" in a mild, inquiring tone.

The Setite felt shame warming the back of his neck, and his face fought to fell in sorrow. He mastered his expression and volunteered nothing. He had suspected the prince was better informed than he pretended, and after this he had no doubts. *He knows Boleslaus is gone. He must have known enough of Spalato to recognize Zoë when he saw her, too. What game is he playing with us?*

Valerian left his place and drew near with somber, serious countenance. He walked into the Caesar's field of vision, and Andreas had another question answered. Ever since Zara, he had grieved for the friend lost, and he felt his failure greatly. On another plane, he had wondered, too, whether the Nosferatu's assassination would irreparably tarnish his reputation as

Andrew of Egypt and jeopardize his appointment to the Grand Court in Paris. Now, Valerian gave Titus a single look as subtle as all the exchange between prince and Gangrel had been. It dispelled the Caesar's curiosity and exonerated the Setite without rubbing salt into fresh wounds or inflating the defeat by lengthy, vocal defense. Andreas knew, then, that the ambassador did not blame. Valerian yet supported him, and "Prince of the Road" had not been meant only for the moment in Zara.

By tradition, Titus held two feasts each year. At the first report of snow in the mountains, he gathered his guests to celebrate the frost. The ice was a sign that no others—allied or enemy— would venture through the Alps from north or east to join them. Nothing larger than a fishing vessel would brave the perils of the leaden-gray seas. The coast and the lowland Marks were a world unto themselves for the next four months. This year, winter came early, but there was time for three more visitors before the festival was declared.

The Tremere envoys arrived three days after the caravan, expecting to take their brother north through the Alps if the weather allowed, or if not, east to the clan chantry house in Ljubljana. They were seen to visit Calleo early one evening, and Andreas, informed by the children who had done the seeing, stood ready to receive them. Soon enough, Magister Thomas of Hamburg and Ole Germanicus Magna came to him, proposing to move the warlock's wagon from the Egyptian's camp to their own. With delicate courtesy, Andreas made clear his position, and the Saxons left with thoughtful haste. Riki and Didier, playing with the local youth in the warlocks' street, saw six messengers leave the next day—one east, one north, and three to the west. Their destinations were easily guessed. The single riders would try the two passes leading to Vienna, and the three rode on Trent, Verona, and the anti-Venetian stronghold of Genoa.

Andreas had warned the crew to expect the Tremere delegation. He had made no provision for the third, and more alarming, interloper.

Dehaan and Jacquy were crossing the courtyard to meet their master. Their route took them past the Ravnos wagons—not closely, but near enough to see the figure moving toward the workshop door. Jacquy blinked, and knew it for a trick of the light; the Rooster saw an unfamiliar shadow across the steps, and gestured quickly. The caravan master left the younger man to wait while he found Andreas.

A board creaked. Slowly, the latch rose and the handle turned. The door would open before Jacquy could hope to reach their lord, and so Dehaan walked out of hiding as though his step had never broken. His eyes fixed on a point five feet higher than the lowest step. He spoke brightly.

"How may I serve you, noble sir?"

The clear air made a startled movement. Suddenly, the Rooster could see clearly the dark-skinned, curly-haired stranger. The man was not breathing, and beneath his tanned color, there was no life-red foundation. He stared at the mortal through gold-flecked brown eyes.

"Are you one of Ankhesenaten's men.?" the stranger asked.

"I am, my lord."

The stranger nodded sagely. "Go, the n, and tell your master I have come to see him."

"Follow me," offered the Rooster, "and I will happily take you to him."

Through a tight smile, the other answered, "I shall await him here. Go now."

Dehaan felt that he should, after all, obey this man who knew his master's priestly name—who was so clearly himself blessed by Set. A slender thread kept him standing where he was. The service was being done already, and Andreas would wish him here. "Another of our band has gone ahead to announce you, lord."

"I do not require your pressssssenssssse," hissed the stranger. His thin, forked tongue flicked threateningly from a widening mouth.

The mortal's feet fought to carry him away. Fear coiled up his spine. He could run or keep still, but he could do nothing else, make no attack, utter no sound. Dehaan thought of his master and stood his ground, praying silently.

Footsteps echoed through the little courtyard. "Alsezir,"

called Andreas, and his worshiper's prayers were answered. "Welcome, brother. You honor me by your visit, Sethnakhte." The Moorish Setite looked to his kinsman, and Dehaan felt the alien compulsion ebb.

Others came behind the Egyptian. The faithful carried gentle lights to greet the guest. Magda offered devotions, took his cloak, washed his feet, and led him away to the shrine.

Andreas remained with the Rooster.

"He was trying to enter the Wonder-Maker's workshop, master."

The Setite nodded grimly. He put a hand on Dehaan's shoulder. The contact was a comfort, a sign of approbation, honor, gratitude, camaraderie. It was a finger on the young man's neck, to be sure his pulse was strong. It brought Andreas close enough to see his servant's eyes and know that they were clear. After a moment, he let Dehaan go, and he joined the procession.

Not keen to worship beside the intruder, Dehaan sat down on the steps with his back against the wagon. Time passed. Busy thoughts slowed to drowsy dreams. He slept.

He woke to a painful pressure on his spine. Someone was trying to open the door from within. Dehaan sprang forward, alarmed to think that Sethnakhte had come so close to invading the shop while the tinker worked, amazed that he had not wondered why the Moor had come so stealthily, and sure that he had trapped one of the Ravnos inside. His weight would have been too much for Gregory's twisted limbs; slightly built Zoë would have fared little better. They might have pushed against him for hours, perhaps even called out and gone unheard while he slept and the others prayed. He looked up, and the moon eased his mind. She had moved in her course, but not far. This might well be the first attempt his unwitting captive had made to escape. Apologies ready on his lips, the Rooster turned to explain himself to whichever Ravnos held the door.

There were no Ravnos. Dehaan faced death-white skin, hell-red hair and light eyes that seemed to tremble. Meribah slipped sideways from steps to ground, staring at him all the while. *She is afraid of me*, thought Dehaan. The little Frank disappeared around the corner of the wagon. *She was afraid of Sethnakhte. She fears my lord.* Pity overwhelmed him, and he darted forward to catch her.

The courtyard was empty. Nothing moved within his sight, and Meribah did not return to sleep in her wagon that day.

The party itself was quite simple. Titus's villa was built around an old Roman dome. From capitals of the original columns, later builders had suspended a gallery, and the entertainers played and sang from the safety of this height. Between the original pediments, masons had shored the arches up with fresh walls, and these made a large niche of each former vault. Each alcove held chairs and couches for guests who wished to speak together, and there were other seats in the center of the room for those who preferred to watch the performers or parley in Titus's company. No blood was offered at these celebrations—no mortals were allowed on the ground floor. Too many passions and enmities—feuds, in truth—simmered beneath the courtesies of the Friulian Mark to risk adding hunger to the stew.

Andreas sat with the Ventrue in the center, listening to them discuss the shifting borders of Thrace, Rascia, and Achaea. He had only half an ear for the politics of the living; he was looking to the encircling alcoves in admiration. From beneath the dome's oculus, the prince on his round, backless throne could see into every one of the "private" booths. A man could do well here if he read lips and had Takouhi s sight, Andreas realized.

The three Tremere now beckoned to him. He made his excuses to his host and joined the warlocks, careful to keep his back to the center of the room. With his body, he shielded Calleo's mouth from view, as well, and hoped that the two Saxons would be silent.

"Abetorius," he said pleasantly. "Magister Thomas." He bowed. "I trust you are all well?"

"Well enough, thank you," Calleo answered. "I called you here to inform you that your payment is on its way. I am ready to fulfill our first agreement, as well, if you can provide the necessary ingredient by Saturday."

"Saturday?"

"On Monday," explained Magister Ole, "we are moving on to Ljubljana."

Andreas raised an eyebrow. "The money will be here on Sunday, then?"

"It will arrive soon enough."

"When?"

"A third by the end of this month," said Thomas. "The rest will arrive in early April, when the roads are better."

The Egyptian shook his head. "Then you will be staying until spring, I fear."

The Saxons opened their mouths to object, but Calleo cut them off. "Very well," said the warlock, looking steadily at his host. "We accept your terms."

Andreas bowed to them all and took his leave. As he left, he saw Hadeon standing in the niche opposite the Tremere, gazing steadily at the warlocks. It seemed that the Gangrel spoke, and the Setite moved forward a little to see with whom the outlander deigned to converse.

She was a gray-skinned, sleek woman with artfully high-arched brows and long, elegant hands. Andreas realized swiftly that the effect was not simply the shaving or training of the hair; the eye-sockets themselves had been curved into their new shapes, perhaps to improve her appearance. The elongated phalanges, the graceful spines on the backs of her wrists, these, too, were sculpted from the very bones, perhaps to improve her skill in battle. This was the Tzimisce envoy to Aquileia, and she was deeply interested in what the Gangrel had to say. She smiled sweetly on the Setite, and Hadeon, too, nodded his acknowledgment.

Andreas looked back over his shoulder. The Tremere had not missed the bear-like sentinel, nor the beautiful Tzimisce. "Consider, Abetorius," the Setite said quietly, "that until your friend's ransom arrives, you remain a traveler under my aegis."

Calleo stared back at him without comment, and Andreas walked away.

Beneath the dome's center, the talk had changed. Lord Valerian held a genealogy of the Theodora's Ventrue lineage, Ewald another showing Iaroslav's legacy. These were the

Caesar's gift to the Tsarika, drawn in his own hand. The Setite drifted by in time to hear how Valerian and Ewald were connected, and he observed that the name of the great uncle who appeared on both had been written in red and gilded.

Andreas left the nobles to their game. There were others here, plotting in the present, to amuse him.

Galatea and a Lasombra shared a couch together. The Neapolitans manner suggested that the Toreador had won another heart, but his eyes were on the Magyar countess a quarter-arc away. Mario di Napoli had come to Aquileia to watch the flesh-crafting Tzimisce; the Tzimisce had come to watch the Tremere. After Calleo had gone, at least one of the warlocks would stay to watch the Giovanni whom Alsezir had cornered, and Alonso Giovanni had come to watch the Lasombra. In their spare time, they would spy against the other three, and the four studied Titus every night for a weakness. The prince studied them all in turn.

Gregory and Zoë kept silent company in the niche beside Hadeon and the countess. The Wonder-Maker watched the acrobats in delight, and his apprentice had found a bit of slate and chalk to draw the dancers with. Only the Ravnos, realized Andreas, were listening to the music. He thought first of Boleslaus, then of his cousin, and found her.

She sat alone, in her own alcove, on a small chair wedged between two columns, and the bulge of the outermost pillar hid her from view. He had overlooked her the first time he strolled by; only the hem of her skirt betrayed her.

"Meribah?"

"Andreas," she returned, not leaving her little hole. He was forced to move directly in front of her to see her face at all.

"May I join you?"

With a foot, Meribah hooked another chair away from the wall and poked it toward him. While he settled in, she used him as a screen—leaning out, she looked past him and ducked quickly back—and he saw their Moorish cousin move. His new position, chatting with Galatea and Mario di Napoli, was the only place in the room from which Meribah could be seen. Andreas seized the arms of her chair, lifted it out of the hollow, and stuck it between the corresponding columns on his other side.

"Better?"

Meribah's eyes were shut. "Yes," she said gratefully.

"You know what he's here for, of course."

"I can guess," she whispered timidly.

"Stop guessing."

The ice-blue eyes opened, and Meribah looked straight at him.

"Thebes is impatient," Andreas said. "They want what Khay'tall hid with Gregory."

The blue eyes blinked blank. "Of course," she agreed.

"He hoped to try his hand before I caught his scent. He will move on, now that we are on guard against him, but I fear there will be others." Andreas left his deeper doubts unsaid: Sarrasine sprang from Khay'tall, who sprang from Nehsi, and Nehsi's second childe had sired Detonate. It was possible that Khay'tall's nephew sought to revive him. It was more probable that Sarrasine's cousin wished to protect the younger man. Most likely, Nehsi's brood knew what prize belonged to him who seized it. Meribah's grandsire was Nehsi's brother. It would be cruel to remind her how nearly her blood tied her to the abominable Typhonists, and it would be a risk to his mission to reveal how closely he had studied those heretics.

"You've made great gains into the Ravnos's confidence, with all the subtlety I could ask for, but we cannot move so cautiously any longer. For Gregory's own safety, we must not let the cache remain in his possession. When Calleo leaves, I will make public that his debt is paid. Sit with the Wonder-Maker on that night. If the question of my fee arises, see if you can suggest the idea of the cache as my price."

The redhead nodded once, earnestly, and her expression inspired him to add the new strategy that had come to him after Zara. "Zoë still haunts you for the secret of the faith?" Meribah flashed a wry, sad smile.

"It's time, I think, to offer it to her. Make her first act against *ma'at* the winning of this prize for Set," murmured the priest into his cousin's ear. "Gregory's sense of honor—his promise

made to a man four years dead—might make him reluctant to
pay me with Khay'tall's commission."

A long silence—a pause, rather, saturated by music—and
Andreas feared his cousin would object.

"If Sarrasine comes himself—"

"I'll do it."

"Good girl."

He patted her shoulder, saw Alsezir homing toward their
tete-a-tete and rose to chase off the interloper. Sethnakhte gave
his promise to leave by week's end, and kept it. And so began a
blessedly uneventful winter.

At the first report of thaws in the mountains, Titus gathered his
guests to celebrate the spring. Snowmelt-swollen streams were
the sign that his winter subjects—allied or enemy—could venture at last through the Alps to north or east and escape each
other. The first fleets from Venice and Genoa would soon arrive,
bearing fresh scandal and diplomacy. The coast and the lowland Marks opened their doors to the rest of the world in raw,
undisguised relief.

Andreas sat with Titus in the center of the round room, listening to the prince discuss the murder of Peter of Castelnau, a
papal legate, by a Cathar in the service of the count of Toulouse.
The crime had spurred Pope Innocent to call for soldiers of
Christ to march on the heretics in the Albigenses. Provence
and Lombardy seethed with religion. Andreas planned a more
northerly route.

Twice, he tried to free himself from the Caesar's attentions;
twice, the old Roman had changed the subject. Abrupt departure might offend, and so the Setite remained the Ventrue's conversational captive. The prince knew precisely what he did. He
smiled, expectantly—wickedly, like a little boy fibbing past the
gate at a fair. Titus didn't care that Andreas saw through the
trick, so long as he himself had a good view.

Not for the first time, Andreas wondered at the prince's
omniscience. The Tremere's retainers had delivered their last
payment that day, and Titus had descended on his guest so
shockingly soon after sunset that Calleo had no chance to claim

his freedom. Thus, the prince forced the warlock to make his farewells here, in public, or sleep another day in Aquileia. The fact that this was precisely what Andreas himself most wished for—that Meribah should have the opportunity to play the gambit he had provided in autumn—made him feel no better.

Some hours into the entertainment, when it was clear to all that Titus would keep the Setite at his side all night long, the warlock approached them and made one scant bow. "I leave you this night, Egyptian."

The prince's hand rose, and all conversation hushed.

"I acknowledge your payment in full, Abetorius Minor. I release you, with honor, from your debt to me, and I deliver you to the safe custody of your own blood kin." Andreas stood and made a deep obeisance to the three Tremere. At the bottom of the bow, he glimpsed Meribah at Gregory's side, and the Ravnos was, indeed, whispering to her briskly. The warlocks returned the courtesy and departed.

Hadeon, grinning wolfishly, replaced them at Titus and Andreas's feet.

"Egyptian."

"Hadeon."

"I find," the Gangrel began loudly, "that I, too, shall take my leave of you here."

Behind him, the Tzimisce shone her sweet smile upon the wizards.

"There is a fine land north of here in need of a protector, and I have agreed to escort the Countess Djula through the mountains to it and to her retinue. We," he showed more teeth, "also leave tonight."

"The coincidence astounds us," chimed the lady, "but what a pleasure, to share the road with our so-young neighbors."

"I owe you nothing," said Hadeon.

"You owe me nothing," Andreas agreed.

Very softly, Hadeon continued, "If ever your travels take you on the road between Nagykanisza and Buda, sound your horn and let me know you are there. I would readily owe you nothing again, and I wish you well."

The Egyptian found his feet, but the two men did not bend

to each other. The Gangrel stalked away once more, and contrived somehow to loom over the wizards from halfway across the room.

"How soon do you leave, Andreas?"

"Tomorrow evening, my lord." *As I told you a week ago, my lord.*

"Then I, too, must make this my goodbye, my friend." The Tsarika's voice rang out clearly and echoed slightly from the marble dome. "My kinsman," said the princess, gliding across the floor to prince and serpent, "has written to my grandfather's brother and his soldiers. They come to Aquileia to take me home."

Feeling Titus's eyes upon him, Andreas only inclined his head. All of his other passengers, past and present, stared dumbfounded at the imperious girl. She took her place, calm and stately, before her hosts—and Ewald, surprised and lost-looking, followed her like a beaten dog.

"My friend," said the girl in Turkish, "are you not happy for me?"

"I am happy for you," replied the Setite flatly, and in Greek. Hearing no protest from his Norman cousin, Valerian clapped Andreas on the back consolingly. "You chose this one well, my boy, and I believe you do the right thing, here. Her own people can teach her best, and your lady-sire will be happier to see you unencumbered. We shan't tell her at all, for a few years, I think."

Theodora shook her head. "No. The boy comes with me, and this Greek girl, too."

Valerian's countenance fell, but Ewald's lifted in joy. Galatea lowered her eyes in resignation, but her face was no less a model of contentment.

"Andreas, my friend," resumed the Tsarika. "My thrall Ewald owes you for his passage and for mine. This debt falls to me now, I believe. What would you ask of me?"

"Release them. Give me Galatea for Ewald's passage and Ewald for yours."

A cat-like smile blossomed on Theodora's face. "Something else."

"You may owe me, for now. When you have regained your

inheritance, or if you change your mind, we will discuss this matter again."

"You have treated me well, my friend. My great uncle, he will show you the gratitude of the Kievan Rus."

"You," Lord Valerian accused the girl, "are the very image of your grandsire, and I thank god you are not coming to France. We don't need two of you."

The Tsarika accepted this as an homage, and the old senator kissed her forehead. The prince nodded his laurels, and others—spies, Tremere, Hadeon—advanced to congratulate her on a game well played. She had no great interest in them, and her eyes strayed often to her thralls. Andreas caught her disappointment, and understood. Theodora had thought to humiliate them, to pay back in part what they had done to her in Constantinople and Durazzo. Yet after the blood oath—so soon—they loved her. They were happy merely to be near her.

When the crowd thinned, the Setite approached the victor. "A word, Tsarika."

"Speak, my good friend."

"Do your good friend a favor—take a lesson from him."

"You have always advised me for the good," she admitted.

"Treat your bondsmen well."

She searched his face suspiciously, but she listened.

"The oath can be broken. Remember that they love you, and be merciful."

Her cat-like smile returned, and the princess promised nothing. Andreas never saw her again.

Chapter Twenty

To the Little St. Bernard Pass, Graian Alps
April, 1208

Spring sped the caravan along the lowlands of Lombardy. Here the roads were well kept, and the Romans had built many of them. Jacquy could choose the route best suited to men and beasts; Leopold coaxed restless, eager animals into greener pastures easily. They entered no cities, for Valerian was not to be awoken again until Lyons and the market towns were rich enough to feed and supply them. They gave Venice and Genoa miles of respect. With five of their own wagons empty and Calleo's gone, the going was easy. Without Hadeon to distract her, Meribah spent more time with the Ravnos. Gregory and Zoë worked while Meribah read aloud, and Gregory and Meribah discussed philosophy and lost texts while Zoë practiced her new-learned magic of illusion.

They entered the mountains amid rain and mists, and the little Frank had not yet, despite Andreas's encouragement, begun the "breaking-together" of her friend. The first clear night, however, was also the full moon. Under that silver light, many things were broken.

Meribah had gone to rest with rain pelting her wooden roof. She opened the windows and laughed to see stars—burst out her front door and into the mud with absolute glee.

The caravan was camped in a valley like the palm of her hand. A glacier trickled down the four fingers. Its thumb, the unprotected cliffside road, was scoured barren brown by sun and wind. The center, though, was lush, green pasture, and here Jacquy had called the halt.

The little Frank thrashed eagerly through the tall, toe-tangling grass. There was a titanic boulder beside the road, a cracked massif around which the wagon-ruts swerved, with a clear path up its side. Meribah scrambled up the rock in one unceasing, four-limbed run. The breeze whistled between her body and the earth. Her skirts were soaked with rainwater, her feet black with soil and blood. Her borrowed kerchief blew away, and she tore her dress. Once, in the last chimney-crack leading up, she fell down hard enough to break her foot, but Meribah had no thought to spare on trifles. Her body healed itself as she hopped to the summit. From the top, she could see clouds beneath her—lightning striking sideways—a field of ice the size of a city.

When she had had enough of the impassable north, she gazed east. All that was left of Italy was a sliver above one ridge-line, and she could not recognize any place that she had been. The road went west into Languedoc, but there were cliffs in the way. She could not glimpse their destination—she couldn't even tell whether the mount in front of her was the peak or a lowly shoulder. To see the caravan, she would have to circle around the crag; the path did not overlook their valley from any impressive height. Meribah found a ledge to walk along which seemed as if it curved the right way. It took her down, not up, but where it ended, another shelf began, and there was a gap in the cliff face above that. The little Frank pulled herself up and gazed out of this natural window.

Her view was narrow; the opening was a small crack in a dike yards thick. By chance, it aligned perfectly with caravan and valley. She could see past the path to the road, past the road to the meadow, above the camp to the glacier, past the glacier to the peaks, and through the peaks to the hard, sweet stars. Wind whipped through the space around her. Here the world was not gentle; it was cold and grand and pure. The air touched heaven; it was burdened by no earthly odor. Meribah leaned against the rock wall with her chin on her folded arms. She became one with the careless air, and she came to a decision.

There was movement on the rock (her rock, the wind's rock), and Meribah returned to thoughts in words.

Zoë. She ran from the camp, glancing back over her shoulder furtively, and her friend shook her head in exasperation. *That child can't sneak. You want to sneak, you've got to look as though you ought to be doing what you are. Bring a basket, girl. Be picking flowers.* She propped her chin on her palm, sighing. *Poor Gregory. She's left him waiting in the wagon again.*

Then Meribah froze, conscious of a presence. First her eyes looked right, then her head. Gregory wasn't in the wagon. He was here, watching his darling childe slip away from him. He slowly turned left, and the two sentinels' eyes met. His were too deep; she could not fathom them. At last, one side of Meribah's mouth quirked up—the heights had made her happy—and she traversed the small, scree-strewn slope between her rough watchtower and the Wonder-Maker's lonely throne.

Gregory made room for her; together, they witnessed the gypsy's difficult climb, saw her emerge from the steep chimney to the plateau above them. Her hair streamed behind her in the wind, and she smiled as if she knew something about the world that no one else could learn. She opened her mouth—shouted. Borealis stole the words, but the tone was jubilant.

The Setite sat helplessly, searching for something to say. If she could make the moment a conversation, an ordinary time... "She's a beautiful girl, isn't she?" Meribah said it as though Zoë were someone neither of them knew. "She would have been a woman, now."

The serpent's neck flashed hot. She had chosen the wrong thing. Trying to rescue them both, she blundered on: "She is one. She's just never going to look it."

"She is not. She has the arrogance of a child, and she will never grow past that." Gregory seemed to be speaking only to himself, and as he went on, fewer and fewer whispers survived the journey to the listener's ears. "I was...I was a very angry young man. I was the servant of Tzimisce, and I was angry that they kept me. I ran away, and they saw to it that I could not so do again." Meribah remembered his misshapen limbs. "That too, fueled my fury. In time, I found a tribe of easterners who would take me on the road with them, and though I had escaped my masters, I raged that I must leave my home. One of the easterners made me what I now am, and I have borne the yoke of my youthful wrath in every year since." Only his lips spoke the last words, and Meribah had to guess their shapes: "Zoë, she will not be humble. She will not listen to me, who has killed her."

Audible once more, he sounded frail and weary. "Please, Meribah, I want to think. Would you mind...leaving me by myself, for a little while?"

Somewhat frightened, she nonetheless kissed him on the cheek and gave him the solitude he asked for. Distaste for Zoë (consciously unreasonable—she knew it was the tinker's own talk of curses that harried the gypsy to starvation, drove her to rebellion, forced the girl to abandon him) spread through her. She determined to reach the path without being seen by her friend, and did, but the path itself was naked rock and gravel. Being inconspicuous was not enough. Zoë hailed her, faintly enough to ignore—ran down behind, tugged her sleeve, and chivvied her back up the great boulder.

"Look!"

Meribah nodded her head and sighed. Obediently, she admired a vista grown finite. The north was her own, not to be shared, the east was Gregory's, to be avoided in pity, and the south was shielded by the boulder on which they stood. To the west, she spied Andreas and the caravan crew holding prayers past the bend of the road. Her eyes burned. "Glorious."

"Mmm. I'm glad I decided to come."

The Setite's eyebrows climbed. "What do you mean?"

Zoë laughed. "Titus. He asked me to stay on in Aquileia—said I was a wonder-maker myself." Her voice grew round and slow, almost purr-like. "I never would have agreed, of course, but he did offer."

Meribah pressed her palms against her eyes. "Of course he offered. Anybody who gets a hold of you, girl, has gotten hold of Gregory. If you wanted to stay somewhere, you don't think he'd just walk off with the rest of us, do you?" She rapped her forehead against the rock and stood there, staring into stone. "Titus is a bad old man, dear heart. He knew all about you. I imagine Jacobi's bearding is known in Taugast by now. Mortals probably gossip the story in the streets."

"I don't think that was it." Zoë stole in beside the serpent, smirking. "Meribah."

"Yes?"

"The Third Pillar."

"Yes."

"It can't be just faith. Any faith. You've been testing me," she accused.

"I have," the Setite answered flatly.

"Aren't I ready yet? Don't you trust me? It wouldn't be the first secret I'd be keeping, you know."

"Do you trust me?"

The gypsy seized the Frank girl's hands. "You know I do."

"Then believe me. I can't teach you the secret bits unless... well, I just can't."

"Unless what?"

Meribah peeled herself off the wall. "Zoë. Think about this. You'd be betraying Gregory."

"He betrayed me. We'd be even."

So they would, thought Meribah, and felt better about her course. "Listen. Be serious. The Third Pillar is called *heqa*. It's white magic—faith magic. There's a spirit, a kind of guardian angel for the Cainites of Egypt." *Keep it as true as you can, Merrier girl, or she'll see through you, and the game will stop right there.* "He's very powerful—very helpful—to anyone who knows how to call upon him properly. But to call on him requires rituals—prayers—an icon of this saint. I don't have an icon."

Zoë's face blazed triumphant. She finally had the truth out of her tutor, and was eager to move on. "How can you get one? Can it be made? What can we do? You said 'unless'—"

"Khay'tall had a shrine, Zoë. A little scroll with the holy image on it. It hasn't been seen since he was killed." Meribah moved on, praying not to be asked how she knew this. "And I think that's what he commissioned Gregory to build that box for, like a reliquary. He must have brought it with him when he hid—well, whatever it was he hid from Sarrasine. You could get it for me, couldn't you?"

The Ravnos flinched at the name, then hesitated. The serpent was glad to see that Zoë balked, unwilling, despite her bravado. *Thank God,* Meribah thought with relief. *She won't do it.* "Or—better still—Andreas owes me a favor. No, I'm not paying him for this trip. It's half of the debt. Suppose you just convinced Gregory to give Andreas the box as the price of your passage? Then I could claim it from him."

"In Paris? You mean you'll teach me there?"

"Of course," lied Meribah.

"I'll do it," said Zoë. "And I'm glad you're going to stay with us. I've been dreading France. I knew I was going to miss you."

"I'd miss you, too." And that, at least, was true.

Meribah let her victim go, to sneak home "before he notices." Alone again, the little Frank laid down on the cold earth and shed her sorrows exploring the brittle black sky.

By the time Meribah joined the congregation, the petitioners had finished their requests of Ankhesenaten and the rosewood cabinet had been hidden away. Annemie and Gertje were herding the faithful off to dinner, but Magda and Dehaan remained behind to discuss the ritual with their priest. The redhead marched straight in past Goreb, grinning forcefully.

"We need to talk," she announced.

Andreas made a sign to the mortals, and the three moved out of hearing. Meribah wistfully watched them go then thrust her hands decisively into her pockets and began her proposition.

"About my boon. You know. If I can get the cache for you."

The Egyptian nodded his encouragement.

"I asked you to teach me the old language," she reminded him. "Will you?"

Andreas gave a twisted smile. "That is a small thing, and your birthright. It would hardly be a fair return for your services."

"I don't care. That's my price. Will you do it?"

He pulled on his braided beard, becoming businesslike. "Time enough to discuss payment when the job is finished, Meribah. After Paris—"

"I see." She bit her lip. "You were ready to discuss it until you knew what it was. And you talk fees with the passengers anytime you want."

"We're family," he explained. It was no answer, and he saw that she knew that.

"Please," cried Meribah from between clenched teeth. "Don't pretend. Don't patronize me. Just, just stop!" Her mouth opened—her fangs were down—her tone carried bleak fury. Goreb and Dehaan stepped forward; Magda pulled torches and coal from her bundle. All three remained where they could listen as the girl recovered, but Meribah paid them no mind.

"Stop," she said again. Her gaze was direct, her voice calm and very old. Andreas had never heard her speak with such clarity. "The first lesson a Follower of Set must learn is the language. I was never taught it. My sire is destroyed. He cannot remedy the error. You will not teach me, though you are my friend and shall be in my debt. I know, therefore, that it is too late to redeem myself by learning it.

"My sire was disgraced by his heresy. I am an alien and outcast. I err toward a god who denies the existence of the one who animates me. I am an infidel, and so a walking waste of the power of the Lord of Storms. There can be no penance, no atonement for this sin. The Destroyer is not a god of mercy."

She paused before adding, "My life is forfeit." Ankhesenaten bowed his head, acknowledging the accuracy of his cousin's construction. In his private heart, Andreas wept.

"I have thought about this a great deal. It was in my mind from the first. I suspected that al-Suti's omission—his neglect—was impossible to remedy. I ask you, my brother, for this boon: Let me choose my executioner. I have..." she choked on her words, "...very potent blood." Her voice broke to a whisper. "It will strengthen him who devours me, and the credit for my destruction will serve him well in Thebes. I want you to do it," she finished quietly. "So...please say yes. It's important to me."

The Egyptian shut his eyes against this strange, inexorable child. He had known since Spalato that duty demanded he expunge the sin of Sutekh in the person of this Frank, but he had prayed fervently that this moment might not come. He had thought it kinder not to tell her. One night, on the road to Flanders, she simply would not wake. *Set rewards my cowardice with this ordeal. Lord, forgive me my weakness, but what has Meribah done, to be brought to suffer here?* His lips parted, and against the will of Ankhesenaten, Andreas spoke:

"Why do you want this? Why not run away?"

He wavered, but she was sure. "I was born to Christianity. I was baptized. Christ forgives the truly repentant—I believe that. To repent being a Follower of Set, I must cease to be one. Suicide is forbidden. Someone else will have to do it. Perfect logic or perfect faith—neither of which I possess—would take me to a priest or Templar. But the blood in my veins is Set's, and I must return to him his gift. He has no mercy, but he does accept sacrifice. The best service I could do him would be to give up the waters to someone worthy." Meribah did not smile, but she ceased frowning. "You. You're a good man and a good Setite. You believe. You have faith," she whispered, with awe and envy. "You deserve to rise in the hierarchy. You could make use of what al-Suti wasted on me.

"This way, you see...I could satisfy both gods. Even if one doesn't exist. Hedge my bets. Pray for a happy little limbo, somewhere. Oblivion."

"Why tell me now?"

"Sethnakhte didn't come to Aquileia to snatch Khay'tall's papers, Andreas." Meribah's hands rose to her mouth in a guarded gesture. "They aren't pleased with me."

"Who?" asked Andreas, although he understood perfectly. Habitual secrecy put forth the question, and it was no doubt wise. But under the shattering moon, after the girl's petition, his caution was insulting. He regretted it instantly.

"Your prey," said Meribah. The words were a slap. "I am neither fool nor child, brother."

Andreas remembered their meeting in Venice, when he had thought her innocent—in Philippopolis, where she had seemed young—in Aleppo, where she had been nicknamed "the little Frank." She was none of these. *I do not know her.* All through their journey, he had felt her will working in channels of his own—easily manipulated, a fine tool to use upon the Ravnos. Underneath that, this hardness. *What does the shell I now see hide?* He was suddenly furious with Sutekhankharen. *What a crime, to condemn this woman. May he burn forever. May the Devourer swallow his soul.*

Taking his silence for contradiction, Meribah spoke on: "Rome appoints bishops; the bishops investigate heresy in their diocese. Thebes has no bishops; they have you. Isn't that right, inquisitor?"

Suspicion arrested sympathy. *All this has been a ruse. The heretics suspect my mission. They placed the girl in my path to infiltrate and undermine me, and confirm their guesses.* "I am not," he said aloud.

"Who killed Sutekhankharen?"

"Not I."

"Who tested me?"

"I never asked a question."

"No," retorted Meribah. "You made Kadjadja do it, because you suspected her."

Out of the corner of his eye, Andreas saw Magda lighting her torch and Goreb's swords gleaming redly. Instinctively, he stepped between the Hand of Set and the girl—his instinct battered down the ignoble suspicion. *I would like her to be my enemy,* he realized, *that I might kill her without conscience.* He took her hands, and his eyes felt strangely wet. "I did," he said softly. "But we will not speak of it now." Ankhesenaten put his arms around the infidel and held her until she stopped shaking. His priestess blew out her torch. The Hand of Set sheathed his great scimitars. The Rooster stood by with tear-streaked cheeks. After a little while, Andreas led his followers in to their great pavilion for a feast, and Dehaan half-carried Meribah to the seat of honor at his lord's right hand.   ~

Chapter Twenty-One

Chambery, Savoy
May, 1208

In Savoy, even villages built walls to fortify their homes, and their nobles similarly built *castra* within the town to protect themselves and to offer refuge to lower classes should the first defenses fall. In Chambery, these strongholds surrounded a third—an ancient, round-towered keep that was never used by the ruling family. Villeins and merchants believed it haunted by the ghost of a martyred princess named Clovia. Priests revered her memory and laid cures and miracles to her credit. The abbot spent evenings researching her life and works, determined to present his case for her beatification before he died. Only the nobles knew better. For centuries, the decaying tower had been the home of their patron, the Lady of the Keys.

Clovia received Andreas on the lichen-furred roof of her tower. Her welcome was warm and gracious but unaccommodating. Chambery's fair, concurrent with the Feast of Our Lady, would bring all the countryside in for the celebration, so the Lady of the Keys could offer no hospitality within her walls. If he wished, she would exert her influence over the *seigneur*—he owned fields as yet unreserved. Andreas so wished and found his audience ended.

However well-intended the Lady's gesture, it resulted in an unfortunate juxtaposition. The heretics were here as well. They had traveled faster than the caravan through the passes, having left their wagons behind, and their leaders had begged the same favor from Clovia. The two pastures given to the deathless

travelers were two corners of a fourfold square, opposite the
camps of knights come for the minor tourney anchoring the
fair. Cainite zealots breathed smoke from Setite campfires. Their
camp-followers' tent cords intertwined. They drew water from
the same wells as the princes. Nothing, however, happened. The
heretics seemed less apocalyptic, less mad. If Andreas had not
recognized faces in the crowd, he would have thought them a
different people. *The least sane,* reflected Andreas, *the weakest, the
wildest. They have been killed by the snows or sacrificed. Easter would
have gone hard for the mortals among them.* Most wore flowers, and
some sang hymns to the Blessed Virgin. All in all, the Byzantine
refugees found them friendly neighbors. This change intrigued
the Egyptian, but his curiosity hungered in vain. Takouhi was
not of their number, and Andreas would not risk his flock on
the inquiry. Jacquy laid in provisions and livestock all the first
day and the second. Andreas gave orders to leave before dawn
on the third.

Despite the threat and the short leave, the crew simply rev-
eled. They had conquered the mountains early—the last remaining wide Roman road had been clear of snow in April, an event
unknown in living memory. Now they felt the warmth of summer, smelled green grass and vineyards and listened, as rapt as
Odysseus to the sirens, to the speech of every man, woman, and
child. Many of Andreas's people had good Greek, one or another
vulgar Latin, all a polyglot, trade pidgin. Some few could struggle along in Slavic—Ljudumilu's descendants spoke it perfectly.
Goreb had been born to Arabic, raised to speak Turkish. For most,
their native tongue was a French one. The Flemings might have
found the *langue d'oc* harsh and strange in their own county, but
it was homey and familiar after years in the Marks, Dalmatia,
Macedonia, and Thrace.

They allowed themselves the luxury (as Andreas would not)
of looking on this as their last year on the road. True, Savoy,
Burgundy, and Champagne were lands of jealous Cainite discord, but Lord Valerian was the man who presented such disputes to king and queen. No one would dare cross him or bar
his progress to their court. With good weather and good luck,
the caravan would reach Lyons in a week and Paris itself in

two months. In case of torrents, damaged roads, and September snows, the wagons might winter in some market town on the Seine, but Valerian and the Ravnos pair could be delivered waking, on horseback, by Christmas. Their chattels would arrive by mule soon after, and their bulky goods would come whenever the roads permitted. The crew themselves would be home in Flanders this time next spring, and all but one were happy.

On the last night, Meribah and Zoë wandered the market of Chambery together. Trade had given way to celebration. Few merchants manned their stalls so late as this, but the two carried coin purses tucked in their bodices on the chance. They admired what they could see, to know it again at the fair in Lyons, and watched the people go about their entertainments.

There were bonfires in every square, so the girls went hand in hand—both to borrow bravery and to know on the instant if the red fear overtook the other. The Greek girl never flinched. She was too eager to see these Franks to care about flames. Meribah's lessons had given her the linguistic key to the country. She listened to a troubadour in the church square and understood what was said, much of the time; she played games guessing the rest. The serpent basked in her friend's innocent delights but kept her guard up. She paid more attention to the passers-by than to the minstrels, and she caught their words below the tune:

A bold-faced boy and a pretty maid: "I will ask your father tonight, *cherie*, if you..." Three middle-aged men in fur-trimmed finery: "...seventeen bales of wool by Thursday week, or he won't..." Two noblemen in blue, with liveried squires and pageboys: "...can't ransom his horse, let alone his armor, the dog. I told him..." A priest, a monk, and a nun: "...edict to gather his forces in Lyons, to pursue the Cathars." Four old women in black: "...buried ten grandchildren, poor dear, and her daughter, all in one month..." An old knight and a new one, in red tabards, mounted: "...for daylight; they will be gone by sunup. Two blades won't be enough on the road; I have gathered the more pious chevaliers..." A weary mother with two babes in her arms, driving three children before her: "...because I said so, Guillaume. That's why."

Hoofbeats, and the complaints of the crowd. Meribah glanced over her shoulder. The red knights were riding for the main street. "Zoë," she said, "we're leaving."

"Why?" The gypsy's hand squirmed, and the Frankish girl had to drag her from the square.

"Because I said so, that's why."

The mob, which parted for noble horsemen, closed before two half-grown girls, but news travels faster than feet. They heard of the battle in the fields almost as soon as it was joined. They heard the clamor of the *castra* alarm bells before they could see the walls. Then the crowd's currents helped them. Most within the town tonight were travelers, and their own tents and lodgings lay outside. Precious minutes passed while they battered their way through the crush at the gates—a frustrated, angry vortex, surging toward the exit, being denied it, frothing back into the city to try again at some other portal. Meribah and Zoë swirled up in their turn, and found stony-faced pikemen guarding the great barred doors and the postern gate within them.

"No one in, no one out," said the soldiers in monotonous unison for perhaps the thousandth time.

"My—my father is out there!" screamed Zoë.

"Yours, theirs, everyone's, cherie," said the nearer man, not unkindly. He returned to chanting, and another wave threatened to sweep the two away. Meribah stepped behind her friend to break the force, and saw the younger girl close her eyes. Only a moment later, Zoë opened them with a terrible shriek.

"Look!"

The pikemen were well trained, so only one followed Zoë's frightened gaze. Only one saw the tiny arm trapped between the jamb and door of the lesser gate—life-pink still, bluing at the fingertips, bruised where the cruel wood pinched the skin.

"A baby!" cried the crowd.

"Jesus Christ!" exclaimed the soldier, and he flung open the door.

The Ravnos was through it in an instant, the Setite scarcely a breath behind. Others streamed out behind them for a short while, to the shouts of the pikemen.

"God's wounds! Illusion! Witchcraft!"

An arrow creased Meribah's elbow, and she laughed aloud. "Good one, Zoë."

"Where do we go? Where do we go?"

They ran along the narrow ring between the inner walls and the outer, and there were no gates in sight. The camp, somewhere outside, lay west. Meribah steered her friend to the left, trying to remember where the road pierced the stone. She guessed wrong, and suddenly the open space ended. There were stairs leading up, onto the fortifications of the *castra*, and for want of choices, they climbed the narrow flight.

Now the Setite led the way, pounding along the flagstones, dodging sergeants and bowmen. No one attacked the girls; the defenders stared in silent wonder at the strange battle below. Meribah leaned over the battlements and stretched her senses to their limits.

An oval of fire surrounded the deathless encampments—theirs and the heretics' both. Men-at-arms wielded torches, hemming in the travelers. Priests and other clergy hovered a short distance away, swinging censers and chanting Latin.

Within the ring, a confused mass of refugees, heretics, Cainites, and crew shrank from the fire. Magda and Danica waited at the door of Andreas's wagon—prepared to defend the shrine—but the Egyptian himself was missing, along with Goreb, the Hand of Set. A handful of other women huddled around their priestess. Most stood around two barrel wains drawn side-by-side with dreadful patience, shielding the children who ducked and hid under the bodies of the oxen. Gregory, Annemie and Carl paced between this group and the fighting men. Jacquy, Lieven, and Dehaan held their forces ready at the periphery, but no one heeded them.

The knights advanced on an absolute monster in the other camp—a Nosferatu who had lost his or her cloak. Unmasked, it was so malformed—etched with a blood-red leprosy—that even its followers seemed confused by the apparition. A few fell back from the knights to defend their leaders, more simply retreated. Some, new converts perhaps, not yet aware of their priesthood's natures, began screaming when the cloak failed, and they did not stop. Amid the clamor, there was a moment of stillness, two heartbeats in length—and suddenly, one man ran for the torch-men with an ear-splitting yell.

The lights in that arc winked out, and Meribah scented blood on the wind. One knight reached the Cainites, and she saw a woman lose her head. *They know how to fight us,* she realized. *They know how we die.* Mortals fled the line to pour out of the broken arc, cringing against the still-firm sections, and further in, to the calmer regions of the Setite camp. Many of the caravan's own refugees were running now—Meribah could no longer tell which were theirs, which the heretics'.

Dehaan, Leopold and Ern were closest to the combat, closest to the desperate victims. If the knights had charged them, they would have fought. With women and children rushing their posts, they hesitated—they tried only to deflect the invaders. Rough hands were not enough. A child broke the line; two pressed through behind her; mothers pierced the gaps. Men tried to struggle past, and the Rooster's party smacked them with the flats of their blades. Then the Nosferatu bore down on Dehaan, and Meribah went over the wall.

She climbed red-eyed, her inch-long claws driving deep into the rock. Zoë wailed something after her. Meribah hardly knew what she answered, but she became aware of the gypsy scrabbling above her. She thought of Zoë's short, thin talons just in time to hear the cry and the whistle. She clung more tightly to the wall as her friend plummeted past her. She heard the miserable, wet thump below her and the double greenwood cracks of breaking bone.

Zoë sprawled in the grass like a rag doll, her legs crumpled beneath her. Meribah slung her friend over her shoulder and began to run. Robbed of height, burdened, weaving through the countryside, she could see little. She fought and cursed her way through the tourney camp—tumbled into the shallow stream dividing the nobles from the refugees—lay low and kept the gypsy's head down while she spied upon the field.

The battle had nearly run its course. None of the crew had held their posts. The two barrel wains were gone. Andreas's wagon, Meribah's quarters, the Ravnos's workshop—these remained in place, hacked open and laid bare. Men-at-arms clustered around their captives, forcing them into great hay wagons at the direction of sad-faced prelates. The knights were fighting yet. Knots of two or three dealt with Cainites in far-flung melees. Meribah had a fine view of the largest combat. The men in red tabards, another in green, and one in blue and white, had trapped ten or twelve defenders in the corner formed by the junction of two vineyard terraces.

Grown men held off the attackers barehanded. Smaller bodies rose slowly through the air behind them, and Meribah recognized a dark, blue-robed figure there—Gregory, whose twisted limbs could never climb that wall, lifting the caravan children to Annemie and safety.

Now the defenders were falling, and the eldest, strongest boy, Jozef, offering his arms over the turfed ledge—the little girls screaming for the Wonder-Maker—Annemie bracing herself to pull Gregory up the giant step. The Ravnos backed away, shouting. He could be heard from the stream—heard from the Lady's tower—heard, Meribah believed, in Jerusalem, at the center of the world:

"Run!"

And calmly, the tinker turned to face the knights alone.

An anguished scream pierced Meribah's concentration. Zoë, able-bodied at last, leapt from their cover in the water and raced out onto the field.

Healed, thought Meribah. *All that blood to mend her legs. Blood on the wind. Wounded souls on the ground. And they know how to fight us.* The gypsy sped toward the fires, the steel, and the cross. Her friend prayed her own feet were faster, and leapt out of the stream.

She caught Zoë a scarce four yards from the torchmen—caught her, seized her shoulders, hurled her around. The Ravnos's body was the Beast's. Meribah struck her, saw the raging hunger fix itself on her throat, and ran. The maddened Cainite followed. Praying for speed once more, Meribah ran away from the battle, from the town, from the innocents and from the guilty. She led Zoë into the wilderness, and the two were miles from Chambery before Gregory's childe regained her senses.

"I fear their intentions." Clovia's warning was gently given, her face placid, but her deep-set, dark eyes were as grave as carven saints'. "They came to the *seigneur* and my abbot this morning, and they asked about you."

"By name?"

"No," said the Lady, "but they are looking for heretics fleeing from the East. Your refugees—there are Bogomils among them?"

"Yes," admitted Andreas. "I believe so, but—"

"They intend to join the Cathars in the Albi and Toulouse?"

"I think they do. But those in the field beside my camp, they fled New Rome as well, and they stray much farther than the dualists."

"Will the red knights know the difference?"

A bell pealed below them in the town. It was not from the church or abbey. It was more shrill, more piercing, and it emanated from a watchtower. Another joined the first, jangling out the alarm. Andreas and his hostess hastened to the tower's edge, as close to the first signal as they could judge. The *castra's* guards began to shout, and the two deathless watchers saw a thread of fire—a double line of torches—reach the fields and separate to form a ring.

The Setite sprang for the stairs, and Clovia was a blur on the stairs before him. She led him down past the ground floor and into the donjon—she stopped at a moldering door and opened it. "Here, take my gage," she whispered. Her hand, too fast to see, pressed against his tunic for an instant only. He looked down at the spot and found a tri-cornered, silver knot: three keys, interwoven, pinned to his breast. "Show the boy at the gate, and he will let you out. In again, if need be. I must speak to my *seigneur*. Hurry."

Andreas sped down the tunnel. He slipped on wet earth and slimed rock, barked his shins against unseen steps. His sandals filled with muck; his linen was covered in grime. He righted himself by shelves carved into the walls and felt bones piled within the niches.

More carefully, with the eyes Takouhi had given him, he

moved forward through the catacombs. A large chamber opened to his left—a great room cut from the hillside, covered in charcoal markings. There were fish and crosses, alphas and omegas, texts in Latin. Fresher air came from the right, ahead of him. He left the chapel behind to follow it. The slope dropped away, and he skidded to the bottom at breakneck speed, hands outstretched to break his fall. He found a moss-covered, blank wall—a dead end with a draft. Instinct groped for the catch, and the stones did, indeed, feel loose beneath his touch. The door was open before he knew which movement had caused it, and he emerged from the catacombs into a private tomb. Within, shroud-wound corpses lay on marble slabs. Andreas sidled respectfully between the sleeping souls, pursuing a moonbeam to the exit.

Here stood an iron grating without hinges or handle—a portcullis, looking out over the *seigneur's* vineyards, down into his fields. Eager to join his men and his charges in the camp, the Setite tried at once to raise the barrier. His hands burned on the bars. The portal was warded against someone or something of his ilk. Singed fingers fumbled over the stones, seeking the key; a cord over the lintel, made of fresh, new hemp, invited hope, and Andreas pulled it. In the distance, he heard a bell. He pressed as close as he dared to the gate, peering through the vines.

While Meribah and Zoë watched from the *castra* battlements, he waited for the boy, hunting out the mechanism. Andreas bore witness to his catastrophe, helpless to prevent it. He was in time to see the heretics make their rush against the circle, and he knew what to expect after that—he had trained his people for this. He saw the caravan children busy in their place beside Valerian's barrel wain. They hitched two pair of oxen to it, as they had been taught. When the circle broke, the non-combatant crew rushed to the wagons. The elderly, the infirm and the very young were helped aboard by the oldest children. The women, all of whom had tasted Set's blood within the week, seized the uprights and pushed, running alongside. Their otherworldly strength accelerated one huge cart straight at the confused men-at-arms. Magda held the reins. Beside her,

Danica raised an arm. The women picked their feet up, and the first wagon crashed through the cordon and out to the road.

Another wagon, though already underway and poised to exploit the success of the first, was yet tardy—the knights had time to attack it. Men from the crew advanced to their families' aid. Sergeants and squires cut down some; others freed themselves to oppose the knights' charge.

One man on foot, wearing red, wielding a sword, delivered a titanic blow just above the rear right axle. The whole frame shuddered, and Gertje, driving, cracked the whip furiously. Gregory left his place beside her and crawled along the top of the casks to defend the rear.

The knight's second stroke cleaved the uprights in twain, and the rear third of the wagon sagged behind the wheel. Riders scrambled to safer seats. The wagon lurched forward, and the blade fell again. Splintering planks gave way. Two barrels rolled off, the Wonder-Maker tumbled down, and a handful of women and children were left behind as the barrel cleared the circle. The men-at-arms closed in. Crewmen formed a fighting pocket in front of them, retreating toward the opening in the ring.

Red-tabard rallied the knights, and the warriors disengaged themselves from, or simply dispatched, their opponents to chase the little group back against the hillside.

Now the ring shattered completely. Torchbearers, monks, squires, and pages busied themselves corralling the refugees, herding them into the hay wagons. Crossbowmen galloped from combat to combat, firing large wooden quarrels into pinioned Cainites.

Footsteps approached the tomb. A toothless old man plodded along the weed-choked path. A small child skipped along beside him carrying a lantern.

Andreas had no eyes for them—he watched Annemie chin herself up the earthen wall—and then man and boy blocked his view. Revealing himself, he held Clovia's gage to the grate, and the boy swung the rusty iron open on well-oiled hinges. The Egyptian grunted his thanks and bounded down the hillside.

Not one quarter-hour passed before he reached the lowest terrace, but it was too long, too late.

Andreas found the camp in shambles. The first of five hay wagons lumbered along the road to Chambery filled with refugees, heretics, women, and children. Robert, Carl, Dehaan, Lieven, Jacquy and Isabelle marched to town in iron shackles. Ton Wheelwright, Ern Blacksmith, Willem Scrivener and young Riki were bleeding on the field, left for dead. The victors milled about, looting wagons and bundles. Crossbowmen, knights in red and Cainite prisoners had disappeared completely, and Gregory was gone with them.

Chapter Twenty-Two

Commune of Bergamo, Lombardy
June, 1208

They had ridden hard to make it back across the Alps, following the trail of the red monks. Lady Clovia had thought they would head for Verona, but their trail led here, to Bergamo and its monastery. They had prisoners and prizes in tow including Gregory and his wonders.

The plan was relatively simple. Lady Clovia had seen to the release of those among Andreas' party whom she could and a few had deigned follow, including Dehaan. Goreb remained in Chambery, watching over Lord Valerian. Dehaan had scouted the monastery by daylight and now, Andreas and Zoë were to rescue Gregory while Meribah recovered his prize—the heart of Khay'tall. A simple plan than involved three unliving heretics sneaking into the very fortress of the soldiers of God.

Fog lay on the town. Eerily, it moved as the deathless did. *It is an illusion*, thought Meribah, *the effect of its thickness*. It was impossible to see more than five feet in any direction—that was why this clear space, ten feet wide, seemed to follow them. *Not really a hole in the clouds, walking, intelligently, with us…* Her gaze flickered to Andreas, and she was no longer sure.

Reaching their chosen spot, they found the knotted ropes bid ready for them—Dehaan's work. Meribah did the hard climbing to secure the lines; there were ladder loops for the less-nimble Egyptian and less-strong gypsy. Once inside, they parted in silence. She had an anxious glance for both her companions, but neither looked at her.

Meribah waited for them to clear, then shed her great cloak, fog-white though it was. Underneath, she wore the coarse brown of brotherhood. Her hood thrown back revealed red hair cut short all round and shaved in a tonsure. The dead could not change; her shorn locks would grow back before sunset to disguise her. With humble stride and ethereal serenity—brass-bold—she walked across the yard to the great church.

She slipped in by the side door the monks used, and padded softly, bare-footed, along the cool marble aisles. Ahead of her, a weak light struggled to soften the vast darkness, and a low, ragged snort rumbled through the vaults. She made her way to the nave, her goal and the audible nexus of habitation, with excruciating care. Halfway, she saw them, and grinned ruefully to herself.

Summer nights are short, the vigil between prayers shorter still—but too long for novices. Three half-grown boys slept at their devotions, nodding where they sat (where Meribah had a vague notion they ought not to be—there were empty kneelers before them). In front, a middle-aged, liver-spotted, grizzle-fringed pate shone by candle flame. The older monk prayed too intently to notice the boys' dereliction or her own approach. Slipping past him to the stalls, she looked back to check. His head was bowed, braced against folded hands. Surely some great intent, an unusual cause spurred him to such concentration. Meribah moved on, afraid her envious stare might somehow wake him, and was rewarded by the sight of the crypt door on her left. She dropped to one knee before it and busied herself with skeleton keys and wire. The lock was simple; this crypt, though full of patrons and priors past, held no other secrets, no treasure. Meribah was up again and relocked it before any of the monks noticed.

Prowling behind the choir stalls, she discovered a far more promising possibility: A heavy, iron-strapped door set between two doughty pillars. Its lock was modern and recently oiled; she took her time picking it. Down dark, stooping stairs and along a low tunnel she crept. Another sturdy door and clever lock barred the way, but they were nothing to a snake who'd solved Lakeritos's lotus box.

The treasury overflowed its coffers. Coin, plate, reliquaries, disused altarpieces, jeweled chalices, and outmoded sanctuaries were stacked on purpose-built shelves, on one another, on caskets, on jutting cornerstones, on raw planking. The room doglegged left, widened, bent again, and narrowed, twisting like a snake around the massive vault foundations. The light came from its farthest lobe, opposite her entrance. As she neared it, she heard a man's breathing...slow, steady, slumberous. Meribah dropped to all fours and poked her head around the last corner. At a second door, a lone man, sitting on his keys, slept by a dying lamp. The serpent slunk back into the shadows to explore. Raw stones caught her eye—familiar gems, the contents of the Ravnos workshop. The loot of Chambery was heaped like bricks in the middle of the floor. There—the lotus box, Zoë's cats, a pile of her sketches, the mechanical horse she had never finished, Gregory's papers—the Odyssey. Meribah ran her hands over the binding, remembering.

Underneath Andreas' writing box (which she realized, with a pang, that she would have to leave behind) she found a pale green box, and knew it must be the cache. It was built of six carved, stone slabs unlike anything she had ever seen. Fantastic snakes cavorted with dragons and fire-flumed birds. The material was the color of glass, but opaque, chased in emerald-green enamelwork. It complemented the strange pieces, but the craft was unmistakably the Wonder-Maker's.

Outside the back door of the old distillery building, Andreas crouched to examine the gnawed-out boards. The hole was tiny; his doubled fists would not go through together.

"Your bag," he prompted. "A saw." He accepted it, setting to work immediately. The girl knelt on the ground beside him, hampering his stroke. "Keep watch," he said curtly. The Egyptian concentrated on the ancient, resinous wood, and didn't notice her leaving. Fortune smiled on him; he found a brittle patch around a knot. It would not give, but snapped instantly.

Andreas transformed into his serpent-shape and slithered through. Turning around, he found a key. Something squeaked behind him. Light streamed through a widening crack, silhouetting the girl. She stashed something in her sack, beaming victoriously. Andreas underwent his second metamorphosis—a man-shape with snake's skin tough as brass. He flattened himself against the wall, out of Zoë's way. She groped her way across the unfurnished room, tried the door, felt for the missing key—looked down, finally, at the enlarged hole.

"That was dangerous," murmured Andreas in her ear. The shock startled her into gratifying sobriety. "But very well done," he added, and Zoë flushed. "Now close that."

The first room spanned the entire width of the distillery, yet was only a few yards long. It had three doors without locks, all barred—from this side, to keep in—with wood so fresh Andreas could smell sap. He led the Ravnos to the closest, pulled the bar, and swung it open.

The second room was longer, higher, darker. Two rows of tables stretched its length. Some bore scraps of cloth or bundles of sacking. Others were cluttered with homely, household things. No breath whispered there; nothing within it lived, not even vermin. Andreas, for the first time, allowed himself to hope. The table on their left was piled with food of every kind—meat, bread, fish, and beer, apples, greens, gruel, and garlic. Only the deathless could frighten rats away from a feast like that. Yet on the right, there were knives—blued steel, browned iron, polished silver, gold, bronze, copper...

"Ehhhhhhhhhhh..."

"What was that?" The girl clutched his arm frantically, but she stepped toward the noise, not away. "What do you see? Gregory?!" Zoë wrenched free of her new tutor. She lifted her hand, and there was light—a soft, glowing fog inside the chamber. It did not cloud the vision, but enabled it.

Folded clothing covered the next table on the left; coarse blanked draped and concealed what lay on the right. Andreas snatched away the sacking, revealing the scarlet Nosferatu, naked, pierced with small cuts on every inch of skin. His eyes were open—his, the heavy sigh. His tormentors had not driven a stake into his heart, which would utterly immobilize him. He was, instead, shackled to the oaken slab with new, bright chains. Zoë cried out, then sprinted down the room, yanking the covers off all the tables.

"Egyptian..." croaked the monstrosity. "I do not know...for which of us you come...but they are dead...."

The Wonder-Maker's apprentice stopped running. Andreas hastened to her side, and saw what she did. Gregory Lakeritos's garments lay like a shadow on the blackened wood. His sleeves ended in steel bracelets, his hose in iron hoops. His shoes had fallen empty on the floor. All were scorched black; they were full of loose, white ash.

His daughter stood—stared—closed her eyes—opened them again, immediately, as if not seeing hurt worse than this vision. "Zoë."

Her hand snapped up, warding him away. After another moment, when he believed in her restraint, he returned to the survivor.

The heretic watched him coming. "All dead but me," he explained. "Marie..." His rescuer pulled forth the saw and disappeared below the table. "Appius...Georg...Stefan..." No link or bolt was obviously weaker than any other, they had bound, for nights on end, one of the mighty Nosferatu, whose deformities hid legendary strength. Abandoning the saw, the Setite chose a heavy cleaver from the torturers' stock and brandished it before the prisoner.

"Do it," urged the scarlet man, and Andreas chopped his thumbs off. Zoë jumped both times; she didn't seem to have followed their words. "Now, just my heels...will be enough. Or give me the saw." He took it in his maimed paws. "Thank you. I think this might score through...and let me...snap it." He gestured with his head toward the girl. "Lakeritos's?"

"His childe."

"He was first," said the prisoner sadly. "It gives a little, I think." The sawn link stretched suddenly, then popped. The sound was violently loud; it brought yells from the far doors.

"Blessed Christ and Caine," the heretic's voice quavered in fear. "Leave while you can."

The doors burst open, and three men rushed in. Two wore full plate mail and white Templar cloaks and tabards. Andreas had battled their kind before; he would be wary of them, but felt no fear. The third man, dark-eyed, hawkish, and fervent—his robes were russet in color, and the Setite was certain he posed the greatest threat. He charged up the center aisle, straight for Zoë, and Zoë did not move.

Andreas was easily faster, beginning his attack, but the girl was closer, and had good instincts. She broke her paralysis, leapt for the young monk, and reached him first. He staggered back under the weight of the wild creature, all claws, who climbed his chest. Yet despite her ferocity, Zoë drew no blood; there were layers of fine chain under the brown cloth.

The two Templars joined the fray. Twin swords swung toward the girl; the Poor Knights would cut her open against their companion's steel skin. Andreas hooked his talons into the visor of the nearest.

"Isidro!" screamed the Templar. He bled from his eyes.

The Setite interposed his body between his pupil and the second chevalier. The man left his side open, and Andreas raked open the breastplate's leather straps.

Suddenly, Zoë no longer held the monk. He threw her back, somehow, with a strength his frame belied. She sailed through the air. Andreas, lunging forward to keep her opponent off, found a crucifix in his face.

"In *nomine Parris*," cried Brother Isidro.

The snake staggered back. He felt as though an ox had rushed him. He gathered his will (for it was difficult, even, to think of harming God's chosen) behind one swift slash at the monk's chest. He struck neck and shoulder, and the mortal would bear a scar all his days. Still, the holy man continued. "*Et Filii—*"

Red skin flashed through Andreas' sight. The Nosferatu, freed, fed from the fallen Templar. On the other side, Zoë—quite mad now—buried hands and teeth under the breastplate of the standing knight. Blood streamed down her arms and neck, splashing, wasted, on the flagstones.

The Nosferatu rose with healed hands and feet. His patchwork cuts had vanished, but on his back, Andreas saw dozens of crucifix-shaped burns, blistered and seeping. They did not stop him from scrambling across Zoë to block the monk. "Egyptian. Holy ground. Get out, get her out, get out!"

Andreas seized the girl and dragged her clear. On the table beside them lay the knives in shining rows; an iron dagger offered itself. The Setite turned, aimed, and threw, and the cross fell from Isidro's grasp. Another, copper, missed its mark; a thick-bladed bronze cleaver flew home. It struck the mortal's side under his armpit, where the mail was single-layer, but could not cut the steel. Then the Nosferatu fell, and Andreas picked up his squirming ally and carried her from the room.

Another knight materialized from the swirling mists behind the old distillery. No innocent, he, but the elder red-tabard from Chambery. He had seen battle already; his tabard and his face were torn, and there was blood spattered on his arms. Sergeants ran after him; all three wielded stake-loaded crossbows.

Andreas sliced into the knight's shooting arm, and won out—the wooden missile penetrated his chest too low to reach the heart. A torch broke against his face. Water sizzled across his right side. He lost hold of Zoë's arm. She thrashed away with a stake through her belly, destroying the man at arms who had burned them both. Andreas slit the throat of the second soldier, the holy-water grenadier. The mortal's helmet came free.

Red-tabard raised his cross and began to speak. "*In nomi—*"

Andreas smashed the knight's unhelmeted head with the heavy steel shell, and the man went down. Grabbing his wild ally once more, he steered her out into the fog. *Lord of Storms*, prayed Ankhesenaten. *Do what you will with us.*

The white curtains thickened on every side, hiding the fugitives. Rain fell in torrents, drowning the noise of Gregory's spitting, writhing, fighting childe. The water washed away blood and ashes; it cooled burns; it brought Zoë back to her senses.

With the rope before her, she could speak, and climb, and mourn.

On the hill below Bergamo, Dehaan had heard the church bells ring their alarms. He expected the worst. When his master and Zoë arrived alone, the Rooster held his tongue and gave them time.

Andreas sank to his knees. His friend Gregory was dead, his childe orphaned. Andrew of Egypt's career was probably over. It would be impossible for Valerian, however willing he *had* been, to recommend him for appointment to the court in Paris now. And as for Ankhesenaten's goal—Meribah had not returned, and all the monastery must be on alert by now. The guards would have found the rope, and she could hardly be expected to escape the tightening cordon.

"What happened, master?"

Andreas looked away. "Later," he said. "We'll tell it once, when Meribah gets here." He signed for Dehaan to rescue Zoë's mule, then bit his own beast's neck.

Zoë, sobered, had sat down by the time he finished. She leaned her head against a boulder and watched the road. Andreas, hawk-like, perched atop the rock. The Rooster paced back and forth across the road itself. Slowly, the eastern horizon changed from black to indigo.

"Dehaan—"

The Rooster left his post to saddle Eureka and ready the other beasts for the road. When the noise stopped, Andreas checked the sky; it was indigo at zenith, and the east was royal blue. "It's time," he told them, catching Zoë by the arm. Their progress to the sleeping bags was interrupted by the sound of horse's hooves coming up the slope.

Dehaan sprang back to the boulder, bow and sword at the ready. Andreas regrew his scaly armor, and Zoë scampered back to join them with her claws out.

A cock-crow rang from below, and the three of them swarmed the road to see Meribah riding a mare up the hill. She nodded when she caught her clanmate's eye.

Andreas, still heartsore, found a smile—reluctant, rueful— on his lips. "Right." One *thing, then, is saved from the wreck.* "Well, the sun is on its way."

Chapter Twenty-Three

The Lombard Alps
June, 1208

They were a full day's hard ride from Bergamo when they woke the next night, and well on their way back to Savoy by the time Zoë had taken in enough blood to heal her wounds and clear her head. Her soul, however, was gripped with outrage.

"The priests. They killed Gregory and we're leaving them behind."

"Yes," said Andreas. "We are lucky to have escaped that monastery, girl, much less to have recovered even a portion of what we came for." Andreas took up the pale green box—Khay'tall's cache. "Meribah, can you…?"

"Nope. I tried on the wagon. It's harder than the lotus box—it doesn't have keyholes. I haven't a chance—not with the tools here, anyway."

"I can open it," Zoë offered haughtily. It occurred to Andreas that she might have thought Gregory's locks unpickable. "Goody for you," muttered Meribah.

The Ravnos took the cache from her tutor. All eyes followed her hands through the intricate movements—pressure points in series, sliding panels, revolutions of the entire box. At last, one of the end pieces, not the lid, popped loose.

Reaching inside, Zoë pulled out an ugly, shriveled mass. The lump was the size of her two fists, ruddy brown, and repulsive. She handed it to Andreas as if it were nothing. "What about Gregory?"

He tried not to pay too much attention to the mass in his hands. "Gregory is gone."

"And his memory calls for blood. I want my revenge, Andreas. I *thought* you would too."

"I understand your obligation, but I have obligations of my own." He glanced down at the heart of the greatest heretic of his faith. "I must convey Valerian and yourself to Paris."

"I don't want to go to Paris."

"I think it would be wise," suggested Andreas, "and a surer path to your goal."

"*This* way is surer, she said, pointing back southeast toward Bergamo, "and faster, as well. It will be months before you reach Paris. This Isidro may move by then, and escape me."

"Valerian both entered into a compact to protect the cara-van—to avenge the fallen if called for. Bring your claim to Paris, and he will be a powerful ally to you. King Alexander and Queen Saviarre will join your cause. Their agents can gather information on these monks; they can raise armies to destroy your foes."

"An army? Do the servants of Set need armies?" The Ravnos' eyes flashed. "I will destroy these monsters with my own hands."

"Set has patience," replied Andreas. "He acts with fury *after* he has thought. He understands time and mortality; these monks are doomed—their hearts will not beat forever. He understands war; a girl alone cannot take two militant brothers in the heart of their fortress."

"I will destroy them myself," Zoë declared again, dangerously calm. With slow and steady steps, she crossed the small camp to her horse. Glancing back, she saw Meribah and Dehaan—silent throughout the debate—amazed and saddened. "Meribah. You *are* coming?" The tone assumed assent.

Meribah shook her head. "After Paris—"

"Now," insisted the gypsy. Angry tears reddened her eyes. "You loved him, too—how can you leave me?"

"Andreas is *right.*" She looked from one to the other, licking her lips anxiously.

Zoë swung into the saddle. "I wish you well," she bid them

wistfully. Her heels dug into her mount's sides, and the mare began walking toward the road. Andreas did nothing.

"Zoë!" her friend ran after her.

"Meribah." The gypsy turned her horse back. She glowed with satisfaction, and her voice held profound relief.

"Don't just—run off like this. Listen." She ran her hand through her thick red curls, rumpling them in frustration. "Andreas *has* to go. You—I guess you *have* to go, too, if you feel that way. But—don't part without a plan. If you want to see whether the monks are in Bergamo, that won't take very long. Either they are there, or they are not. If they are there, and you can dispatch them yourself, well and good. Come find Andreas, and finish your apprenticeship. If they are not, or if you find your quest wants extra swords and teeth—come find Andreas and hunt them down with him. But set a rendezvous for either event." Meribah checked the Egyptian's face—he approved. Zoë seemed less adamant.

"After Paris," offered Andreas, "the caravan goes to Normandy and Flanders. We will be at the fairs next year. Find us there."

Zoë blinked three times, staring at her tutor. Eventually, she nudged the horse around again and slowly took the road. As the hoof beats—moving at a walk—receded, Meribah spoke again.

"You're going to just let her go?"

Andreas turned to the redhead. "I am," he admitted softly.

"She doesn't mean it. She hasn't any baggage. She hasn't any plan. Go after her."

"No. Gregory always went after her. She never thanked him for it."

For several minutes, neither spoke. They just watched the young gypsy head back toward the madmen who awaited her. Dehaan joined them putting an arm gently on the small of Meribah's back. She didn't react, but when Zoë had passed over a ridge and out of sight, she spoke again.

"You remember, Ankhesenaten. Our conversation, about my boon. The favor you owe me."

Dehaan tensed. "No."

Andreas walked toward her as if he had not heard.

"You have that which you desired me to steal, brother. You no longer need me to persuade Zoë to anything." Meribah stepped out from behind her lover. "Your duty to your Lord, Ankhesenaten—do it now," she proposed, in a plaintive, hopeful, tiny voice.

"Master—" Dehaan blocked the way again.

He rebels, thought Andreas. *He defies his god.* The mortal attempted to shield the girl with his body, and she fought him off. *Independent little Franj—she fights everything* but *the gods.* "Leave us, Dehaan." Ankhesenaten looked his follower in the eyes, and the Rooster shrank from him. "Ride away. Do not return until I call you."

The two deathless stood face-to-face while the young man hesitated—obeyed—mounted Eureka and galloped into the darkness.

Ankhesenaten put his arms around his cousin and kissed her neck where he should have torn it. "I have come," he said quietly, "to love you like my own daughter, and cannot kill you."

Meribah, in fearful stillness, whispered dryly. "I'm sure the sentiment does you credit, but I doubt it will placate Set or Thebes."

Andreas chuckled. "How many condemned prisoners argue against their pardon?"

"This is not a joke."

"I know." He brushed the hair out of her eyes. "It is a paradox. An unbeliever who desperately desires to die for her gods." Meribah stared at him—opened her mouth to protest. "Quiet. I came prepared to debate you. Let me give you my other reasons, and we shall see whether you can convince me to your murder.

"I promised Ljudumilu," he went on, "that I would make Dehaan one of us. My own blood is weak in the Dark Waters. I propose that you sire him, and I shall raise him as my own."

Meribah shook her head. "Better that you find someone whose lineage is more secure. Suppose other sins are traced to my Grandfather? What would Thebes do to the father of such a heresy? If they slay his name and his memory as well as his body, my name dies too. Dehaan would be an outcast."

"Dehaan would be *my* childe in Thebes' eyes, not yours.

I accept the risk." Andreas paused, then, satisfied that she accepted the point, moved on.

"Moreover, Meribah, you are dangerous. You know too much for the heretics' peace of mind. Therefore, you can do something to the heretics which I cannot. Merely by traveling with me, who hunts them, you draw them to yourself. If I need justify my conduct to anyone, I shall say, 'This girl is bait.'" Meribah frowned, but for this argument, she had no rebuttal.

"The most important reason, I save for last. I have discovered something more important than hunting Sarrasine and burning out the heresy. I feel called to save the wanderers—the lost ones, like you. Europe swarms with the red-headed bastards of Crusade and Egypt. We must win them for the Lord of Storms before the heretics convert them."

She had no answer for this, either. Releasing her, he reached for his horn. A death-white hand arrested his.

"Thebes will send another inquisitor, and you will be exposed."

"I have a new priestess to whom I must teach the language of her office, and a candidate for the Dark Waters who needs instruction. You will assist me in their lessons and help them with their studies. Remember—as far as Thebes is concerned, you have always known the mysteries."

"But my *name*—" she insisted in anguish.

Andreas stopped with the horn at his lips, frankly confused. "What?"

"I was christened *Meribah*. Al-Suti never called me anything else. In the genealogies, it will show that I have no name in Set's ears—he does not know me. Sethnakhte and the others—the heretics hidden in the Temples—must have kept it to themselves until now, so that they would be the ones to catch me. But if I help you against them, they will have that—which you cannot change by any amount of teaching, training, or lies—and they will use it against me to bring you down."

Ankhesenaten blew the horn in fury, and his wrath echoed from the hillside. *Her sire never told her,* he thought. *Sutelkhankharen, I spit on your name. I will salvage what you wasted. I will tend what you neglected. She will outlive your memory and destroy it.*

Andreas gazed down on his new student, smiling wickedly above his beard. He took a malicious pleasure in his next words. For many years after, he remembered them as his first strike against the heretical Followers of Typhon. Dehaan arrived— nearly falling off his horse to see the girl unharmed—in time to hear them.

"The crusader priests named you Meribah, Temptation, a thing of evil, sprung from the waters of strife, but they also gave you your name in Set. The Destroyer calls you mre-ba, the Beloved-Soul, and he has always known you."

About the Author

Kathleen Ryan has worked for, with, and around White Wolf Publishing since 1993. Her first fiction pieces, about a young mage named Amanda, appeared as book- openers in *Mage: The Ascension*, first edition. Through cajolery and threats she has managed to get an Amanda piece in every major Mage release since then, wrangled all the fun parts of *Tradition Book: Euthanatos* for herself, and snuck most of *Changing Breed Book: Kitsune* into the back of *Hengeyokai: Shapeshifters of the East*. She is also the author of *Clan Novel: Setite*..

Curious about other Crossroad Press books?
Stop by our site:
http://store.crossroadpress.com
We offer quality writing
in digital, audio, and print formats.